We Will See You Bleed

ALSO BY RON CURRIE

The Savage, Noble Death of Babs Dionne

The One-Eyed Man

Flimsy Little Plastic Miracles

Everything Matters!

God Is Dead (stories)

We Will See You Bleed

RON CURRIE

Atlantic Books
London

First published in hardback in the United States of America in 2026
by Putnam, an imprint of Penguin Random House LLC.

First published in trade paperback in Great Britain in 2026
by Atlantic Books, an imprint of Atlantic Books Ltd.

1 2 3 4 5 6 7 8 9

A CIP catalogue record for this book is available from the British Library.

Trade paperback ISBN: 9781805466468
EBook ISBN: 9781805466475

Printed and bound by CPI Group (UK) Ltd, Croydon CR0 4YY

Atlantic Books
An Imprint of Atlantic Books Ltd
Ormond House
26–27 Boswell Street
London
WC1N 3JZ

www.atlantic-books.co.uk

Product safety EU representative: Authorised Rep Compliance Ltd., Ground Floor, 71 Lower Baggot Street, Dublin, D02 P593, Ireland. www.arccompliance.com

MIX
Paper | Supporting responsible forestry
FSC® C013604
www.fsc.org

For Gary David Socquet, 1969–2018

Joyce had Dublin. Faulkner had Lafayette County, Mississippi. Hemingway had the Upper Peninsula, the Keys, and, of course, Paris. Steinbeck had Salinas and Monterey. And we, my brother, had a dying, decaying mill town perched on the edge of a river.

Places as desperate obsessions, grimy windows on the near world.

Rags
Make paper
Paper makes money
Money makes banks
Banks make loans
Loans make beggars
Beggars make
Rags

—ANON., CA. 18TH CENTURY

Maine Sucks.
Tell All Your Rich Friends.

—BUMPER STICKER FOR SALE AT DEBBAHS CLOTHING & GIFTS, BAR HARBOR, MAINE, 2024

We Will See You Bleed

PART ONE

PRÉLUDE

August 27, 1984

A hot, humid, and intermittently thunderstormy day, latest in an endless string of them, the kind of Maine summer that left you feeling moldy, like there was zero point to bathing or washing your clothes or doing much of anything other than lying as still as possible somewhere shady and waiting until the calendar flipped to October. In this weather you never started or stopped sweating but were just *sweaty*, it was a state, an immutable fact of your existence, like the color of your eyes or the size of your feet, and everything—bath towels, sofa cushions, the floor—was and remained ambiently damp to the touch. It was fucking gross, in a word. Every time you turned your head you caught a faint whiff of blue cheese, moldy shower curtain. Blackflies and mosquitoes ruled the streets and laid relentless siege to window screens, found gaps and holes, attacked when you thought you were invulnerable. Days like this, it was hard to believe Maine was the same place that five months of the year was as pitilessly cold as Siberia.

Your name was Babs Dionne, and for the first time in your twenty-nine years of existence, you had reason to worry you might be losing your mind.

The thing threatening to displace your mind was, of course, the Mill. What else could it be? Nothing else mattered as much. Nothing else mattered *at all.* Sickness or health, good times or bad, all were meaningless except in the context of the Mill. Since 1900 it had rolled out every page of every newspaper in the United States: 240 tons of paper a day, 365 days a year, for nearly a century. The Mill had fed and clothed everyone in your family for generations; its power was so absolute that even during the Great Depression not one person in Waterville had lost their job. It burned your lungs with sulfur and, when the wind was right, coated everything in weightless bits of particulate like black snow. The Mill's smokestack loomed over all, casting a shadow that moved steadily across the downtown every day like a sundial.

Put most plainly, the Mill was God. And like God it sometimes grew angry, turned deaf to prayer, demanded blood sacrifices. You and your neighbors and the generations who came before you had done all that the Mill asked, without question or complaint. And now it had forsaken you.

What were you without the Mill? Any of you? The answer, which you all had become too acquainted with in the past year, was: Nothing. You were nothing without the Mill.

And so you sat swatting bugs in the heat, trying to figure a way to hold everything together now that the Mill had cast you all out, growing ever more convinced you were losing your mind. You were home alone. Home being the modest bungalow, in the Little Canada neighborhood of Waterville, Maine, where you were raised. The house had belonged to you since your mother died of Huntington's disease when you were nineteen. Your husband, Rheal, had gone to the north woods the day before, to take a break from the tension and sadness that had enveloped the neighborhood for the last year and a half, canoeing the Allagash River and drinking whiskey by firelight with the Saucier brothers. And so you had the place to yourself. Or at least you did until your mother, Rose, showed up and took a seat at your kitchen table as though, rather than having been dead for a decade, she'd merely been out having her hair set for an extremely long time.

There was precedent, of a kind, for this haunting. You'd always had a sort of sixth sense that gave you glimpses, whether you wanted them or not, of things you could not otherwise know. For instance, on the first day of February 1968, when you were thirteen, you'd awakened with the knowledge that your older brother, Jean, had been killed by sniper fire at Da Nang, hours before the first reports of the Tet Offensive reached American eyes and ears, and three days before grim-looking men in army dress showed up at the front door and set your mother to wailing like a wounded animal. More recently, in late March 1977, you had a vision of a dog floating down the swollen Kennebec atop its doghouse, and three weeks later, that very image was printed in the Central Maine *Morning Sentinel*, as part of their coverage of the worst flood the area had seen in a hundred years.

There were other examples. You'd always been tuned, for good and for ill, to a frequency other people didn't seem to pick up. But you'd never had a visit from the dead, until today.

Your mother appeared to you much as she'd looked just before her death: nearly skeletal, eyes sunk in their sockets and clouded as if made from smoked glass. Now, though, despite looking like literal death, and despite actually *being* dead, your mother had the vigor of someone very much alive and well. The first thing she did, after appearing at the table, was ask for a cup of coffee.

"What will you do with a cup of coffee, *Maman*?" you asked. "You're not even here."

"Of course I'm here," she said. "You see me, don't you? You hear me?"

"I do."

"Then don't argue with an old lady."

"You're not old. You're dead."

"Barbara. Coffee."

You rose from your seat and went unsteadily to the Mr. Coffee on the counter next to the stove. Pulled a mug from the cabinet, lifted the carafe, gazed back at her for a second before pouring.

"*Noir, oui*?" you asked.

"Same as always," your mother said.

You nodded, poured half a cup, and replaced the carafe on the hot plate with a clatter. When you turned away from the counter with the mug, you saw that your mother already held an identical mug between her thin, veiny hands.

"Why did I just pour you a cup," you asked, irritated, "if you already had one of your own?"

"But I didn't," she said. "Not until you got it for me."

You stared silently.

"It's complicated," your mother said. "Suffice to say the dead need help from the living with certain things. But none of that matters. Come, sit."

You did so, leaving the mug of fresh coffee on the counter. "You need me to light you a cigarette, too?" you asked.

"Oh, that would be heaven. It's been an eternity."

"It's been a decade."

"Time passes differently when you're dead. I don't know what I want more, the coffee or the smoke."

"They're only properly enjoyed together," you said, shaking a cigarette from your pack. The moment it was lit, a Marlboro appeared between the fingers of your mother's left hand.

"*Merci, chérie,*" she said. She shut her eyes and dragged on the cigarette slowly, emaciated cheeks so concave her face resembled, for a moment, little more than a bare skull. You lit another cigarette for yourself and watched as your mother held the smoke in, exulting. When she finally breathed out and opened her eyes, they were wet with tears.

"You've made me so happy, Barbara," she said. "You always did."

"That's a slightly different tune than you sang when you were alive, *Maman*."

"What can I say?" she asked, flicking her cigarette in the ashtray. "Death has a way of sharpening one's perspective. But even when you were a pain in the ass—even when you broke my heart—you were always a joy."

"Now you tell me."

"Are you saying you didn't know?"

"Am I hallucinating?" you asked. "Have I lost my mind somehow?"

"Hardly."

"Then what is this? How did you come to me? Why am I seeing you now?"

"I've always been here, Barbara," your mother told you. "The difference is in you, not me."

"What does that mean?"

"You'll find out soon enough. It's not my place to say."

"I don't need riddles right now, *Maman*. I need answers. I've lost the ground under my feet. So please, tell me: Why are you here?"

"I'm here because I'm your mother, and because you need to know the biggest test of your life is on its way."

"Bigger than Sacha?"

"Sacha prepared you for what's coming next."

"That's a generous way to describe raping me."

Your mother sipped her coffee. "I'm only speaking plainly," she said. "You want sympathy, go to your father."

You laughed. "Oh good, is he around here somewhere, too?"

"We all are."

Something about her tone made you go silent for a moment.

"My point," your mother said, "is I never had the luxury of telling you anything other than what *is*. That was my duty to you. Fathers can coddle their daughters. Mothers—we know too much."

You gazed at her a moment, then rose from the table, cigarette dangling from your lips, and refilled your cup. "Fair enough," you said. "So tell me what is."

"Things are about to get much harder," your mother said.

"Difficult to imagine how that could be possible," you said.

"Don't feign naivete, *chérie*," your mother said. "You know better than most that it can always be worse."

You returned from the counter and sat at the table once more. "Yes," you said. "Which is why I don't need to hear about it."

"But you do," your mother said. "Because your neighbors are going to need you to lead, in the way only you can. So you have to be ready."

"Ready for what?"

Your mother sat back, dragged on her cigarette, exhaled the smoke with a sigh. "To be the woman Sacha made you."

You blinked at her. "A victim?" you asked.

Your mother stared. "*Saint-ciboire de tabarnak*," she said. "Don't be stupid. If you were a victim, it was only for the few seconds between when Sacha finished his business and you stabbed him in the lung."

"I swore I wouldn't hurt anyone again," you said. "I promised."

"Promised who?"

"Myself."

"Good. No kind of promise is more easily broken."

Your mother stubbed her cigarette in the ashtray, folding the filter over the cherry and pressing down with her thumb to smother it.

"It's too easy for me to be cruel, *Maman*," you said.

Your mother laughed. "You say that as if I don't know for myself."

"It scares me," you said.

"That it scares you is a good thing," your mother said. "It shows you're the right person to decide when it's time to be cruel and when it's time to be merciful. For the good of all."

"I can't do it," you said. "I can't go back to being that way."

"There's no can or can't," your mother said. "Sacha made you a killer. The only choice you have is whether to accept what you are, and what you must do. Knowing it will make you hated, and hunted. Knowing it will eventually cost you your life."

You said nothing, afraid that if you opened your mouth you would begin to weep.

Your mother gazed at you for a moment and her face softened. "Your burden, *chérie,*" she said, "is to be someone bursting with love who is also capable of terrible things. The world needs people like that. Because you have what it takes to protect us from the true sadists."

You stared at her a moment, then blinked hard several times to clear the tears away. "You never talked like this when you were alive," you said. "This is just me having a conversation with myself, isn't it?"

"It's natural you would think that," your mother said.

"I don't think that," you said. "I know it. I'm like Scrooge, hallucinating after a bad meal. There's more of gravy than of grave about you, *Maman*."

Your mother smiled. "Believe whatever you need to," she said. "But like it or not, now you can see. And you will see others, assuming the change in you holds."

"What *change*?"

Your mother finished her coffee and rose from the table. "I hope we'll speak again, *chérie.* But if not, know that you are loved. That was always the thing you had a hard time believing."

Then she was gone.

You sat there for a minute after, your breath coming fast even though you'd done nothing more vigorous than drink your coffee. You were frightened and confused but the promise you'd made to yourself, alone in the woods with Sacha's stiffening corpse, remained. Even when pushed, even when it would have been more than justifiable, you hadn't hurt anyone since that day. And you were not about to start now just because of a hallucination brought on by the heat.

Instead, you got up from the table and carried your coffee mug and the ashtray to the sink. You dumped the butts in the garbage, hit the hot tap, and rinsed the mug and the ashtray and put them in the dish drainer. Then you reached for the other mug, the one you'd poured for your mother and left on the counter, but when you turned it upside down over the sink you found that it was now impossibly, inexplicably empty, just a few drops of coffee tapping against the stainless steel of the sink.

CHAPTER ONE

When the guy with the chain saw walked in, Babs's husband, Rheal Dionne, was seated alone at the Chez Paree Bar and Nightclub, three whiskeys deep and lost in a stir of thoughts. It was slow for a Thursday, or at least would have been considered slow for a Thursday before the strike; now it made sense that Rheal was the only person at the bar, given that it was two in the afternoon and most people in the neighborhood couldn't afford to eat, let alone drink. The jukebox was silent for want of a few quarters and the only other people in the place, besides Jeannie the bartender, were a couple in a booth against the far wall, whose conversation Rheal could make out over the hum of beer coolers behind the bar. So when he heard the squeak and clang of the door opening Rheal half turned toward the sound, on reflex, and spotted the guy with the Stihl as he crossed the threshold, headed straight toward him.

This was new. Rheal'd been shot at, stabbed, beaten with a baseball bat on two occasions. He'd been punched and kicked more times than he could count. He'd had his nose broken twice, lost five teeth, and once got his forearm snapped in two when

Denny Albert took a swing at him with a pressure-treated two-by-four after hearing an erroneous report that Rheal had fucked his wife, Carrie. Rheal even had three pieces of steel shrapnel in his neck from a mortar round that'd had at least half his name on it fifteen years earlier. But on all the occasions somebody had tried to kill, maim, or simply beat the ever-loving shit out of Rheal, no one had ever come after him with a chain saw.

The novelty of it brightened his mood a bit. He rotated on his stool and watched, smiling and still holding his whiskey glass, as the man closed the distance between them and came to a stop five feet away.

"You Rheal Dionne?" the man asked.

"I am," Rheal said.

The man nodded and made a show of yanking the saw's starter cord several times—to no avail. He paused, looked down, fumbled with the choke, then started pulling again, glancing up at Rheal and appearing more than a little embarrassed.

"Take your time," Rheal said, lifting the whiskey to his lips. Over his shoulder, he could hear Jeannie on the phone out back, calling the police.

More adjustments to the choke, more yanking on the cord. The man was breathing hard now. Rheal imagined the skin on his fingers was starting to sting and blister.

"A friendly word of advice," Rheal said. "If you're going to attack someone with a chain saw, you may want to get it tuned up beforehand."

"Just—hold on a second," the man said. "It works fine."

"You gas it up?"

"*Yes*, I gassed it up. You think I'm an idiot?"

Rheal shrugged and finished his drink while the man continued to pull and curse. Finally the saw sputtered to life, hacking out a cloud of two-stroke smoke that billowed upward and spread across the ceiling like a black liquid. The motor was running, but barely; it chugged and hiccupped, threatening to stall.

"Hit the choke!" Rheal yelled over the racket. "You're going to flood it!"

"I know how to run a goddamn chain saw!" the man hollered, fumbling for the choke as the engine paused mid-chug, seemed for a second to quit, then turned over again and continued to cling to life. Behind the man, the couple in the booth got up and ran out; Rheal waved cheerfully to them as they went.

The man finally got his fat fingers around the choke knob and opened it up, and the saw's motor smoothed out and idled at a growl. The man took the saw by the handles and goosed the trigger a few times, trying to approximate a menacing glare. He said something to Rheal, unintelligible over the grind of the saw.

"I can't hear you!" Rheal said, cupping a hand behind one ear.

The man let the motor come back to idle and yelled, "What happened to the lady behind the bar?"

Rheal looked over his shoulder toward the door to the kitchen. "She probably ran outside, don't you think?"

"Well, go get her back in here," the man said.

Rheal gazed at the man for a moment, then shook his head. He reached back and pulled the bottle of Jameson from the rack and poured himself another drink. "Let's just walk through this, step by step," he said. "I assume you're here to cut me up, right?"

"That's right," the man said.

"That being the case . . . if you let me go outside, what makes you think I'm foolish enough to come back just so you can take that saw to me?"

The man didn't have a ready answer for this. He stood there mute, the chain saw still rattling in his hands.

"Let's try another line of inquiry," Rheal said, placing the bottle back in the rack. "Why is it so important that Jeannie be behind the bar to see you chop me up?"

"Because I've got a message someone needs to hear."

"Why not just tell it to me?"

"Because you're going to be dead."

"Oh, right," Rheal said. He took a long drink of whiskey and made a show of pondering, rubbing at the stubble on his chin. "Well, it's just the two of us in here, and you can't send me out to grab Jeannie, because no way *I'm* coming back," he said. "Seems like you've got yourself one heck of a dilemma."

"Shit," the man said. "I told them I should just use a gun. But no, they said, it's gotta be a chain saw, has to be scary and bloody and all that."

"Way I see it," Rheal said, "there are two possible solutions, and neither of them is perfect. One—and this is probably the better of the options—you could just write the message down. You know, for someone to find after I'm dead."

The man looked doubtful about this, and Rheal realized he must be illiterate.

"Or two," Rheal said, "and you're really not going to like this one—you could wait for the cops to show up, which I'm guessing they will within two minutes at this point, and give *them* the message."

"The cops?" the man said. "Who called the cops?"

"Jeannie," Rheal said, hooking a thumb over his shoulder. He finished his whiskey. "Tick-tock, friend. What's it gonna be?"

The man dropped the saw and turned to run the way he'd come in, but Rheal was quicker, he was always quicker, he was in fact a grand master when it came to life and the violence it visits upon us, having learned everything he needed to know and then some from his own father, and he leaped up and grabbed two fistfuls of the man's hair, hauled back hard enough to lift him clean off his feet, and slammed the back of his head into the bar.

The man went slack but Rheal held him upright, depositing him on a stool and leaning over to turn off the saw. He straightened up again and slapped the man's face a few times, lightly, to bring him around.

"What's the message?" Rheal asked.

"Huh?"

"Listen, you seem like a hapless shit caught up in something you don't understand," Rheal said. "I want to get you out of here before the cops show, but first I need to know who sent you."

The man finally focused his gaze on Rheal's face. "Harold Aucoin," he said.

"That was my first guess. And what message, pray tell, did Harold want you to give us?"

The man put a hand to the back of his head; it came away slick with blood. "That this town is his now, by order of both God and Clay Sutton."

"I see." Rheal brushed off the man's shoulders, clapped him on the arms. "Okay. You good? Can you walk out of here?"

"I think so."

"You give old Harold a message for *me*," Rheal said. "Tell him we've got enough problems without him trying to poison our neighborhood with drugs. And if he keeps sending people our way, we're going to start sending them back to Lewiston in body bags, regardless of what God or Clay Sutton has to say about it. Got all that?"

"No."

Rheal hauled the man to his feet. "Doesn't matter," he said. "Tell Harold I said to get fucked. Now scoot."

The man wobbled out the door, and Rheal turned to the bar and poured himself another couple fingers of Jameson. Two minutes later, Jeannie came back in with Captain Daryl Bates in tow.

"Did you kill him?" Bates asked.

"Kill who?" Rheal asked without turning around.

"The guy that saw belongs to."

"No idea what you're talking about, Daryl. I was cutting some dead branches off an elm in my backyard when I got thirsty."

"Uh-huh." Bates looked to Jeannie, who'd resumed her spot behind the bar. "That how you remember it?" he asked.

Jeannie shrugged. "If that's what Rheal says."

Bates slid between two stools and leaned against the bar top, facing Rheal. "I want to help you," he said, "but I can't if you won't talk to me."

"If and when I need help from a no-good Anglo cop," Rheal said, "you'll be the first call I make, Daryl."

Even a quick glance at the classics demonstrates that, throughout human history, going home after a long absence has always been at best a mixed bag. Odysseus came back from twenty years at war to find a bunch of guys trying to bed his wife; the Prodigal Son's return, celebrated by his father, was received with considerably less joy by his older, more responsible brother. The very word *home*, for most of us, is freighted with ambivalence, and certainly that was the case for Rita Doyon as she came down the steps of a Greyhound bus and emerged into Little Canada, the place that had birthed and weaned her, for the first time in five years.

Rita had gotten word about hard times at home during the paper mill strike—that was, in fact, part of the reason she'd returned. But the squalor and decay she encountered as she walked south on Water Street and shifted her suitcase from hand to hand far outstripped what she had imagined. It looked like some kind of natural disaster had hit the place and no one could be bothered to clean up. Stores that had thrived her entire childhood were closed, display windows covered with plywood and FOR LEASE signs pleading from their front entrances. Trash cluttered the sidewalks and gutters, drooped from power lines and tree branches. Most ominously: every third house had a sign in the front yard offering it for sale at a price one would expect to pay at a tax auction. It was more important to people, evidently, that they flee Little Canada as soon as possible than get anything resembling a fair price for their homes. And it seemed it was a struggle even to give them away.

As Rita walked and the scope of the damage wrought by the strike sank in block by block, she was surprised to find herself weeping. But there was little time for such things, because here now was a home stolidly *not* for sale, a home that, unlike the ones around it, had been kept up with great care and precision. This was the home that Rita's best friend, Babs, lived in, the home Rita herself had grown up in after Babs's parents had rescued her from her drunken, sadistic father. And inside that home, now, awaited a reckoning.

She climbed the front steps, set her suitcase on the porch landing with a thump, and wiped the tears from her cheeks. Not for the first time since getting on the bus at Forty-Second Street in

Manhattan, she wondered if this had been a mistake. Things were far worse than she'd realized, and not only did there seem to be nothing Rita could do to help—whatever she'd imagined she could do was lost to the destitution on display—but now she had to face the prospect of Babs's ire at her having left in the first place. The two of them hadn't spoken since that day in 1979 when Rita had followed her ambitions south, and if she meant to be a part of this community again, she would first have to settle accounts with her best friend and adoptive sister.

Lacking the energy to walk all the way back to the bus stop, not to mention the money to pay the return fare to New York, Rita took a breath, fixed her posture, and knocked.

A few seconds later the door opened and there stood Babs, indelibly herself. The only difference five years had made being the length and cut of her hair—it was below her shoulders now, and aggressively feathered. Before she had a chance to catch herself, Babs's eyes went wide at the sight of her best friend, and in an instant Rita found herself enveloped in an embrace that lasted long enough for her to consider that this was not at all the reception she'd anticipated.

"Come on," she said finally. "It's not like I've risen from the dead."

Babs pulled back and looked her up and down. "No," she said, "and I can't tell you how glad I am that you're *not* dead. Because it means I can kill you."

That was more like it, Rita thought.

"Should I translate that as 'Great to see you, come on in'?"

"Has it been so long," Babs asked, "that you've forgotten my words never require translation?"

"An elephant's faithful one hundred percent," Rita said. She lifted her suitcase again. "I assume there's coffee on?"

Several minutes later the two sat together at Babs's kitchen table, cigarettes sending up smoke signals and mugs of black coffee steaming. Famished after more than a dozen hours on the bus, Rita worked over her second slice of Babs's *tarte au sucre,* alternating bites with drags on her cigarette.

"I saw you were in some plays," Babs said.

"Off-off-off-Broadway," Rita said. "Don't be too impressed. How'd you hear about that way up here?"

"You're my sister," Babs said. "I kept tabs. So why are you back?"

"Blunt as always."

"You chose to leave. Those of us who've been here all along have a right to ask why you returned."

Rita looked at Babs for a moment. "I knew there was trouble. I wanted to help."

Babs squinted. "How, exactly?"

"Not sure," Rita said. "I thought I had some idea, but it blew away on the ride up."

"Of course it did," Babs said. "Because you didn't come home to help."

"No?"

"You said it yourself. Whatever idea you had fell apart when faced with the reality here. So what really brings you home?"

A pause, the two of them staring at one another. "Because," Rita said finally, "I need to regroup. I took my shot. It didn't work out. And here I am."

"Good," Babs said. "Now you're being honest. And that's the bare minimum for getting back in my good graces."

"Babs, I don't need forgiveness—from you or anyone else—for trying to live my life."

"No you do not," Babs said. "But you *do* need my forgiveness if you want to be part of this community again."

"Such as it is," Rita said. She dragged on her cigarette and tapped it in the big glass ashtray on the center of the table. "From what I've seen, you should be turning cartwheels that anyone wants to move back here."

"Are you moving back here? Or just using us as a pit stop while you 'regroup'?"

Rita leveled her gaze. "I'm here right now," she said. "Take it or leave it."

And it was, improbably, Babs who broke off the staring contest. She looked down at the nub of her cigarette, took one last drag, and crushed it out in the ashtray.

"Since we're being honest with each other," Rita said, "I don't know what I'm doing, or how long I'm going to be here. Might be two weeks. Might be the rest of my life. I may or may not go back to New York and try again."

"You're still young enough," Babs said, "to think you can walk through a door without it locking behind you."

"What are you, five months older than me?" Rita said. "Give me a break."

"Killing ages a person," Babs said. "That's why I swore off it."

"Babs, get serious. What's going on? What's happening with the strike? Why is everyone leaving?"

"Each of those questions has the same answer, and it's a long one."

"Just tell me how I can help," Rita said.

"Do you still pray?" Babs asked. "Because I've got a very important meeting this afternoon, and I don't think it's going to go well."

"I do pray, as a matter of fact," Rita said. "And in the meantime, I'll give you a bit of free advice: Stop trying to do everything on your own. You have friends. Or at least you did, last I knew."

An hour later Babs was at her very important meeting in the basement of the Forest J. Paré post of the VFW, which had served as the de facto strike headquarters from the beginning. No one at the meeting had yet spoken beyond preliminary *hi howya-doins*, but nonetheless, as she'd predicted, it was not going well. Mostly because five minutes before it began Babs had been waylaid by what felt like a sudden fever, and now she sat shaking and sweating and trying her damnedest not to puke up the chicken salad sandwich she'd been eating before Rita had knocked on her door.

Babs sat alone on one side of a folding banquet table. Opposite her: five representatives from the United International Papermakers Union, of which the twelve hundred striking employees of the Hollingsworth & Whitney mill were dues-paying members, Babs included. She served as the president of Local 116 and was there in that capacity. This made the men at the table ostensibly her allies, but they felt every bit like enemies, peering at her with a mixture of disinterest and distaste. These men had smooth hands and looked like they'd never once needed a shower after work. They'd arrived from the Portland airport in separate late-model rental cars, two of them convertibles, as though on vacation, as though they'd never once had to consider the value of a dollar. If the strike failed, none of their lives would change a whit. They would not need new jobs, or wonder how they'd feed their children. Nothing they'd planned on or hoped for would be lost. The only world they'd ever known would not suddenly cease to be.

As she eyed the union brass and swallowed hard against the turmoil in her belly, Babs mused that for all the complex and minute ways people organized themselves into tribes, there was really only one distinction that mattered: you either had money, or you did not. When it came down to it, you could only ever share common cause with the people on your side of that line. Yet here she was with these men who were pretending to have her interests, and those of her neighbors, foremost in mind.

"Coming here, I have to drive past Connie Fecteau's place," Babs said finally. "Do you know Connie? 'Course you don't. Connie's divorced, got two little girls. She crossed the picket line last week. Couldn't take it anymore. Couldn't feed her girls one more meal of buttered noodles. Strike fund's dried up, the company's not budging, and you guys are doing jack shit about any of it. So she crossed over."

Babs observed the men, who remained as impassive as God.

"So just now, when I drove past Connie's," Babs said, "I see someone's taken a can of spray paint to her place. On one side of the porch, in letters six feet high, it says 'Superscab.' On the other side it says '*Putain*.' Do any of you speak French?"

Heads shaking on the other side of the table—vigorous denial, as though Babs had asked if they were into pederasty.

"It means 'whore,'" Babs told them. "Her girls have to see that. And kids are smart. They've been in this with us. They know one of their neighbors did that to their mother's house."

The oldest of the men, the only one Babs knew by his name,

which was Robert Reynolds, spoke up. "Mrs. Dionne," he said, "it's not clear to me what this has to do with us, or, I guess, what you expect us to do *about* it."

"I expect you to expand the strike to International Paper's mills in Memphis and De Pere," Babs said.

"How will that help Miss . . . Fecteau, is it? And why *should* we want to help her? You said it yourself—she crossed the picket."

"She crossed the picket because she lost hope," Babs said. "And she lost hope because the company's got no reason to negotiate. The Mill runs day and night. Paper goes out and money comes in. We're losing everything, and the company hasn't skipped a beat."

"Mrs. Dionne," Reynolds said. "We cannot *make* other Locals strike. That's for their membership to decide."

"Then we need the national union's support in convincing their membership," Babs said.

"And you've had it."

"So you say," Babs said. "But when we sent a contingent of Local 116 members to Memphis, they didn't even know we were coming. We spent two days trying to set meetings on our own, and when we finally did get one, they booed us out of the auditorium."

Reynolds put his hands out in a shrug. "It's hardly within our ability to control how you are received by other Locals," he said.

"They believe the lies the company tells them about how we're soft and greedy," Babs said. "And they'll keep believing those lies, because *you* haven't told them the truth. That the contract the company offered was designed to cause a strike. That when the company's finished with us, the other Locals are next."

An impasse. Babs was quiet for a moment, looking at each of the men in turn.

"When this strike started," she said finally, "you told us we had to do things the 'right' way. It's been a year, and what has that gotten us?"

Silence from the men.

"Anyone?" Babs said.

Still nothing.

"I'll take your silence to mean you agree it's gotten us nowhere," Babs said. "The law is written to benefit the company. We follow the law, the company wins. It's that simple. As such, I can't promise my membership will have patience for the 'right' way much longer."

Reynolds's eyebrows knitted. "That sounds like a threat," he said.

"No, it's just a fact. I'm not the only person in this town who remembers how our fathers and grandfathers dealt with strikebreakers. People got hurt. People got killed. As someone who knows all too well what violence looks and feels like, I want to avoid it even more than you do. But you're giving us no choice."

"Babs—"

She couldn't believe they were making her say this and *mean* it, that after a year of suffering, families broken like cheap plastic toys and friendships turned to dust, the strikers were going to end up doing what they should have done to begin with, bricks through windows, fists in faces, the hard way, the *only* goddamn way, the way she'd sworn off while listening to Sacha gasp his last.

But of course these men were making her say it, because it wasn't their windows or teeth that would be broken, same as it wasn't them queuing up at the union food bank or buying five gallons of kerosene with rolled change to keep their pipes from freezing. These men weren't the ones who would end up in jail, so they didn't care.

"Mrs. Dionne," Reynolds said now, "I hate to be the one to say this, but it must be said: The national union is withdrawing its support for your strike. And our strong recommendation is that you call an end to it yourself."

Babs had known this was coming, had known it in her heart even before she'd arrived at the VFW today, and yet hearing the words still took her breath away, made her gasp audibly. And looking at these men now, seeing on their faces the smug certainty that this decision would not hurt them one bit, Babs felt the first stirrings of a long-dormant beast in her chest, the animal that could make these men pay for their treachery and double-dealing. It wanted out. It wanted to taste their innards, burn their houses and their vacation homes and make their children wail. And this horrified Babs even more than the prospect of Little Canada being no more.

Her stomach heaved suddenly into her throat, and she rose from the table and walked out of the room with as much composure as she could manage, glad that it would appear as though she was storming away on a wave of righteous anger. She hit the vinyl tile in the hallway and lurched right, soles slipping and squeaking, toward the sign, hanging over a doorway fifteen feet distant, that read LADIES. Her head swam and she kept her jaw clenched against the insistent acid surge, her diaphragm knocking like a landlord looking for three months' back rent. She hit the bathroom door with both forearms, opening her mouth before she even reached the nearest sink, an electric, liquid rush—and twenty seconds later her vision cleared and she was breathing hard over the basin, holding herself up with hands on either side, staring down into what had been her lunch, wondering, *Oh my God what is wrong with me?*

CHAPTER TWO

Rheal had a meeting of his own, but because he was intent on continuing to drink (particularly given the nature of this meeting), he sat in the basement at You Know Whose Pub, nursing a Schlitz that had started warm and only gotten more so as he waited for Claude to show up. On the floor, next to his stool, rested the chain saw he'd taken from Aucoin's errand boy, which Rheal had every intention of keeping. His mind should have been on Claude, not to mention Aucoin and the fact that the two-bit gangster from Lewiston was apparently working for the company, but instead he was thinking about his wife, Babs. In the previous year, they'd lost each other. This was the simplest, most honest way to think about it. That peculiar thing where you lived with somebody and shared just about every significant experience but, despite all that, one day you looked up at them and realized you had no earthly clue who they were.

The reason Rheal felt distant from Babs seemed straightforward enough: they were so preoccupied with the strike that even during the few hours a day when they (a) found themselves in the same place and (b) weren't asleep, they rarely talked about anything but the strike itself: how it was going (poorly), what they might do to improve things (not much), who among the strikers was getting antsy to either cross the picket or murder a scab (just about everyone).

But that wasn't all of it. Something else was at work between them, some lever ratcheting them apart. Rheal couldn't name it, but he could feel it unmistakably. His wife was becoming a stranger to him, and he to her. And there seemed to be little he could do about it.

Rheal finished his Schlitz at a pull and motioned to Remy the bartender for another. At the same moment this fresh pint hit the mahogany, rude sunlight blasted the basement as Claude Rancourt, Rheal's best and oldest friend, came in.

Claude mounted the stool to Rheal's left and pointed at Rheal's beer to indicate to Remy he'd have the same. Rheal and Claude had been so thick for so long that the two of them, knowing they'd be drafted before the ink dried on their high school diplomas, had volunteered for the Marine Corps on the buddy program back in '68. They did two tours together, the first with the 5th Marines and the second with the 3rd Force Recon, both out of An Hòa, though with recon they were in the bush so often and for so long they barely saw the village that served as their base. As one might imagine, serving together for two years in the place where North Vietnamese Army units regularly infiltrated the South via Laos meant Rheal and Claude did and saw and endured some unthinkable shit together. Throughout, they remained loyal friends, which was why Rheal still had a hard time believing the conversation he was about to have was actually necessary.

"*Salut*," Claude said.

"How's things?"

"I haven't had a paycheck in forty-seven weeks," Claude said. "That's how things are." He took his Schlitz from Remy before the bartender had a chance to set it down.

"Beer's on me," Rheal said.

"Merci mille fois."

"Sophie worried about money?"

"No," Claude said. "We're not broke. Yet. It's not about that."

"What's it about, then?"

"The way it all feels," Claude said. "When you wait long enough for the other shoe to drop, eventually you find yourself wishing it would. Get it over with, *tu vois*?"

Rheal did, in fact, know the feeling Claude was talking about. To keep struggling, you had to hope. And hope was a burden—one so onerous that Rheal and Claude had abandoned it fifteen years before, discarded in the An Hòa valley along with the cigarette butts and empty bug spray cans.

"And then the other thing," Claude continued, "is you worry the shoe has *already* dropped, and you're just too stupid to realize it."

Another feeling Rheal was familiar with. But he was not here to commiserate with Claude, particularly over when and how the struggle should be abandoned, so he kept his agreement to himself.

"What's the word with our friends at the police department?" he asked.

Claude's brother-in-law was Daryl Bates—the young captain on the Waterville police who had wanted to "help" Rheal. Bates fed Claude information about the department's posture regarding the strike, and how that posture shifted day to day and incident to incident. Generally, because the strikers were mostly Franco—which was to say poor and Catholic and thus disregarded—and the company was the alpha and omega of the local economy, the cops deferred to the company and leaned in their favor when making decisions. For example, in the first few weeks of the strike, seemingly decades ago now, chief Roy Davies decreed that no more than two dozen picketers could gather at the gate to the Mill at any time. This, of course, kept most of the strikers sidelined, and hamstrung their ability to draw media attention to the cause. Three or four hundred picketers made for good copy; a couple dozen did not.

"They're nervous about the rally," Claude said. "Bringing in off-duty bodies from Fairfield and Winslow. Sheriff's deputies, too. State police are on call in the event of trouble. Davies's talking tough. Zero tolerance for shenanigans of any kind, is the word."

"And how do they define 'shenanigans'?"

Claude snorted. "I'd tell everyone to avoid jaywalking, if they can help it."

"There's a good chance people will get up to worse than that, depending on how Babs's meeting with the union honchos went," Rheal said. He lit a cigarette and ashed in one of the little disposable aluminum ashtrays scattered around the bar.

"Why? Are they refusing to expand the strike?"

Rheal turned and peered at Claude. "I don't know yet," he said. "But I'm not sure I'd tell you if I did."

"Quoi?"

"You heard me."

"What is this bullshit, Rheal?"

"People think you're talking to management."

"Who said that?"

"Doesn't matter. Are you?"

"I'm not going to dignify that with a response."

"Why?" Rheal asked. "Because it's not true and never would be in a thousand years? Or because you don't want to lie to your best friend?"

The two men tested each other's gaze, Rheal dragging on his Pall Mall.

"This is your one chance to come clean," Rheal said finally. "After today, I think you're working both sides, it's your ass. You know how this goes."

"Yeah, I do," Claude said.

Rheal drained his beer, then looked at his friend again. "One last chance, Claude," he said. "Be straight with me."

"Fine," Claude said. "Guilty as charged."

"*Tabarnak*," Rheal said. "Why?"

"*Un centime*," Claude said. "Why else?"

"You just said you weren't broke."

"Exactly," Claude said. "That's *why* I'm not broke."

"You're betraying us all for *money*?"

"Must be one hell of a view from up there on your high horse," Claude said. "It's simple: my wife's kidneys are shit and without money she would die. I give the company nothing. Just because they think the information is worth paying for doesn't mean it actually is."

"An example. I'll decide whether it's nothing."

Claude drank from his beer, thought a moment. "Last week I told them Peter Chasse was planning to take water samples from up around the sludge dump, try to prove the company didn't line the dump the way regulations said."

"You gave them his *name*?"

Claude scowled at Rheal. "Of course not. I'm using his name with you. I told them 'someone' was going to take water samples—on Thursday."

"And Peter went to the dump Tuesday."

"Exactly," Claude said, lighting a cigarette.

"It's still dangerous, what you're doing," Rheal said. "They normally have one guard up there, asleep in the gate shack. Peter said he saw half a dozen, walking patrols, carrying goddamn carbines."

"Chasse's slick enough to deal with that."

"Not the point, as you damn well know."

"I'm not a fucking turncoat, Rheal," Claude said.

"No. You aren't. And you're going to prove it."

"Meaning what?"

"For starters, you're going to cease and desist telling the company anything."

Claude shook his head. "I need that money, Rheal," he said. "Do you have any idea how much dialysis costs? I didn't either, until we went on strike and I lost our insurance."

"We'll figure out how to pay for Sophie's treatments."

"How?"

"I just said we'll figure it out."

Claude dragged on his cigarette and rounded the cherry against the wall of the ashtray. "I don't know, Rheal," he said.

"You don't know?" Rheal said. "Let's talk about what you do know. You know I'm not much of a crier. If I was, you'd understand how much this conversation has hurt me. You broke my fucking heart, Claude."

Claude looked down into his beer. "I know," he said. "And I'm sorry. I was doing what I had to do."

"We'll take care of Soph and the girls, one way or another," Rheal said. "But I have to know you're going to toe the line."

There wasn't much left to talk about after that, and the two men passed several minutes in silence. Then Claude finished his beer and left without a word. When he was gone Rheal rubbed at his eyes and asked Remy for a shot of Canadian Club. He tossed it back, put a ten on the bar, then rose from his stool, hoisted his new chain saw, and headed for home.

Bernette Bergeron had always thought of marriage like a sine wave: Sometimes you were up, sometimes you were down. The cycle repeated itself at more or less regular intervals and you learned to ride the wave and made it—or you didn't, and didn't. Bernette and her husband, Hugo, had, like any other couple still together after a decade, for sure ridden the wave. Married when she was seventeen and he eighteen, they'd had three kids and made it through the lean times when Hugo pieced together a living slinging eggs in the mornings and loading long-haul trucks at night, and the flush times after he'd gotten hired to run a log picker at Hollingsworth & Whitney. Through that decade, Hugo had been several nautical miles from perfect, but he was on balance a good husband and father, and Bernette had never had reason to question whether she loved him. Until now.

Like most of the other men in the neighborhood, Hugo had been out of work for over a year, and like most of the other men in the neighborhood, he'd been slowly transformed by the erosive force of the strike into someone whose chief personality trait was self-pity. This was, needless to say, from his wife's perspective, not sexy. Still, at first Bernette had been sympathetic. But as time went by and Hugo spent more and more of his waking hours staring forlornly out the kitchen window or pretending to read *The Wars of America*, sympathy was incrementally displaced by impatience.

And then impatience had turned to disdain, which didn't seem to Bernette at all compatible with love. Thus her misgivings about the state of her and Hugo's sine wave, which from her perspective had crashed headlong into the earth like an airplane missing a wing. In recent months she'd found herself thinking more and more about how every man she'd ever known—her father included—had invariably behaved like a big fat baby whenever anything didn't go their way, while simultaneously never seeming to notice the gigatons of shit the women in their lives managed and tolerated without complaint. More recently, she'd found herself considering what had previously been unthinkable—taking the kids and moving somewhere else. Lewiston maybe, or north to Bangor. Hugo could stay or he could come along, his choice. By the time Rita showed up at her front door that morning, Bernette had just about decided to leave what was left of Little Canada, come what may.

"Which is ironic," she said to Rita as they sat at the kitchen table sharing a jug of Carlo Rossi Chablis. "Because here you are."

"You're not really going to leave," Rita said.

"Why not? You did."

"I didn't have a husband and three kids."

"If you were still in New York, and we were talking on the phone," Bernette said, "I could see why it'd be hard for you to understand how bad things are. But you've had a look for yourself. There's nothing left for us here. That's the plain fact."

"Bernie," Rita said, "since when do the women of this neighborhood just up and call it quits?"

"Since no one's husband has pulled a paycheck in a year."

"Please," Rita said. "Let's not get evangelical about money. On the rare occasion my father had a paycheck, he drank it. My mother still found a way to feed us."

"Sure, but you left home in grade school."

"Not because my mother couldn't feed us," Rita said. "And anyway, you're making my point for me. I'm tired of leaving. I want to do what I have to do to stay."

"You picked a hell of a time to decide to grow old here."

Rita laughed. "Yeah, well, what can I tell you? My timing has always been impeccable."

They were quiet for a minute. Bernette poured more wine while Rita gazed out the window, adrift in memory.

"My mother stole," Rita said finally. "From the supermarket, the gas station, the department store. She stuffed lunch meat in her bra and frozen dinners down her pants. She jimmied open the change dispenser at the laundromat. She figured out how to rig a pay phone to make free calls. She stole bags of bottles from behind the redemption center and walked them back in the front door to cash them in a second time. She was a goddamn bandit. Butch and Sundance had nothing on her."

Bernette lit a cigarette, a smile her only response.

"When all else failed, she even sold her body a few times," Rita said. "Of all the things she did to provide, not one of them was legal, but she worked harder than anyone I ever knew with a job. She raised five kids with no paycheck and a husband who beat the piss out of her on the regular."

"So what are you saying?"

"She did all that alone. Imagine what she could have done with a few other women as tough and smart as she was?"

Father Clement Thibault, who Babs had chosen to save her on the day she killed the cop in 1968, and who as a result had become her spiritual caretaker whether he liked it or not (and he didn't), was seated at his desk in the rectory across the street from Notre Dame du Perpetual Secours when he heard the doorbell ring.

He looked up from the photographs on his desk, trying to remember if anyone had ever rung the rectory doorbell in the two decades he'd been living there. When people wanted to see Clement they sought him following Mass, or Saturdays after CCD; all other inquiries and entreaties came via telephone, without exception. Which made sense, when you thought about it—just walking up and knocking on God's door unannounced seemed impertinent, if not downright sacrilegious.

When the doorbell rang, Clement had been feeling melancholy for days. God seemed so distant as to not exist, a palpable absence that came over Clement from time to time and which he could only admit, ironically, to God Himself. When Clement doubted God he naturally doubted the life he'd chosen, and when that happened he often would find himself going through old photographs from another life altogether, which no one in Waterville knew anything about. A life that only a handful of people in the world knew about—because most who'd been central to it were long-since departed.

Here was a black-and-white of his parents, 1935 or so, posed in the gravel driveway of their modest Cape in Madawaska where Clement would be born a year later. His older brother, Richard, stood between them, the crown of his head level with the belt on their father's high-waisted pants. Scarlet fever would ensure that Clement had no memory of his only sibling, but he didn't need a photo to confirm his brother had existed—as the firstborn son Richard had been owed to God and thus slated for the priesthood, and on the day he died and every day since, Clement had taken his place.

Farther down in the scattering of photos, the pine trees and smokestacks of Madawaska gave way to the gleaming vertiginous towers of postwar Manhattan. As a young man in his twenties Clement looked no older than fourteen, jeans cuffed and hair duckassed, carrying his trumpet case down a crumbling sidewalk in Harlem, as far from the cassock and crucifix as one could imagine. *Mon Dieu*, all the incriminating, godless shit in these photos: Clement performing behind a scrim of cigarette smoke at the Palm Cafe, the only white face in the joint onstage or off; laughing with friends at an after-hours bacchanalia, fine-hewn drinkware in hand; standing on his wedding day at the eastern foot of the Brooklyn Bridge, in the same black suit and skinny black tie he wore to play, arm in arm with Simone, the woman who had died and taken their baby with her.

Married and with a pregnant bride, yes, these were among the biggest secrets in Clement's secret unpriestly past, that lost decade when he ran as hard and as far from his obligations to his parents and his brother's ghost as he could. And then Simone's death had sent him running right back, all the way to the seminary.

The doorbell rang again, and Clement shuffled the pictures together and stuffed them into the Phillies Perfecto box (itself a relic of that other life), which went atop the hutch in the dining room where no one shorter than six foot six would be able to see it. As he put the stepladder away the doorbell rang a third time, and Clement finally went to the entryway, wondering who in hell would be so insistent, then realizing the answer with abrupt certainty just as his hand hit the doorknob.

And sure enough, it was Babs he found standing on the rectory's top step, smoking and looking impatient. "Mind if I bring this in?" she asked, waving her cigarette absently and striding past Clement before he could answer.

"'Course not," Clement said to her back. "Why would I mind?" He closed the door again and followed Babs to the dining room, found her pulling a teacup from the hutch for use as an ashtray.

"I was really hoping to see you in confession this past Sunday," Clement said.

"Don't start."

Clement smirked. "What's up, Babs?"

"I assume you plan to be at the meeting tonight?"

"As I have been at every weekly strike meeting to date."

Babs sat in one of the sturdy, modest oak chairs at the table and pulled the teacup to her. "Tonight will have to be different, Father."

Clement sat opposite her. "I'm not welcome anymore?" he asked. "Hey, do me a favor and don't burn the dining room set. It's the only furniture in the whole place I like. Rescued from a Dutch monastery in the 1800s."

"No, of course you're welcome," Babs said. "It's just your stance of neutrality has to change."

"Why's that?"

"You can't be neutral on a moving train, Father."

"Don't quote Zinn at me, young lady."

A hint of a smile crossed Babs's face. "The national union has pulled the rug out from under us. We're on our own."

"Baptême."

"You said it."

"So, game over."

"Maybe not," Babs said. "There are a few cards left for us to play."

"Not sure I like the sound of that," Clement said.

"And that's why I'm here," Babs told him. "I need your help to keep the strike going—and to keep it from spinning out of control."

"Feelings are running way too high. Not even you will be able to control things, and I'm not sure what help you think I'll be."

"You wield the imprimatur of the Almighty. That seems helpful."

"No," Clement said. "Tell people the truth, Babs: you lost. It'll hurt like hell, and they'll be angry. But if you string this out, it's only going to keep escalating."

"Are you kidding?" Babs asked. "You expect me to just say it's over, your jobs are gone and there's nothing to be done about it?"

"If you're smart, that's exactly what you'll do."

"Whose side are you on, anyway?"

"Babs," Clement said, "you know damn well whose side I'm on."

"Doesn't matter, if you won't say so publicly."

"Regardless of my personal feelings, the Church has to remain above the fray."

"Clement," Babs said. "This is me you're talking to. Save the PR."

They stared at each other in silence for several moments.

"If you're going to insist on smoking in here," Clement said finally, "the least you can do is offer me a cigarette."

Babs smiled and slid her pack across the table.

"And open that window, will you?" Clement said, lighting up.

Babs went to the window looking out on the driveway and slid it up a few inches, then leaned against the sill.

"Look, let's cut the bullshit," Clement said. "We've talked about this on more than one occasion. I'm not allowed to endorse the strike, period."

"Is that according to the bishop?"

"The man himself."

"And what happens if you do it anyway?"

"That would be pointless speculation, since I'm not going to."

Babs flicked her cigarette through the window into the driveway, and Clement gave her a look. "What's really going on with you?" he asked.

"I'm presiding over the end of this neighborhood, the only home I've ever known," Babs said. "There needs to be something else?"

"There doesn't need to be," Clement said. "But there is."

Babs gazed out the window and took a deep breath. "I'm afraid," she said finally.

"Of what?"

"What I'm going to do—what I'm going to become—if this strike fails. I need your help making sure that doesn't happen, Father."

Clement closed his eyes for a moment, face full of regret. "I can't help you, Babs," he said.

She stared at him for a beat, her eyes flashing, and then stood up from the windowsill. "You know how despite the fact that you've been here for twenty years, and despite the fact that your Franco bona fides are impeccable, you still don't really feel like part of this community?"

Clement narrowed his eyes.

Babs crossed the room and snatched her cigarettes from the table in front of him. "If you want that to change, you should start finally *acting* like part of the community."

"That's low, Babs, even for you."

"See you tonight, Father," Babs said, and went out.

Rheal's Mustang was in the driveway when Babs pulled in around five, but when she stepped through the front door the house was silent and still, the only evidence of Rheal's presence his keys on the kitchen table—and, inexplicably, a chain saw on the floor next to the shoe mat.

She found him in their bedroom, asleep on top of the covers in his stockinged feet. Her first impulse was to wake him so he could shower and get ready for the meeting—but then she noticed how serene he looked, his face relaxed and lips slightly parted, hands threaded together loosely over his chest as though he were giving thanks. Rheal's sleep was normally violent and haunted—by his father, by the war—and Babs often had to dodge blows in the middle of the night and kick Rheal awake, or poke him with a broomstick, before he hurt her or tore the bedroom apart. It was rare to see him this at peace, as the sun angled toward evening through the window and a breeze stirred the curtains. So instead of waking him, Babs sat in the baby-blue suede wing chair that had been her mother's, and her grandmother's before that, and watched over her husband as he slept.

She did love Rheal, somewhat desperately, in fact, though she of course would never let that desperation show, to him or anyone else. She loved his patience, his confidence, his unflagging good humor, and his steady conviction that right was right and wrong was wrong. She loved that he was able to put up with her shit, of course, but also that, at a certain threshold, this deference ceased like a crash test car ramming a concrete wall—Rheal was the only man in three counties (whose existence she was aware of, anyhow) who would not wilt before her. She loved his eyes, and the ridge of muscle that ran along either side of his lower abdomen, in front of his hips. The man also had improbably beautiful feet, smooth and sinewy and somehow expressive, nary a callus or bunion. Babs never would have imagined this important, but now that she'd been married six years she knew that as much as you saw (and smelled) your husband's feet, it helped a great deal if they were easy, even pleasant to look at.

None of which was to say the man was without flaw. Drank too much (though it only made him funnier, never mean). More than a little loose with a dollar (though, in fairness, this was usually because he spent it on something for Babs). Refused, too often, to treat a given situation with the seriousness it was owed. In fact, taken as a whole, Rheal could be fairly characterized as somewhat immature, really. The kind of man likely to be described as suffering from Peter Pan syndrome.

Of course, given all he'd seen and done, not to mention what had been done to him, Rheal could have been nasty as a honey badger, and few would have blamed him. In that context, so what if he treated everything like a joke? Babs wasn't the only person who loved Rheal—everyone did, precisely because he wore the world and everything in it so lightly. And Babs knew that wasn't because darkness didn't exist within him. It was because, in response to the example set by his own father, and all the suffering he'd seen and caused, Rheal refused to cede one inch of space to that darkness.

Except, of course, when he slept and no longer had control over the matter.

Now, as Babs watched, the darkness began to rise. Rheal murmured and stirred, unlaced his thick fingers and raised his hands as if getting ready to grapple with someone or something. She'd seen it a hundred times, Rheal preparing for bloodshed in whatever grim, cursed place he went to in his dreams. He curled his fingers into fists, whisper-growled something unintelligible yet easily recognized as a promise of harm. Next, Babs knew from long experience, came the blows.

But as she stood to grab the broomstick before the real trouble could begin, Rheal suddenly opened his hands and raised them in front of his face, as if warding off an attack. He trembled and whimpered, begged for mercy, for peace, sounding every bit like a frightened child. This was entirely new to Babs, and far, far worse than any violence Rheal had ever committed in his sleep—even the times that had left marks on her. She crossed the space between the chair and the bed quickly, put both hands on Rheal's shoulders and shook him hard, yelling at him to wake up. Normally it was dangerous to bring him around in such close quarters—thus the broomstick—but she was so alarmed that her own safety didn't figure into it. She just wanted the pleading to stop.

Rheal opened his eyes with a gasp, suddenly both awake and not, both here and, for a few moments, wherever he'd been in the dream—on the banks of the Thu Bôn, maybe, or locked in his father's toolshed for the night in the dead of winter. He remained in limbo for several moments, gazing about blindly as Babs rubbed his arm and called him back to her, and finally his eyes fell and focused on Babs's face, and he was home again.

Rheal put his head back and closed his eyes once more, gathering himself. "What time is it?"

"Time to get ready," Babs told him. "What had you in such a state?"

"Bad dream," he said.

"No kidding. Want to elaborate?"

"I'd rather not," Rheal said.

"Which means now you have to," Babs said.

He smiled at her, crookedly: *Careful what you wish for, darling.* "You and I had a baby," he said. "Someone was trying to hurt him, and there was nothing I could do about it."

"Who was trying to hurt him?" she asked.

"No one we know," Rheal said. He sat up and swung his feet to the floor, grabbed for his cigarettes on the nightstand. "How'd it go with Clement?"

"He thinks we're cooked."

"From God's lips to our ears," Rheal said. He reached up and pulled Babs onto the bed with him, put an arm around her chest, and proffered the newly lit cigarette, which she smoked from between his fingers. "Asking him to endorse the strike now is like trying to sell a car after you drove it with no oil."

"Am I the only person around here who thinks the union screwing us could actually be an opportunity?" Babs said.

"An opportunity for what?" Rheal grinned. "To work at McDonald's for two bucks an hour?"

"People are angry," Babs said. "But if we can control that anger—direct it—we can make the company look bad. The only thing corporations care about as much as making money is pretending to be good citizens while they do it."

"Well, if it's anger you're after, don't fret—you'll have plenty of it after you give everyone the bad news in a couple hours."

Babs stole Rheal's cigarette and dragged on it. "What's the story with the chain saw, by the way? You planning some renovations I need to know about?"

"I've got good news and bad news," Rheal said.

"I'll take the good news first," Babs said.

"I found out who's been sending all those coke peddlers our way over the past six months."

"Yeah?" Babs said.

"That's the bad news, too."

"You think you could stop talking like the goddamn Sphinx and tell me what's going on?"

"It's Harold Aucoin," Rheal said.

"Ostie qu'il m'énerve," Babs said.

"My thoughts exactly," Rheal said. "And apparently ol' Harold's not happy that we sent his dealers packing. The guy I got the saw from was supposed to cut me up with it. If he wasn't half-retarded they'd be selling pieces of me at Marcoux's Meat Market right now."

"Where is he?" Babs asked.

"Back home in Lewiston, I imagine," Rheal said.

"You let him go?"

"He was a kid, and an idiot," Rheal said.

"An idiot sent to kill you."

Rheal took his cigarette back and tapped it in the bedside ashtray. "There's more," he said. "Aucoin and his crew are on the company's payroll. Way off the books."

"What does that mean?" Babs asked.

"Not sure," Rheal said. "But if I had to guess, I'd say it means in addition to trying to expand his drug operation to our neck of the woods, Harold's going to be gifting us with strikebreakers soon."

"*Saint-ciboire*," Babs said. "Fellow Francos, doing the company's dirty work. *Dieu ne pardonnera pas cela.*"

They were quiet for a moment.

"So we need to be ready for trouble at the rally," Rheal said. "And we need to send a message to Aucoin that betraying your own comes at a cost."

"Who's the messenger?" Babs asked.

"Claude owes me a favor."

"No bloodshed," Babs said.

Rheal slid from behind Babs and sat forward, looking her in the eye. "*Chérie*," he said, "obviously I know how you feel. But this is reaching a point where we have to be willing to break a few eggs. We're standing in the middle of the road right now. And the only thing that accomplishes is, you get squashed."

"No bloodshed," Babs said again. "Make sure Claude knows."

CHAPTER THREE

Over the year-plus that the strike had dragged on, the regular Thursday union meeting had transformed from a sparsely attended bitch session into a quasi-religious display of solidarity that had outgrown several previous venues. Now it was held in the gymnasium of the old Gilman Street school, which could squeeze in around two thousand people if you also used the floor for seating and the fire marshal looked the other way. The meeting had moved there the previous fall, when Jesse Jackson, who was running for the Democratic nomination for president, had come to support the strike while campaigning in the New Hampshire primary.

Some in the union had qualms about inviting Jackson, given that he was quite prominently black and Maine was the whitest state in the country. But Babs had pointed out that if anyone should have a problem with that dichotomy it should be Jackson himself, and perhaps those strikers who had misgivings about him might ask themselves if maybe they weren't racist assholes who were missing the whole point. Jackson was the man who'd said recently it was time to stop thinking about black and white and start thinking about employed and unemployed. Besides, it wasn't like Walter Mondale or Gary Hart were clamoring to support the strike. The union's fight was Jackson's fight, and black and white didn't figure into it.

So Jackson came, and stood before a packed house wearing a Union of International Paperworkers ball cap. No dummy, he went right to the heart of what most were thinking.

"A few weeks ago," Jackson said, "the workers in Cudahy, Wisconsin, called me and said, 'Mr. Jackson, we've been locked out, and we're hoping you can support us.' I said, 'I will come and support you because I think that workers, and their families that have been destabilized, deserve support.' And then they said, 'But you must understand, we're white.'"

Here Jackson paused and gazed around the gym, a knowing smile on his face. The crowd murmured uncertainly—were they being invited to find this funny, as Jackson apparently did?

"So I said to them," Jackson continued, "'Let me get this straight. You're telling me that most people in Cudahy, Wisconsin, are white?'"

The crowd laughed heartily, almost in relief, while Jackson smiled again and waited for the laughter to die down.

"So I told them, 'I understand, but I'm still coming.' And they said, 'Okay, Mr. Jackson, but there's something else you should know. The scabs they brought in are from Milwaukee, you see.' And I said, 'Okay. So what?' And that's when they got real nervous. They said, 'Mr. Jackson, the scabs are black.'"

Silence now in the gym, the tension suddenly even thicker than before. Those assembled knew that many of the scabs in their own mill, having been brought up by the company from the Carolinas and Georgia, were black. Jackson, no doubt, was aware of this fact as well.

"And I told them," he said, his voice rising now, "'I'm still coming!'"

The workers cheered, and Jackson smiled and gazed around the gym, nodding his approval of their approval. "You see," he said over continued applause, "the fact is, it's no accident that management has brought in black workers to replace white workers. Because they want you to see each other as enemies, and the easiest way to do that is to pit black against white. But you aren't enemies. You are all brothers and sisters. It hurts me to see you divided. I have a profound sense of pain for those trapped in poverty who lose their self-respect. So I'm going to talk to the workers inside the Mill, the same as I'm talking to you right now. And I'm going to help them understand that you all have a common enemy—the people who own this mill, the people who exploit both of you for their own gain."

The meeting that day ended with Jackson leading the workers in a rendition of "We Shall Overcome," and dozens of strikers, cash-strapped though they were, wrote checks for Jackson's presidential campaign. Even Babs had felt tears sting her eyes as she watched her neighbors, hand in hand, swaying and singing. Because Jackson had given them something they previously lacked: a sense that they were not on their own, that they were in fact part of a much larger struggle against oppression and iniquity everywhere.

Now that sense of connection to a higher purpose was either AWOL or DOA, depending on your read. Rheal watched from stage left as his wife faced a crowd that sat largely silent, brooding like boulders on a mountain slope as they awaited confirmation of the rumor that had been circulating through the neighborhood all day. No one was holding hands, and they definitely weren't having a sing-along. Grim faces all around and, beneath the veneer of composure, a year's worth of well-earned discouragement, despair, and, deeper still, a primordial fury.

Babs stepped up onto the dais and tapped the microphone several times with a finger, though there was hardly any need to bring the meeting to order. "I'll dispense posthaste with the bullshit," she said after a moment. "What you've heard by now is in fact true: the union has withdrawn its support for the strike."

She paused to allow for grumbling that did not come, and that it did not set Rheal immediately on edge. Complaint, commiseration, even yelling and throwing things would have been welcome, nay reassuring. This silence, though, this tacit submission to their fate—Rheal couldn't imagine anything worse.

"The way I see things," Babs continued, "our choices are simple. We can do what the company and apparently the union want, and give up. There are no guarantees any of us get our jobs back—as you know, the scabs are considered permanent employees by the company, so jobs will only become available again if and when a scab leaves or gets fired. And even if that happens, the pay will be for shit, health and retirement gutted, safety practices ignored altogether. We'll have to accept that everything our parents and grandparents and great-grandparents bled for is gone. You'll only get time-and-a-half on weekends, and then only if you're already over sixty hours for the week. You'll work on Christmas Day, and you'll do it with a smile on your face, or you'll be out on the street again. That's option number one."

Judging by the continued silence in the gym, this option did not much appeal.

"Or," Babs said, "we can keep fighting."

And now the answering silence was broken, finally. "Is that what we've been doing?" a woman's voice called out from somewhere in the bleachers. "Because it seems to me we've just been lying down and taking it."

"She's right," another woman said before Babs had a chance to answer. "I've got an idea: tomorrow we grab every Louisville Slugger we can find and have some batting practice when the scabs come rolling out after second shift."

At this prompting, for the first time in more than a year, order at the meeting broke down and the rabble began to rouse—and even the most casual observer would have noticed that this mob was comprised entirely of women. To a man, the men stayed seated and silent and slumped, but the women rose from their folding chairs, bared their teeth, and shook their fists, sounding every bit as though they were at last in the market for trouble, if not blood. The men, quick to anger at the beginning of the strike but not much for endurance, had burned out months earlier, while the women's greater perspective and self-restraint had preserved their energy for this moment, when they had nothing left to lose but the last thing: the dignity of every person who'd ever walked through the gates of the Hollingsworth & Whitney mill to punch a clock. Dignity: you couldn't eat it and it wouldn't keep you warm, but *par Dieu* the bastards weren't going to take that, too, not if these women had a say. Their righteous fury came roaring forth in a great and deafening wave, more focused and potent and plain dangerous than any foot-stomping the men had ever gotten up to after a few beers. And look at those men now, gazing up and around, bleary-eyed and bewildered, as their wives and sisters and nieces beat the war drums on their behalf when they couldn't be bothered to do so for themselves. As it had always been, so it still was: when it came time to stand up and be men, those who got to their feet were the women.

Rheal watched carefully as Babs waited for the anger to subside. But it only grew further, spreading across and around the gymnasium, a deep, ominous lowing punctuated here and there by incomprehensible shouts. Rheal thought, once more, that Babs's belief that this anger could be harnessed and used to good effect had been naive.

After a few moments, Babs leaned into the microphone again and spoke over the din. "I understand you're angry," she said. "But we've got to be smart about this."

None of those assembled seemed interested in being smart. The din only grew louder.

Rheal was about to walk onstage and commit the cardinal sin in their marriage—behaving, in public, as though his wife needed his help—when Father Clement rose from his seat on the floor and mounted the stairs to the stage. He came to the podium, lifted the microphone from its stand, and jammed it against the amplifier, silencing the women with a blast of feedback loud enough to make people's eyes water.

Satisfied, Clement pulled the microphone away from the amp, and the feedback ceased with one final electric squeal. The priest looked out on the crowd as quiet settled over the gym. Then he brought the mic to his lips.

"I had a visitor earlier today," Clement said. "You may think this is the sort of thing that happens all the time, people coming to the rectory to hit up the priest. But I realized, when I heard the doorbell ring, that this was the first time anyone had come to visit me at my home. I had no idea what my own doorbell sounded like.

Actually, now that I think about it, I didn't even know I *had* a doorbell."

A few chuckles among the strikers.

"When it occurred to me I'd never had a single visitor," Clement went on, "at first I assumed it was because people are naturally reluctant to knock on God's door. But then this visitor helped me understand the real reason no one calls on me. And that's why I'm standing in front of you now, instead of sitting down there quietly like I have every Wednesday since this began."

Clement paused here to gauge his audience, which remained quiet and attentive. He turned briefly to Babs, and she nodded.

"In Psalms," Clement continued, "God asks, 'How long will you judge unjustly, and show partiality to the wicked?' In my case, the answer turned out to be around eighteen months. And I'm sorry it's taken so long. Because I know what's unjust. I know who's wicked, in this fight. And I want to get off the sidelines. But in order to do that, I need to ask something of all of you."

Clement paused again, less to measure the effect his words were having, than to measure the words themselves, make sure they were exactly the ones he wanted to use.

"Sorry to throw a bunch of lousy Bible quotes at you," he said, "but there's another one that explains better than I could what I need to ask. It comes from Paul, when he's laying down church doctrine for the Romans, and despite how that worked out I still think it's essential advice. 'Do not repay anyone evil for evil, but take thought for what is noble in the sight of all.' Paul doesn't make specific mention of putting a baseball bat through the windshield of a Chevy Cavalier, but I think it's the kind of thing he had in mind as something less than noble."

Now the strikers laughed aloud.

"I'm going to come out publicly in support of the strike," Clement said, "and that's going to land me in pretty hot water. What I ask is you don't turn the heat up further by doing something Paul would disapprove of. Because in that case, in addition to needing new jobs, you're almost certainly going to need a new priest."

Clement turned to Babs again. "Thank you, and God bless you, and I'll see you all at the rally," he said into the microphone. "In the meantime, if anyone has anything they want to talk about, it turns out my doorbell works just fine."

Babs came toward the podium again while people in the audience began to stand, commiserate in small groups, and file out of the gym. As she approached, Clement flicked the power switch on the side of the microphone and said, "Jesus Christ, what did I just sign myself up for?"

"There are two ways I can see to hold this place together," Babs said. "You signed up for the one that doesn't involve a bunch of people getting hurt. Or worse."

"Are you sure that's even possible, at this point?" Clement said.

"I have to believe it is," Babs said.

"Well, let's pray to God you're right," Clement said, looking out over the slowly dispersing crowd. "Because otherwise I'm going to be out of a job, same as everyone else."

If Saint Paul wants to come down from heaven and pay for my groceries, I'll be happy to take moral instruction from him," Carmeline Bérubé said. "Until then, he and Father Clement can both go pound sand. Hold on." She turned her head toward the living room, where two of her five boys were horsing around. "Patrice and Chris, if you throw that football in the house *one more time* I'm going to nail your dicks to the floor and push you backwards! Also, why the hell are you conscious? It's ten o'clock at night!"

A voice, thick with sleep, came down the stairs from the opposite side of the kitchen. "It's not me, Ma! I'm in bed!"

Carmeline looked in the direction of the stairs. "Which one are you?" she yelled.

"Chris!"

"Fine, fine," she said, turning back toward the living room. "Whichever one of you little shits is in there with Patrice, knock it the hell off!"

Rita chuckled into her glass of wine. She was not surprised by Carmeline's view of continuing to strike "the right way." In fact, she'd come to Carmeline precisely because among the friends she and Babs shared from childhood, she was the most pugnacious and the least tolerant of bullshit.

Carmeline turned back to Rita and fished her cigarette from the ashtray. "Where was I?" she said.

"You were saying how you'd tell Saint Paul to get bent."

"Right," Carmeline said. "He can fuck off all the way back to Jerusalem. I've got kids to feed."

"Noted," Rita said. "Have any ideas what to do about feeding those kids, then?"

The thunk of a football hitting hardwood came from the living room, and Carmeline whipped her head around again. "If they don't *stop screwing around in there and go to bed* I might just let them starve!"

Muffled, furtive giggling drifted into the kitchen in response.

Carmeline looked at Rita. "*I* still have a job," she said. "At the moment, it's my no-good husband who's useless as tits on a boar. Unless you consider sulking useful."

"Seems that's the general strategy among the men," Rita said. "Granted, I've only been back in town for a few hours."

"Nope, sulking is pretty much it," Carmeline said. "They piss sitting down these days, most of them."

"I was hoping we could come up with a plan a bit more likely to accomplish something."

"Like what?"

"No idea. Just seems obvious that collective bargaining ain't what it used to be. So, fuck it."

"Fuck it?" Carmeline said.

"Fuck it."

"I appreciate the spirit," Carmeline said. "But what's this 'it' we're fucking? And how are we fucking it?"

"All I've got so far," Rita said, pointing toward the living room, "is to take a cue from your boys in there. Stay up past our bedtime. Throw the football in the house."

Carmeline smirked, took a drink of wine, and swallowed, wiping her mouth with the back of her hand. "You know I'm happy to stir the shit," she said. "But good luck getting it past Babs."

"I already talked to Bernette and Stella," Rita said. "They're in. If we go to Babs together . . ."

Carmeline shrugged. "I just hope you're ready to be disappointed. She's a regular albino Gandhi these days."

"I don't believe it," Rita said. "You know as well as I do who Babs really is."

"You've been gone awhile. People change."

"Most people change. Babs isn't most people."

Carmeline shrugged again and dragged on her cigarette. "You

heard her at the meeting tonight," she said. "She expects us all to be good, law-abiding citizens."

"We'll see," Rita said. "All I know is, when I got off the bus this morning and looked around, the first thought that popped into my head was: if Babs hasn't killed anyone over this yet, she's sure as hell going to."

At that moment Claude drove alone through Auburn, Maine—sister city of Lewiston, on the opposite bank of the Androscoggin River—looking for Harold Aucoin's house. In theory the place shouldn't have been hard to find; word was that Hickory Drive, the road Harold lived on, had come into existence solely to accommodate his desire for a country estate, and still had just the one house on it. But there was no sign of any such byway in Claude's *Maine Atlas and Gazetteer*. And Claude didn't want to stop and ask directions, lest whatever helpful citizen he enlisted later be interviewed by the police. Despite Babs's insistence that he merely put a scare into Aucoin, things could easily escalate.

So he drove, following the cracked, rutted pavement of route 202 south out of town, until most signs of habitation ceased. The only thing Claude had to go on was a note that Aucoin's home was "out by the airstrip," meaning the tiny Auburn-Lewiston Municipal Airport, which serviced a handful of charter companies and weekend-warrior Cessna jockeys. But that wasn't very helpful, because there was plenty "out by the airstrip," including Marston Corner and Rumford Junction, the sprawling new Martindale Country Club, and about a thousand meandering country roads, some of which proved to be dead ends, some of which went in circles, and none of which bore a sign reading HICKORY DRIVE.

It went on like this for hours. So long, in fact, that Claude had to gas up again, deciding to drive two towns over to Gray to avoid being seen in Auburn. He kept driving long after dark, a steady stream of WTOS cock rock on the radio to keep himself alert after three deer flashed across the road mere feet in front of his Bronco. He'd smoked an entire pack of Marlboros and was two deep into the next one when his headlights illuminated the DANVILLE CORNER ROAD sign for the fifth time, and he thought briefly about going home, telling Rheal that the message to Aucoin had been sent. But he'd already lied once to his best friend, the man who'd saved Claude's life and Claude his, and he'd resolved that he would not do so again.

Then Claude realized something, as though God had cuffed him on the side of the head. And the moment he had this realization, he wondered how his instincts and intuition, once sharpened to a lethal edge, could have gotten so dull that it took him this long to figure it out: for the past six hours he'd been looking for a road marked Hickory Drive, when in fact he should have been looking for a road that was not marked at all.

Claude had passed such a road several times, three-quarters of a mile north of Danville Corner on Route 4. At a glance it looked like little more than a skidder path: gravel and dirt disappearing just a few feet into the trees. Now he suspected that impression was intentional—and misleading.

Claude pulled to the side of Route 4 and killed the Bronco's engine, reaching into the mesh pouch on the back of the passenger seat for his Maglite. He got out, glanced around, walked over to where the gravel road began. He clicked the flashlight on and saw that ten feet beyond the line of trees, the gravel became brand-new pavement. Casting the flashlight beam skyward revealed power lines strung from Route 4. And to the right side of the road at the intersection, obscured in overgrown crab grass, he found the jagged stump of a street-sign post that had been chopped off near the ground. The city of Auburn had dutifully put up this street sign, and someone else had taken it right back down. Claude was looking, finally, at Hickory Drive.

He went back to the Bronco and, with the lights off, pulled slowly onto Harold's private road. He pulled into the brush, grabbed his KA-BAR and .45, his lock pick, and a package of stew meat he'd purchased before leaving town. At war Claude had never been fond of the pistol—if you had need of one that meant things had really gone to shit. But civilian life rarely called for carrying a long gun outside of deer season, so Claude had gotten more comfortable with the Browning. And he was glad to have it now.

He set out on foot, staying to the trees on the shoulder. The night was moonless, black as squid ink, and, to a former Force Recon Marine, ideal. People made the mistake of thinking that being SpecOps meant that you were a badass; but what it really meant was you were remarkably skilled at seeming to not exist. Claude made his way mostly by senses other than sight, could almost identify the species of tree by the grit of the bark under his hands as he moved from trunk to trunk. There was just enough ambient light to distinguish the strip of charcoal, barely discernible from the black surrounding it, that comprised the road to his left. In this way he kept from wandering off into the woods.

And then the road made one last long turn, and the trees, previously as dense as the north woods, came to an abrupt end, giving way to an undulating emptiness. Floating in the middle of that emptiness: a single light. An upstairs window in a structure that otherwise seemed made of the formless dark surrounding it.

Claude moved toward the light like a moth: silently, compulsively. The house seemed not merely unoccupied, but as if it had never held people at all, which made the back of his brain tingle—in Claude's experience, such a convincing sense that a place was empty was usually cultivated with purpose. Someone awaited.

A hundred meters out, Claude cut across to the other side of the road and approached the house from an angle, gazing up to see where the power and phone lines went in. He scanned the exterior of the building's southeast side, searching for the telltale red lights that indicated a camera or motion detector. Satisfied that there were none, he cut the phone line at the junction box anyway, in case he discovered a security system inside. It might still go off, but now the signal wouldn't reach the Auburn PD, or Aucoin's muscle, or whoever was meant to receive it.

Claude knew Aucoin had at least one dog, a Doberman. This presented two problems: one, no matter how he breached the house, the dog was likely to detect Claude's presence and try to take a bite out of his ass; and two, Claude was not supposed to kill anything, per Babs, which meant making friends was going to be paramount. Thus, the pound and a half of beef cubes crammed into the back pocket of his Wranglers.

He searched around the front of the building and, finding no ominous red lights, went to the door. Peering down through the window, he clicked his flashlight on and saw no alarm sensors, so he used his lock pick—a tool resembling a ballpoint pen—to make quick work of the slant lock in the doorknob. He nudged open the door with his fingertips, winced . . . no lights, no siren. Also, importantly, no growling.

Claude slipped into the garage and took note of the late-model Lincoln parked in one of the garage's four bays. He went over and put a hand on the hood, found it cold. He climbed the three steps at the back of the garage and slowly opened the door that let into the house proper. Both the latch and the hinges were silent—praise God for new construction—and Claude found himself in a kitchen that appeared to have never been used. The rest of the ground floor, as he moved through it, felt the same, less like someone's home and more like mock-ups of rooms from the Sears catalog. And still no Doberman.

He discovered a staircase to the second floor and paused at the bottom to turn his head and listen for any sound; there was none. He checked his sidearm and the stew meat in turn, then began to climb, lightly, on his toes. He put each foot down with great care, but the new stairs had no soft spots, produced none of the cracking and snapping he'd been conditioned to expect by every old tenement in Little Canada he'd ever been in. Before long he had ascended soundlessly to the second floor, and could see, down a hallway and around a corner, a sliver of the same jaundiced light he'd spied in the window upon emerging from the woods.

Claude pulled out the .45 and sidestepped toward the light, his back to the hallway wall, pistol gripped with both hands in front of him. He paused at the corner to listen once more, and was able to pick up a faint sound that took him a moment to place: the tinkling of tags on a dog's collar.

Claude pivoted around the corner on his left foot, gun raised—and found Harold Aucoin lying in bed, massive belly straining the buttons on his pajama top, his right hand stroking the neck of a Doberman on the bed next to him. The dog was the size of a Shetland pony, and Harold himself reminded Claude of a grizzly bear; together they strained the California king mattress to capacity. Neither reacted much to Claude's sudden appearance, though the dog did pick its head up in a way that suggested more decisive action could be forthcoming in a flash.

"You must be Babs's errand boy," Aucoin said, barely bothering to lift his gaze from the television on the dresser opposite his bed.

"I'm the guy with a .45 aimed at the spot between your eyebrows," Claude said.

With much huffing and puffing, Aucoin pushed his bulk into a sitting position against the headboard. "I thought she was smarter than this," he said. "But apparently not."

"Smarter than what?"

"Taking a shot at the king," Aucoin said. "She's out of her league, and she has to know it."

Claude slid into the bedroom, his back to the wall, keeping an eye on the dog. "Maybe she decided to step up to the majors after you tried to kill her husband," he said.

Aucoin snorted. "That was a warning, not a hit," he said. "If I wanted Rheal dead, I wouldn't have sent someone with the mental age of a toddler. So, what is this? Babs doesn't do violence."

"Babs isn't here," Claude said. "I am."

"Indeed. And obviously you've got the drop on me, so if your purpose was to send me on to my eternal reward, I'd already have wings."

"My purpose," Claude said, adjusting his grip on the pistol, "is to demonstrate that, should you push your luck, we can get to you."

"But to what end?" Aucoin asked. "You're not going to do anything, so what do I care? Come on in, pull up a seat, watch *Magnum, P.I.* with me."

A moment passed, then another. Claude stared at Aucoin and Aucoin stared at the television and the dog stared at Claude.

"Are you aware you and I are cousins?" Aucoin asked finally, turning his eyes back to Claude.

"You don't even know who I am."

"Sure I do," Aucoin said. "You're Claude Rancourt, Rheal Dionne's best friend, Babs's errand boy—and my second cousin."

"If that's true," Claude said, "we're all inbred enough that it's hardly a shock."

"Well, once removed. My grandfather Jules was the brother of your great-grandmother. We're family, Claude. We shouldn't fight."

"I'll make sure to say hi at the reunion," Claude said. "Since you brought it up, that's Babs's problem with you, Harold old boy. Siding with the company against fellow Francos? *Tu devrais avoir honte.*"

"Don't come in here and lecture me about loyalty," Aucoin said. "Didn't you report on your neighbors for that same company? *Quelle honte*, Claude."

Claude had nothing to say to this, but something like shame appeared on his features like a radar blip, which Aucoin did not fail to notice.

"Don't worry, I don't judge," he said, smiling. "It's a dog-eat-dog world, cousin. You saw an opportunity, you took it. Anyone who'd fault you for that doesn't understand how the world works. Like our friend Babs. She fails to understand that life is, in the end, about force. Or, I suppose she understood that once, but then lost the stomach for it. Just like a woman."

"Women were some of the best soldiers I fought in Vietnam."

Aucoin waved this away. "Claude," he said, shifting his bulk against the headboard, "you've done your job. Babs's message has been received. And now I'd like to ask a favor, cousin to cousin."

"What's that?"

Aucoin gazed at Claude in silence for a moment, something like regret on his face, and then he said, "*Fass*" quietly, almost in a whisper, and before Claude could even think to take proper aim and squeeze off a round the Doberman was airborne, covering half the distance between the bed and Claude in a single Olympian leap, the dog was massive and impossibly quick, one more long stride and he was in position to leap and seize Claude's throat in his jaws, and Claude had time only to register the beginning of acceptance and a strange curiosity regarding how long it might take to actually die when a dog such as this used your trachea like a chew toy, how much of it he was going to be alive and awake for and how much it was going to hurt, when Aucoin said, equally quietly, "*Stoppen*," and the dog froze with a suddenness almost as improbable and terrifying as that with which he had come unsprung. He sat at Claude's feet, staring up at him, still fairly vibrating with a lethal readiness, and Claude realized suddenly that the animal had not made even the smallest sound.

"Come work for me," Aucoin said. "I have plenty of men in my employ, but none as smart or capable. Unlike Babs, I can appreciate your skills and make use of them. I'll pay you well. You'll not have to worry about your wife's health care again, I can promise that."

Claude looked up at Aucoin, then back down at the dog. "Sorry," he said, "but I'm still hoping to get my job back at the Mill."

"Sure you don't want to give it some thought?"

The dog continued to stare up at Claude, its jaws open and eager, festooned with gleaming white points.

"I'm sure."

Aucoin sighed. "*Platz*," he said, and in an instant the dog lay down at Claude's feet. "Too bad, cousin. Consider it an open offer. In the meantime, go home and give Babs my response. Tell her the company came to me to break the strike because I have power. And

I've had power in Lewiston for forty years for one simple reason: Because people know if they don't do what I want, I will hurt them. As I will hurt Babs, and her husband, and anyone aligned with them. Not just because she has angered me, but because my entire business—indeed, my very survival—is dependent on everyone knowing there are no exceptions to the rule. Each person I hurt is an investment in my own future. And Babs will be no different."

CHAPTER FOUR

"I trust this isn't going to take long," Babs said to Rita, Carmeline, Stella, and Bernette. "I've got plenty to do today, as you're no doubt aware. And I feel like shit."

They were seated at Babs's kitchen table, smoking and drinking coffee and discussing the business of Little Canada. This activity was to become a regular feature of all their lives for the next four decades, though of course none of them knew that yet.

"What's the matter?" Rita asked.

"Ate something bad, I think," Babs said. "Stomach's gone sideways."

"That's weird, because you look terrific," Stella said.

"Sorry?" Babs said.

"You're right, she does," Bernette said, peering at Babs. "I can't put my finger on what it is, exactly. Just kind of an aura. No offense, but you don't normally look that good."

"No offense, sure," Babs said.

"Did you have your hair done?" Stella asked.

Babs glowered over her coffee cup. "I did not have my hair done," she said flatly.

"It's more than that," Bernette said. "She looks like she had a spa day."

"Jesus Christ," Babs said, lighting a cigarette.

"*Resplendissante*," Carmeline agreed.

"Hey, I've got an idea," Babs said. "How about one of you tell me why you're here."

"Good question," Carmeline said in French, stirring sugar into her coffee. "Some of us still have jobs, you know. I'm missing first shift for this."

Carmeline worked at the Hathaway Shirt Company, which sat several hundred yards downriver and on the opposite bank from Hollingsworth & Whitney. Hathaway had begun by outfitting Union soldiers in the Civil War, and management and labor had good relations, rubber-stamping a new work agreement so reliably every five years you could set your watch by it. No one alive could remember the last time the shirtmakers had gone on strike, a fact that Carmeline and many of the others would attribute to their being exclusively women. They knew how to give and take, and they knew how to get what they needed without having to turn it into a dick-measuring contest. But the women of Hathaway were also, like it or not, eyeball-deep in the fight at the Mill—whether through husbands, fathers, sons, uncles, or nephews, every woman in Little Canada had a man she loved walking the picket.

"I asked everyone to come," Rita said, "because it feels to me like if something doesn't change soon, this community is no longer going to exist."

"And you feel confident in that assessment," Babs said, "after being back for a whole twenty-four hours?"

"I'd argue being gone so long helps me see things you've long gone blind to," Rita said to Babs.

"Like?"

"Like, this place is dying," Rita said. "*Dying*, Babs. On your watch. Businesses, gone. Families, gone."

Babs looked around the table. "I assume the rest of you agree with her, otherwise you wouldn't be here."

"I would maybe word it differently," Stella said.

"'Dying' is perhaps a smidge too strong," Bernette said.

"Maybe it's more like the neighborhood is gutshot and bleeding pretty bad, but if you get it to the hospital quick enough it might pull through," Stella said.

Bernette turned to Stella. "That's a lot more detailed than anything I'd thought of," she said. "But I can see where you're going with it."

Babs just stared.

"Don't get mad at us," Carmeline said to Babs, "for pointing out what's obvious to everyone but you."

Babs continued to stare in silence for a moment longer, then pushed her chair back and went to the counter with her mug. "Okay," she said, pouring fresh coffee. "Then what would you have me do?"

"Be yourself," Rita said simply.

"The hell does that mean?"

"It means I don't recognize the person in front of me," Rita said. "Where is my sister? She wouldn't stand by and let this happen."

"No?" Babs said. "What would she do?"

"I don't want to scandalize you all," Rita said, "but while I was gone, I dated an Italian guy."

"Gross, but okay," Carmeline said.

"At least he was Catholic," Stella said. "Wait. He *was* Catholic, right?"

"Technically, I guess," Rita said. "He was a professor. Well, a PhD candidate. His field of expertise was the Mafia."

"Of course it was," Carmeline said.

Babs sat at the table and put her mug down with a thump. "Oh my *God* do I not have time for this."

"Once, I asked Luca how the Mafia got start—"

"*Luca?*" Carmeline asked. "What, there wasn't a Geppetto handy?"

"Sorry, Carm," Rita said. "I would have fucked a Tony to spare your feelings, but they were all taken."

"More's the pity," Carmeline said.

"I asked Luca how the Mafia got started all the way back at the beginning, and he told me lots of people want you to believe it's really complicated and arcane and hard to figure out, but really it boils down to a formula any third grader can understand."

"Don't leave us in suspense," Babs said.

"The cost-to-benefit ratio of committing crime," Rita said. "If the cost is smaller than the benefit, people will—and logically should—break the law. To survive. To keep their self-respect. To make life better for their kids when there's no other way of doing so."

"I don't get it," Stella said.

"It's basically a fancy way of saying when you've got nothing to lose, you're free to do whatever you want," Rita said.

"So the Mafia is a *good* thing?" Stella asked.

"It's not a question of good or bad, exactly," Rita said.

"Let me make sure I understand," Babs said. "You want my blessing to start some kind of half-assed Franco mob?"

"No." Rita pulled a cigarette from her pack, lit up with a practiced flick of one thumb, and exhaled a blue funnel of smoke toward the ceiling. "I want you to lead it," she said.

The ladies all stared at Babs, and she stared right back, incredulous.

"Are you serious?" she asked finally.

"Mostly," Stella said.

"We are," Carmeline said, glaring at Stella.

"Do you have any idea what you're asking for?" Babs said.

"Something other than lying down and taking it," Rita said. "That's all."

"No," Babs said. "None of you knows. That's the problem with the tree of knowledge. You think you want to eat the apple, but only because you have no idea what it means until you do."

"Well, that's gibberish to me, sorry," Stella said.

"I spent *five years* in a convent," Babs said, "in a town where I knew no one, and no one knew me, and it had to stay that way. No friends. No one to talk to. Barely sprouted tits and I had killed a man. Most people go their whole lives without knowing what that feels like. But I was fourteen, and I knew. Took a big bite of the apple and I'm telling you I *liked* it. Despite losing everything. While you were all worrying about grades and football games and whether God would forgive you for letting Louie LaCroix finger-bang you in the back of his Chevelle, every morning I opened my eyes expecting to see cops standing next to the bed. I dreamed about blood, every night. Buckets of it. I'd wake up and wash my hands until the skin peeled off in strips. I *still* dream about blood, all the time. Is that what you want?"

"Everyone's broke, tired, and scared," Rita said. "The law's against us. The union's against us. The town and the state are in the company's pocket. We have no recourse except that which we make for ourselves."

"Rita, I love you," Babs said. "And I'll give you credit—if you're willing to defy me like this, in my own house, that must mean you've come home for the right reasons. But don't ask me to do this. It's madness, and it will end badly."

"How else does anything ever end?" Rita said.

Babs stared at her for a moment, then closed her eyes and took a deep breath. "So you come to me now and say you want to play at being gangsters? Okay, fine. But understand this—if you get what you're asking for, you will spend every day, for the rest of your life, looking over your shoulder. You will never really sleep again. It will be my way in all matters, all the time, and you will hate and fear me."

"And that's different from the present state of things how, exactly?" Carmeline said.

"If it's between that and the only home we've ever had crumbling away," Rita said, "seems like an easy choice."

Babs looked around the table for a moment and then suddenly her eyes went wide and she shot up from her chair, bolted across the kitchen, and made it to the sink just in time to vomit a jet of coffee into the stainless steel basin.

"Ew," Stella said, and Rita gave her a look: *Shut up, you ninny.*

Babs stood for a few moments with her hands braced on either side of the sink, breathing hard, waiting to see if that was it. Finally she straightened up, wiped her mouth with the dish towel that hung on the drawer handle beneath the sink, and returned to the table, pale and quiet.

"I have a rally to lead tonight, and there's going to be trouble,"

Babs said. "If you want to help with that, feel free to stick around. Otherwise, get out of my house. All of you."

"Tell us what you need," Rita said.

Half an hour later Babs rang the doorbell, once more, at Father Clement's home. This time no one answered, so after a minute Babs crossed the street and went into the church. She searched the hallways, the two small classrooms where CCD and Sunday school were held, and the sanctuary, finding no one and nothing. The church was dark and cool and silent and seemed abandoned, unless you counted Jesus hanging from the cross behind the pulpit, gazing down wearily as he bled.

Babs selected a pew at random and sat, glanced around the sanctuary, wondered if Clement had finally had enough of the drama around here and skipped town, or else been sacked by the bishop and sent to wherever disobedient priests got sent. But neither of those things made sense—trying as he sometimes found Waterville and his congregants, Babs in particular, Clement wouldn't just leave; she knew that as surely as she knew her own name. And it seemed unlikely the bishop had heard about Clement's support of the strike less than twenty-four hours after he'd offered it; that shoe would drop tonight, sometime after coverage of the rally hit the eleven-o'clock news.

Finally, here came Clement now, emerging from the one room in the church—the sacristy—that not even Babs would dare enter. He looked up, saw her in the pews, and waved as casual as you like, as though not a bit surprised to find Babs in his church on a Friday morning. He went to the pulpit and futzed with something in the cabinet under the podium.

"What are you doing?" Babs said.

"Priest stuff," Clement called out, his head still down.

"Likely story."

Clement stood up, closed the cabinet, and descended from the pulpit. "I see you're finally ready to talk about whatever's been on your mind," he said.

"Actually," Babs said, "I'm here to give you a chance to save your job."

"How's that?"

"Turns out you picked a bad time to come to Jesus regarding the strike. Going to be trouble today and there's very little I can do about it."

Clement waved a hand for Babs to make room for him at the end of the pew. "Doesn't that just figure," he said, plopping down next to her.

"My recommendation is you stay away from the rally."

"It'll be awfully hard to give a rousing speech in support of organized labor from my sofa," Clement said.

"That's kind of the point."

"What manner of trouble," Clement asked, "is beyond the great Babs Dionne's ability to control?"

"You know the name Harold Aucoin?"

Clement looked at her. "Cardinal Law himself probably knows the name Harold Aucoin," he said. "There is no greater benefactor of the fund to restore Saints Peter and Paul Basilica in Lewiston."

"I don't imagine Cardinal Law troubles himself with wondering where all Harold's basilica money comes from."

"I don't imagine he does, no."

Babs reached into her purse, removed a cigarette, and held it, unlit, between her fingers. "Word is the company has hired Aucoin to do a little strikebreaking," she said.

"What?"

"His men will be crashing the party this afternoon. And I don't think you want your name attached to what happens when they show up."

Clement leaned back and blew a raspberry. "Well, that *is* shit news. But I don't see why it should change my plans."

"No?"

"I can defend my decision to endorse the strike. No one can blame you—or me—for the actions of outside agitators."

"The bishop will blame you."

"The bishop is a political animal. I'm not that smart. I'm just listening, hoping to hear what God thinks is right." Clement rubbed at his eyes and sat up straight again. "And now, for the love of all things holy, would you tell me why you're really here?"

Babs had been hoping Clement wouldn't ask again, but praying he would; didn't want to talk about it, but also very much did; wished to deny what she knew, but could not any longer.

Babs was not a fan of strange faces.

With familiar faces you had a sense of what lay behind them, the love and perfidy and plain human mess, but you could only read that shorthand after knowing the person the face belonged to for some time. People were so instinctively adept at arranging their features in an inscrutable neutral, hiding what they felt to keep it safe and/or secret, that with most strangers you had no hope of inferring what lay behind the scrim of indifference.

They could be planning to cut your throat and you wouldn't know it until the blade was out.

And what happened when you basically airlifted two thousand strangers into a town like Waterville, where normally everyone knew everyone else? Well, Babs was looking at it now as she stood at Head of Falls along the Kennebec and watched car after car pulling in and disgorging unfamiliar faces. All of whom were ostensibly here to support Local 116, some of whom might have been on Aucoin's payroll, and none of whom could be read or, consequently, trusted.

Head of Falls, where Benedict Arnold had portaged boats during a comically ill-fated invasion of Quebec (before revealing what lay behind his own inscrutable visage), was now a dirt parking lot across the river from the Hollingsworth & Whitney mill. The stretch of land was forever being mentioned as the lynchpin of one grand civic development scheme or another, yet remained the same several acres of gravel and thistle it had been since urban renewal swept the Francos downriver and bulldozed their homes three decades before. These days it was used principally as a place for the carnival to set up rides and games twice a year, and a spot for the city to dump snow cleared from downtown streets and sidewalks; the mountain of ice and trash produced often persisted into June. The only thing that remained from that time when Head of Falls had been a neighborhood was the Two-Cent Bridge, which connected Head of Falls to the campus of the paper mill. The bridge was so named because it had cost two pennies for workers to cross, on foot, to report for work. It was the last standing pedestrian toll bridge in the country, and though it hadn't been used by workers in a generation, figured prominently in the plans for the rally.

The simple version of those plans went like this: The bulk of the rallygoers would follow trucks from the Waterville Fire Department (which was a Teamsters shop) and cruisers from the Waterville Police Department (which was emphatically not) from Head of Falls down Front Street along the river, across Bridge Street, then back north along Mill Street to H&W's gate number one. At the same time, the members of Local 116 would make the symbolic (and much shorter) walk across the Two-Cent Bridge, where half would sit in at gate number one and the other half would continue to the east side of the Mill and block gate number two. And they would stay there, resisting all entreaties and orders to disperse, until the police came and carted them off in zip ties. Dignified, sympathetic, and above all peaceful.

Except there was, before Aucoin's goons had even shown up, already a problem. Or the beginning of a potential problem, at least. From the dais that had been hastily constructed from studs and plywood for the occasion, Babs could see people, after being directed into parking spots by volunteers with orange flags, dragging coolers from the trunks of their cars. Which in and of itself wasn't an issue—Babs had hoped, after all, that those in attendance would bring their own beverages to supplement the donations from Scottie's Variety—but as they gathered in small groups and waited for directions, she could see emerging from those coolers not water and soda, but beer and wine and, in some instances, hard liquor.

Ill-advised, but also, upon a second's reflection, utterly inevitable. Who were we talking about here, after all? If you wanted good manners and highballs before dinner, that crowd was on the other side of this fight, on the other side of the river. No one, least of all Babs, should have been surprised that the people on *this* side of the river—her people—had come equipped to do some serious day-drinking. In the heat. With Aucoin set to start trouble at any moment.

And Babs wasn't surprised—after all, Francos drank. That's how it was, how it always had been. To the ignorant eye it might appear those gathered were just having a party, but she knew well that her people drank when they were happy *and* when they were despondent, to excite passions *and* to ease nerves, to pass the time *and* to make time stand still; they drank, in short, as a way of life and as a way to ease life's burdens. Today they drank out of defiance, fear, tattered camaraderie, and a weariness that few, hard as they used to work, had ever been acquainted with. Still, despite the fact that she knew in her dark heart that Rita and co were right, Babs would have preferred things go as close to plan as possible today, and people getting wasted before the whistle blew for second shift at the Mill did not augur well in that regard. The Waterville cops were looking for any excuse, and it would do nobody any good to get arrested for drunk and disorderly.

But it was what it was. Babs did not, as a matter of personal policy, ever resign herself to anything, did not settle or compromise or, the ultimate capitulation, *accept*—but as she watched more cars pull in and sheriff's deputies cluster at the edge of the gathering crowd like insecure boys at a school dance, she knew that, booze or no booze, it was anyone's guess which way the wind would end up blowing today, or how hard, or what might get wrecked as a consequence.

She gazed across the river to the windowless brick facade of the Mill, impregnable as a medieval fortress. She sensed the malign presence of Aucoin's people and knew the fight would commence before the sun set. She couldn't change that, whether her friends and neighbors were drunk or not, any more than she could bring Sacha back from the dead.

Besides, there was another feeling that thrummed in her, contradicting her dismay at the people drinking, and that was: a joyful, defiant pride at the people drinking. Her kin talked too loud and told crass jokes and everything they did and felt was outsized as a way of staving off misery, denying death, rejecting the mores of those who had rejected them. They loved too much and laughed too much and worked too much and died too much and, yes, drank too much, thank you very much.

"Mrs. Dionne," a man's voice said from behind her. "I'm told you're in charge of this gathering?"

Babs turned to see Captain Bates standing there. "Guess so," she said.

"Then you're aware that the permit issued by the city explicitly forbids the sale, possession, or consumption of alcohol."

"I am aware," Babs said. "And people were told."

"Were they?" Bates pointed to a sign outlining rules for the rally, none of which mentioned alcohol at all.

Rita walked up, and Babs turned to her. "Who made the signs?"

"What? Why?"

"Because they were supposed to include a really prominent notice that there's no drinking allowed."

Now it was Rita's turn to look around. "Well, shit," she said.

"Who made the signs?" Babs asked again.

"Stella, I think."

"Stella?"

"What?" Rita said.

"The woman who hasn't been sober for five minutes since eighth grade was responsible for making sure the rule against alcohol was highlighted?"

Rita shrugged. "I guess so," she said. "What do you want me to do about it now?"

Babs turned back to Bates. "It's a good question. What do you want us to do about it now?"

A pause, and then Bates said to Rita, "Could you give us a minute?"

Rita glanced at Babs, who nodded, and she headed back toward her station at the entrance to the parking lot.

Bates looked out over the gathering crowd. "I ran into your husband yesterday," he said.

"He mentioned."

"Someone came after him with a chain saw, but he didn't want to talk about it."

"Rheal's not one to make a fuss."

Bates chuckled. "No one in your neighborhood is. I've been on the force almost a decade, and it occurred to me that during that time, I've only been called to Little Canada on three or four occasions, including yesterday."

"What can I say? We're a law-abiding people. And we take care of our own problems."

"Like you've taken care of Aucoin's coke dealers?"

"You keep your ear to the ground, don't you?"

"I consider it part of my mandate to serve and protect."

Babs smiled wanly. "What do you want, Daryl? I'm a bit busy today."

"I want to be your friend."

"Uh-huh."

"I want to help you plan for the future. Of Little Canada. Of Waterville."

"And how do you propose doing that?"

"That's for another time, I suppose," Bates said. "For now, there's the small matter of all the drinking going on here," Bates said.

"I'll make an announcement. Can't guarantee it'll accomplish anything."

"You misunderstand," Bates said. "I just want to let you know it's not a problem. That's how easy things can be, when you have friends in the right places."

Babs considered him for a moment. "Good to know," she said. "Now if there's nothing else?"

"That's it," Bates said. "Good luck out there today." He touched the brim of his hat in parting, and was gone.

The twin marches to the Hollingsworth & Whitney mill were set to begin at 4 p.m. (for the longer trip around) and 4:15 (for the straight shot across the Two-Cent Bridge). When the clock hit 4:00 the crowd was already plenty lubricated, and demonstrating such in a handful of ways not exactly befitting a labor rally. Crowd-surfing, for one example. Beer-shotgunning competitions, for another. The cops were, thus far at least, good to Bates's word and did not intervene or confiscate drinks, did nothing in fact but stand by and watch, amusement cracking the facade of sternness on some of their faces, as the vibe careened further and further into rock-festival territory. And while it was good that the cops hadn't gotten jumpy about the drinking, the upshot was the strikers had to police themselves—no one was going to keep them out of trouble but them. Which meant Babs and the other ladies, in addition to keeping an eye peeled for any incursion by Aucoin, had been busy discouraging the more exuberant strikers from, say, slap-boxing or setting fire to empty twelve-packs just for the drunken fuck of it. Carmeline, in particular, had excelled in this role, dragging more than one young man out of the crowd by a painfully twisted earlobe, as though he were a wayward schoolboy.

So it was that when the first, larger march got underway—the head of the column, two dozen people wide, turning left onto Front Street to much fanfare—what Babs felt more than excitement or anticipation was simple relief. Relief that no one had (yet) fucked things up. Relief that, during what to her seemed the most likely time for Aucoin's goons to descend, things had remained festive and peaceful, not a strikebreaker in sight. Maybe Aucoin had heeded Claude's warning after all. Maybe, she let herself half believe, this day would end peacefully.

Once her relief crested and began to recede, Babs was able to take a breath and simply enjoy the sight of two thousand of her people marching in jovial lockstep (Had she ever seen them so happy? Not for a very long time, if ever), filling Front Street curb to curb and moving against the normal one-way flow of cars—that was the thing, she realized, that she enjoyed about this sight more than anything else, the way everyone moved so calmly and determinedly *opposite* to the direction that traffic was, by law, supposed to move. Like an army they marched, in sync despite the collective buzz, and like an army they carried standards: Old Glory, of course, but almost as many Fleurdelisés, the flag of Quebec with its white lilies on a background of Mariana Trench blue. The wind blew steady into the face of the procession, making the flags stand as if they'd been starched. Taken as a whole, the scene made it feel, for a few minutes at least, as if the strikers had taken over the whole town, just like that.

As the larger procession continued down Front Street, the head of the column out of sight now, Babs made her way off the dais and down a slope of scrub grass to where the smaller group, still five hundred or so people, had come together to begin the march across the Two-Cent Bridge. Cheap domestic lager flowed, and several boom boxes scattered throughout the crowd competed for dominance; at the moment, Quiet Riot's "Cum On Feel the Noize" was throttling "Hello" by Lionel Richie. Babs found Father Clement, Rheal, and the ladies near the ramp that led to the toll-house.

"The music's got to go," Babs said to the group.

"On it," Bernette said, and began to push through the crowd in the direction of the Quiet Riot.

Babs turned to Clement. "You sure you want to be seen leading this bunch?"

Clement smiled. "I'm picturing the expression on Cardinal Law's face when he opens the newspaper tomorrow, and it feels worth getting shitcanned, to me."

"Okay then." Babs checked her watch just as, twenty or thirty yards distant, the paint-by-number guitar solo of "Cum On Feel the Noize" was cut short by the crash of a boom box meeting its fate against the pavement. Two minutes later, Bernette reemerged from the crowd.

"You didn't have to break their radio," Babs said.

"It was Rick Begin," Bernette told her. "He was acting like a drunken asshat."

"What else is new," Babs said. She turned to Rheal. "Can you get everyone's attention, please?"

Rheal jammed two fingers in his mouth and cut loose a whistle loud as a rifle shot. Silence gathered in its wake.

"*Écoutez!*" Babs said as heads turned in her direction. "We're going to start the walk across the bridge in two minutes. You all know the plan—the first half stops at gate one, the second half continues to gate two. We sit until they move us, and we don't cause any trouble otherwise. Got it?"

Nods and affirmative murmuring. Babs gazed around, smiling at her people—and then the smile melted when she noticed, here and there, faces she did not recognize. The larger march included all kinds of people who weren't part of Local 116—Teamsters out of Dover, rank-and-file AFL all the way from Maryland, even some sympathetic students from Bates and Bowdoin Colleges downstate—but this group was supposed to be comprised entirely of strikers, and it was not.

"Who is that?" Babs asked Rheal.

He followed the plane of her pointed finger, looked at the man in question, and shrugged. "Don't know," he said.

"What about this one?"

"What about him?"

"There aren't supposed to be any strangers here, Rheal," Babs told him.

"Maybe not," Rheal said, still scrutinizing the second man, "but they're here now, and we've got a march to get underway."

"I don't like it," Babs said. She pointed again. "There's another one."

"Relax. They're somebody's cousins or something." Rheal placed his hands on his wife's shoulders and turned her gently toward the ramp to the bridge. "Let's get moving."

The Two-Cent Bridge was unchanged, save for a fresh coat of

paint every twenty years or so, since Babs's father and grandfather and great-grandfather had used it to report for work at the beginning of each day and return home at the end. Though of course the workday never really began or ended—the Mill's great stack had pumped forth steam and carcinogens without interruption for a century, save for when a chlorine spill had shut things down during a few tense hours in 1955. The trucks arrived endlessly with raw timber and departed endlessly with rolls of newsprint around the clock, seven days a week, 365 days a year, no pause for the birth of the savior or the nation, and barely any bathroom breaks. Time was paper and paper was money and even now, as the rightful stewards of the Mill's machinery began filing onto the bridge that had carried their families to work for five generations, the smokestack smoked and the discharge pipes glopped forth and the truck engines grunted and idled and jake-braked without cease, and moreover, the black snow continued to fall, as it had since before anyone alive could remember. This was a fine particulate matter, which no one could (or would) say really what it was, that drifted out of the sky and coated everything—cars and trucks, the leaves of trees, your very skin—with bits of black like flecks of dried blood. When it rained, the flecks turned to mud and left dark smears on windows and clothing. Occasionally someone would worry out loud about what breathing the black snow must do to the lungs, but no one knew for sure it was necessarily *bad*. What people did know for sure was that as long as the black snow continued to fall, you had a job. At least, until recently.

The bridge was only wide enough to walk two abreast, and Babs and Clement took the lead with Rheal and Rita immediately behind them. Beneath their feet wood slats popped and creaked, and as more and more human weight loaded onto its supports the bridge began to sway, a slight, almost imperceptible rocking not unlike a boat in gentle swells. Halfway across, the head of the larger procession came into view to the distant right, a few hundred yards away from gate one on Mill Street. The timing would work out well, with the two marches reaching the Mill almost simultaneously. And the press, having been informed that the union had bailed out and a new, more aggressive, intermittently illegal phase of the strike was in the offing, had shown up to cover the moment. At the far end of the bridge, photographers snapped pictures of Babs and Clement as they made their way slowly across the river, and not one but two camera crews, from WMTW and WGME, had earlier gotten footage and conducted interviews among the gathering crowd, and now were set up on the Mill side of the river, filming the strikers crossing the bridge.

So, naturally, this was when nausea hit Babs like a snakebite. It came on so powerfully that she nearly buckled, like a fighter caught flush by a liver shot. Clement grasped her arm.

"What is it?" he asked, talking out of the corner of his mouth and keeping his eyes ahead, so as not to put on any more of a display for the cameras than had already occurred.

"I'm going to throw up," Babs told him.

"Like, this instant?"

"Help me hustle past the cameras. I'd rather not blow chunks on the six-o'clock news."

"Everything okay up there?" Rheal asked from behind them.

"We're going to pick up the pace," Clement told him, dragging Babs along.

Flashes popped like starbursts ("It makes the composition more dramatic," one of the photographers had told Babs earlier when she asked what the point was on a sunny day) and the unblinking eye of the TV cameras glared as the two of them double-timed the last twenty yards to the end of the bridge. Babs did her best to approximate a smile for the press, to make any expression other than one that said with utter clarity, *I am about to vomit* a lot. What she couldn't know was that the footage and photos the press would capture in the next couple of hours—some of which would be spectacular enough to garner national attention—would ensure that nothing preceding it would really matter.

Still, in the moment, unaware that events were about to occur that would render puking on camera the least of her worries, Babs was grateful to get off the bridge and find a modicum of privacy down the riverbank to the left, where, in partial cover provided by the tall grass, she heaved and kept heaving long after her lunch was gone. Tears wet her cheeks and her vision trilled with stars as she sucked at the air. Rheal came and put a hand on her back, rubbed small circles, waiting with her for it to be over.

After another minute Babs straightened up, used a finger to extract a wet tuft of hair from the corner of her mouth, and accepted the thermos of water Rheal offered. She rinsed and spat, then again, but each time, after a few seconds the burn of stomach acid returned to her throat and the back of her nose.

"*Ça va aller, chérie?*" Rheal asked.

"Better now," Babs said.

"Maybe we should get you home."

"It's just a touch of food poisoning," Babs said. "I'll be fine."

"What did you eat?"

"*Cretons* did it to me, I think."

"The one that's been in the fridge for two months?" Rheal asked.

"I thought it tasted a little funky."

"*Crisse*, Babs."

In the next instant, from the direction of the bridge, they heard a collective gasp—the sound of mingled alarm and excitement—and they turned their heads in time to see a man falling headfirst toward the river. But not falling, exactly; the man did not pinwheel or flail as he dropped, but kept a straight, composed, inverted line, hands clasped below his head, feet tucked neatly together and toes pointed at the sky; a textbook front dive, complete with minimal splash when he entered the water.

Up on the bridge, a cheer erupted. This, more than the diver himself, was what alarmed Babs. The timbre of the applause: drunk, anarchic, desirous of much more. She looked to the end of the bridge, where all the cameras had trained their lenses on the man as he resurfaced and pumped a fist.

"Shit," Babs said. She scrambled back up the hill, Rheal close behind.

By the time they got to the ramp two more people had already leaped into the river. They found Clement calling for calm, pushing fruitlessly against several men who blocked his way back onto the bridge. These men had faces Babs didn't recognize. Behind them, a chant had gone up among the hundreds of strikers, led by other men she did not recognize. These agitators began to jump up and down in unison, landing hard on the deck with every other syllable, and soon most everyone else joined them. Forty tons of human heedlessness, rising and crashing over and over, and the old bridge began to creak and moan as more people scaled the metal railings and launched themselves into the river.

Meantime, the larger march had arrived behind them at gate one, but instead of waiting peacefully for the strikers to arrive and begin their sit-in, this group started chanting as well. Babs turned and saw beer bottles and rocks going airborne, arcing like artillery fire toward the Mill. The cops that had chaperoned the march scrambled out of their cruisers and approached the tumult, but they were outnumbered two thousand to four, and could do little but holler impotently for the crowd to cut the shit. Before long one of the cops took a bottle to the head and went down, and that, for whatever reason, was the thing that suddenly clarified Babs's mind: Aucoin's men, infiltrating the march here and there, hadn't come to strikebreak; they'd come to fool the strikers into breaking themselves.

Babs turned back toward the bridge just as one of the men holding Clement hit the priest across the face with a big calloused hand. Rheal leaped forward in front of Babs, stepped over Clement, and broke the attacker's nose before catching a punch in the side of the head from the other man who'd been harassing the priest. Rheal caught the offending fist, grappled for a few seconds, then got hold of the man's upper arm and it was over, a step forward, a quick gruesome twist, the man's elbow and shoulder a sudden mess of impossible angles, and he went down screaming. Rheal moved forward onto the bridge as the strikers and Aucoin's saboteurs kept jumping up and down and hollering nonsense. Babs bent over and helped Clement to his feet, left him clinging to the railing to hold himself up, and then she followed Rheal, who was now shoving aside those he knew and brutalizing those he didn't with a vigor and efficiency that reminded her why she loved the man.

Meantime the cameras saw everything, impassive, unblinking, flawless in their recall but deeply wrong in the story their footage would tell when it was over.

Babs continued to follow Rheal. The only people she encountered who were still upright were her neighbors. And though these people were friends and fellow strikers, they were still jumping up and down like angry monkeys, still perching on the narrow steel railings and diving into the river, still effectively doing Aucoin's bidding as they exulted in chaos as if they did not know, or no longer cared, what it meant for their jobs, their families, their lives. Under their feet the bridge swayed and shuddered, and they seemed to pay no attention to that, either. But then Babs realized they felt the bridge faltering just as surely as she did—and that was precisely why they continued to jump. They wanted destruction, craved it as a release of the anger and grief they'd held within themselves the past year. They wanted to know they were potent in the world, that they could make someone pay even if that someone was themselves. In ten minutes they'd gone from a lifetime of powerlessness to the absolute power that came when you realized you could destroy whatever was in reach and not even God could stop you.

Here was Eddie LeTourneau, a machine operator since before Babs's father had started at the Mill out of high school, Eddie himself a father and grandfather, Little League ump and Meals on Wheels driver, all-around stand-up non-rioting guy, gripping the rail for maximum leverage as he leaped and stomped, his eyes and bald head both gleaming viciously.

There was Armand Frappier, a young father about whom the most common sentiment was he wouldn't say shit if he had a mouthful, shirtless and sunburned with a can of Budweiser in each hand, his arms spread wide as he screamed at the sky like a Viking on a cocaine bender.

Roger Doyon, a mill maintenance supervisor who took care of the ice on Little Canada's outdoor rink for the kids every winter, bellowed as he hauled on a loose section of railing over and over, trying to pry it from its bolts for some nefarious purpose, or none at all. He was joined in this effort by a gay pipe fitter named Stanley Picoult, who made extra scratch by styling the hair of neighborhood women in his kitchen, and Luc Lafarge, who was not the best cylinder machine operator on the planet but got the job done adequately more often than not. Together, it looked like they had an outside chance of actually freeing the section of rail from its moorings, and then God knew what they would do with it.

Babs pleaded with these men to stop, use their heads, think about their families and their neighbors and those who came before and would come after, but this had so little effect she might as well have not even been there. The men did not see her or hear her. They continued to grunt and scream and heave on the railing, and when it finally broke free of its rivets the men lifted it overhead in triumph and hurled it down into the river. They were far, far beyond responding to reason or good sense, and Babs knew now that this was her fault. She'd thought she could shirk her duty. She'd refused, ever since returning to Little Canada, the responsibility of deciding when to be cruel and when to be merciful, for the good of all.

This, then, was her mistake—which she'd been warned against by her dead mother, but too late—playing out disastrously in front of her: thinking she could be something other than what she was. Trusting her neighbors to behave as they should, instead of making them behave for fear of her wrath. It was not their fault Babs had refused so long to accept her fate—but *par Dieu,* now she was going to make them pay for it all the same.

And so she reached into her boot, where she'd put Rheal's expandable nightstick earlier that day, after talking with the women who had been her friends since childhood and seeing their judgment, and feeling their sorrow and fear, and knowing, though she was still reluctant to admit it to herself, that the vision of her mother had been real. Babs pulled the nightstick out, gave it a flick to extend it to its full, lethal length—and started swinging.

"Jesus Christ, Babs!" Roger Doyon cried when the baton landed across his upper arm, but that was all he managed before Babs cracked him one on the right temple and turned his lights out and he went down under the feet of the others. Next was Stanley, and when he hit the deck people started to pay attention in a way all her pleading had not achieved; they saw Babs coming toward them, swinging like Reggie Jackson, and they stopped delighting in their petty chaos and backed away from her, slowly, hands up to ward off blows but also in entreaty for a mercy Babs would never again be willing to extend. But the crowd on the bridge was too thick for anyone to escape more than a few feet before being relegated to sardine status, trapped against one another and the structures of the bridge, wedged in tight and one hundred percent fucked with Babs bearing down. On the other side of this bottleneck hundreds of others continued to leap skyward and crash back onto the deck of the bridge, fully synchronized now, united in purpose, and Rheal was in that scrum somewhere, and farther along at the far end the Waterville PD was fighting its way past the tollhouse and onto the bridge, wrestling strikers to the ground and cuffing them, but too late, Babs knew, far too late. It was all about to quite literally come down, she could feel this unmistakably beneath her feet, but she would get her licks in before that happened. She took another step toward the sardines, who stared at her with terrified unblinking sardine eyes, and she lifted her nightstick (it was hers now, forevermore) and that was when she felt hands grabbing her from behind and dragging her back, away, off the bridge entirely, and she heard voices that sounded familiar and realized they belonged to Bernette and Rita. Babs's friends pulled her to solid ground just as one and then several of the bridge's support cables gave way with a sound like massive bullwhips being cracked across the sky, and then the far end of the span broke free and collapsed into the water to a chorus of screams from both banks of the river.

The bridge that had stood for a century, surviving floods and ice floes and even the occasional hurricane, that had brought five-plus generations of Francos to work and home again over and over, day upon day, had borne the weight of their bodies but also of their lives, was undone in one afternoon while the cameras—and the ghosts—bore witness. And now hundreds of strikers, Rheal among them, were being swept downriver by the current toward the falls, and the turbines of the Lockwood dam.

CHAPTER FIVE

Twenty-four hours later, the best that Waterville police chief Roy Davies could say for the entire tawdry debacle was that no one had died—at least, not that they knew of. It was impossible to account for every person who'd attended the rally, and equally impossible to know whether they'd fished every last idiot out of the water. But so far no one had called to report someone in their family failed to come home from the rally, and so far no floaters had been found in the dam or farther downriver, thank God for small miracles, though in searching the banks of the Kennebec as far south as Sidney yesterday, state police had stumbled on a man's badly decomposed body, an apparent suicide that now had to be dealt with alongside everything else. Still, as far as they knew, despite the best efforts of every half-wit in Little Canada, no one had died as a result of the previous day's events. Now Davies just had to hope, over the next week or so, that this continued to be the case.

The way his luck was going, he didn't feel super-optimistic.

The DA had already told Davies that neither the motivation nor the resources existed to charge most of those who'd been rounded up at the rally. Fifteen or so were hospitalized, dozens of others would get off for want of witnesses willing to testify, at least ten were related one way or another to men in Davies's department, one was a goddamned priest so good luck with that, and finally the people who could perhaps be successfully prosecuted weren't worth going after for a grab bag of Class D misdemeanors. Not to mention the DA had less than zero interest in screwing himself with every judge in the county by tying up their courts with this shit-show for the next five years.

Which left none other than Babs Dionne to deal with.

Babs herself, having spent a night in the drunk tank, now sat across from Davies in his office, on the other side of the desk. To her right sat Captain Bates.

"Daryl," Davies said to Bates, "are you aware of how far back Babs and I go?"

"Not sure that I am, Chief," Bates said.

"Way, way back," Davies said. "My first beat, twenty-odd years ago, was in Little Canada. I remember Babs when she was still in pigtails."

Babs stared at the floor in front of Davies's desk, silent and impassive, to all appearances deaf to the conversation.

"Remind me when you first came on the force, Daryl," Davies said.

"Ten years ago, Chief," Bates said. "Fall of '74."

"Right," Davies said. He pulled a cigarette from a pack of Pall Malls and lit it, leaned back in his chair, and continued talking to Bates while staring at Babs. "So you probably don't know anything about our friend Babs here, or her history before you came to town."

"Afraid not."

Davies shifted his gaze to Bates, seemed to gauge whether he was being honest about this. "There's not much to tell, really," Davies said after a moment. "In fact, there's *nothing* to tell, which is kind of the point. There's just a big stretch of time when Babs kind of . . . disappeared. Like she'd never even existed. No one seemed to know where she got off to. Not her family, not her friends, not her teachers or her priest or anyone else in Little Canada. No one could say where she was. And believe me, we were asking."

"And yet, here she is now," Bates said.

"Yes," Davies said. "Came back just as mysteriously as she disappeared. But what's interesting is when you consider the timing. Babs went away at *exactly* the same time that my first partner, Scott Markee, was murdered in the woods down by the sewage treatment plant. That was 1968. And she reappeared five years later, just a few months after the previous chief shut the case down."

"Why'd he do that?" Bates asked.

"No witnesses, for starters—except for one little boy who said he saw Babs walking down Grove Street covered in blood, but later, after being coached by his parents, said he just dreamed it. No real physical evidence, no weapon, no leads of any kind."

Now Babs unstuck her tongue. "Those were the official reasons, anyhow."

"Shut up," Davies said.

But Babs ignored him. "Unofficially," she said, "the chief didn't want to have to answer questions about what Sacha was doing at the time of his death. Which no doubt would have come up if they'd tried someone for his killing."

"Sacha?" Bates said. "I thought his name was Scott."

"In Little Canada, we knew him as Sacha," Babs said. "That was the name his parents gave him."

Davies smiled grimly and leaned forward again. "So Babs got to come home," he said, flicking his cigarette in the ashtray. "And she never had to spend a minute in prison for killing my partner."

"Classic case of what you know versus what you can prove," Babs said.

"Indeed," Davies said. "But I've got you now, Babs, don't I?"

"You've got me for what, exactly?" Babs asked. "Smacking a couple people with a nightstick?"

"Well, let's see," Davies said, shuffling papers on his desk. "Yes, as an appetizer, at least three counts of assault, one of which will be bumped up to a felony—when you see Roger Doyon's face you'll understand why. That's ten years, all by itself."

"Only if Roger presses charges," Babs said.

"And why wouldn't he?" Davies asked.

"Because he won't want two broken legs to go along with his face."

"Are you telling me you intend to intimidate a witness, Babs?"

"I'm telling you things are about to change around Little Canada," Babs said. "From now on what I say goes, and anyone who doesn't like it can take the train. Or end up like poor old Roger."

"That's actually very good news," Davies said.

"How's that?"

"Well," Davies said, "while I would love to put you away for the next three decades, Babs—and really, I would—I have something else I need done."

Babs scoffed. "Three decades. Please."

"Did I neglect to mention criminal conspiracy, incitement to riot causing shall we say *serious* property damage and bodily harm, unlawful assembly, et cetera et cetera? I'm guessing the feds will want to get in on this, considering you brought so many people across state lines to take part in your little pep rally."

Babs said nothing.

"Thirty years," Davies said. "That's door number one. Door

number two, given your new status as supreme ruler of Little Canada, should be very easy for you."

"And that is?"

"Simple," Davies said. "End the strike."

"I'd sooner cut off my own tits."

"You say that now. But what's the point in keeping up the charade? It's over. Time for you and your neighbors to move on."

"Move on to what?" Babs said. "Do you have twelve hundred jobs we could take?"

"City can always use more prisoners to pick up trash and paint fire hydrants."

"Such a wit."

Davies smiled broadly and stubbed his cigarette out in the ashtray. "Oh, I've been waiting a long time for this, Babs. A long, long time."

Babs turned her eyes to Bates. "The chief told you my history. Any interest in hearing about his?"

Bates looked to his boss, who shrugged.

"He and Sacha were regular rank-and-file Waterville cops—by which I mean they were thieves and dirtbags. They had the keys to every business in Little Canada, took whatever they wanted whenever they wanted."

Davies looked at Bates, shook his head, dismissive. "Wasn't nearly as bad as she makes it sound," he said. "We were kids."

"My guess is these days the chief has become a bit more sophisticated in his graft. Everything has the patina of legality, no doubt. Property seizures, fat donations to the police officers' union. Hard to believe he can afford that big house up on Cherry Hill Drive on a cop's salary. Anyway, I got sick of watching Davies and his bestie Sacha steal from my uncle's corner store, so I piped up. And Sacha didn't like being challenged by anyone, let alone a little Frog like yours truly. So he decided to teach me a lesson."

"And you killed him," Davies said.

"He definitely died," Babs said. "Like the pig that he was. I can confirm that."

Davies glared.

"You know, Chief," Babs said, "over the years I've sometimes wondered why you carry such a torch for a no-good scumbag like Sacha."

"He was my friend."

"Right," Babs said. "Remind me—how's that old saying go about the company one keeps?"

Davies glared. "Obviously you need more time to think this through," he said. "Captain Bates, would you return the prisoner to her cell?"

Clement opened his front door on the second ring, his left cheek a blossom of purple and red in the rough outline of a handprint. The bruising extended around the arch of his left eye socket, and the white of the eye itself shone demon-red from burst capillaries. Just shy of noon, the priest already had a glass of whiskey in hand, which he held against his swollen jaw.

"Two visitors in less than a week," he said when he found Rheal on his stoop. "I am blessed beyond all measure."

"How's the face?"

"Sore. Hardly my biggest problem."

"Babs asked me to check on you," Rheal said. "Mind if I come in for a minute?"

Clement stepped aside. "You want a drink?" he asked.

"Always," Rheal said.

The priest led the way into the kitchen, where a bottle of Wild Turkey sat uncorked on the counter, next to a clear plastic container of ice. "Babs still in the pokey?" Clement asked, reaching into the cupboard for a second rocks glass.

"For now," Rheal said. "Trying to figure that out."

"What's to figure out?"

"Bail was set this morning at twenty-five grand."

"Yikes." Clement scooped a handful of ice into Rheal's glass, poured a couple fingers, and handed it over. "Any chance of coming up with that? Short of divine intervention?"

"Think you could put a word in?"

"I could try, but I wouldn't count on it to help any."

"Then the only option I've got is taking a loan against the equity in the house. And even then, I'm short."

"So what happens if you can't come up with bail?" Clement asked.

"They transfer her to county until she's tried."

"Baptême." Clement leaned against the counter and sipped whiskey over the top of the ice. "If I tell you something, Rheal, can I trust you to keep it between us?"

"I'm a lot of things, Father, but a gossip isn't one of them."

"I spent a couple weeks in jail, once," Clement said.

Rheal smiled, somewhere between delighted and incredulous. "What'd you do?"

"I was playing around with being a junkie," Clement said. "I deserved to be there, and if it hadn't happened I might not have lived long enough to find my way back to God."

"Well, then I'm glad you went to jail. There's something I never thought I'd say to anyone. Mind if I smoke?"

Clement waved a hand. "Neither one of you can go five minutes without a cigarette. It's unseemly. Use the sink."

Rheal lit up and slid over to the side-by-side basins.

"I'm touched that Babs could spare a thought for me, when she's in such a bind herself," Clement said.

"It's her way," Rheal said. "Besides, she thinks she's tough enough to do prison standing on her head."

"She might be," Clement said. "Still, it'd probably be better for both of you if she didn't have to."

They were quiet for a moment. Rheal smoked, started to speak, seemed to think better of it, then plowed ahead anyway. "Father, I know you and Babs talk sometimes."

"She and I have always been pretty frank with each other, it's true."

"When she came here a few days ago, did she mention anything other than the strike meeting?"

"You know I'm not allowed to tell you about private conversations, Rheal," Clement said. "Whatever she said or didn't say, that's between her and God."

"Except she doesn't believe in God. Shouldn't that mean all bets are off?"

Clement grinned. "Doesn't really work that way." He poured himself another splash of whiskey. "Can I get one of those cigarettes?"

Rheal handed over his cigarettes and lighter.

"This is maybe a stupid question," Clement said, "but if you're wondering about something, why not just ask her?"

Rheal paused. Then: "Because I'll know if she lies. And then that'll be between us for the rest of our life."

"I see."

"Having been lied to recently by someone I love, I'd rather not deal with that again anytime soon."

Clement stared out the window and drank, thinking. "I've got some experience with that kind of thing myself," he said.

"A woman? Or a friend?"

"She was my best friend. And my wife. This is also, probably goes without saying, information I'd like you to keep to yourself."

"A married priest."

"I wasn't a priest at the time."

"Why are you telling me this?"

Clement took a drag of his cigarette. "Oh, I don't know," he said. "It's been years. I guess I'm ready to tell someone."

"So what happened?"

"She died," Clement said. "And then I became a priest. And here we are."

Rheal shook his head. "This life," he said. "Who can figure it?"

Clement finished his whiskey at a pull, sighed. "I think the hardest thing about life is never really knowing the people we love."

"Obviously you've never had dysentery."

Clement laughed. "That's harder?"

"Shitting blood for a month?"

"Well, when you put it that way . . ."

"I won't lie, Father," Rheal said. "It's the kind of thing that makes a man wonder if maybe God hates us."

Clement smiled and nodded. "Every one of us is a locked box, Rheal. Nothing to be done about it. Babs will always elude you. You will always elude her. Even when you're not trying to."

"That's heartening."

Clement didn't respond for a moment, lost in thought. He brought his glass to his lips, then lowered it again without drinking.

"It's something to do with language, I think," he said. "The inadequacy of it. Laughter is much more eloquent. So's suicide. Each one of us is trapped in our own skull, alone at the center of all creation. Even when we're with those we love. All we can really do is decide to love them anyway, even if we have no clue who they are."

Rheal ran the water and stuck his cigarette under the stream to snuff it. "Shit, I'm supposed to be checking on you, and here I am going on and on. Anything I need to know about? Anything I can help with?"

"Not unless you've got pull with the Pope."

"Uh-oh."

"I got a call bright and early this morning. My presence has been requested in Boston by no less than Cardinal Bernard Law."

"Thus the a.m. brown liquor."

"Not that I need much of an excuse."

"It probably says something about your employer that you'd have a better shot to keep your job if you'd just diddled some kids."

Clement smiled and shrugged. "You said it yourself. This life—who can figure it?"

"I'll let Babs know," Rheal said. "She won't be happy."

"Tell her not to worry about it," Clement said. "I could use a vacation. Besides, my relationship with God can't be severed by anyone. Not even his Most Reverend Eminence Law."

"She won't be worried for you, Father," Rheal said. "She'll be worried for us."

A few hours after the meeting in Davies's office, Bates appeared outside Babs's cell. He looked up and down the hallway, found it empty, and said, "You should take the deal Davies is offering."

"I won't sell out to save my own hide."

"That's not what I'm suggesting."

Babs sat on the bunk and looked up at Bates, weariness tugging at the corners of her mouth. "What are you suggesting?"

"Tell me something first."

"Maybe."

"What *was* Scott—Sacha—doing at the time he was killed?" Bates asked.

"He'd just finished raping me," Babs said. "A few minutes later, he'd been stabbed to death, though by whom is anyone's guess. I didn't see a thing."

Bates fished a pack of Marlboros out of his chest pocket and offered one to Babs. "And you were how old?"

"Just turned fourteen."

Bates pulled a Zippo from his pocket and lit Babs's smoke, then his own. "I don't know what's more incredible," he said. "That Scott was the kind of monster who would rape a little girl, or that a little girl could stab a grown man to death. Of course, this is you we're talking about, so."

"I just said I had nothing to do with it."

"Right." Bates took a breath and blew it out. "I'm sorry he did that to you, Babs. Truly."

"Anyway. Now I've told you what you wanted to know," Babs said. "Your turn. What are you suggesting?"

Bates sat on a folding chair against the wall opposite Babs's cell. "You're never going to get what you need with Davies running this department," he said. "He's a Company man all the way."

"He lacks the imagination to be anything but."

"So what if he wasn't running this department anymore?"

"Naked, shameless ambition," Babs said. "I like it."

"You weren't wrong in there about him being a corrupt scumbag," Bates said. "Or about how he hides it."

"So you want to do something corrupt to get rid of Davies's corruption?"

"I'd be a better steward of the people of this town than he ever could."

"The bar is low," Babs said. "But regardless, I think Davies is still a few years from being able to collect a pension."

"And yet," Bates said, "I can envision a scenario in which he could be encouraged to resign."

"In this vision of yours," Babs said, "who is it that takes his place?"

"I might offer myself up. With the appropriate measure of humility."

"Natch." Babs flicked ash on the floor of her cell. "What I'm not tracking is how any of this is dependent on me being in or out of jail."

"Encouraging Roy to resign is going to involve activities that I, as an officer sworn to enforce the law, cannot take part in."

"You want me to set him up."

"You said it, not me."

"And then what?"

"And then," Bates said, "you and I enjoy a long and fruitful partnership."

"Meaning?"

"You can run Aucoin's dealers out of town a hundred times, and they'll come back a hundred and one. Unless you start doing their job yourself."

"I'm not going to sell drugs to my neighbors, Daryl."

"If you don't," Bates said, "someone else will. That's just life in the market economy."

"Cute."

"Here's something I learned from my time working vice," Bates told her. "There's only one person who controls a place. It isn't the police, and it sure as hell isn't the town council or the neighborhood watch. It's whoever runs the rackets."

"I may not be the smartest person in the world, but it doesn't seem wise to start dealing drugs just so you can blackmail me for a cut," Babs said.

Bates smiled. "Do you know the theory of mutual assured destruction?"

"The Russians won't blow us to hell because they know we'll blow them to hell. And vice versa."

"You got it," Bates said. "I'll have very little interest in seeing you, or any of your people, in jail. Because you will easily be able to put me in the cell next to you."

Babs peered at him. "All that aside," she said, "I don't see how any of this helps with the strike."

Bates leaned forward, his hands on his knees. "I'll encourage you to think of it this way," he said. "When you have a friend in charge of the police department, it can, in theory, open up a whole new suite of options for dealing with the company."

"Extralegal options."

"Again, you said it, not me."

Babs leaned back against the cell wall, thinking. "I have to admit, Bates," she said after a moment, "I appreciate the moxie, if nothing else."

"Great minds, and all that. So should I tell Davies you're prepared to reconsider?"

The local legal ecosystem had a reputation for ponderousness, especially when it engaged the people of Little Canada, but that afternoon it demonstrated it was capable of moving with great speed, at least when everyone involved wanted to be shut of Babs and the events of the previous day as soon as possible. By three the DA's office had produced a plea agreement, which Babs stoutly rejected because it required her to admit guilt; by close of business she had an agreement that allowed her to plead nolo contendere and that had already been signed by the district attorney when it arrived. Half an hour later, with her cigarettes and lighter, her watch, and even her nightstick returned to her, Babs was a free woman.

But there was no rest to be had—when Babs arrived home with Rheal, Rita was waiting for them with the news that the previous evening, just hours after the bridge collapse, somebody had burned Connie Fecteau in effigy on her own front lawn. While her little girls were home, no less. Similar incidents had occurred simultaneously at the homes of three others who'd crossed the picket, and one of those homes had lost a porch before the fire department arrived on scene and managed to keep the house itself from burning—hardly a given since most of the fire personnel had bedrock sympathies that might keep them from trying their absolute hardest to save the home of a scab.

"Get the ladies here now" was the only thing Babs said in response to news of the fires. Rita went off to work the phones, Babs dispatched Rheal north to find the Saucier brothers, and half an hour later Rita, Bernette, Stella, and Carmeline were all seated at Babs's kitchen table, smoking grimly over their cups of coffee.

"I've known the four of you longer than I've known anyone else," Babs said. "We've been friends since kindergarten at Sacred

Heart. We got our asses beat by the same nuns for years. We covered for each other, fought shoulder to shoulder, helped each other mend broken hearts. We share blood that goes back to Trois-Rivières, and before that Acadia, and before that Occitania."

"We came from the lost continent thing?" Stella asked.

"That's Atlantis, dummy," Carmeline said.

Babs eyed them both in turn. "What I'm saying is you are the only people in this kitchen because you are the only people I trust. And you were right. I let you down. That ends now."

"This is starting to sound pretty heavy," Stella said.

"I told you to be careful what you asked for," Babs said. "I'm proposing nothing less than a complete overhaul of how we do things in Little Canada. Yesterday demonstrated people can't be trusted to act in their own interests. So from now on, we'll make sure they do so. Beginning with calling an end to the strike."

This yanked a collective gasp from the ladies, as if Babs had proposed cooking a live beagle on a spit. On reflex Stella reached for her flask of vodka, and Bernette fumbled with her pack of cigarettes before realizing she already had a smoke going between her fingers.

"Hear me out," Babs said. "The basic agreement between labor and ownership that we've worked under for, what, seventy, eighty years, has been broken. Nobody bothered to tell us. We've been playing by the old rules as if they still apply—march around and sing songs and hold the line and sooner or later they'll have to give us our fair share. But that's not happening. We've acted as though we're only fighting the company, when in fact we're fighting three different institutions, all of them equally powerful: the company, the city, and the Church."

"I thought Clement was on our side," Stella said.

"He is," Babs said. "The Church, not so much. It's just another company, when you get down to it. That most of its revenue comes from shaking down parishioners doesn't change that. And what about the city? You see it right on the sign coming into town: 'Waterville, Incorporated 1882.' It's a company. A company with police powers it uses against us, for the benefit of the Mill."

Carmeline rose from her chair and went to the Mr. Coffee, mug in hand. "So what do we do about it?" she asked over her shoulder.

"The details will come," Babs said. "For now, I need to know you all have what it takes to make this work. We're going to break the law pretty much every day. Sooner or later, one of us could very well get hurt or end up in prison. If that sounds like something you'd rather not to be a part of, you should leave now."

"Normally I would say 'no thanks' to such a proposal," Carmeline said, coming back to the table. "But you make it sound so appealing."

"Hey, this wasn't my idea," Babs said. "I'm just telling you how it's going to go. You have to decide if you're in or out. Right now."

"Is this one of those deals where once you're in the only way out is death?" Stella asked.

"Don't be dramatic," Babs said.

"I'm not," Stella said. "It's a legitimate question."

"This isn't *The Godfather*, for Christ's sake," Carmeline said. "Take a pill."

"How do you know?" Stella asked.

"If it'll help you stop worrying, I could just kill you right now and get it over with," Babs said.

Stella peered at her, trying to determine if she was serious.

"If we could get back to the business at hand?" Babs said to the group. "Who's in?"

They all looked at each other.

"Are we doing like a secret ballot or something?" Stella asked.

"I think a simple show of hands would suffice," Babs said.

She raised her own hand, and each of the other women followed suit, Bernette last and somewhat tentatively.

"Then it's decided," Babs said. "First order of business is to tell everyone the strike is over. What we're not going to tell them is that doesn't mean we're giving up. Not by a long stretch."

As younger men the Saucier brothers had done the kind of messy geopolitical work that, by comparison, made CIA spooks seem like model candidates for good sportsmanship awards. This work involved exotic locales and a marked moral flexibility and could never be talked about because it would never be declassified, owing to the fact that the United States government was definitely not supposed to be doing the things it trained the Saucier brothers to do. And the long psychological tail of the Sauciers' previous work made it unrealistic to expect those who did it to go back to a normal civilian life and, say, drive a timber truck or work a road crew.

As such, the Sauciers' current employment was related to the job they'd held previously, though not quite as shady and off-the-books. When Rheal pulled into the long gravel drive of the Sauciers' shared home in Dallas Plantation and was greeted only by the two Karelians they used to hunt bear, he knew right away that the brothers were at work a few miles away in Rangeley, at the United States Navy's SERE training facility, and he knew they might be gone for another two hours or another two days, so he fed the dogs and unloaded the whiskey he'd brought and made himself comfortable.

The Sauciers were originally from Waterville, which was how Rheal knew them, and though the brothers' work (and post–Vietnam/Cambodia/Laos/Nicaragua disposition) had brought them to the solitude of Maine's western reaches, old friendships were, among Francos, sacrosanct, inviolable, and to the grave. And the Sauciers were as Franco as they came—they'd been raised in a home where English was forbidden, resulting in pronounced accents. Because they spoke like logrollers from the nineteenth century, people sometimes assumed they were from the St. John Valley and environs, the far north bastion of Francohood.

Together with Rheal and Claude, the four had been inseparable all the way through high school. They'd played hockey together, raised hell together, raked blueberries and baled hay together. They'd learned hunting and tracking from the Sauciers' father, Otis, and grown to love each other sitting shoulder to shoulder in the woods with rifles across their laps. They'd brawled regularly with boys from the well-to-do side of town, and once, when the cops had chased them half the night following just such a brawl, Ray Saucier had given himself up to allow the other three time to escape and notched a year at the Long Creek Juvenile Detention Facility while his brother and friends walked free. Rheal would do anything for the Sauciers, and they for him—which was precisely why he'd come to their home today, and why he intended to wait however long it took for them to return.

The Sauciers had spent the previous night chasing three naval aviators through the woods and, having captured all three when they'd made the mistake of teaming up, were now back in the SERE facility's mock POW camp, loading the unfortunate pilots into hotboxes, which were exactly what they sounded like: steel containers set in a small clearing so the sun beat on them unabated all day. The dimensions of the hotboxes were such that a grown man could only fit inside with his arms wrapped around his rib cage and his knees tucked into his chest. If you imagined yourself unbothered by tight spaces and/or thought you did well in the heat, as many of the sailors and Marines who came through the SERE facility did, the hotbox most often disabused you of either notion in little more than the time necessary to padlock it shut.

As SERE instructors, the Sauciers' job was to hunt, interrogate, and torture students, with the objective of demonstrating what life would be like should they ever find themselves prisoners of war. What this meant, in practical terms, was that half the gig involved being an effective actor. This being the tail end of the Cold War, instructors wore Eastern Bloc uniforms and deployed fair-to-lousy Russian accents, but the Sauciers' natural accents were odd enough that they were allowed to simply speak like themselves.

"When we bang on de box once," Normand said to the aviators, loud enough to be heard through the steel, "you will give us de war criminal number you have been assigned. When we bang twice, you will give us your soshal securitee number. Understand?"

"I can't breathe," one of the aviators said, sounding on the edge of panic already.

"Dat is not one of de prescribed responses," Ray said. "Continued disobedience will result in correction."

"Seriously, you guys, I feel like I'm suffocating," the aviator said.

"It only feels dat way," Normand told him. "Just relax and you be fine."

Ray looked at his brother, incredulous. Normand shrugged.

Ray went to the box in the middle and slammed it with his palm, once.

"War criminal number zero-one-four," the aviator inside said.

"Oh my God, I think I'm dying," the frightened aviator cried from the box farthest to the left, and before he was finished speaking Ray strode over and slapped the side of his box twice, hard.

"Help me!" the aviator said. "Please!"

"Soshal securitee number!" Ray told him.

A pause, punctuated by some whimpering, almost too faint to hear through the box. "One six . . . zero . . . oh Jesus, I'm going to puke."

"Git him out of dere," Normand said.

Ray slapped the box twice again, then hooked a thumb over his shoulder to indicate he desired a word with his brother in private. They moved together across the camp's dirt courtyard as the panicked aviator continued to try and fail to recite his social security number.

"What de hell is going on wit you?" Ray asked.

"I don't know, brudder."

"What is dis, you don't *know*?"

Normand answered in French. "I'm trying to tell you I don't know *myself*, lately," he said. "All I can say is it hurts my heart, to hear him beg."

Ray scoffed, refusing to dignify Normand's sentiment by speaking French himself. "It hurts your heart," he said. "Dat's rich."

"I tell you something true about myself," Normand said, "and you make fun? Are we not brothers? Can we not say anything?"

Ray stopped walking and stared at Normand. "Dat boy," he said, pointing toward the hotboxes, "in six months he gonna be flying off a carrier in de Artic Circle. What happen if he goes down in Bulgaria and dey trow him in a cell? How your heart gonna feel den?"

Normand said nothing.

"We have a job," Ray continued. "In dat job, cruel and kind are upside down. I shouldn't have to explain dis."

"You don't."

"Den what's de problem?"

"Maybe I don't want the job anymore. Maybe I'm tired of being upside down."

Ray looked at his brother. "Well, den," he said, "I guess we should take de rest of de day off, at least."

And so the brothers did that, because they never did anything except together, and this, at least, was an arrangement neither of them needed to discuss. They informed the camp commander that they were leaving and someone needed to look after the men in the hotboxes, and then they drove through the gate in their F-150, Normand at the wheel, and went home together along the sinewy backroads of Maine's mountain country, finding Rheal on a lawn chair in the front yard, the Karelians posed on either side of the chair like they were modeling for an oil painting.

"Mr. Dionne!" Ray said, smiling broadly as he dismounted the truck and slapped his thigh to call the dogs. "If you here to recover your losses at cribbage, you going to be disappointed, you."

"We'll see about that," Rheal said.

"To what do we owe?"

"Believe it or not," Rheal said, "I'm here to offer you more money."

"You just gonna give it over?" Normand asked. "Not even gonna make us work for it?"

Rheal stood and shook the brothers' hands. "Oh, you're going to work for it," he said. "Whiskey's on the counter inside."

"Well, let's not stand on ceremony," Ray said.

For several hours, nothing else was asked or offered about what had brought Rheal north—these men were friends, and they knew whatever needed to be said would make its way out between them in due time. First, there was drinking and bullshitting to attend to. Normand started a fire in the pit out back, while Ray, who always did the cooking, found a moose-meat chili in the chest freezer and made a salad with greens from the garden. The men ate and drank and smoked and were well into their second bottle of whiskey when Rheal, apropos of seemingly nothing, asked what was going on between the two brothers.

"Whatchoo mean?" Normand said.

"Don't play dumb," Rheal said in French. "There's something in the air. I know it isn't about me, so it's got to be something with you two."

"Nothing wrong wit me," Normand said flatly.

Rheal glanced over the fire at Ray, who picked at his fingernails with a pocketknife and said nothing.

"If you want to know why I came," Rheal said finally, "first you're going to have to tell me what the problem is. It matters, for what I'm here to ask. I can't have the two of you carrying around some bullshit about each other."

Ray finally spoke, not looking up from his hands. "Don't know how many diff'rent ways we can say it, Rheal," he said. "No problems here, us."

Rheal absorbed this, then sat back and jabbed at the fire with a stick of cedar, charred black at the business end, that served as the brothers' fire poker. "Okay," he said. "Well, listen, I think you're full of shit, and let me tell you why. There's only one other time, in the thirty years we've known each other, when I felt the kind of tension between you two that I feel right now. You remember?"

The Sauciers both gazed at Rheal, but neither said anything.

"I'll give you a hint," Rheal said. "It was down at Art's."

Art's, a Little Canada institution, was officially known as Le Petit Canada Colisée, an Olympic-size outdoor ice rink and nickel arcade where teenagers had hung out since the place had been built in the early 1920s. Local boys had been doing their part to maintain the ice, scraping and flooding the rink every night after games, for generations. There was no finer place to skate anywhere in Maine, which was why the best hockey players in the state—and sometimes other states, as well as Quebec—flocked there all winter long.

Both the Saucier brothers knew what night Rheal was referring to, but neither of them had any interest in discussing it. So Rheal went on as if he didn't know that *they* knew exactly what he was talking about.

"This was, I don't know, '64 or '5," he said. "I'm surprised you guys don't remember this. Me and Claude walked down to your place with our skates hanging on our sticks, just like any other night. But when we got there the two of you weren't talking. You just got your gear and we all went down to Art's in silence. It was the first time we'd ever gone anywhere together without anyone saying a word. I had no idea what to make of it. Ringing any bells?"

The brothers remained quiet.

"So *then*, when we show up at Art's we've got enough guys to play four-on-four with goalies and a sub, but for some reason Normand says he wants to switch up the teams. He'll play with three of the four Thibodeau boys, and Ronnie Thibodeau will play with me and Ray and Claude. Which was *really* weird, because in nine or so years of playing hockey together, I'd never once seen the two of you on opposing teams."

Still nothing from the brothers. Ray got up and went to a stack of split maple, grabbed two pieces off the top, and tossed them on the fire. A burst of sparks flew up into the dusk, flaring and fading in seconds.

"But it didn't take long," Rheal said to Normand, "to realize why you wanted to play against Ray. What was it, a minute flat before you put the blade of your stick across his nose?"

Now, finally, the hint of a smile on Normand's face. "More like tirty seconds," he said.

Rheal laughed. "Next thing I know, it's fight night at the Colisée. Instead of playing hockey, we all gotta stand around watching you two beat the living shit out of each other."

In Little Canada, then and now, one didn't intervene in a fair fight unless and until it seemed like someone might get killed, so Rheal and Claude and the Thibodeau boys had just watched and waited as the Sauciers traded blows for ten minutes, blood bouncing on the ice, before finally Art Gagne came out of the arcade, scruffed them apart like a pair of ill-behaved dogs, and kicked everyone out for a month.

"Still one of the most vicious fights I ever saw," Rheal said.

"Dat was over a woman," Normand said. "Dis is different."

Rheal laughed. "A woman? Rose Arsenault was all of, what, thirteen? *Twelve*?"

"She was a two-timer."

"She couldn't tell you apart!" Rheal said. "No one could, except me and your ma."

"Brudder Ray could tell us apart, *par Dieu*," Normand said. "And he still kissed her anyway."

"*Kissed* her!" Rheal said, really laughing now. "You *mangeux de marde* nearly killed each other over a junior high kiss? Ray, I hope you at least got some tongue."

"I got no tongue," Ray said. "I did lose two teeth, dough."

Now all three were smiling, the brothers in spite of themselves.

"So." Rheal looked from one to the other in turn. "You wanna tell me what the fuck is going on?"

Ray took his seat again, kicked at one of the chunks of granite that ringed the firepit. "Brudder Normand's going soft," he said.

"Unthinkable. How so?"

"Have to ask him."

Rheal turned to Normand, eyebrows raised.

"I would not characterize it as 'going soft,'" Normand said in French.

"Then how would you characterize it?" Rheal asked.

"I guess I'm tired of being cruel to people for no good reason."

"I see." Rheal jabbed the poker into the fire, levering the new wood up so air could pass underneath. "In that case, how would you feel about being cruel to people for very good reasons?"

"Way tings are going all of a sudden," Ray said, "I tink we will be in need of work. If dat's what you're offering."

"It is," Rheal said. "It's also complicated, be aware."

"How's dat?"

"For one thing, you'll have to come home for a while," Rheal said. "For another, we can't pay you right away."

"Sounds great so far," Ray said.

"The downside is no pay up-front, or maybe ever," Rheal said. "The upside is an equity share in what Babs and I are building."

"Drugs?" Normand asked.

"Not just. We're taking over everything. Putting our own guy in charge of the police. We've got a fight brewing with Harold Aucoin out of Lewiston. And we have to convince management at the Mill that it's in their best interests to give everyone their jobs back."

"Got your hands full, you," Normand said.

"That's why I'm here."

Normand and Ray shared a glance over the fire. "I spent tree months in prison in Ban Naden," Ray said. "Not exactly eager to go back."

"That's where the 'our guy in charge of the police' part comes in. Besides, I don't know for sure, but it seems reasonable to assume accommodations in Thomaston are somewhat better than in Laos."

"I don't plan to find out."

Rheal smiled and leaned back in his chair, kicked his boots up on the edge of the firepit. "Look, fellas, we could really use you. The cause is righteous. The work is well-suited to your skill set. And if we do it right, we all could end up making a lot of money. But it's your call."

Normand looked at his brother and smiled. "Brudder Ray," he said, "you tink Ma would let us stay in our old room for a few monts?"

CHAPTER SIX

The following afternoon, at a special meeting of Local 116—in the same gym where union members and neighbors and family had linked arms and shed tears and exchanged reassurances that all would eventually be well, the same gym where Jesse Jackson had led a rendition of "We Shall Overcome" and it had seemed, for a while, that the unity and kinship they felt *would* in fact overcome, no matter how rigged against them the fight might have been—Babs announced that the strike was over. She told everyone assembled that she couldn't explain how, but she was already working on a way to save them from the abyss that now yawned beneath all of Little Canada.

No one believed her, and Babs didn't expect them to. The vibe as people filed into the gym had been funereal with a tinge of grade-school shame; after her announcement, it was apocalyptic. And the truth was, Babs's sympathies were not entirely with the strikers. Not after the rally debacle. The way Babs saw it, she was going to save her neighbors in spite of themselves, and that was more than they probably deserved. How they felt about the *manner* in which she saved them ranked very low on the list of things she gave a shit about. Which was fortunate, because they clearly didn't feel good about anything they were hearing. Not the end of the strike, nor her stern warning that there were to be no further attacks on people who had crossed the picket. When she said the strike was over, that meant entirely. There were no more strikers and no more scabs—only neighbors.

The sole comfort, cold as February, was that being this comprehensively fucked seemed to preclude anger among the now-former strikers. Instead, it was resignation that floated in the rafters, mingling with the cigarette smoke, and under that some scattered grumbling about how a scab was always a scab.

Babs let this settle down for a moment. She had one more message to impart to her neighbors and kin, and it was, to her mind, the most important thing she would say that night.

"As we set about doing what we have to to get your jobs back," Babs said once the crowd had gone quiet again, "people are going to come here. People from outside this community, who don't speak our language, don't understand us and don't care to. They'll flash badges and say scary official-sounding things, trying to get you to talk about what's going on here. I'm not going to tell you what you should say to them. You're free to say whatever you will, without any threat of reprisal. I merely ask that you give it some thought, before the time comes. Don't get caught flat-footed. Think about who actually has your interests in mind. Think about whether these people who want you to give up your neighbors have any stake in what happens to this community. And then, having given it thought, I want you to speak your conscience. And that's all. Thank you, friends."

As she came offstage, Rheal pulled her to the side. "You sure that's the best idea?" he asked.

"Which part?"

"Letting people say whatever they want when the cops come sniffing around?"

Babs looked around for anyone in earshot, and moved Rheal farther away from a cluster of people in front of the stage before responding. "I'd invite you to think about two things," she said quietly. "First, we can't control what people will say even *if* we tell them it's their ass. Second, and more important: If we're in this for the long haul, we've got to have people's support. We need to be hard-asses only for as long as necessary, and not a minute longer. Until people see we're actually getting things done for them. After that, this neighborhood has to hold itself together through common purpose, the sense that the only people we can count on is us. Otherwise, we might as well let it all go to shit right now and save ourselves a lot of trouble."

That evening, Charlie St. Pierre was splayed across his ratty couch wearing nothing but a pair of basketball shorts, a half-forgotten joint smoldering in his fingers and *Dynasty* playing on the TV, when all hell broke loose.

The door to his apartment, to the left of the TV set, burst inward with a crash, shards of wood flying through the air as the doorjamb splintered. In rushed five figures dressed in black, ski masks obscuring their faces. The first person through the door, who was also the tallest, carried the sledgehammer that had circumvented Charlie's dead bolt; behind them four others followed, two with baseball bats, one with a pistol, and the last carrying a slender black nightstick which they used to push the door shut again.

Having been a bully all his life, Charlie was much more accustomed to doling out beatings than receiving them. He'd only been hit with a baseball bat once before, and that had been an accident, a glancing shot to the mouth on a backswing during Little League practice that relieved him of a couple baby teeth that were falling out anyway.

This was very different. It's been said that the hardest thing on earth to do is hit a round ball with a round bat squarely, but squaring Charlie up proved quite easy. The blows fell flush as he twisted and whimpered and cried out and pleaded incomprehensibly. It seemed to go on forever.

"Don't cave his head in, for Christ's sake," Nightstick said. "We're not trying to kill him. Yet."

After another thirty seconds, one of Charlie's two assailants tapped out, but the other, the smallest among the five, seemed inexhaustible. Her bat rose and fell with the precision and impassiveness of a metronome. Before long, Charlie was too hurt and exhausted to even bother continuing to cover up; he relaxed out of a protective fetal curl, defenseless as a boxer KO'd on the canvas.

"That's probably enough," Nightstick warned.

No sign that these words were heard or heeded. The bat swooped upward once more.

"Stella, I said that's enough!"

This time the order got through. The bat hovered overhead for a moment, then came down slowly, harmlessly, to rest at the one called Stella's side.

"Sorry, I was miles away there for a second," she said, breathing hard and smiling through the hole in her ski mask.

"Okay, well, good job, stand down now."

"Did anyone else know this was going to be so much fun?" Stella asked. "It's like when you go to the fair and get three swings at an old Buick for a quarter. Except way better. And you don't have to pay."

"Okay, we can probably reflect more on that later," said Nightstick.

"I'm just saying," Stella said, "I think this is going to be really good for me."

Nightstick crouched alongside the sofa so she was eye to eye with Charlie. "Look at me," she said.

Charlie did, trying to focus through the tears and pain, and as he gazed at Nightstick she pulled the mask up to reveal her face.

"Now you know who did this to you," Babs said. "And you've got a lot more batting practice to look forward to if you're still here when we come back tomorrow. You like dealing for Aucoin so much, move to Lewiston and do it there."

Charlie squinted at her. "Babs?" he said. Then he started to laugh, which turned into a coughing fit. "I don't know what you think you're doing," he said, "but Harold's going to eat you and your girlfriends for breakfast."

"We'll see," Babs said. "For now, I'm telling you as plainly as I can: Don't let me see you in this neighborhood again. Ever. Your ghetto pass has been revoked."

At the same time, Rheal, Claude, and the Saucier brothers fanned out across town to let Aucoin's other dealers know their time selling dope in Waterville had come to a definitive, nonnegotiable end. They walked up on street corners, approached cars parked conspicuously in otherwise empty lots, and kicked in the doors of tenement apartments to deliver the same simple message Charlie had received: Get gone, or get hospitalized.

The men of the Little Canada crew encountered no resistance at all—Aucoin's minions, seeing both lethal weaponry and the flat gazes of men expert in its use, abandoned their posts and dens and faded into the dark. These were not people being paid well enough to risk their lives, or even to take a beating, and they clearly neither loved nor feared Aucoin enough to do so. And so in one evening the drug trade in all of Waterville belonged to Babs, both the market and the existing supply, which included enough coke, pot, and pills to get them started while they figured out arrangements for more.

In the meantime, once the evening's main business was concluded, Babs and Carmeline paid a visit to Rick Roy's bungalow on Halde Street, two blocks from Babs and Rheal's house on Carrean. The porch light was off at eleven o'clock, and the rest of the house was dark except for a single light in an upstairs window, but Babs leaned on the doorbell three, four, five times until Rick finally threw the door open, wearing only boxer shorts, his mouth a rictus of irritation.

"You woke up my kids," he said. "You got any idea how long it takes to get a three- and five-year-old to sleep?"

"I do," Carmeline said. "Not her. She's smart enough not to have kids."

Rick turned to Babs. "What do *you* want?" he asked.

"Thirty-four-D boobs," Babs said. "My father to not be dead. The Red Sox to win a World Series in my lifetime. Though I'd sooner put money on my father rising from the grave."

"You know what I meant," Rick said.

"Yes, I know what you meant, but it's not what you *said*, and one of the many things about to change around this neighborhood is people saying what they mean and doing what they say."

"Didn't realize you were the grammar police," Rick said.

"Like for example," Babs went on as if he hadn't said anything, "this afternoon I was very precise in saying that there would be no further attacks on anyone who crossed the picket."

Rick continued glaring at her, not yet convinced he had anything to really worry about.

"And yet," Babs said, "no sooner were the words out of my mouth than someone goes and kills Connie Fecteau's dog. Or rather, her kids' dog."

"Dogs die."

"This one died from eating rat poison," Babs said.

"Not sure why you're bugging me about it."

"Because you did it," Babs said.

"The hell I did."

"Rick," Babs said calmly, "you walked past Connie's house after the meeting, and you tossed something over the fence and onto her lawn."

"The hell you say."

"Three hours later, that little Jack Russell was dead. So you can come clean or not, your choice. But we both know what you did."

"This has been real, Babs," Rick said, "but I'm going back to bed. Case you didn't notice, it's eleven thirty at night."

He tried to swing the door closed, but the tip of Babs's nightstick stuck in the jamb, propping it halfway open.

"I'm not like everyone else in this neighborhood, Babs," Rick said. "You don't scare me."

Babs looked past him, to the stairs. "Those kids still awake up there, you think?" she asked.

"Never mind my kids."

"Because it would be a shame for them to hear their father catch a beating," Babs said. "Or worse, for them to see it. Should they hear you screaming and come to the top of the stairs to see what's going on."

Carmeline took a step back and glanced up and down the street, then stepped forward again.

For the first time, Rick seemed to understand that Babs was not fucking around. "Fine," he said. "What do I need to do to make you go away?"

A pause, Babs's expression as inscrutable as the Mona Lisa's. She turned to Carmeline, who nodded, then back to Rick.

"Bleed," she said finally.

When it was over, Babs wiped her baton clean on the front of Rick's boxers as he lay on the floor of his own foyer. The sound of children crying drifted down the stairs, but they remained out of sight. Instead, Rick's wife, Stacy, stood on the landing to the second floor. Her own cries having been cut short by a sharp gesture from Babs, she held a hand over her mouth, tears glimmering in her eyes in the soft light of a hallway lamp.

"Tell anyone who needs to hear it," Babs said to Stacy. "I see everything, just like I saw your husband poison that dog. Nothing happens without me knowing, and from now on, nothing happens without my say-so."

In the wake of being screamed at and ultimately fired by Cardinal Law, the newly defrocked Clement Thibault was his own man for the first time in over twenty years. He wandered around Boston's Theatre District after dark, squinting in the rainbow strobe of marquees, nothing to do, nowhere to be. It turned out that, although defrocked, by a quirk of theological law Clement could not be stripped of his ordainment, by the cardinal or the Pope or anyone else, so as he strolled east along Stuart Street he was technically still a priest (whether he or the cardinal liked it or not). But though still ordained, Clement could no longer conduct Mass, administer sacraments, or hear confessions (this last being the far greatest relief of both burden and boredom, if Clement was being honest). He no longer had an obligation to perform the Opus Dei five times a day, and though he did often enjoy the meditative aspects of that ritual, it still felt, more often than not, like a thing required of him rather than given joyfully. Now, suddenly, his time and his mind were his, for the first time in over twenty years.

And yet all he could think about was his daughter, the one forever without a name because she'd died before she was born.

And so he walked, not just because he lacked anything else to do before returning to Maine the following day and assessing what was next (packing his few earthly belongings and clearing out of the rectory, most immediately), but because he was tormented. His heart ached, and he worried he might break spontaneously into tears. He was also gripped, suddenly, by a hunger that had hit him as violently as a mugging. He strode out of the Theatre District and into Chinatown, and found the lights there were somehow even brighter, the asphalt glowing red and yellow, paper lanterns hanging from every streetlamp, music and chatter and the honk and hum of vehicles drifting up to mingle with the smells that hung in the air: the bite of dried chilis, the smoky warmth of five-spice powder, the delicious cacophony of seared duck and sautéed garlic and scorched anise, all carried on clouds of steam that billowed from doorways and kitchen vents and food carts.

Every time someone in his life had needed him—truly needed him—Clement had failed.

He realized, with a suddenness that felt like divine inspiration, that he hadn't had a Chinese meal since before Simone died and took their baby with her in 1964. He veered, without thought, into the next doorway on his right, sat at the counter and scanned a menu, looking for a dish he'd had innumerable times at a Hell's Kitchen restaurant as small as a living room, trying to remember the name of the meal, bone-in chicken thighs braised in wine and soy sauce and sesame oil, served over rice with scallions and basil. The name had something to do with the ingredients in the sauce—three-something chicken. This menu had several candidates, none of them quite seeming right: Three Treasures, Triple Delight, Three Dancing Dragons. Triple Delight sounded appealing, though, so Clement ordered, had a beer while he waited, and ate unheedingly, like a man rescued from a month in a life raft, when the food arrived. The plate was big enough to feed two, and when he finished Clement was full but, somehow, not sated. He asked for the bill, paid, and stepped back into the street.

Many times over the past fifteen years Clement had reminded himself, forcefully, that Babs had a father, and he'd been a good one, Armand, kind and loving, all the father a girl needed. And yet, when she needed to be rescued, Babs had gone not to Armand, but to Clement.

As he'd feared, Clement began to weep. A menu on a food cart listed something called Three Pandas, with a little photo of a bowl that held chicken mixed with rice and bamboo shoots, and though Clement was almost positive the meal he remembered from Hell's Kitchen did not include bamboo, he ordered it anyway. It came two short minutes later in a plastic bowl with chopsticks, and one bite, rich with anise and black pepper, confirmed that it was not the meal Clement sought. But it was, all the same, quite good. He ate, crying all the while, and when he was finished he stuffed the bowl and chopsticks in an overflowing trash can near the cart, and went seeking more.

It was impossible, of course, not to think from time to time about where his own daughter would have been in her life, had she lived. Six years after she'd died, Clement was the guest of honor at a dance recital and realized his daughter could have been in it. Five years after that, chaperoning a junior high dance, he imagined her standing in a cluster of girls on one side of the gym, while the boys shoved and chased each other on the other side, pretending they weren't aware of an audience, pretending not to perform for that audience's benefit.

Recognizing he was not entirely in possession of himself, Clement continued to eat. The night wore on and the streets began to empty and finally, at the last place he could find open, he ate bullfrog hot pot with celery root and fried rice cakes, as the two men running the restaurant mopped the floors and upended chairs onto tables around him.

He stepped outside and the men turned the lights off in the restaurant. Clement was alone, nearly crippled with satiety, standing on the sidewalk with no idea which direction his hotel lay and little ability to get there even if he'd known. The streets were abandoned, no pedestrians, no cars, and, most alarmingly, no cabs.

Clement sat on a nearby bench, sweating though the night had grown cool. He ran a hand over his face like a squeegee, wiped it on his pant leg, and looked without hope at the empty, silent plaza, and the street beyond. He felt himself alone and helpless beneath the stars. And so, relieved of all illusions and vanity once more, he began to pray.

During the five years Babs spent at the convent in Vermont,

Clement had taken a father's responsibility for her. She didn't ask him to and he never said it out loud, but they both understood it to be so. He alone knew where she was hidden, so he alone visited her, at least once every couple of months, more often when he felt it was safe. He brought news from home, and letters from her friends, Rita and Carmeline and Stella and Bernette. He took Babs for meals and ice cream and listened to her talk for hours, an endless, desperate stream of chatter from this child, as though he were the only other person on earth to talk to. And she was still very much a child, despite having a death on her hands. He told her when her grandmother died, and her beloved uncle Paul, and he held her close, though she never, ever cried. Each time he left to return to Waterville without her she simply said goodbye, but her eyes pleaded with him not to go. And each time he swore to himself, and to God, that when this was over he would never leave her alone again, so long as he drew breath.

Sitting on the bench, Clement felt the clear, uncomplicated guilt of a father who had failed. He'd failed his daughter, the one without a name, and she had died. He'd failed Babs, his other daughter, when she'd come to him just days earlier for an ear and for guidance, when she'd talked to him once more as though he were the only other person on earth. She needed him, and now he'd allowed himself to be taken from her side.

As sick and sad as he'd ever been, Clement let himself drop off the bench to his knees, then lay face down in the dark, empty plaza, nearly weeping with relief as the coolness of the marble spread into his body and his bare cheek. After a while he rolled over so he faced the sky. Above him the streetlamps waved and swam, tracing blurry streaks of light across his vision, and by and by he passed out beneath the Chinatown gate. Several hours later, just before dawn, he came to and found his pockets turned out and his shoes and watch missing, and the first thought that occurred to him, inanely, was that this was the poorest he'd been since taking the vow of poverty nearly twenty years earlier.

CHAPTER SEVEN

The deal was as simple as it was widely known around Little Canada: bring Phineus the Drunk a can of Milwaukee's Best beer (a tallboy, mind you, *not* a standard-issue twelve-ounce can, and *froid*, as cold as possible while still remaining this side of frozen) and he would tell you whatever you wanted to know.

In a previous life, Phineus the Drunk had been Dick Bolduc, a contemporary of Rheal's father who worked in chemical recovery at Hollingsworth & Whitney. In the winter of 1962 Dick had taken a blast of quicklime to the eyes, and like that he had seen his last sunset. A few years later Dick started telling people the loss of his vision had come with a trade-off—he'd been gifted vision of a different kind, and now was a psychic. This was around the same time Dick started insisting people call him Phineus.

Naturally, his neighbors wrote Dick off as gone cuckoo from the accident, and the fact that he'd been denied a settlement by the company for failing to wear his safety goggles. Not to mention, people said, that Dick'd hardly spent an hour sober since losing his sight, and that did things to a man's mind, too. But then stories started circulating: Dick had warned Phil Frappier to cut down a towering old maple on his property; Phil ignored him, and two weeks later the maple fell and pulverized half of Phil's house. In early 1965, Dick told people he had visions of the House of Pancakes closing, and that spring the owner was hauled off by the feds for tax evasion. Heart attacks, burst water pipes, car accidents—Dick called them all. Before too long, people started listening to Dick when he told them something. And they started calling him Phineus, as he'd asked them to.

Like the oracles of antiquity, Phineus the Drunk did his best work in an altered state. Ancient Greek seers inhaled vapors from the body of a slain serpent; Phineus got hammered on Milwaukee's Best and Old Crow. Different technique, same result: cryptic insights and predictions; unforeseen consequences well-nigh guaranteed; caveat emptor, no refunds, no exchanges.

Except in the most inhospitable of weather, Phineus could be found on the sidewalk on Water Street, the main drag of Little Canada, directly in front of his tenement at the top of the hill, just past Scottie's Variety and the VFW. Allegedly a veteran (no one alive could remember if Dick had served or not), Phineus often repaired to the VFW bar around dusk, and was usually in such a state when he left—or was told to leave—that residing within crawling distance was a necessity. He always got an early start, setting up his lawn chair and TV tray around 6 a.m. and cracking the first beer of the day shortly thereafter. By noon he had his shirt off and his buzz on, ready to advise and foretell, and all were welcome so long as they came bearing the prescribed twenty-four-ounce offering.

On this bright, clear morning, Phineus's first supplicant of the day was Rheal Dionne. Though plenty of other people availed themselves of Phineus's services on the regular, Rheal never had, in part because he believed the blind old man was a nutter, and in part because Rheal himself, at least until recently, had never worried much about the future—or anything else, for that matter. Life had taught him, through a steady diet of pain and terror that began in his earliest memories and continued straight through two combat tours in Vietnam, that everything was random, devoid of meaning, and thus ridiculous. You could choose to be in on the joke, or you could default, as most did, to being the butt of it; either way, it was still a joke. This refusal to take anything seriously made Rheal a perfect counterbalance for Babs, who would fight a bull moose given the slightest provocation.

Rheal didn't need a meaningful purpose, for existence as a whole or for himself as a man. He'd been girded in good humor, always. What was the sense of getting upset about life's fickle randomness? You sure weren't going to change anything. Have a drink, have a laugh, watch the clown show.

Except something had changed since the strike began. He couldn't say what or why, just that he'd become aware of a feeling that resembled what others had told him about worry. He slept like shit. His thoughts fluttered around his skull like moths in a lampshade. He was cranky all the time but often didn't realize it until he'd already snapped at someone.

And then Claude had lied to him, and Rheal's worry, previously ephemeral and free-floating, became quite specific: Could he trust his best friend again? Could he trust anyone? What else was being kept from him, and by whom?

Now look at the state of things: in his desperation, Milwaukee's Best in hand, he approached Phineus the Drunk for counsel.

The sun had barely cleared the trees on the riverbank side of

Water Street, and already Phineus had his second beer going, the first dead soldier of the day in its customary spot on the sidewalk underneath Phineus's TV tray, soon to be joined by others. As someone who enjoyed a drink himself, Rheal appreciated the brio, though he did wonder how in hell Phineus was still alive after decades of this. The man probably hadn't had a glass of water his entire life.

Phineus heard Rheal's boots gritting against the sidewalk and looked up, his eyes like opals. "Thank you, friend," he said as Rheal placed the tallboy, dripping with condensation, in his hands. "Are you here for *l'enluminure*?"

"That what you call it? I guess I am."

Phineus dumped the remnants of his open beer on the sidewalk, where it splattered and foamed. "Shit gets warm fast once the sun's up," he said with a grimace.

Rheal watched as Phineus put the empty with its brethren under the tray, then removed a pocketknife from his jeans, lay the fresh tallboy on its side, felt around to measure the can's dimensions, and poked a hole near the bottom with one deft stab of the blade. Phineus plugged the hole with a thumb, raised the business end of the can to his mouth, popped the tab and lifted his thumb simultaneously, and twenty-four ounces of icy, lousy domestic lager flowed down his throat in just a couple of seconds.

"Ostie de calisse de ciboire de tabarnak," Rheal said.

"That ain't nothing," Phineus told him. "You want to see some real drinking, stick around." He took a fresh beer from his cooler and shoved it into a foam Koozie that read FIESTA, SIESTA, TEQUILA—CANCUN, MEXICO.

Rheal plunked down in the webbed lawn chair that sat to Phineus's left.

"I'm Rheal," he said.

"I know who you are. I'm a goddamn psychic, guy."

"Right right. My mistake."

Phineus let loose a belch like a gunshot, gathered himself in its wake, and took a drink of the fresh beer. "You're skeptical," he said. "I understand."

"A little," Rheal said.

"A lot," Phineus said. "And you should be. Been a long time since you believed in Santa Claus and the Easter Bunny."

"Nice that you don't take it personally," Rheal said.

"Why would I?" Phineus reached under his TV tray and pulled out a bottle of Old Grand-Dad. "I already got what I wanted out of this transaction. It couldn't matter less to me if you think I'm a fraud."

Rheal lit a cigarette. "That's not entirely true," he said. "The only way you stay in free beer is if people believe you're for real."

Phineus squinted at him, odd and unnerving with eyes blind as marbles. "Hard to understand what you're doing here, since you know everything already," he said.

Rheal sat back, looked across the street at the trees on the riverbank. "I guess I'm a little lost."

"People are always lost by the time they sit in that chair," Phineus said.

They were quiet for a few moments. Several vehicles passed, all heading in the direction of the Mill upriver. Scabs, reporting for first shift.

Phineus took another slug of whiskey, swallowed, and groaned. "Shit, that's tough first thing," he said. "Okay, do you want me to just tell you what you're here to find out, or do you want a bit of a show first? Like, I can pretend to go into a trance. Make funny noises. Some people like to see me flop around a little bit, like I'm having a seizure. I want you to get your money's worth."

"The beer was seventy-five cents," Rheal said. "No seizures necessary."

"Roger that," Phineus said. "Okay. I've got an eight thirty, so let's get on with this. You say you're lost, but that's not quite right. You know exactly where you are. What you're less sure about is everyone else. All of a sudden, you don't know if you can trust your best friend. And then there's your wife. You're missing each other coming and going, and you've started to wonder if she's keeping something from you. How am I doing so far?"

It took Rheal a couple of beats to unstick his tongue. "Pretty spot-on," he said finally.

"I've got good news and bad news," Phineus said. "The good news is you can absolutely, one hundred percent trust your buddy. Same as you always believed you could. He was desperate and he made a mistake. But that's over."

"And what's the bad news?"

"Your wife is a slightly different story."

"I'm gonna need more than that," Rheal said.

"Well, that's the problem," Phineus said. "There's definitely something between you—I can see it, she's like a running back throwing a stiff-arm—but whatever it is, she's locked it away so deep in her mind there's nothing for me to read. Is she wildly strong-willed, this woman?"

"You could say that," Rheal said.

Phineus closed his eyes for a few moments, furrowing his brow with effort. "Nope, I got nothing," he said finally, opening his eyes again.

"Nothing at all?" Rheal asked.

"Nothing specific," Phineus said. "Nothing, you know, *actionable.*"

"Then tell me what you do have."

"You're not going to like it."

"Try me," Rheal said.

"Okay," Phineus said. "Whatever it is she's keeping from you, it's going to cause you more pain than you've ever experienced in your life."

Rheal stared at him. "That's going to be a lot of pain," he said.

"I told you you weren't going to like it."

"That's it? Just pain?"

"I'm seeing some good, too," Phineus said. "It's gonna go like this: a wicked lot of pain, then it'll be pretty nice for a stretch, and then the worst pain you've ever had in your life."

"Wait. The first stretch of pain isn't even the bad part?"

"Oh, it's still plenty bad," Phineus said. "But no, not the worst."

Sophie had told Claude she didn't want treatment anymore, but when she said things like that, especially when she was only going to dialysis once a week, Claude couldn't know if it was his wife talking, or the poisons building up in her blood. Because when you weren't getting cleaned out as often as you needed, it messed with your thinking. They'd seen it plenty of times. Before they knew her kidneys were bad, she suddenly couldn't keep people's breakfast orders straight, when she used to be able to hold orders for four or five tables in her head at a time, no problem. Then a year later, when Sophie had grown tired of watching her own blood pass into and out of a machine that reminded her of the robot from *Lost in Space*, they'd tried to get by with diuretics and iron supplements and hope. That effort ended one afternoon when Claude came home from an early strike meeting to find his wife had no idea who he was, and he spent the next nine hours in the emergency room at Thayer hospital, his own mind whirring with existential confusion, wondering if maybe the woman he knew as Sophie was right and they were strangers to each other, if in fact Claude's whole life had been nothing but a dream and he was not and never had been a boy, a man, a Marine, a husband, or a father.

In any event, even if Claude believed, now, that Sophie was in her right mind, he wouldn't have accepted her deciding to just die. One, because they had the kids to think about. Two, because he knew all too well what death was, and Sophie did not. Like most people, she imagined what was grievous about death was its permanence, that the person who died could never be seen or heard from again. But Claude knew what was truly terrifying was the irreconcilable contrast between a living person and a dead one, a contrast so vast as to seem impossible. Claude himself hadn't understood where the notion of a spirit could have come from, until the first time he saw the absence in a dead friend's mangled body, the sudden *unthere-ness.* The only explanation for such a transformation was that something other than—greater than—the physical had been removed. And so death was, for Claude, the enemy. Death he would not accept.

Which was why he'd asked his brother-in-law Daryl Bates to meet him at the Villager for breakfast—though Claude, being broke, only ordered a coffee.

"Have some breakfast," Bates told him. "It's on me."

"I'm fine with the coffee."

"Eat something," Bates said. "You look like death warmed over."

"I was up late."

"Doing what?"

Claude glanced out the restaurant's front window at the parking lot, where people went into and out of the Shop 'n' Save supermarket. "Hanging out. With Rheal."

"Hanging out."

Claude met Bates's gaze. "What are you, my mother?"

"No, I'm your police captain. And I question the wisdom of spending time with degenerates like Dionne."

"Mind your own business. And mind how you talk about my friend."

"You are my business. Being married to my sister and all."

Kim Vachon burst through the saloon doors from the kitchen, pen and pad in hand. "You guys know what you want?"

"Couple of Sunrise Samplers, over easy, bacon, white toast," Bates said. He handed the menus to Kim, and she disappeared back into the kitchen as quickly as she'd come.

"I didn't ask you here to get a free meal, Daryl," Claude said.

Bates sipped his coffee, frowned, added more creamer. "Then why did you ask me here?"

"It's about Sophie."

"What about her?"

"She's not doing well."

Bates stared, coffee mug in mid-lift. "Tell me," he said.

"She doesn't want to do dialysis anymore."

Bates frowned again, dismissive of the very notion. "She has to."

"Well, no, she doesn't," Claude said. "Nobody can force her. Doctors tell us that all the time. Fact, they say it so often you'd think they *want* her to call it quits."

"I'll talk to her," Bates said.

"I've talked to her plenty," Claude said. "Talking won't make a difference. She's tired of being sick, Daryl. And I don't blame her."

"Well, she *is* sick. And since there's nothing to be done about it, she's just got to keep dealing with it."

"I think there might be another option, is what I'm trying to tell you."

"And what's that?"

"A transplant."

A pause, Bates staring at Claude. "I thought a transplant wasn't really on the table."

"It wasn't. But they've got these drugs now. They keep the body from rejecting the new organ. A game-changer, they say."

"If Soph doesn't want to go get her oil changed anymore, what makes you think she'll be so eager to have the sawbones cut her open?"

"Because she said so herself," Claude said. "Dialysis is a stopgap. No one wants to live their life hooked to a machine. But a transplant is a chance to be whole again."

Now it was Bates's turn to gaze out the window at the people going into and out of the Shop 'n' Save, traffic passing and pausing by turns at the light on Main Street. "I'm hesitant to ask," he said, topping off his coffee from the urn Kim had dropped on their table earlier. "But what unholy amount of money does it cost for a kidney transplant?"

Claude looked down at his paper place mat, which featured a crossword bordered by advertisements for local businesses. "A lot," he said.

"No shit, a lot. How much?"

"Depends, but around a hundred and fifty thousand."

"Jesus Mary and Joseph."

"And that's just the surgery," Claude said. "We'd need to stay down in Boston for a week, tons of follow-up care. For years. None of it's free."

Kim came swooping in again, plates in her hands and a plastic bottle of pancake syrup tucked under one of her arms. "Two Samplers, sunny-side *down,*" she said, plunking the food in front of the men. "Anything else you fellas need?"

"Got any ketchup?" Bates asked.

"Funny you should ask," Kim said, pulling a bottle of Heinz from the pocket of her apron and placing it next to the coffee urn. "You good?"

"Thank you, Kim," Bates said. She left, and Bates and Claude sat looking at each other, neither making a move to start eating.

"Claude, look," Bates said, leaning forward with his elbows on the table. "You know me and Melinda have been happy to help where we can. But this . . . this is a whole other thing."

"I'm not asking for money, Daryl," Claude said.

Bates didn't seem to hear him. "I mean Jesus, I guess we could refinance the house or something. Cash out my IRA."

"You're not listening," Claude said. "I don't need money."

"The hell you don't," Bates said. "I know damn well they're not just going to bill you. What do you have to pay to get her through the door?"

A pause. "Thirty up-front."

"Claude," Bates said, not unkindly, "how are you going to come up with thirty grand, when you can't even pay for breakfast?"

Claude used the tips of his fingers to push his plate away, untouched. "I told you I didn't want breakfast," he said. "And I'm telling you now that I don't want your money. I'm here to ask for something else."

"If you say so," Bates said. He reached, finally, for his fork and knife, unfolded the little paper napkin and spread it on his lap. "But don't be an asshole. Eat."

Neither spoke for a few long moments, Bates slicing his pancakes in a grid while Claude continued to ignore his own food. Bates poured syrup, lifted a dripping forkful of pancake to his mouth, paused, and said, "So?"

"The thing is," Claude said, "even though the drugs keep the body from rejecting the transplant, you've still got a much better chance if the organ donor is related to you. Something about blood types and genes and such."

Bates paused mid-chew, starting to grok what Claude was proposing.

"So I'm not here to ask for a free breakfast, or to ask for money," Claude said. "I'm here to ask for a kidney."

Bates stared. "*My* kidney?"

"You've got two of them. You only need one. I can get the money, but before I do I have to know you're going to help. Because once I start, there won't be any going back."

"Says the guy who's not being asked for a kidney."

"Trust me when I tell you," Claude said, "that I'd rather be in your position than mine."

"Claude," Bates said, "it's hard for me to imagine how you can legally get thirty thousand dollars on short notice."

"If you're too scared to do it, just say so. Don't hide behind your job."

"I'm not scared."

"Good. Then don't worry about what I have to do to get the money."

Bates lowered his voice to a hiss, glancing around the dining room. "Don't talk like that. I'm a cop, for Christ's sake."

"Daryl, look at me."

Bates did, and Claude held his gaze.

"This is my wife. The mother of my kids," Claude said. "Your sister."

"I know."

"I'll do what I have to," Claude said. "Will you?"

Chief Davies showed up at the Dionne house in time for morning coffee, but Babs certainly wasn't about to invite him in. She stayed in the doorway holding her own mug by the handle, eyeing the chief with amusement as he stood with both hands on his utility belt, feet spread wide, command presence all the way.

"I assume if you were going to arrest me I'd already be in cuffs," she said.

"You'd already be back in that cell," Davies said.

"Then beat it. I'm busy." Babs went to close the door.

"I'm just here to let you know," Davies said, "that whatever you think you're up to, you should stop. Or else I'll nail you sooner or later. Whether Rick Roy is willing to press charges or not."

Babs paused, considered. "I'm happy to talk about what I'm up to," she said after a moment. "See, I've got a problem, but I think I've figured out how to deal with it."

Davies crossed his arms over his chest. "Do tell," he said.

Babs smiled at him, sipped her coffee. "It's like this," she said.

"Someone's giving me a hard time about something that's ancient history. And I need to get rid of that person, because they're fucking up my efforts to take care of things in the here and now."

"I know," Davies said, "that I am not standing here listening to you threaten me."

"This person, who is definitely *not* you," Babs said, "has a position that would make most assume he answers to the mayor. But that's not really the case. Like everyone else in this town, he actually serves at the pleasure of a fellow named Clay Sutton."

Davies's eyes narrowed at the mention of International Paper's senior vice president.

"My guess," Babs went on, "was that Mr. Sutton was probably ready, after dealing with a strike for a year and a half, to have some peace and quiet around here. So I took a drive down to his nice summer home in Kennebunk, told him he'll have no further problems with us little people—if he's willing to take care of my problem for *me*."

"You're out of your mind," Davies said.

"Maybe," Babs said. "Still, he seemed pretty receptive to my pitch, and maybe you should mull it over, too, Chief: Who's a more valuable ally to a man like Sutton? A stuffed uniform, who only appears to be in charge? Or the person who's going to really decide what happens around here?"

Davies didn't respond, though his face had gone red with some mixture of worry and rage. The two of them stood staring at each other for a long moment.

"Now either arrest me," Babs said finally, "or get the fuck off my property."

And rather than slam the door in his face, she let it close, slowly, while Davies watched and fumed.

WE WILL SEE YOU BLEED

Davies had been to Clay Sutton's compound in Kennebunk once before, nearly two years earlier, when the strike had loomed on the horizon like a thunderhead and Sutton had called a meeting of various officials, local, state, and federal, ostensibly to try to figure out a way to avoid a work stoppage. In a room that featured the secretary of labor, the governor, and Maine's Republican senator, Davies had barely rated above the men circulating trays of hors d'oeuvres, and so had neither talked to nor even officially met Sutton. He'd just stood around for two hours feeling vaguely ridiculous in his dress uniform, thinking ungenerous thoughts about the kinds of men who divvied the world up a bit more finely among themselves while eating shrimp cocktail and miniature quiches. But then, when the portion of the gathering intended for the public came to a close, and the reporters from the *Press Herald* and *Morning Sentinel* had gone home, Davies had been asked to stick around for a private meeting, where he proved himself just the kind of man Sutton was looking for: easily flattered and ethically labile, disdainful of the genteel power Sutton wielded only until that power was dangled in front of him. Davies had been made to understand that his future would be much brighter if the Waterville Police Department favored International Paper in its policies going forward, and then he'd been bid adieu, and that was the last he'd seen or heard of Sutton. In the ensuing year and a half, Davies had done everything expected of him and then some, up to and including bringing the strike to an end with one single, brilliant stroke. Now here he was, pulling up to the guard shack at Sutton's compound and demanding an audience. Indignation, it turned out, had a way of making even cowards bold.

Davies didn't know he expected to be turned away until he

wasn't. The gate went up and the guard waved him through, but for a second or two he just sat there. Finally, he put the car in drive and moved slowly up the gravel driveway, struck anew by the sheer size of the place. The compound took up the entirety of Point Vesuvius, nine acres, twelve buildings, an indoor and an outdoor pool, boat-house, guesthouse three times the size of Davies's own home, two tennis courts, a four-car garage, and finally the compound's center-piece: a brooding nine-bedroom mansion, anchored by six stone fireplace chimneys and done up with a forest's worth of cedar shin-gles, giving the impression of a summer cottage on steroids. As he approached the main house Davies could see Sutton's boat, a seventy-foot carbon fiber catamaran that kept a crew of five busy shuttling back and forth between Maine and the Caribbean with the seasons. In toto the estate was nearly a quarter mile long, bor-dered on three sides by jagged rocks and splashing surf, as absurd an affirmation of the greed-is-good ethic of the current moment as one could hope to find. This, then, was what it looked like to have a generous equity stake in the world's largest private landowner, otherwise known as International Paper.

Davies followed the driveway as it looped into a small cul-de-sac in front of the main house, then parked near the entrance. He turned the car off and sat there for a minute, not knowing what protocol was in such environs—should he expect to be greeted by a valet or other servant? Was he even supposed to park here in the first place? Enough time passed without a clear answer that he started to feel more than a little silly, sitting there like the world's most obvious stakeout. Already simmering with doubt and anger—the faithful servant betrayed—now embarrassment was added to the stew as he dismounted his vehicle and took the stairs, still gaz-ing around to see if anyone at all was present.

Davies stood before the double glass doors for only a moment, looking at his own stupid reflection, then thought fuck it, tried the door handle—and found it unlocked. The entrance let onto a small foyer, which Davies remembered from his first time here, mostly because it was so modest, just a regular old mudroom, really. If not for the very old hand-carved woodwork around the doorframes, it could have been the entryway of most any house in Waterville.

Beyond here, though, Sutton's summer home became something Waterville had never dreamed of. Which Davies also remembered well.

A huge sitting room lay on the other side of the foyer's interior door—fifteen-foot ceilings with exposed oak beams, custom windows as tall as a man and twice as wide looking east toward the breakwater and, beyond that, the open Atlantic. This was where Davies found Sutton, seated on the one piece of furniture—a chocolate leather lounge chair—that seemed like anyone had ever actually used it.

Sutton looked up from his newspaper and smiled. "Chief Davies," he said. "Can I offer you something to drink? I'd suggest a cocktail, but it's early and you're in uniform. Coffee, tea?"

Davies found himself surprised that Sutton remembered him, and felt a flush of pleasure that he immediately quashed. "Not at the moment, thank you," he said, keeping his voice even.

Sutton removed his reading glasses and looked Davies over, appraising. Then he extended a slender hand toward the sofa opposite his seat. "Join me."

Davies sat and, though he had the urge to look everywhere but at Sutton, forced himself to keep his eyes steady on his host. On the drive here, Davies had been thinking about one of the many axioms his father had drilled into him: that there were moments, in certain kinds of conversations, when silence became a test, and the position of strength went to the man who could tolerate that silence the longest. This felt like one of those moments, and so even though every bit of his brain was screaming at him to say something, to not be rude, to not make this more awkward than it already was, Davies kept his mouth shut.

Sutton, a man for whom meaningful silence appeared as comfortable as fleece-lined slippers, stared back placidly for several moments. And then, smiling again, he set his newspaper aside and said, "So. To what do I owe the pleasure, Chief?"

Davies, feeling like he'd won this round, forced himself to swallow a smile. "You must have heard by now that the strike is over," he said.

"Of course," Suttton said.

Quiet, again. That was it? No happiness, no relief, no *gratitude*, for the guy who'd actually brought the strike to an end? But then, did Sutton even know he was talking to the man who had forced Babs to call it off? Davies thought of his father again, heard him saying: *If you have to draw attention to your accomplishments, they aren't accomplishments at all.*

"I thought you'd be a little happier," Davies said, trying not to sound petulant.

Sutton cocked his head a quarter of an inch, and Davies couldn't tell if this indicated amusement or annoyance. "Certainly I'm glad the public relations headache is over," he said. "But is that why you drove, what, two hours, Chief? To gauge whether I was appropriately pleased by the conclusion of the strike?"

"Well, no," Davies said. "I'm here about something else."

"Now that the strike is officially over, though," Sutton said, "I feel like I can tell you something that may come as a surprise. Can I speak to you in confidence?"

"Mr. Sutton, I do want to talk to you about something—"

"A couple of years ago, I managed to corner President Reagan at a cocktail party. A fundraising thing, you understand. It's not like we were old buddies or anything. Anyway, long story short, I was complaining about some collective bargaining issue, and Reagan says to me, 'Why don't you just fire them?' Like it's the easiest, most obvious thing in the world. And I say, 'Well, that's the thing, Mr. President, you can't just fire these people. They're highly skilled. They've been doing this work for generations. You can't pull someone off the street and put them at the controls of paper machines and log pickers.' And he looks at me and says, 'Clay, if I shitcanned every air traffic controller in the country and managed to keep the skies open, I'm sure you can find people to make toilet paper without too much trouble.' And he was right, of course."

Davies, not entirely certain he was following, kept his mouth shut.

"I tell you that anecdote," Sutton continued, "by way of explanation for my . . . tepid reaction to the end of the strike at Hollingsworth and Whitney. As far as I was concerned, your fellow Watervillians could go on marching around and shouting slogans until the second coming. Because I had already achieved my aim: an entirely nonunion labor force."

"You *wanted* them to strike?" Davies said.

"How else could I fire an entire operation's worth of union workers? Of course I wanted them to strike. In fact, I made it impossible for them not to. We appeased the Locals at other mills to keep them on the sidelines, but soon enough they'll get the same treatment."

Disbelief kept Davies from responding.

"Obviously that sounds terrible," Sutton said. "But your mayor, and your town manager Mr. Daly, and most of the city council understood it had to happen."

"Why is that, exactly?"

"Because it was either this, or I would have been forced to move operations to Indonesia. And then where would Waterville be?"

"In the shitter?" Davies said.

"Not how I would have phrased it," Sutton said, "but yes."

"Mr. Sutton, I'm going to be plain with you," Davies said. "I think you're telling me all this because there's something else you don't want to talk about."

Sutton's eyebrows went up ever so slightly. "What is that?"

"Babs Dionne."

"I'm sorry. Who?"

Davies smiled, to let Sutton know he wasn't buying this for a second. "I just want to warn you—don't think that because you've gotten what you needed out of me I can just be thrown away."

"Chief," Sutton said, "I think maybe we're talking past each other right now."

"You expect me to believe you don't know who the leader of the union Local is?"

"Why would I?"

"Because you've been fighting her for the last year and a half."

"You misunderstand. I know the key players with the national union. It's not my custom to have dealings with the Locals."

Davies studied Sutton's face. "Babs Dionne," he said after a moment, "is a person I have history with. I'm the one who forced her to call off the strike, basically on *your* behalf. And now she's threatening to use you to get rid of me."

Sutton leaned back and gazed out at the water crashing against granite. "Ah, I see," he said. "And how did she propose to convince me to *get rid of you*, exactly?"

"You really don't know anything about any of this?"

Sutton raised his hands, palms skyward, and shrugged.

"I'm not sure I believe you."

"Well, consider, Chief Davies," Sutton said, "that it doesn't really matter what you believe. If what you're saying were true—which it is not—I could be shut of you quite easily even if you knew that was my intention. Your awareness of this alleged scheme would hardly confer any protection from it."

Davies tried to think of a response, came up with nothing, and stayed silent.

Sutton leaned forward again in his chair, clasping his hands together between his knees. "You were right to think I owe you a favor, Chief," he said. "Can I offer some insight, gleaned from years of operating—pretty successfully—within the Machiavellian ecosystem of corporate America?"

"I suppose so."

"If I had a rival who told me something that wasn't true, I would think they did so for a reason," Sutton said. "Both the fact of the lie and its content, I would assume, were purposeful. Meant to confuse and distract me. To get me chasing my tail, while they were busy doing something else entirely that I wasn't paying attention to. Something that *was* a real threat to my position. Do you understand what I'm driving at, here?"

"I . . . think so?"

"This Mrs. Dionne? No doubt she does intend to dislodge you from the power structure in Waterville. However she's planning to accomplish that, it's nothing to do with me. But even though I have no knowledge of her plan, I feel confident saying that so far it's working. Because here you are, talking in circles with me, instead of back home in Waterville minding the shop."

Davies blanched.

"One last thing," Sutton said, "and understand when I say this I mean for it to be a comfort, though it will likely feel the opposite."

Oh Jesus, Davies thought, cursing himself now for being so stupid as to come here in the first place.

"You are nothing to me, Chief Davies," Sutton said. "Which means I have no cause to waste time on some bumpkin plot against you. The only reason I would bother to have you gotten rid of is if you somehow became an inconvenience or a liability. Do you anticipate being either of those things?"

"No, Mr. Sutton," Davies said.

"I'm glad to hear that," Sutton said. "For your sake. Rest assured, if this Mrs. Dionne becomes a problem, she'll get the same treatment. Now if you'll excuse me? I trust you can see yourself out?"

Davies hesitated for a moment, then stood up and smoothed the front of his uniform, uncertain. Obviously it was time to leave, but it seemed odd to do so without saying anything further, so he just stood there like a dummy.

Sutton opened his newspaper again. "I hope this conversation has put your mind at ease, Chief," he said, keeping his eyes on the paper as he spoke. "And in the meantime, I wish you the best of luck in trying to hold on to your job. I'd hurry home if I were you."

For Babs and Rheal nothing short of a nuclear exchange with the Soviets was allowed to interfere with Tuesday-night league bowling at Spare Time Bowling Center. In fact, league bowling was inviolable for not just the Dionnes but most of Little Canada's residents. The league took a pause during the summer, but from September to May, the only other place the neighborhood went with such Swiss-timepiece reliability (if somewhat less enthusiasm) was Notre Dame church for Sunday mass.

So it was that, even as the Saucier brothers were at Davies's home committing several felonies on their behalf, Babs and Rheal were at the lanes for the league's opening night, drinking Miller Lites and carrying on with the other members of their team, of whom only Rita and Claude were present. Sophie, Claude's wife, was too ill to bowl, and no one seemed to know where Father Clement had gotten off to.

In a league that boasted a dozen scratch bowlers, Babs was among the best, her game a synthesis of power and finesse that a professional would have admired. Her average, at the conclusion of each year, was consistently above 200 on a house shot, 185 if the Spare Time people had been feeling sadistic and opted for a sport oil pattern that season. She approached the game as all the best bowlers did: dispassionately, analytical as a mainframe, with a quick eye and mind. Bowling was a game of adjustments, and Babs could see and execute the correct adjustments two or three frames before most others in the league recognized what was wrong with their shot and finally moved their feet or changed out balls.

Rheal, on the other hand, bowled like Fred Flintstone. He had one ball, a sixteen-pounder with a crack in its coverstock that he'd been using since the second Nixon administration, and he delivered it as hard as he could down the middle of the lane, every time. No spin, no hook, no nothing. Just league-leading velocity, often upward of thirty mph according to the lane speedometer. When his throw hit the pocket just right the pins seemed to vaporize, and often came bursting out of the pit onto his and, occasionally, others' lanes. But a point of impact even half an inch astray often left him with ugly, unmakable splits. As such, by scoring average Rheal was the weakest bowler on their team, man or woman. Which was fine with him. He was there to knock back beers, throw the ball as hard and straight as possible, and forget about anything other than having a good time.

But it was difficult for even Rheal to have a good time when the vibe on the lanes resembled an afternoon viewing at Veilleux's Funeral Home. Normally a hum of laughter and Quebecois chatter ran in the background of league Tuesdays, increasing in volume and exuberance as the night went on and the drinks went down. One would expect that on opening night this din would be even more boisterous, but tonight there was only the dutiful rhythm of the game itself: the rumble of balls as they traveled down the lanes, the clap as they hit the pins. Beneath that, a grim silence. When people spoke they did so closely and quietly, shoulder to shoulder, as though telling secrets. Instead of sharing pizzas and big plates of poutine, people ate from brown paper bags like elementary school kids, sitting alone and nibbling sandwiches as they waited their turn to roll. Rheal's team wasn't the only one missing members; near as he could estimate, probably a third of the league hadn't shown up.

And then there was the energy directed toward him and Babs: in a word, icy. People glared and talked behind their hands, and if looks could kill, the Dionnes would have been dead a dozen times over. Their opponents, a team of seamstresses from the Hathaway Shirt Company called the Gutterballs, barely spoke, conspicuously avoiding any shared time at the ball return. Meantime, Rick Roy limped around the alley like a walking indictment, too busted up to bowl; he sat nursing a Budweiser at the high-top table on lane five while his team got savaged by last season's champions, a group of erstwhile H&W machine operators who called themselves Roll Another. People disliked bowling against Roll Another, not just because they got their asses kicked, but because the games took an hour longer than usual owing to Roll Another's frequent excursions to the parking lot to smoke pot.

Between the second and third games, Rheal pulled Babs onto his lap and said, "Should we be worried for our safety?"

"*You* should, if you don't manage to roll above a hundred this time."

"Everyone hates us all of a sudden."

"So?"

"So these are our neighbors. Our friends."

Babs put her hands on either side of his face. "We'll talk about this later, in private," she said. "Right now you should be thinking about two things. One, winning this last game. And two, whether those Saucier maniacs are going to pull this off."

Rheal wasn't worried about the Sauciers, who had once assassinated a Khmer Rouge prefect with a chopstick and lived to tell about it; they could handle their assignment without much trouble. So he buckled down on the bowling, taking a bit off his throw in the hope it would result in greater control over where the ball ended up downlane. This seemed to work at first—he managed a turkey in frames two through four, and the team jumped out to a sixty-pin lead. But as they were sure to demonstrate any time you got cocky, the bowling gods were fickle, and from then on Rheal left every frame open but the eighth. By the time they'd lost by only seven pins he had cursed, in French, every last thing in heaven and earth that was holy.

The Gutterballs changed their shoes and packed their gear and departed without a word, though once they were off the lanes and into the bar area, much whooping and exchange of congratulations took place among them. Rheal finished his beer and watched the women order a round of celebratory shots.

Babs came up beside him, her bowling bag in hand. "No one likes them," she said.

"True," Rheal said, still gazing at the Gutterballs as they raised their shots for a toast. "They're definitely the second-least popular team in the league."

"Are you ready?" Babs asked.

"I'll have Claude drop me off," Rheal said. "He asked me to stick around for a beer."

"Tonight, of all nights?"

Rheal looked over at his friend, near the ball return packing his things, and he turned to Babs and lowered his voice. "Not a terrible idea to extend my alibi. As long as I'm here, I'm not at Davies's house."

"Fair enough," Babs said. "I'll be at home, in my nightgown, innocent as a lamb."

"Okay. I won't be late." Rheal lifted his bag, took a step toward the bar, then paused. "Hey," he said.

"Yes?"

"Is it my imagination," Rheal said, "or did you not take a single smoke break tonight?"

"Guess I got caught up," Babs said. She pulled her cigarette case, a leather pouch with a clasp top, out of her bowling bag. "Taking one right now."

"And you've got your piece?"

Babs looked at him. "Of course," she said.

"Just making sure," he said. "We started something the other night, and we need to be careful. Two steps ahead. Always anticipating."

"I'm aware of what we've started, my love," Babs said. "I'll see you at home."

She left, and most of the other league bowlers followed over the next ten minutes. By the time Rheal and Claude had settled into a booth with fresh beers the place was mostly empty, with only the occasional thump and rumble of a ball hitting the lane as a handful of people got in extra practice.

"What's on your mind?" Rheal asked after a few moments of silence between them.

Claude laughed into the neck of his beer bottle. "What's on my mind?" he said. "Nothing much. Just what the hell is next. How anyone in this town is going to feed their family. Just that."

"We've got a plan," Rheal said. "As I told you."

"Sure. But you didn't tell me what the plan *is*. Makes it tough to judge for myself whether it'll take care of me and mine."

Rheal lit a cigarette and threw the expired match in a disposable aluminum ashtray on the table. "You really think I'd let your kids go hungry, C?"

"I think your wife would."

"See, that's where you're wrong. She cares more about doing right by everyone—including you—than I do. I'd let all these assholes soak in their own bathwater, but she's determined to fix things for them."

Claude didn't respond. Instead he lit his own cigarette and gazed over at the lanes. Finally, he spoke.

"Here's what I know," Claude said. "We ran all of Aucoin's dealers out of town and took their merchandise. We're sitting on three or four kilos of coke, a couple kilos of weed, and what, four or five hundred pills, mostly quaaludes. I assume the plan is to turn all that into money."

"Eventually."

"I'm broke now."

"So are we. So's everyone."

"Not everyone's wife has late-stage kidney failure."

Rheal hung his head over his beer. "We've got to do this right, Claude. That takes time."

"How much time?"

"The next step is happening as we speak," Rheal said. "And that's all I can tell you."

Claude leaned forward and tapped his cigarette in the ashtray. "What's the long game? Does this plan that I can't know anything about include getting our jobs back?"

"We mean for it to."

"Because I don't know about you, but I'm not interested in being a full-time drug dealer."

They were quiet for a moment.

"We missed Soph tonight," Rheal said finally.

"She misses you guys, too."

"She's feeling lousy, eh?"

"It's gotten pretty bad. I'm sort of at wit's end."

"What do you mean?"

Claude glanced around to make sure no one was within earshot. "She doesn't want dialysis anymore, and no one's going to convince her otherwise. It's kidney transplant or bust."

"Merde."

"So now you know why I need money. A lot of it. Right now.

Everything's been such a drag on her," Claude said. "It's bad enough being sick, but with the strike and everything . . ."

"You can't convince her to keep up with the dialysis for another six months? Just until we get things off the ground?"

"It's way past that," Claude said. "She ain't herself. Half the time I feel like I shouldn't leave her alone with the kids. I'm afraid I'll come home and find her hanging in the garage."

"Don't talk like that."

"She keeps saying 'you don't understand, you don't understand,'" Claude said. "And she's right, I don't. I can't. That's the worst part. We can't reach each other. She's over there in the land of the sick, and I'm in the land of the healthy."

This was not something they could fight and kill, or neuter by making fun of it over drinks. Rheal didn't know what else to say.

"You want to hear something terrible?" Claude asked.

"I want to hear whatever you have to tell me," Rheal said.

"The truth is, I'm with Soph," Claude said. "I can't live this way anymore, either."

Even with only the dim light of a streetlamp to see by, the circle of scorched grass in Connie Fecteau's front yard was easily visible from the street. In the shadows it looked more like a hole than a burn mark, perhaps even a portal to hell. Like it could—and wanted to—swallow you whole. Or so it seemed to Babs, at least, as she pulled to the curb in front of Connie's house and put her station wagon in park.

She came up the walkway, paused to eye the blackened grass and shake the persistent, unnerving impression that it might be a bottomless hole in the earth. She took the stairs to the front door, noticing as she went that the word *Putain*, spray-painted crudely in black on the vinyl siding weeks ago, had been half-scrubbed away and now read just *ain*.

Babs raised a hand to knock, but paused when something off to the right caught her eye. On the floor of the porch, tucked into a corner, was a small lump like a loaf of bread, wrapped neatly in a blanket. The Jack Russell, Babs realized. They hadn't buried him yet. Babs felt a fresh surge of anger at Rick Roy as she turned back to the door and knocked.

In the quiet of the slumbering neighborhood Babs could hear footsteps approach from inside the house. The curtain on the door was pushed aside briefly as whoever stood there, hidden in darkness, assessed Babs's presence. A moment later the porch light blazed to life and Connie opened the door.

"Sorry to call on you so late," Babs said.

Connie whispered through clenched teeth. "If you're here to lecture me about scabbing, you can turn right around and leave," she said. "I get it. Solidarity. All for one and one for all. But I have to work. It's that simple and I don't want to hear about it anymore."

"Connie, I'm—"

"No. Enough's enough. Your point's been made. My girls watched their dog die yesterday. He was making these terrible noises and throwing up everywhere and there was nothing I could do about it and they *saw* that, Babs. Saw their mother couldn't make it stop or make it better."

Babs lowered her eyes to the transom between the porch and the interior.

"So I hope you're all satisfied," Connie said. "Because now they know I can't protect them or the things they love. Mission accomplished. I sure have learned my lesson. But I'm still gonna get up and go to work tomorrow, because I have to."

"Connie," Babs said. "Listen for a sec. I want you to go to work."

"What?"

"The strike's over. You probably didn't hear."

"I . . . what happened?"

Babs sighed. "We lost," she said. "Everyone's fired, and that's all she wrote. But it's hardly your fault. And it's not why I came."

"Then why did you?"

"I want to try and help your girls feel a little safer again. Can I speak to them a moment?"

Connie stared at Babs for a beat. When she realized she could trust what Babs was saying, all the fury drained from her in an instant, and Babs saw how hollowed out and stricken she was. Connie moved to one side, closed the door as Babs stepped in.

"You want some coffee?" Connie asked.

Babs shook her head. "I'm not going to bother you long," she said. "You look like you could sleep for a week. Just want to see those girls a minute."

Connie nodded and left the mudroom as Babs looked around, shifting her weight from foot to foot. Fully in evidence was the loving chaos of a household with two small children and only one parent: tiny shoes and boots kicked off in haste and scattered everywhere except the shoe mat; toys and Barbies and a visibly deflated soccer ball gathered into a loose pile in one corner; matching My Little Pony backpacks crumpled on the floor. Looking at the bedlam wrought by only two children, Babs marveled at how her parents and so many others could have managed to raise a dozen or more. The mothers in particular, who not only did the majority of the real, contact-sport parenting, but did it most often while pregnant with yet another child. The mind reeled, the heart swelled and ached.

And as Babs's heart swelled and ached, Connie came back to the mudroom with her daughters in tow: eight-year-old April and five-year-old Tiffany, scuffing the floor in their footie pajamas. Both girls were impossibly thin, and neither had the puffy eyes and flyaway hair of children who'd been suddenly awakened. They looked sleepless and haunted, and considered Babs with a plain skepticism that was startling on such young faces.

Babs looked to Connie for a moment, then crouched in front of the girls. "Hi there," she said.

"Hi," April said. Tiffany kept silent, eyeing Babs as though she were responsible for all her family's trouble. And in a way, Babs thought, she was.

"I heard about what happened to your dog," Babs said, looking back and forth between the girls. "What was his name?"

"Tippy," April said.

"Tippy," Babs said. "That's a good, solid name for a little dog. I heard that Tippy was in a lot of pain, and I know that was probably pretty scary and sad."

April nodded, but Tiffany continued to keep her own counsel.

"And listen, I've heard things just generally have been scary and sad for a while now. But I came here tonight to tell you it's going to get better. Those people who set the fire out front? And hurt your dog and wrote on your house? They won't be doing any of those things again."

"Yes they will," April said. "They always come back."

Babs smiled. "Do you girls know my name? Do you know who I am?"

They shook their heads.

"Good," Babs said. "Because you don't want to. You know how awful the people are who hurt your dog? Well, believe me when I tell you: I'm much, much worse."

For the first time, Tiffany's expression shifted, from open hostility to a blip of concern.

"That's the bad news," Babs said, looking directly at Tiffany now. "The good news is, I'm on *your* side. I'm here to protect you and your mom, to fight for you. And because I'm so much worse than those other people, now that I'm here, they're never going to bother you again."

CHAPTER EIGHT

Father Clement finished packing his few belongings into a secondhand hockey bag he'd bought at Goodwill the previous evening upon realizing that, along with many other basics, he no longer owned anything resembling luggage. The bag wasn't even half-full, but it held everything. Six button-down shirts, four pairs of slacks, and some ratty jeans he wore when spreading mulch and pruning trees on the rectory lot. An ancient pair of tennis shoes, which ditto. Socks, tighty-whities, some threadbare, pit-stained undershirts he used as a layer between his skin and the polyester of his stole. Which of course was not *his* stole at all, but rather one of the many things that had been on loan to him from the Church. Including his car and this very house, which Clement was expected to vacate today to make room for the new priest assigned to the parish. He had until noon, when a housekeeping crew was scheduled to show up and clean the place top to bottom, as though Clement had fleas, or leprosy.

By 10 a.m. he was ready to go, and saw no reason to linger. So he slung the hockey bag over his shoulder, left the keys to both the house and the car on the kitchen counter, and set out on foot down Silver Street toward Kennedy Memorial Drive, at the end of which, near the interstate, three miles distant, the Budget Host motel awaited.

And it was at the Budget Host that, one way or another, Clement's future would begin to take shape. As he trudged along, keeping his face averted from passing traffic to avoid being recognized, a reporter with *The Boston Globe*, an old friend from Clement's jazz days who'd been a cub reporter with the *Daily News*, was driving north to meet him. The old friend, whose name was Steve Heron, now worked the Church beat for the *Globe*, and he'd called after seeing a notice that Clement had been defrocked. Steve hadn't known Clement was a priest in the first place, and it was about the last job he would have expected him to have. Clearly they needed to catch up. And lacking anything else to do or any sense, really, of what was next, Clement agreed.

Before hanging up, Steve had asked Clement where they should meet. Clement told him he had to clear out of the rectory the next day, and while he was reluctant to say so, he could use a lift to the Budget Host, having been rendered carless as well as homeless. But Steve had demurred, saying he'd prefer not to be seen together, and especially not anywhere near Church property. In this way Clement understood that, whatever Steve's stated motivations for wanting to talk, this was not entirely a social call.

And so he walked. Which wouldn't have bothered him, except that the far end of Silver Street, and the entirety of Kennedy Memorial Drive, had in the years since urban renewal become a de facto extension of the interstate, an artery that drew the lifeblood of commerce from the town's heart and dispersed it here and there in the form of ugly, prefabricated buildings, chain stores and strip malls. Traffic whizzed past Clement, gusts of wind stirred by log trucks and tractor trailers tugging at his clothes. The din of horns and jake brakes and tires speeding across blacktop made it near impossible to hold a thought in his head, and bits of trash swirled at his feet and gathered in the gulley to the side of the road, held fast by overgrown weeds. At the Cinema Center, still a mile distant from the motel, the sidewalk disappeared, and Clement trudged along the bare hint of a shoulder, cars passing so near that if he'd extended an arm he would have lost it.

The overall sense was, fittingly enough, that of disconnection, exile: he had been cleaved from his place in the community and watched as it went about its business without him. And he understood now he needn't have worried about being recognized—from the perspective of those driving back and forth on KMD he was just one more anonymous figure, dispossessed and nameless, receding steadily in a mirror until he vanished altogether.

By and by he arrived at the Budget Host and completed this vanishing act by checking into his room.

An hour later, he was jarred from the purgatory between wakefulness and sleep by a sharp knock at the door. He opened up to find Steve standing there, older, for sure, and sporting a ponytail he hadn't had in their New York days, but Steve nonetheless.

"Come on in," Clement said.

Steve stepped inside, and Clement closed the door behind him, and the two of them stood looking at each other for a moment.

"First things first," Steve said finally. "Are you a pedophile?"

"Excuse me?"

"It's a simple question, Clem. Are you, like so many of your brethren, a pedophile? The kind of conversation we need to have is entirely dependent on the answer."

"The conversation will be a short one," Clement said, "if it goes on this way."

"Don't act so scandalized," Steve said. "Water's wet. The sky is blue. Priests regularly diddle altar boys. Maybe the worst-kept secret in America, yet no one seems to know anything about it."

"Sorry to disappoint," Clement said, "but no, I am not a pedophile."

"And I'm sorry to ask so plainly," Steve said. "But I believe you. And I'm glad. Goddamn relieved, is what I am."

"So now that that's established," Clement said, "what kind of conversation do we need to have?"

Steve sat on one of the beds and pulled the strap of his messenger bag over his head. "Why did they shitcan you?"

"I was disobedient."

"God forbid. How so?"

"Given strict repeated instructions not to pick sides in a labor strike, I did so anyway."

"That's it?"

"That's it."

Steve laughed and shook his head. "You mind if I take some notes?"

"I guess not."

"I've been covering the Church for eight years," Steve said, flipping open the flap on his bag and pulling out a spiral notebook and a pen. "You'd think by now I'd be incapable of shock. And yet."

Clement sat on the bed he'd been in before Steve arrived. "What's so shocking," he asked, "about a priest being fired for defying an order?"

"In and of itself, it's not," Steve said. "What's shocking is what happens to priests who do much, much worse. Or rather, what doesn't happen."

"Yes, well."

"You ever hear of a guy named Michael O'Brien?"

"Not sure I have."

"Father Michael O'Brien, straight out of Irish Catholic central casting," Steve said. "Recently assigned to St. Mary's in Presque Isle. For the last two years, near as I can tell, Father O'Brien was unattached to any particular parish. Before *that,* he was at St. Patrick's in Lowell, Mass. He disappeared from St. Patrick's suddenly and without explanation in late 1981. A year later, the church very quietly settled a civil suit with the families of two altar boys. The details of which are, of course, sealed."

"So?"

"So, priests who stick up for strikers get fired, and priests who fuck kids get reassigned. That seem right to you?"

"And you know for sure he was molesting kids."

"Of course I know. I can't prove it, but I know. And so do you."

"I don't *know* anything. Except rumors and innuendo. Same as anyone else. The cardinal doesn't confide in me."

"Bullshit. You know. And you rationalize inaction by telling yourself the Church is an institution made up of men, and to drag those men into the light would rob people of their faith in God. Who, naturally, is not responsible for any of this."

Clement cast his eyes to the carpet. "I'd like to ask a question that will probably seem rude," he said.

"Shoot. I'm not easily offended."

"Why do you care so much about this?"

Steve paused and looked at him. "You know I'm from South Boston, right? That ever come up back in the New York days?"

"Maybe? My memory of that time is spotty, for reasons that are probably obvious."

"I ended up back home about a decade ago, after my father took sick," Steve said. "When he died, people in the family started talking. Quietly. About how something had maybe happened to my dad when he was a kid, around the time he was confirmed. And about how later he had maybe done some things to his younger sister, my aunt Delores. When he was sixteen and she was only eight."

"*Baptême*," Clement said.

"To this day, I still don't know the whole story," Steve said. "So look at it from my perspective. My father's just died, but that's not even the worst part. The worst part is I'm only now learning about what was done to him, and what he did in turn. Because the power of the Church was such that we wouldn't even talk about it among ourselves. They muzzled us in our own house, Clem."

"I'm sorry," Clement said. "Really. I mean that. But what do you want from me? I know nothing. I'm as on the outside as you are."

"Are you?" Steve asked. "They offered you a job, didn't they? Doing clerical work?"

"How do you know that?"

"That's usually where ill-behaved priests who aren't pederasts end up. Filing paperwork, answering phones."

"I have a friend with the diocese in Portland. They offered me a job at a records storage facility. But I said no."

"Well, now you can say yes."

"What do you imagine I can do for you?" Clement asked.

"If you don't take the job, nothing," Steve said. "But if you do, you'll have access to information I can't otherwise get. Information I need to write about this."

"It's hard for me to imagine a newspaper in Boston publishing anything even mildly critical of the Church. Let alone what you're proposing."

"Well, they definitely won't publish it," Steve said, "if I don't write it in the first place."

Clement thought about this.

"But I'm not naive, Clem," Steve went on. "Maybe the best we can hope for is to create a kind of time capsule. Make sure there's a record, for some shining day in the future when the *Globe* no longer serves at the pleasure of the Church."

"I don't know," Clement said. "My life has come apart in the last few days. I'm not sure I'm capable of making any big decisions, at the moment."

"Your life didn't 'come apart,'" Steve said. "Cardinal Law blew it up. This is the same guy who shields pedophiles as a matter of policy. Doesn't that piss you off? Don't you want to do something about it?"

Clement said nothing.

"If nothing else, Clem, don't you want to try and help these kids?"

That week was easily, bar none, the absolute worst of Chief Davies's life—though it would not retain that distinction for long, as the following week would turn out to be worse still.

It started with an article in the Central Maine *Morning Sentinel* that asked readers to consider whether several generous donations to the Waterville Police Benevolent Association by Kennebec Towing was at all related to Kennebec Towing having received a lucrative, noncompetitive contract with the police department.

The following afternoon, Davies was invited to meet with the mayor in private and explain whether the contract was or was not the sort of quid pro quo it very much appeared to be. Davies did his best to assure the mayor that it was not. The mayor, for his part, didn't even pretend to believe him. He had an election in two months, and he informed Davies, at high volume, that the last thing he needed at the moment was the stink of Davies's obvious, unimaginative, cut-rate corruption on him.

But the worst part of Davies's worst week to date came two days later, at the monthly town council meeting—though he wasn't there to see it firsthand. He'd never been to a council meeting and had no reason to break his streak and attend this one. It was only the following day, once again in the *Morning Sentinel*, that he learned a dozen Little Canada old-timers had lined up, during the portion of the meeting when citizens were granted three minutes to address the council, and outlined in detail everything they remembered about Davies's larcenous past as a beat cop. One of them, Pat Michaud, had serial numbers of merchandise that had been stolen over the years from his stereo shop; he gave copies of the list to council members and invited them to find out if they happened to match an amplifier or set of speakers in Davies's home.

The following day, Friday, Davies had been invited *back* to the mayor's office, where the mayor wondered aloud if it would behoove him to shitcan Davies and find a replacement whose relationships in town weren't quite so fucking complicated and cozy, someone who hadn't spent his whole life here, someone like, say, Captain Bates. And that was when Davies surprised himself by locating his backbone. He told the mayor he could fire him if he wished, but that he could expect a wrongful termination suit from the Police Benevolent Association in response. And then he left the mayor sputtering behind his desk and headed straight to Babs Dionne's house.

"You should have known better than to fuck with me," Babs said when she opened the door. "I killed your partner. What did you think I was going to do to you?"

"I'm not even going to bother putting you in prison," Davies said. "I'm just going to take everything you've got. Your house, your cars, the clothes off your fucking back. When I'm finished you'll *wish* I'd put you in prison, so at least you'd have a place to sleep."

"I certainly don't want to tell you your business, Chief," Babs said. "But if I were you, I'd pump my brakes on bogus property seizures. You're liable to be under a bit of scrutiny these next few months. Assuming you still have a job, that is."

"Sorry to be the bearer of bad news," Davies said, "but the mayor doesn't have the stones to fire me."

"Then you should resign," Babs said. "I'm telling you that as a courtesy. One you don't deserve, but that I am nonetheless extending."

Davies laughed. "That's rich. Thanks, Babs, but I think I'll just stay right where I am. There's nothing else you can do to me."

"Sure there is," Babs said. "In fact, it's already done. Simply a question of when I decide to pull the trigger."

Davies flinched, blinked.

"It's in place," Babs said. "Ready to be used at any time. Up to you to decide whether I treat it as an insurance policy, or a kill switch."

"You're bluffing."

"Don't make the mistake of thinking you can head this off," Babs said. "You'll never see it coming. But for now, I'm going to give you some time to worry about how and when I plan to finish destroying your life. If I were you, I'd also use that time to reconsider your stance on resigning."

Has anybody heard from Clement?" Babs wanted to know.

Babs and the ladies had been joined for that evening's meeting by Rheal and the Sauciers; folding lawn chairs had to be brought in from the garage to accommodate all in attendance. Everyone shook their heads.

"Are we supposed to hear from him about something in particular?" Carmeline asked.

"No," Babs said. "But he wasn't at bowling on Tuesday. I swung over there today and got no answer. And he's probably in hot water with the bishop over the rally. Someone should go check again."

"Me and Bern can head over there after this," Rita said. "On our way to Appleton."

"Good," Babs said. "Now. Everyone's clear on what they're doing tonight?"

"Not exactly," Stella said.

"Which part do you not understand?"

"The part where I sit in the street behind the dry cleaner and sell cocaine."

Babs stared. "You remember the summer you worked the register at my uncle's store?"

"Yes," Stella said. "You fired me."

"Regardless. It's exactly the same. People come looking to buy something. You get the money, and they get what they paid for. And that's it."

"It feels different."

Babs looked at Rheal. "Maybe we should just have her be the secretary or something," she said. "Keep the meeting minutes."

"At the risk of stating the obvious," Rheal said, "I'm not sure we want to have written records."

"We'll be fine," Carmeline said, putting an arm around Stella's shoulders. "I'll walk her through it. Over and over again."

"Okay, so, once more for the cheap seats," Babs said. "Carmie and Stella at Grondin's Cleaners. Rita and Bern over on Appleton, in front of the Masonic temple. This is where Aucoin's established customers will be expecting you. If they have questions, tell them we're under new ownership. If they have other questions, tell them to get lost. If they've got a problem with that, call the brothers or Rheal and Claude on the radio. They'll be roving security, going back and forth. It's only two miles between you, so they'll never be more than a couple minutes away. Meantime, I'll be here monitoring the scanner. If the cops get squirrelly, you'll be the first to know. And what do we do if the cops show up?"

"Tell them to take a flying fuck at a rolling doughnut," Bernette said.

"That is correct. You're sitting in your car on a public street, parked legally. They can't do shit as long as you're not driving and you don't offer them an 8-ball."

"You sure about that part?" Carmeline asked. "Last I knew, you weren't a lawyer."

"I'm sure," Babs said. "And anyway, before long we won't have to worry about the cops at all. What we should be worried about—what I want you to be very much on the lookout for—is any trouble from Aucoin's men. Much more likely, much more dangerous."

"And how will we know when that happens?" Bernette asked.

"If someone points a gun at you," Babs said, "chances are they're working for Harold."

"Great," Bernette said. "That's super-helpful."

"Hey," Babs said. "This is what you wanted. Do you trust me? Do you trust yourselves?"

"I don't totally trust myself," Stella said.

"And that's why Carmie's your wingman," Babs said. "Okay then. Go forth."

The ladies and the brothers got up, put their coffee mugs in the sink, and went out, leaving Babs and Rheal alone.

"This is obviously going to be a disaster," Babs said.

"It'll be fine," Rheal said. "Easy money. Not even Stella can screw it up."

"Sure, it's easy," Babs said. "Move product, make change. But you know as well as I do Aucoin's not going to sit and take it for long."

"That's what me and the boys are for," Rheal said. "We live to serve. The one thing I don't like is you here by yourself all night."

"Once Davies is gone, I can show my face in the streets again. Did you manage to track down the guy at the fish market in Portland?"

"I did."

"What's his take on doing business with us instead of Aucoin?"

"He cares not about any pissing match between a bunch of Canucks. What he does care about is cash."

"Of which we currently have none."

"We sell out the stuff we kept from Aucoin's men, we can get what we need from the fish man. We'll be self-sustaining and then some."

Babs sat back and let out a long breath. "*Esti'd tabarnak de calisse, de ciboire de crisse*," she said. "What the hell am I doing?"

"What you have to," Rheal said. He rose from his seat and came behind her, pressed the tips of his thumbs into her shoulders, kneaded the marbles of muscle he found there.

Babs groaned. "So we're drug dealers now," she said.

"That's not how I'm thinking of it," Rheal said.

"No?"

"Drug dealers have no conscience and no rules. We're more like . . . stewards. Or Robin Hood. We sell the muckety-mucks on Mayflower Drive their nose candy, and we take their money and use it to help our own. Unlike Aucoin, who puts it in his pocket. Then cuts a check to the governor's reelection fund."

They were quiet for a moment. Then Babs said, "You know nothing's the same after this. We're walking through a door that closes—and locks—behind us."

"Every night you go to bed," Rheal said, "nothing's the same as when you got up that morning."

"You get that from a fortune cookie?"

Rheal laughed, and after a moment, Babs joined him.

"Since when, by the way, are you so full of self-doubt?" Rheal asked when the laughter subsided.

"I haven't been myself."

"I noticed."

"But that's about to change."

"How so?"

Babs hesitated—minutely, but enough for Rheal to notice. "I mean, everything's about to change. Obviously."

Rheal thought about pressing her, then let it go. "How are you feeling?" he asked. "It seems like we haven't talked in a week."

"Excited? Glad to not be in prison."

"Let's keep it that way, huh?"

"That's the plan, *chéri*," Babs said.

"I'd feel better if Davies was out of the picture. Not sure why we went to all the trouble—and risk—of breaking into his house if we aren't going to drop the hammer."

"Bates is working on him," Babs said.

"Working on him?"

"A little psychological warfare," Babs said. "Better to give Davies time to come around before we trigger the nuclear option. Besides, I'm enjoying the thought of him lying awake at night, staring at the ceiling until his eyes bleed. With no idea the thing that's going to do him in is right above his pointy little head."

Davies wasn't the only one losing sleep, though. Babs herself lay awake too early the next morning, while Rheal, after not getting home until three, slept the sleep of the dead next to her. She was thinking about how even while so much had changed, nothing had changed. Night and day, the Mill churned and fumed. Logs arrived on massive flatbeds to the timber yard, and paper left hour upon hour by the ton. That the paper was in every way inferior to the product made for generations by the people of Little Canada was of zero consequence. The company sold this inferior paper at the same price as before. Newspapers didn't complain about sheets that tore more readily or failed to hold ink quite as well, for the simple reason that their customers didn't complain. And their customers didn't complain because who had time to care about a smudged photo, or an illegible line? The age of making things well because those things needed to last, or because your reputation and livelihood rested on it, had concluded. This was a new age of disposability—and what a wondrous time, when things need not be mended or cared for or repurposed once their useful life was used up, but could instead simply be thrown away and replaced, over and over, world without end, amen.

Such were Babs's thoughts as she lay next to Rheal, hoping his sleep remained peaceful. When first light began to seep in around the blinds she rose eagerly and went to the kitchen to get the day's coffee going.

The previous night, Rita had gone to the rectory and reported back that the place was dark and she'd gotten no answer at the door. Now Babs waited only until six thirty before driving to Clement's herself. Receiving no response after rapping on the door several times, she let herself in and found the place unoccupied and smelling of Pine-Sol, the keys to both the house and the car on the kitchen counter, Clement nowhere to be found.

Then on Sunday she went to Mass, which she hadn't done in so long she forgot to cross herself with holy water upon entering. Babs figured the one place she was sure to catch Clement was here, but then she, along with the rest of the neighborhood, was greeted by the jarring fact of Father Brennan giving the morning service. Father Brennan, who knew no one and didn't speak a lick of French and gave a lousy canned homily about faith in tough times, a message so generic and anodyne it could have been conveyed to equal effect (which was to say, none) in Fall River or Poughkeepsie or anywhere as well as here. The denizens of Little Canada needed to hear about how they, quite specifically, might carry on, and instead what they got was the oratorical equivalent of a *Hang in There, Baby* poster.

Afterward, Babs was the only person to approach Brennan as he stood outside Notre Dame's main entrance and tried, without much luck, to bid parishioners goodbye.

"Where is Clement?" she asked.

"I'm sorry, who?" Brennan said.

"Father Clement Thibault," Babs said. "The guy whose vestments you're wearing. The guy who's been saying mass here for fifteen years."

Brennan gave an uncertain smile. "I don't know anything about that," he said. "I go where God tells me to go."

"Let's not get God and the bishop mixed up."

"Obviously not," Brennan chuckled. "In any event, the diocese doesn't tell us much when we're reassigned. Just where to be, and when. And now here I am in your fine little city, Miss . . . ?"

"Never mind who I am," Babs told him. "But rest assured, I'm going to find out who *you* are."

With that she left Brennan standing there, smiling impotently at her back.

That afternoon Babs scorned the speed limit all the way to Portland and found the diocese was, more than a little absurdly, closed on Sundays. She pounded on the door, hollered up at the windows on the second story. People passing on the sidewalk stared, and then she stared back, and they quickly returned to minding their own business. Babs then tried the churches: Sacred Heart, Immaculate Conception, even the squat and homely Polish joint St. Louis, which if not for the tacked-on modest spire could have been a dentist's office. No one knew or had even heard of Clement—or at least, no one would admit to it. The man had vanished. Which was a problem, because Babs had never needed to talk to him more than she did now—not even when she'd killed Sacha. And short of getting an audience with the bishop himself, she couldn't think of a single other way she might find him.

When Bates let himself into Davies's office that afternoon, he was surprised—and not pleasantly—to find the chief seated behind his desk as though waiting for him. Neither of them was on duty; one of the privileges of being elevated in the command structure was that of not having to serve or protect shit on the weekends. Such garbage shifts were the exclusive purview of first- through fifth-year patrol officers and the sergeants unlucky enough to supervise them. And yet, here was Davies, looking haunted, even a bit crazed, on a Sunday afternoon when he should have reliably been anywhere else. Bates had been counting on Davies's absence to do what he'd come here to do. Now he needed to fabricate a reason—fast—for why he'd let himself into Davies's office.

"Hey, Daryl," Davies said, eyeing him.

"Chief. What are you doing here on a Sunday?"

"I might ask you the same thing, Captain."

"Oh," Bates said, stepping toward the desk and looking around as though searching for something, "I thought maybe I'd left my lighter in here."

"Zippo?" Davies asked.

"Yeah," Bates said. "Sort of a charcoal-colored chrome. Can't find the damn thing anywhere."

"Haven't seen it," Davies said. "But I think you know that, Daryl."

The two were quiet for a moment, Davies's eyes boring into Bates.

"Daryl," Davies said finally, "I don't suppose you've seen anyone fucking around in my office over the past week?"

"Fucking around how, exactly?"

"Just acting suspiciously, you know? Like they're up to something?"

Bates mimed thinking this over for a moment. "No, can't say as I have."

"I ask," Davies said, "because about a week ago I started finding pennies."

"Pennies?" Bates asked.

"Pennies," Davies said. "At first they were in places that made sense. On my chair. In this little junk tray here. But then they started showing up in odd spots. My spare set of shoes. The breast pocket of the extra shirt I keep in the closet. On Friday, I found one in the bottom of my coffee mug, the hard way."

"Yikes," Bates said.

"Then I realized something: These pennies started popping up around the same time I let Babs Dionne out of jail."

"You think Babs is coming in here and planting pennies?" Bates asked.

"No," Davies said. "But it occurred to me that someone might be doing it on her behalf. Trying to make me feel like I've gone crazy. Let me ask you: As a seasoned investigator, does that theory check out at all?"

"I don't know. Seems kind of thin to me. For one thing, why would someone with access to your office be doing anything for Babs?"

Davies sat forward. "That *is* the million-dollar question, Daryl, isn't it?" he said. "Got any thoughts on what the answer might be?"

"Afraid I don't."

"I think that you do."

Bates laughed. "Chief, look, I gotta be honest."

Davies smiled. "By all means. Be honest, Daryl."

"You don't seem entirely yourself."

"So that's your theory?" Davies asked. "I am, in fact, going crazy? It's all in my head?"

"I didn't say that."

"Not in so many words, no," Davies said. "But you're implying it pretty strongly."

"I guess I'm just saying you seem like you've been under a lot of strain."

"Oh, I have," Davies said. "But that doesn't mean I'm wrong that someone in the department is fucking with me, on Babs's orders."

"Well," Bates said, "it just seems unlikely to me, is all I'll say."

"Unlikely, yes," Davies said. "But I've got an idea that can prove whether I'm right or not."

"And what's that?"

"Empty your pockets," Davies said.

"What? No."

"Why not?"

"Because it's ridiculous," Bates said. "And because I'm not going to validate this craziness by playing along."

"Well, how about this?" Davies said. "As your commanding officer, Daryl, I'm *ordering* you to empty your pockets."

A pause. Then Bates sighed, shoved his hands into his hip pockets, and placed three items on the desk: his wallet, a Zippo, and a penny.

Davies looked at these normally innocuous things, then back up at Bates himself.

"Mind if I sit?" Bates asked.

Davies leaned back again, said nothing. After a moment, Bates sat in the chair on the left.

"Chief," Bates said, "I'm going to give you some advice. For your own good."

"I don't know what your angle is, Daryl," Davies said. "But if that bitch thinks she can drive me crazy and make me resign, she's got another thing coming. I don't break that easy. And I know she's bluffing."

"But that's the thing, Roy," Bates said. "She isn't."

"Why should I believe you?"

"You can believe whatever you want," Bates said. "But I'm telling you, there are two ways this can go, and neither of them ends with you still sitting in that chair."

"Let me guess—they both end with *you* sitting in this chair."

"That's for the mayor to decide," Bates said. "All I can tell you is, if you don't resign, you're going to have plenty of time to regret it. You got outplayed, Roy. Just accept it, and move on. While you still can."

"Fuck you," Davies said. "No goddamn way. They're going to have to drag me out of here."

"Then that is exactly what's going to happen," Bates said.

The call came in to the Maine State Police major crimes unit in Augusta early the next morning, and initially the desk sergeant, who hadn't even finished brewing the day's first pot of coffee, listened with something less than full interest. Crank calls about municipal police departments, after all, were endemic; this was the second he'd fielded already this morning, and it was only nine thirty. In seven years on this post, only twice had he gotten legit complaints about dirty cops: once when a sheriff was selling seized firearms at gun shows and pocketing the money, and once when an officer on the Bangor department had been smacking his wife and kids around for years while his sergeant, his captain, and his chief looked the other way. Otherwise, these kinds of calls were almost always fabrications, from people who had some personal beef with the cop in question, people who were tired of being arrested by the cop in question, or people who were plain off their meds.

As such, the State Police sergeant was perhaps not taking this particular caller one hundred percent seriously. He propped the phone between his shoulder and ear and poured a cup of Maxwell House, murmuring "Uh-huh" and "Mm-hmm" as the Mr. Coffee dripped and hissed. He replaced the carafe on the hot plate and crossed the office to his desk, sat down, and pulled a pad of paper and a pen out of a drawer. At the top of the sheet he wrote *Waterville—Roy Davies*, then proceeded to draw spirals in the margins as the caller went on talking.

And the caller's story was, the sergeant had to admit, good theater. If even a quarter of it were true, this would be the biggest scandal Maine law enforcement had seen in a long time, maybe ever. A shame, really, that it was all an elaborate pile of bullshit.

But then something clicked in the sergeant's head, a distant, indistinct association between this name—Davies—and something he'd read or heard about lately. But nothing specific rose in his mind, and after a second he wrote it off as a brain fart.

Entertaining though this had proved to be, the sergeant had other work to do, so he took advantage of a pause to ask the question that almost always brought such calls to an abrupt conclusion: "Can I ask," he said, "who it is I'm speaking with?"

Rather than hanging up, the woman on the other end laughed. "You know I'm not going to answer that," she said.

"It would make it easier to substantiate your claims," the sergeant told her, "if we knew who you are and could follow up."

"Sure," the caller said. "It would also make it easier for you to have a smokie outside my house in five minutes. Listen, I know you think I'm some clown who's mad at the chief for bouncing my head off the hood of his cruiser. But I encourage you to take what I'm telling you seriously. This time next week, if you haven't moved on Davies, I'm going to give the same information to the FBI. And then your boss is going to want to know why the first he's hearing about this is from the six-o'clock news."

With that, she hung up. The sergeant returned the phone to its cradle and looked down at his notes, the entirety of which read thusly: *Waterville—Roy Davies. Drugs. Guns?* He slid the pad of paper away across the desk and forgot all about it.

But in the afternoon, that click again, completely out of the blue: *Davies. Waterville.* What was his mind trying to regurgitate? It was right there, just out of reach, teasing him.

The sergeant got up from his desk and went into McNulty's office across the hall.

"Mac," the sergeant said. "Why does the name Roy Davies seem familiar to me?"

McNulty looked up from a file on his desk. "Who?"

"Roy Davies. Waterville chief."

McNulty searched the ceiling for a second, thinking, then shook his head. "Never heard of him," he said, looking back down at the file.

That might have been the end of it, but now this was really bugging the sergeant, in a way that made clear it would continue to do so. So he went on lunch and crossed the capitol grounds on foot to the State Library. He found his way to the periodicals room and asked the librarian how far back the newspapers went.

"We keep the physical copies for the calendar year," she told the sergeant. "Then everything gets transferred to microfilm."

"This would have been just in the last couple of weeks."

"Oh, that's easy, then." The librarian pointed toward the far opposite corner of the main room. "All this month's city papers are stacked over there, newest on top. Have fun."

And it wasn't fun, exactly, that the sergeant experienced as he dug down through a week's worth of *Morning Sentinels* and found, first, coverage of a Waterville town council meeting at which a dozen citizens accused Davies of being a corrupt piece of shit all the way back to his days walking a beat, and second, an article that pretty convincingly connected the dots between donations to the Waterville Police Benevolent Association and sweetheart deals with the WPD. What thrummed through the sergeant's synapses was something adjacent to fun, yet far more complicated. A slowly building excitement, coupled with something that felt like nausea. The giddy nervousness one might feel at the outset of a roller-coaster ride, creeping toward that first big drop. As a whole, the feeling could perhaps best be summed up by the thought that blared like neon in the sergeant's mind as he finished reading: *Holy fuck.*

And then the sergeant was up, newspapers in hand, apologizing to the librarian as he rushed out, promising to return the papers just as soon as he could. He double-timed it back across the capitol lawn to the Major Crimes building, hustled down the hallway, and, in his excitement, neglected to knock before throwing open his captain's door and blurting out breathlessly, "Marty, you gotta look at this."

So it was that a few days later, just after 5 a.m., the Maine State

Police tactical team queued up outside the home of Waterville police chief Roy Davies to execute a no-knock warrant. They would find, in the crawl space above Davies's bedroom, right where the anonymous caller had told them it would be, right where the Saucier brothers had planted it, the portion of Aucoin's stolen drugs that had been held in reserve for this purpose: one hundred grams of uncut cocaine, half a kilo of pot, and two hundred pills of various kinds, all requiring either a prescription or a watertight explanation or else it was your ass. Packing materials for these drugs—plastic bags, tiny squares of cellophane, et cetera—put a bow on trafficking charges. What was more, the tactical team would discover two TEC-9s with fifty-round box magazines and an old .38 pistol. All three of the firearms had their serial numbers filed to dust, and the TEC-9s had been illegally converted to fully automatic. Before long, ballistics testing would connect the pistol to a 1979 murder that had cast suspicion on Harold Aucoin but for which neither he nor anyone else had ever been charged.

All told, it was enough to earn Davies a bunk bed in Thomaston until well past social security age. Which in turn cleared the way for Babs's war on the company to begin in earnest.

PART TWO

CHAPTER NINE

Acting chief of police Daryl Bates was not a perfect man, and had never seen any point in trying to pretend he was, for his own benefit or anyone else's. His flaws were legion and he admitted to them more or less freely, even in mixed company. For example: He was, when you got right down to it, selfish by nature. And he knew this about himself. He wanted what was his and, sometimes, under the right circumstances, he might take a stab at what was yours, too—especially if you were in his view a scumbag or an asshole who didn't deserve nice things.

But Bates, though fundamentally selfish, was not without an instinct for largesse. He kept a jar of change in his car for the exclusive purpose of giving it away to panhandlers on street dividers and outside the 7-Eleven. With other officers in the department he put on an annual Toys for Tots benefit at the Elks Club, and one year even had the idea of selling a gag "Men of the Waterville PD" calendar, in which he featured as Mr. July, to benefit the organization. He tossed in a twenty whenever he passed a Salvation Army kettle during the holidays, and he and Melinda cut modest checks to the food bank and the Maine Home for Little Wanderers every spring. Bates was selfish, sure, but not, in his estimation, any more or less than the average American. He took some and he gave some, like anyone else.

But then there was this kidney thing that Claude had dropped in his lap like a grenade. Bates hadn't yet managed to get beyond a loop of thought that played endlessly whenever the prospect came to mind: *She's your sister. But a kidney! She's your sister. But a kidney!* Chief Davies's arrest and the hoopla that followed had quieted these thoughts for a few days, but once Bates had settled in behind the big desk himself the obsessive loop came back, more insistent than before and every bit as insoluble. And he was forced to grapple with the possibility that he was more selfish than he ever had imagined, that he might be the kind of man who kept two good kidneys to himself when his little sister had none.

After two straight nights during which he barely slept at all, Bates did what he always did when faced with a dilemma he couldn't sort out on his own: he sought his wife's counsel.

"You're scared," Melinda told him, rolling over and turning on her bedside lamp. "And who wouldn't be?"

Bates shimmied up against the headboard and reached for the glass of water on his nightstand. "I'm not *scared*," he said.

"Sure you are."

"Maybe we could use a different word," Bates said. "How about 'concerned'?"

"If that makes it easier for you to admit to it, sure. You're *concerned.* Have you talked to Sophie?"

"Just Claude," Bates said. "He told me she doesn't want to do dialysis anymore. Like, really doesn't want to. Like, she'd rather die."

"You need to talk to her."

"I don't think I can change her mind."

"That's not what I mean," Melinda said. "You need to talk to her and see where she's at, for yourself. Before you can decide."

"Would you want me to do it?"

Melinda gazed at him. "In principle?" she said. "In a vacuum? Yes, absolutely. But the details matter. As in: What's the risk for you, how much does it improve her chances to get a kidney from a relative, what will recovery be like, can you live normally with just one kidney of your own. And so on. Also, Jesus, how much is this going to cost?"

"A lot."

"And Claude lost his health insurance."

"Long gone," Bates said.

They were quiet for a moment. Outside, a horn sounded distantly as a freight train rumbled into the intermodal facility out on College Avenue.

"This'll sound shitty," Bates said, "but it's also really lousy timing. I just took over the entire department. Not an ideal moment to be laid up in the hospital."

"Didn't you just tell me the only difference between being a captain and being the chief is now you don't have to leave the office at all?"

"Well, sure, but that's a bit of an oversimplification."

"How so?"

"Things are still unsettled out there," Bates said. "I need to be keeping my finger on the pulse."

"From your office?"

"Mel. Give me a break."

"Besides, last I heard things have been very quiet in Little Canada."

"Who do you think is keeping it that way?"

"I'm just asking, what's happening in the world of the Waterville PD that's so important you can't take a week off?"

Bates had no intention, of course, of telling his wife about the fledgling drug operation he was now providing cover for. Two reasons: One, Melinda would immediately become an accomplice, and two, she would almost as immediately file for divorce. She would not be moved by the argument Bates had made to himself regarding why it was okay, even necessary, to do what he had done: Davies might not have been crooked in the way for which he would soon go to prison, but he'd been crooked his entire career in the worst possible way—he'd repeatedly betrayed the trust of the people he was sworn to protect, culminating with effectively giving away the powers of his police department to some rich asshole who was never going to repay the favor. Not to mention that Davies remained loyal to a long-dead partner who had raped a little girl. In short, Davies was a piece of shit, and he had to go, and the ends justified the means. A textbook instance of when the character of the person in question made the things that belonged to him—including his job and his freedom—fair game in Bates's mind.

Melinda would not see this as an argument at all, but a base rationalization. Especially in the context of the two of them benefiting financially from the whole scheme. There was an infinitesimal chance that ridding Waterville of Davies would pass muster with her, but the drugs, Bates knew, were an absolute nonstarter. Like a lot of people, Melinda didn't give much thought to drugs except to assure herself that they were bad and could and should be eliminated. Never mind that a decade of police work—including three years on vice—had taught Bates that harsh criminalization had zero effect on either the supply of or demand for drugs. It may have been easy for Nancy Reagan to just say no, but here in the real world the best one could hope for was to regulate the kinds and quantities of drugs that came into a community, and who did and did not have access. All things Bates planned to control, by controlling Babs.

"Nothing I can talk about," he said to Melinda. "You'll just have to take my word for it."

Melinda gazed at him a moment. "If you say so," she said, rolling over to turn off her lamp again. "But do me a favor and go see your sister, Daryl. Then you'll know what to do."

Though she may not have been the most cunning or competent drug dealer around, Stella proved quite good at planning logistics for the first neighborhood rally put on by Babs and Rheal. In fact, the very things that made her less than ideal for the business side of the burgeoning operation—perpetual drunkenness, a complete lack of guile, and an abiding desire for people to have fun and be happy—made her the perfect choice to run the community outreach side of things. Under her direction, the rally was meant to have the feel of a street fair—music, a bounce house and balloon animals for the kids, even a seasonally dicey dunk tank that Rheal had volunteered to man, on the promise that he be staffed at all times by someone with a good supply of both dry towels and whiskey. A fifth-wheel food trailer, hired from an outfit that did mobile concessions at concerts and race tracks throughout the state, provided hot dogs and hamburgers free of charge. All this noise, frivolity, and distraction were meant to serve Stella's basic organizing principle: to obscure, however possible, the fact that the rally actually functioned as an open-air food bank and community support program.

And Stella's instincts proved sound. A good time had been so hard to come by for so long in Little Canada that even the adults showed up eager to have their faces painted, and had to be repeatedly shooed out of the bounce house lest they blow a hole in the thing. The section of street directly in front of the PA transformed into a dance floor, while to either side people clustered in groups chatting over their hot dogs and hamburgers. At the same time, nearly everyone partook of the bags of groceries being handed out of the back of a panel truck, while others perused several racks of free clothes that had been purchased wholesale from an overstock auction. Sign-ups were brisk for a used-furniture exchange, as well as free dental checkups for kids.

Rheal's decision to offer himself as fodder for the dunk tank proved hugely popular, as he'd suspected it would; people waited in line for over half an hour for the chance to make him take a bath. He'd intuited that those on the receiving end of Babs's new hard line were harboring resentments they'd be happy to take out on him, particularly since they knew there would never, in this life or any other, be an opportunity to take them out on Babs. The dunk tank gig could be considered an extension of Rheal's long-standing role in their marriage: He smoothed feathers, mended fences, and took the blame for both of them. He alone observed the social niceties that served as adhesive in relationships. He made himself human, available, put himself on a level with friends and strangers alike. Babs, on the other hand, was so aloof she gave people the impression they were always looking up at her, no matter if they were in fact taller. Even those she loved would have agreed, at least after a few drinks, that if you cut her she likely wouldn't bleed.

And Babs stood apart from everyone now, bloodless and calm, surveying the proceedings alone from the top step of the old King Street School, where anyone who wanted to gaze at her from the street would indeed have to look up. The only person who would have ventured to join Babs, probably, was Father Clement, but he was still nowhere to be found—though his replacement, Brennan, milled gamely about the crowd, trying and mostly failing to make nice with parishioners. What Brennan didn't understand, perhaps, was that these people remembered well how Micks had treated Francos back in the day, and wanted nothing to do with his royal Irish ass as a consequence. More broadly, though, he was just an outsider. Simple as that. Nobody knew him, where he'd come from, or whether he could be counted upon, and this was not and never had been a crowd that offered anyone the benefit of the doubt. Earning trust was among the steeper hills to climb around here.

Watching Brennan try so hard to ingratiate himself, like an overeager dog, Babs almost felt bad for him. There was something beyond the fact of his being Irish and a stranger that she had strongly disliked on sight, but it occurred to her now that, while she usually trusted such an unequivocal gut feeling, in this case it might be mistaken, an instinctive response to Brennan suddenly being where Clement had always and should still have been. So instead of wasting time and energy investigating the man, she resolved to put her suspicions aside, at least for now. Certainly there was plenty else on her plate at the moment.

Babs looked away from Brennan to the scene at large. She noted the line at the dunk tank, fifty people long, and allowed herself a tiny smile, both at people's eagerness to give Rheal what-for and his willingness to take it. He'd already gone in the drink a dozen times, the poor man. And Babs was not unaware that there was purpose to Rheal subjecting himself to this good-natured abuse. Just as there was an overarching purpose to the rally itself. Having one's leadership accepted without question or complaint, in the long term, required more than just acquiescence. People had to believe she had their needs in mind, and would tend to them. They needed to see her strength tempered with humility and grace. And so Babs had spent the bulk of her time, over the last week, helping Stella organize the rally and lay the groundwork for more to follow. She'd negotiated an ongoing relationship with the operators of the overstock auction, whose lots included every kind of merchandise people in Little Canada could need. She'd allowed free rein to Stella's instincts for fun. And she'd given two enthusiastic thumbs up to the idea of Rheal in a dunk tank, for reasons both personal and strategic.

As she stood watching from the top step of the old school, Babs allowed herself the indulgence of a moment's satisfaction, even let the smile come broadly enough that her pleasure would be evident to anyone who looked her way. For the first time in nearly two years, her friends and neighbors had stepped out from under the cloud that had hung over all of them since the day they'd been locked out of their jobs. Soon she would do something about that circumstance, as well. But for now it was enough to see people dancing and eating and laughing, and especially to see the children playing, chasing one another without direction or purpose, properly carefree, bellies full. She'd made a plan and begun to execute it and against all odds, *par Dieu*, it seemed like it might actually work. Like life in Little Canada could eventually be, again, something more than grim, grinding survival.

Then Babs spotted Charlie St. Pierre in the crowd. And like that her smile disintegrated, and the cloud returned.

She did not hesitate; she did not even really think. As she came down the stairs, forgoing both her baton and her knife and reaching instead into her waistband for the 9mm she'd started carrying as a matter of course, Babs watched Charlie elbow his way to the front of the line for hamburgers and hot dogs, spurring much protest but little resistance. Charlie was six three, two fifty if a pound. He had a notorious mean streak, a head like the cap on a fire hydrant, and no neck. Even hobbled by the lingering effects of the beating the ladies had put on him, he cut a fearsome figure, and as such, few wanted any trouble with him, especially over something as petty as line-cutting. So as usual he got what he wanted, the way he usually did: by bullying those unable to meet his challenge. By the time Babs reached the food cart Charlie had turned his massive back on those he'd cheated out of their place in line, and stood grinning with self-satisfaction as he contemplated a free lunch.

"Charlie," Babs said.

He turned his head, looked down, and spotted her standing there with her arms folded behind her back. The bruises on his face and arms had faded to yellow, and he smiled and turned back to the counter. "Give me a cheeseburger and two dogs," he told the attendant.

"Charlie," Babs said. "This food is for people who live here. Last I remember, you were told to leave town."

Now Charlie turned fully to face her, still smiling. The food attendant looked at Babs, and she shook her head, once: *Nothing for this guy.*

"You know, Babs," Charlie said, "maybe it's because you were a few years behind me in school, but I never saw you as anything except a little girl, and an ugly one at that. Look at you now, though."

In the immediate vicinity, people started to take notice of the charge between them, and backed away.

"My husband," Babs said, "would not appreciate you talking so suggestively to me."

Charlie looked over his shoulder at the dunk tank. "You mean Rheal over there?" He laughed. "He doesn't look so tough when he's got nothing on but his skivvies. Looks like a plucked chicken, actually."

Babs smiled, noticed Rheal noticing them. "When you were told to get out of town," she said, "maybe you didn't think we were serious. But you are really and truly no longer welcome here, Charlie. You sold drugs for Aucoin. That is disqualifying, now and forever."

"So you get to decide who lives here and who doesn't?"

"Yes."

"I grew up in this neighborhood, same as you," Charlie said. "Where am I supposed to go?"

"I don't care," Babs said.

Awareness of the standoff continued to spread throughout the crowd, and most of those who'd been dancing to "1999" moments earlier now stood and stared. Even the kids in the bounce house had stopped to watch.

"You know what?" Charlie said. "I don't think you, or your husband, or anyone else here has what it takes to make me leave. So I think I'll stick around and have a burger after all."

Babs let the hand holding the pistol drop into view at her side. "There are two possible outcomes here," she said. "One, you're going to leave. Or two, I'm going to kill you. Either way, no one has any intention of *making* you do anything."

Charlie looked down at the gun, then back up at Babs. "So, what," he said, smiling, "you're just going to shoot me? Right here in front of everyone?"

"Yes," Babs said. She brought the pistol up, cocked the hammer, jabbed the barrel into Charlie's cheek, and pulled the trigger.

A collective cry of alarm went up from the crowd, everyone ducking and scurrying away with their hands over their heads. It took several moments, and lots of wide-eyed staring around, before people began to realize the gun hadn't actually fired, and to realize why: Because Rheal had, at the last moment, reached out and put his thumb between the hammer and the firing pin. Keeping his hand on the pistol, he wrapped his arms tight around Babs while she kicked and cursed. Charlie, for his part, just stared for several seconds while his life took its time flashing before his eyes.

"Charlie," Rheal said, gritting his teeth as Babs continued to writhe, "you've got about five seconds before I lose my grip on her, and then you're on your own."

He's gone, isn't he?" Rheal said later, in the kitchen, as the fight that had started in his Mustang on the way home spilled over into their house. "You wanted him gone, and he's gone."

"I wanted him *gone* last week," Babs said. "Now I want him dead. Every breath he takes encourages people to think they can ignore us when we tell them how it's going to be."

"I don't know, Babs. I think you did a pretty good job of convincing everyone you mean business."

Babs leaned back against the counter next to the fridge, her arms crossed over her chest.

"And by the way," Rheal said, "so much for the *entire point* of this thing. Whatever good feelings people had, they disappeared the moment you tried to add Charlie's brains to the sautéed onions."

"Charlie doesn't have any goddamn brains," Babs said.

"You know what I mean, and you know I'm right," Rheal said. "I spent all afternoon soaking wet in my underwear for a reason. And you blew it."

"We have an agreement," Babs said. "You don't challenge me when others are around."

"*Challenge* you?!" Rheal stared, incredulous. "Maybe think of it less as a challenge and more as a favor. Considering I kept you from murdering a guy in front of three hundred witnesses. In front of a bunch of kids, *Crisse d'esti d' la marde.*"

They glared at each other across the kitchen, and for whatever reason that was the moment when Rheal almost asked his wife, straight-up, the question that had been on his mind ever since he'd consulted with Phineus the Drunk. This question rose unbidden, apropos both nothing and everything all at once, the thing that had hung in the air between them every second of every day for weeks, the thing each of them did and desperately did not want to talk about. Rheal didn't know what he feared more: That Babs would lie to him, or that she would say no and be telling the truth. Either way, he couldn't bear it. So before the question could escape his lips he swallowed it back down, instead asking something that, in retrospect, he would understand was really a version of the same question: "What is *wrong* with you?"

"What's wrong with you?"

"Really?" Rheal said. "We're going to play I'm-rubber-and-you're-glue?"

"It's a real question, Rheal. You're too soft. Too worried about everyone liking you."

"I don't care if people like me or not," Rheal said. "I just don't take pleasure in being a bastard for its own sake."

"And you think I do?"

"It sure seems that way, sometimes."

"Well, I don't. At all. And goddamn you for thinking that. But you have that luxury. Of thinking your feelings, or anybody's goddamn feelings matter."

"What on earth are you talking about?"

"You make decisions based on *emotion*, Rheal. You think that's a valid way of moving through the world."

"Give me one example."

"I can give you several," Babs said. "Let's start with your buddy Claude. Why is he still involved in anything we do? He demonstrated that he can't be trusted. So why are we trusting him?"

"How do you know about that?"

"I know about *everything*, Rheal. I am a woman in this neighborhood, which means I have eyes and ears everywhere and always have. So why are we trusting Claude?"

"We're not. I tell him nothing, except when to show up for work."

"And that's trust. We're trusting him to keep our people safe. Because *you* couldn't bear to cut him loose."

Rheal looked at Babs for a moment, then sat at the kitchen table and lit a cigarette. "You know my history with Claude," he said quietly. "That's real. As real as it gets."

"But it's not, *chéri*," Babs said. She pulled out the chair opposite

Rheal and sat down. "It's the past. Ancient history. And making decisions today based on the past isn't smart. It's just sentimental."

"Call me sentimental, then."

"Listen to what I'm telling you," Babs said. "The past doesn't matter. Our feelings don't matter. What matters is doing what has to be done, every time, without hesitation or apology. That's our responsibility. To ourselves and everyone else."

Rheal took a drag of his cigarette and offered it to Babs. She demurred.

"Well, the way I see it," he said, "this afternoon it was my responsibility to save you from yourself. I think you'll agree I didn't hesitate. And you'll notice I ain't apologizing."

If he was being completely honest—the way he'd endeavored to be honest with God while still a fully frocked card-carrying priest, as opposed to what he was now, little more than a secretary who could, in a pinch, administer last rites—Clement had to admit that, when it came to the Church and rumors of sex abuse, he had always been happy to let that particular dog lie. He was not a crusader, did not have the hypertrophic sense of justice necessary to tilt at monstrous, invulnerable windmills like the Holy See. It had been easy for him to simply mind his own yard when the idea of sex abuse was still just that, a kind of ambient concept that drifted on the wind, no firm accusations, no confirmable instances, just an abstract notion that people sort of knew was maybe something that went on somewhere but probably not really because who could believe such a thing?

Now, Clement was beginning to suspect that it was precisely

this brand of willful ignorance—the brand he and many other clergy were guilty of—that had to this moment allowed the abuse to happen in the first place. And he reminded himself, even as he had this thought, that the word *abuse* was far too anodyne and sterile. A bullshit word, meant to obscure rather than illuminate. Long ago he'd learned if you wanted to know when people were up to no good, all you had to do was look for the euphemisms. This was not *abuse*. There was one proper way to describe this, the way his old friend Steve Heron had described it back at the Budget Host: priests were fucking kids. The proof—circumstantial and indirect, to be sure, but convincing nonetheless, once you knew what to look for—rested on a shelf in the basement of the very building where Clement now worked, in plain sight and available to anyone who wanted to have a look: seventy-four volumes of *The Official Catholic Directory*, going back to 1910.

This was the lynchpin, the decoder ring that revealed which priests were pederasts. *The Directory* was also the way by which Heron had convinced Clement to help him. Look at the directories for the last twenty years, Heron had said. Make note of every time you see a priest unassigned for "sick leave" or "further ecclesiastic education." Then watch for the pattern: These same priests always remained sick or in school for a couple of years, then popped up again at a new parish—far from the last one to which they'd been assigned. More often than not, these new gigs didn't take, and the priests continued to bounce around, a year here, nine months there. Sometimes they went back on sick leave, or to further remedial classes. But conspicuously, they were never, ever—not even once, that Heron could find—removed from the priesthood.

Clement had done his own search of the directories, and had to admit a pattern was undeniable. But he had still been resistant to making any assumptions about what the pattern meant. Maybe the priests really were sick. Maybe they really were lousy at the job. He knew, after all, what kind of reception an inept or otherwise deficient priest would receive in Little Canada, and knew without question that such a priest would not last long in the face of that reception.

Clement's resistance to interpreting the pattern disintegrated when Heron suggested he go to the public library and wind through microfiche to find whatever recent articles he could involving the Fall River, Massachusetts, diocese.

Just six months earlier, the archdiocese of Boston had settled a civil suit with a Richard and Carol Shanahan of Fall River. The only public details of the suit were that it involved alleged incidents that had taken place at the Cathedral of St. Mary in 1981. After reading the scant two articles on the matter from the *Fall River Herald News*, Clement had walked back from the library to the diocese office, his feet heavy with dread. He thought he knew why Steve Heron had picked this particular case to highlight. And sure enough, when Clement arrived back at the office and went into the basement and pulled *The Directory* for 1981 off the shelf, he confirmed what in his heart he already knew: The priest at St. Mary that year had been one Father Joseph Patrick Brennan. Then, in 1982, Brennan had gone on sick leave. And now he was in charge of Notre Dame in Waterville. Living in Clement's house. Tending to Clement's people. Including, of course, the youngest of them. With whom, being a priest, he would be trusted implicitly.

Clement had to tell someone. But the first person he thought to tell was also the person he one hundred percent could not; if Babs knew Brennan was a pedophile she would skin him alive. And then

Clement would have two murders to ensure were scoured from her soul, instead of just the one.

He sat at his desk for several minutes, his brain going like tires stuck in mud. Then he lifted the phone and dialed Heron's desk.

"You find out anything interesting about our friend Father Brennan?" Heron asked.

"I've got to let someone in town know," Clement said.

"We'll figure that out. I want to protect those kids as much as you do."

"Did they fire me," Clement asked, "because they needed a place to stash Brennan?"

A pause on the other end. "You certainly gave them a convenient opportunity to do so," Heron said.

"Oh my God," Clement said. "I put all those kids in danger."

"Cardinal Law put those kids in danger," Heron said. "And the kids in Fall River. Before that, the kids in Brattleboro. I've been tracking Brennan for years. You're not responsible for the fact that he landed in Waterville. But you could be responsible for making sure this is the end of the line. And at the same time, get back to a community that pretty desperately needs you."

Clement took a breath, glanced around the office. "What can I do?" he asked finally.

"You can recognize, first, that the pattern *is* the scandal," Heron said. "The reason the settlement in Fall River barely got noticed was because of the assumption that it was a one-off. Anomalous. That's always the assumption. One that the Church is extremely good at perpetuating. And frankly, so is everyone else. People don't want to see that Brennan, or O'Brien, or any of these other bastards is just a tiny part of a whole constellation of abuse. Because to see it would be to admit you really saw it all along, and allowed it to happen."

Clement was quiet for a moment. Then he said, "So how do we shove their noses in it?"

"That's the spirit," Heron said. "Fortunately for us, the Church is even more meticulous about keeping records than the Nazis were."

CHAPTER TEN

"She did *what*?" Bates said into the radio.

"I repeat: she put a gun to Charlie St. Pierre's head and pulled the trigger," Officer Farley said on the other end. "In front of, oh, let's just say several hundred witnesses. Over."

"Jesus Christ. And St. Pierre's still alive how, exactly?"

"Rheal karate-chopped the gun or something. Not totally clear. All I know is it didn't fire. Over."

"Thank fucking God," Bates said.

"What do you want me to do? Over."

"Stop saying 'over,'" Bates said. "Other than that, nothing. I'm on my way to a thing, then I'll deal with Babs."

"Roger that, Chief. Over and out."

Bates threw the radio handset, which hit the floor of his cruiser and proceeded to bounce jauntily at the end of its cord. He hauled the wheel to the left just in time to make a tire-squealing turn onto Claude and Sophie's street. He was supposed to be having a calm, contemplative talk with his sister, and now here he was, so worked up he could barely think, distracted to the point he nearly forgot where his sister and her family had lived for the last ten years.

Babs Dionne, he was learning, could have that effect on a person.

He pulled to the curb outside Claude and Sophie's house and put the cruiser in park, took stock, and decided he needed a minute to get himself calmed down before he could face whatever awaited him inside. It'd been, what, two or three months since he'd seen Sophie. Theirs was not a particularly close family, though they did love one another, and so life happened and you looked up one day and realized you hadn't talked to someone you shared blood with since last Thanksgiving, or whenever. Had Bates known how bad things had gotten, he would have made time. He was, in point of fact, making time, now that Claude had alerted him to the state of things.

He was also sounding awfully defensive to himself. Nobody was judging him but him. He needed to get his head together. He took a deep breath, let it out slow, took another. He checked himself in the rearview mirror, decided what he saw bore a close enough resemblance to an adult human with his wits about him. Thus satisfied, he got out of the cruiser and made his way up the walk to the front door.

When Bates saw Sophie at the kitchen table, his first reaction was not sorrow or even surprise, but fear: it was chilling to see so plainly that someone had given up. Sophie's eyes were dead, and the air in the kitchen vibrated with how badly the rest of her wanted to follow. Her hair lay limp against her skull and her skin glowed yellow, but she still mustered a wan smile for Bates as he came in. He put a hand on her shoulder and kissed her forehead, which was dry and cold as though she were already a corpse.

Claude brought two cups of coffee from the counter as Bates sat and asked, "How's my kid sister?"

"Exactly how I look," Sophie said.

"Beautiful, healthy, full of life?"

"Give me a break, Daryl," Sophie said. "I have zero need for cheerful bullshit, so don't bother."

"Brass tacks it is," Bates said. "How are the kids?"

"Worried about their mother."

"I would imagine," Bates said. "So why are you doing this to them?"

Sophie stared.

"This is what 'no bullshit' looks like," Bates said, holding her gaze.

Sophie nodded—*fair enough*—and Claude put a hand over hers on the table. "They're the only reason I'm going to dialysis even once a week," Sophie said. "Otherwise this would already be over."

"Can you explain to me why you want to die?"

"Who said I want to die?"

"Don't you?"

"No," Sophie said. "I want to live, and I can't. It's a good day when I'm just exhausted. Everyone else gets seven days in a week, and I get four—after dialysis, I'm too tired to even cry. Let alone get out of bed. Let alone be a mother. How do you think *that* is for the kids, to see me like that?"

"Not good," Bates said.

"Not fucking good is correct," Sophie said. "Kyle's got a thing he does when he comes home from school on dialysis days. It's like a little ritual. He only has half days because kindergarten. So he rolls off the bus around one and finds me in bed, and because he knows adults drink coffee to wake up he makes a pot, all by himself.

No one taught him, he just watched us and learned and then decided it was on him to start making his mother coffee on those days when she can't drag herself out of bed. He brings me a cup, even though most of the time I can't even stand the smell. And I've got to watch my fluid intake, right, so even if I wanted the coffee I couldn't have it. But he keeps bringing it to me anyway. It doesn't matter if I drink it. Just makes him feel good, like he's doing something that's good for his mama. And then he sits in bed with me and reads his *Highlights for Children* until his sister comes home and he finally has someone sentient to spend time with."

"Jesus," Bates said. "Soph."

"So don't get it mixed up," Sophie said. "And don't talk about my kids as if they've somehow slipped my mind. I want to live, and I can't, and here we are."

Bates looked at Claude, and Claude returned his gaze, like: *Now do you see?*

Sophie, meantime, looked out the window and sighed. "Listen, I'm sorry, Daryl," she said.

"No, don't apologize . . . ," Bates said.

Sophie waved a hand. "None of this is your fault, and I don't mean to take it out on you. I'm just tired of talking about it. It's not your fault you can't understand."

"I think I understand as well as I ever could," Bates said. "Have you actually talked to the kids about what you've decided?"

Sophie let out a bitter puff of a laugh. "It's hard enough with adults," she said. "But obviously I have to figure it out. Because they already sort of get it, which is a problem. They know I'm not going to the clinic as often as normal. They see the shape I'm in. The longer I let them go on being alone with what they're figuring out, the more they're going to hate me twenty years from now."

"Stop," Claude said. "They're not going to hate you."

"They will if I don't figure out a way to be straight with them," Sophie said. "They may regardless."

There were two broad possibilities for what Bates could say next, and he did not yet know which was right, which he actually felt, which he would ultimately say. What he did know was that whatever came out of his mouth next he had to be dead certain of. There could be no ambiguity or doubt. The easier thing, the cowardly thing, would be to rub the back of his head regretfully and say how sorry he was that they were going through this. He could also, in this instance, throw in some pabulum about how it made a man wonder if there even was a God and, if so, how He could possibly do things like this to people and still claim He loved them. If Bates said these things, there was something else he had to be extremely careful *not* to say: that he wished there was something he could do.

Because of course there was something he could do. And that comprised the meat of the other thing he could say but had to be absolutely certain he meant. It might begin with a line that seemed fairly innocuous: *So Claude tells me you're thinking maybe a kidney transplant.* Which was an implicit commitment to offer his help. Because what kind of sadist would bring up the fact that somebody needed a kidney and then effectively say *Sorry, I'm keeping both of mine?*

Sophie was still looking out the window, but Claude's eyes were steady on Bates. Not pleading, not insisting, not even really asking. Just waiting, for Bates to decide—or discover—what kind of man he wanted to be.

And it was Claude's predicament, rather than his sister's, that Bates felt really burrowing into him. The man had lost his livelihood with zero prospects for getting it back. He was watching his wife die slowly right in front of him. He had two grade-school kids he soon would have to raise by himself. The universe had dealt him an impossible hand, and he had no choice but to play it, knowing full well that he'd already lost. Dying, it seemed to Bates, would be easy by comparison.

Though he had no desire to, Bates imagined himself in Claude's shoes: Melinda blinking out of existence while the kids watched, the house coming down around his ears, not enough money to keep food in the fridge, and not a single reason to expect any of it would get better in this lifetime. Would he hold up as well as Claude seemed to be doing? Fat fucking chance. Bates didn't know what kept Claude on his feet, if it was character or pigheadedness or simply intimate enough acquaintance with suffering in its myriad forms, but whatever it was, he knew he didn't possess it in the quantity needed to survive what his brother-in-law was going through.

But what Bates *could* do was help. By merely saying yes.

There was just one thing that continued to give him pause, even more than the prospect of having his side unzipped and one of his kidneys yanked out: What was Claude going to do to get the money? The thirty grand alone would almost certainly involve multiple felonies, to say nothing of the one-hundred-twenty-thousand-dollar balance. More troubling was the type of people Claude would be dealing with—and possibly running afoul of—to get that kind of dough. Babs and Rheal weren't pulling it yet, and in any event they were overextended, trying to feed and clothe all of Little Canada. But looking at the state of things now, breathing the fermented air of illness in this kitchen, Bates realized that whatever risks Claude ran to get his wife healthy must seem paltry compared to how things would turn out if he didn't.

"So," Bates said before he could hesitate or second-guess or be a coward even a second longer, "Claude tells me you're thinking maybe a kidney transplant."

Steve Heron had been sitting in his car outside the Dionnes' house for several hours without seeing a single person come or go. He'd checked the address several times—Clement had written it himself to avoid any mistakes in transcription—and confirmed, each time, that he was at the right place. The only sign of life was a remarkably cross-eyed white cat that had taken up a perch in the living room window over an hour before and sat staring at Heron. Nothing else moved or breathed—until somebody slipped in behind Heron's car, came up along the driver's side unseen, and pressed a pistol behind his ear through the open window.

"Jesus Christ!" Heron said when he felt the steel against the side of his skull.

"Don't move," a man's voice said. "Don't turn to look at me. You with Aucoin?"

"Who?"

"You a fucking owl, friend?"

"My name is Heron," Heron said. "I don't know who Aucoin is, I swear it."

"Then why are you staking out this house?"

Suddenly, Heron realized the surest way to avoid having his brains splattered across the dash of his Gremlin. "Clement sent me!" he said. "I'm looking for someone named Rheal Dionne!"

There was a pause, and then the pressure behind Heron's ear vanished, leaving a mild radiating ache. "Well, good news, you've found him," the man said. "Come inside. You look like an asshole sitting out here in this ridiculous car."

"I might need a moment to catch my breath," Heron called to Rheal as he went up the walkway to the porch, tucking the pistol into its holster under his arm. "Possibly to change my pants, as well."

"Take all the time you need," Rheal called over his shoulder.

A few minutes later, Heron peeked around the corner into the kitchen, where Rheal was seated, a cigarette going in the ashtray and a cup of coffee in front of him.

"You didn't shit yourself, did you?" Rheal asked.

"By some miracle, no."

"Then have a seat. Mugs are in the cupboard above the coffee maker," Rheal told him.

"Little late in the day for coffee," Heron said. "I'd take some water."

Rheal waved in the direction of the sink. "Mugs hold water just fine, too."

Heron found a commemorative Mayor McCheese glass from McDonald's behind the legion of mugs, filled it from the tap, and sat at the table.

"So where's Clement?" Rheal asked.

"The diocese has him doing clerical work down in Portland," Heron said. "Nothing public-facing. He's been defrocked."

"Which is the Church's way of saying 'shitcanned,' yeah?"

"Correct."

"*Tabarnak,*" Rheal said. "What the hell for?"

"Supporting the strike," Heron said. He gestured toward Rheal's Marlboros. "You mind if I steal one of those?"

"Go ahead. So what now?"

"What do you mean?" Heron lit a cigarette, noticeably absent the grace of the practiced smoker.

"How do we get Clement back where he belongs?"

"That might not be possible," Heron said.

"Very few things on this earth are impossible," Rheal said.

"Maybe. But the Church is pretty much the definition of an immovable object."

"The Church hasn't met my wife."

"Oh, speaking of," Heron said. "The thing Clement sent me here to tell you, he wants to make sure she doesn't catch wind of it. Which is why I was looking for you specifically."

"What's your connection to all this?" Rheal asked.

"Clem and I are old friends."

"And what's your connection to all this?"

"I'm a reporter for the *Globe*. Church beat."

"Ah, I see. Sort of."

Heron ashed his cigarette so clumsily it nearly broke in half. "That's why I'm here," he said. "I have information about your new friend Father Brennan that's pretty important for somebody to know."

"And that is?"

"He's almost certainly a pedophile."

Rheal looked at Heron, his gaze suddenly flat. "What?"

"True story."

"Now I know why Clement didn't want Babs to find out. Her policy with suspected pedophiles is generally to cut their balls off first, ask questions later."

"Right. Bad news for everyone."

"My own policy is only slightly less severe."

"Clem felt confident that you would know what to do to keep people safe."

Rheal shook his head, took a sip of coffee. "I don't yet," he said, "but I'll figure it out."

They heard a car engine approach, and Babs's station wagon flashed into view in the driveway.

"You're about to meet my wife," Rheal said. "You better have a good story about who you are and why you're here."

"Can't I just be an emissary from Clement?"

"Sure. But why are you here?"

"Definitely not because Father Brennan is a degenerate who's into little boys."

"Right. Not that."

Babs came into the kitchen with plastic grocery bags slung over each arm. She stopped at the door and eyed Heron with naked suspicion. "Who is this?"

"A friend of Clement."

At the mention of the priest's name, Babs's entire countenance changed. "Where is he?" she asked.

"He's in Portland. Working for the diocese."

"I went there and couldn't find him," Babs said, still standing in the doorway, still holding the bags of groceries.

"He's in a kind of . . . detention. Supposed to have limited contact with the public."

"According to who?"

"The bishop, I guess. Under orders from the cardinal."

"Well, both the bishop and the cardinal can go pound sand," Babs said. She finally moved to the counter and deposited the bags. "I need to talk to him."

Heron saw an opening. "Funny," he said, "because that's why I'm here. Clem wanted me to convey the message that *he* needs to talk to *you*."

Heron looked to Rheal, who shrugged, like: *That'll work.*

Babs stiffened and turned to face Heron. "About what?"

"He didn't say."

Babs looked at Rheal. "Is there any reason I need to be here?"

"Not during daylight," Rheal said. "But we've got that new thing we're doing tonight . . ."

"I'll be back later," Babs said, and left without putting away any of the groceries.

Rheal and Heron gazed at each other in silence as they listened to Babs's car fire up and back out of the driveway.

"So that's Babs," Rheal said.

"She's exactly as I imagined," Heron said.

"That was as effective a job of getting rid of her as I've ever seen. She may never come back."

"How far do you think she'll get," Heron said, "before she realizes she didn't actually ask me where Clem is?"

"All the way to Portland," Rheal said.

"You want some help with those groceries?" Heron asked.

"Nah, don't trouble yourself," Rheal said. "But I'd be happy to hear any suggestions you have for dealing with Monsignor Brennan."

An hour later Babs screeched into the parking lot of the diocese office on Congress Street. She didn't know who to harangue, but she knew for certain that someone required haranguing. So she started with the laywoman receptionist, who insisted she knew nothing of a Father Clement Thibault or where he might be or if he even in fact existed, but further that if she *did* know of a Father Clement Thibault and his whereabouts she would not be at liberty to divulge that information, as internal Church personnel matters were just that: internal.

"Let me talk to your supervisor," Babs said.

Another layperson, a man this time, who came out of the office behind the reception area but did not invite Babs into his office to discuss the matter; clearly he meant to dispense with her posthaste. He gave her the same line as the receptionist, and it seemed evident he expected that, coming from a person in his position of authority, Babs's reaction to the same line would somehow be different. He was disappointed in this expectation, of course. At the same time, it had become clear to Babs that if she wanted to get anywhere she needed to find somebody considerably holier to harass.

"How many properties does the diocese have in Portland?" she asked the lay supervisor.

He looked at her quizzically. "That's publicly available information."

"Then it shouldn't be a problem to tell me. Or better yet, give me a list."

"Ma'am, I'm very busy . . ."

"Are you?" Babs asked. "It sure doesn't seem like it. In fact, I'm standing here trying to figure out what it is exactly that you're supposed to be or do. You're like the guy on the road crew who stands around watching some other guy dig. Makes you wonder why the Church is constantly hitting up poor people for money on Sundays, if it's just to pay your salary."

The man stared at her. "If I give you a list," he said, "will you go away?"

"It is, in fact, the *only* way that I'll do so," Babs told him.

Based on Heron's statement that Clement was no longer "public-facing," Babs was able to eliminate the four churches from the jump, which left only two offices, aside from the one where she'd started. Both those offices were for recordkeeping and other clerical work, with zero public function. Clement had to be at one or the other.

And Babs got it right on the first guess: an old clapboard building on St. John Street, past a Mexican restaurant and a chicken-processing plant heading out of town. Built around the turn of the twentieth century as a school for the children of Irish dockworkers, now it served as a depository for church records, as well as wholesale supplies of various staples for celebrating Mass: case upon case of as-yet-unconsecrated red wine, boxes of eucharist wafers stacked floor-to-ceiling, hymnals and lectionaries and the various linens used to cover altars and wipe chalices and so on. All of it was "managed" by a priest named Father Doyon, who'd been put out to this particular pasture thirty years earlier and had stoutly refused to die ever since. Now ninety-eight, deaf even with hearing aids and blind in his left eye, Father Doyon was fast asleep behind his desk when Babs threw open the front door and marched in.

"Hey," she said, approaching the desk. "You. Old-timer."

Nothing from Father Doyon.

Babs leaned down and peered at Doyon's crumpled face. "Hello? Anybody in there?"

Still no response.

"Would be just my luck," Babs muttered as she came around the desk, "to walk in here and find a dead priest. Hello? Wake up, Father." She shook Doyon by one bony shoulder, and by and by, to her relief, he demonstrated he was still alive by opening his eyes.

"Can I help you?" Father Doyon croaked, struggling to sit up.

"I need to speak with Father Clement Thibault."

"Do you have official business regarding Church records, and can you provide documentation of such?"

"No."

"Are you delivering something?"

Babs frowned. "Do I look like the FedEx guy?"

"Then you're not supposed to be in here. This place is closed to the public."

"I'm going to cut right to the chase," Babs said. "Tell me where Clement is, or I'm going to burn this place to the ground. Maybe with you in it."

"Young lady," Father Doyon said, "I've been sitting in this room since before you were born. In fact, there are days when I'm convinced I'm actually dead, and this place is purgatory, and it's my fate to spend eternity at this desk. So don't make the mistake of thinking you can come in here, stomp around, and put a scare into me."

They stared at each other in silence for several moments, irresistible force and immovable old object. Babs realized that not even she could make good on a threat to such a defenseless old coot. Which meant it was advantage Father Doyon.

"What if," Babs said, "I asked politely?"

"That might work out better for you," Father Doyon told her. "Hard to say for sure. But it's worth a try."

Babs gave him a warning look—*don't push it*—and cleared her throat. "Father," she said, "do you happen to know where I might find Clement Thibault?"

Father Doyon sat back, crossed his arms over his chest, and closed his eyes once more. "Clement's in the basement, through that door and down the stairs," he said. "Do yourself a favor and don't wake me up again."

For a moment, Babs continued to stare, incredulous. Within seconds the old priest was snoring, and she couldn't help but laugh—quietly—as she made her way to the stairs.

In the basement she found Clement under a single dim light, going through a box of files. He looked up, and real surprise—and pleasure—registered on his features.

"Babs Dionne," he said. "As I live and breathe."

"I've been told you needed to talk to me."

"Who told you that?"

"Your friend who came to our house today. I didn't catch his name."

"Ah. Steve."

"Sure."

"I don't know why he would have said I needed to talk to you," Clement said. "I've actually been enjoying my vacation from all things Waterville."

"I've missed you, too," Babs said. "But either someone got their wires crossed, or someone's not being honest with me. Because Steve definitely said the entire reason he came to Waterville was to relay the message that you wanted to talk."

Clement suddenly got it. "*Oh*, right right right," he said. "I wanted to *talk*. With *you*. Of course, absolutely, one hundred percent. That is, in fact, why I sent Steve to your place. Yes. No other reason, for sure."

Babs frowned. "What's going on?"

"Nothing. What."

"Why are you talking like you had a lobotomy?"

"This is how I always talk."

"Uh-huh." She scrutinized Clement, one eyebrow cocked. "Something's up, and I'm going to find out what sooner or later. So you might as well just tell me now."

"Maybe I'm acting strangely," Clement said, "because I'm still getting used to the fact that I'm no longer a priest."

"That's official?"

"You don't seem surprised."

"You disappear and suddenly some Mick's living at your place. I put two and two together."

"I suppose somebody was bound to notice sooner or later."

"How do we get you back?" Babs asked.

"You're assuming I want to come back," Clement said.

"You're assuming I care what you want."

Clement smiled. "Putting all that aside for a minute," he said, "how are things?"

"I couldn't make a decision without you."

Clement's face softened. "Then I'm sorry I've been gone," he said.

CHAPTER ELEVEN

The first Hollingsworth & Whitney papermaker to go missing was an engineer named Stewart Qualley. He left work after the swing shift at half past eleven, drove out into a drizzly night, and vanished as thoroughly as if he'd been abducted by aliens, car and all. Qualley had been, until six months before, a lifelong resident of Georgia, and his family had joined him in Waterville just two weeks before he was abducted, when his scab job had become permanent. The family's reception in the community had been such that Stewart's wife, June, was working up the courage, just before he disappeared, to tell him she was taking the kids back to Decatur. A person just couldn't breathe air so thick with hostility. Even something as mundane as a trip to the Shop 'n' Save left the girls crying, not because anything in particular happened—no one confronted them, and certainly no one attacked them, verbally or physically—but because their presence was so palpably offensive to every other human being they encountered, it was as if each of them wore a giant scarlet *S*. And June had no interest in being so branded until Stewart retired. But now, with her husband gone under mysterious circumstances, it seemed she and the kids weren't going anywhere, at least until the mystery of what had happened to Stewart was sorted out.

Though they were about to become common as pigeons, disappearances were normally rare enough in the Waterville area that Stewart's was immediately on everyone's mind and lips. Separate pools of rumor boiled and churned: among the scab workers, some thought he'd missed a curve in the rain and ended up in the Sebasticook River; others suspected a darker series of events involving vengeful strikers, a trap, an ambush, a spiriting away by faceless men to a grim fate that might never be known.

The prevailing theory among the locals, by contrast, was that this was likely just another case of a shitheel abandoning his family. After all, it stood to reason that the kind of man whose character allowed him to scab without conscience might also walk out on his wife and kids. Why not? These were, from the perspective of the former strikers, equally unforgivable acts, and if you'd demonstrated you could do one, there was no reason to think you would not do the other.

Acting police chief Bates, however, had a third theory. He got Babs on the phone the morning after June Qualley first reported her husband missing.

"This is the second time in four days," he said in greeting when Babs picked up, "that I've had to ask what in hell you think you're doing."

"Right at this moment?" Babs asked. "I'm finishing a peanut butter and mayonnaise sandwich."

"What?"

"Never mind. What's the problem, Daryl?"

"You know exactly what I'm talking about. Somebody went missing after second shift at the Mill last night."

"I heard."

"You're going to bring him back, Babs," Bates said. "You're going to do it right now. And he better still have all his fingers and toes."

"How can I bring him back, if I didn't take him in the first place?"

"Listen. This is way, *way* beyond anything I'm prepared to sign off on. You can't be *kidnapping* people, for Christ's sake."

"See, that's where you're mistaken," Babs told him. "You signed off on whatever I choose to do. A bit of advice, Daryl: you'd better get used to the fact that our relationship is now one of mutually assured destruction. I can put you away and you can put me away and that's how it is and will remain. We are equal partners. We are in this together. This is what you wanted."

"Bring him back, Babs. I mean it."

"I'll do some poking around," Babs said. "See if I can turn anything up."

"You do that."

At the same time, here is what the actual experience was like for Stewart:

Swing shift normally ended at ten, but he'd been dealing with a digester pump that had died midafternoon and refused, despite everything he could think of, to come back to life. So he stuck around when his replacement came on and they brainstormed together for an hour or so. Then Stewart left when it became clear that the issue was software, not hardware, and would require intervention by a tech from Aptean who would have to fly in from Virginia. This was not good news, as anything that delayed production for two seconds was about the worst thing that could go wrong aside from, say, a chemical spill that killed half a shift's worth of workers (his supervisor Roger might consider that a smidge better than a pause in papermaking, actually). Stewart's job responsibilities could be distilled down to "don't allow anything to delay production," and he had failed in that, and so he hit the gate two parking lot in a less-than-stellar mood, anticipating the earful he would catch from Roger tomorrow afternoon when he came back in, as if he could do anything about the crap software Aptean put out.

It was a wet, cold, shitty night in this wet, cold, shitty state. The windshield wiper on the driver's side was essentially useless, which he'd noticed the last time it rained and had meant to get a replacement for but had forgotten, and now, as he pulled out of town onto the inky undulations of Route 201, the left half of the windshield was just a dark smear, like he was trying to see the road through a shower door. Then the inside of the glass began to fog over, because wet and shitty, and as Stewart fumbled with the climate controls to turn on the defroster a pair of headlights blazed suddenly in his rearview mirror, as though the car behind him had simply materialized rather than approached.

Asshole was right up on his bumper, too, and to say Stewart was not in the mood for such shenanigans was the understatement of the month, so he hit the brakes, hard, and felt the car behind him actually make brushing contact with his rear end, sending his back tires sliding sideways on the wet blacktop. Now Stewart was really heated, his already shaky judgment fully compromised. He'd grown to hate the townies who'd harassed him and his fellow workers every day for six months, and he'd be damned if he was going to spend the rest of his career turning the other cheek for their pleasure. So he yanked the car over to the side of the road and, when the headlights behind him slowed and followed, grabbed the Maglite he kept in the driver's door for just such an occasion, and got out.

The car's headlights continued to blare, and Stewart had to shield his eyes to see two figures emerge, one from either side. Immediately they began moving in sync toward him—none of the cheap horror-movie-type standing silent and still as an intimidation tactic—and for a moment Stewart felt his throat tighten up, wondering if he'd made a mistake. But then he harnessed his anger again and walked forward into the space, lit blinding white by the headlights, between the two cars.

"What the fuck is your problem?" Stewart said, letting the Maglite's weight swing loose beside his hip.

The men didn't answer, just kept walking steadily and with purpose toward Stewart, their shadows dancing on the pavement to either side of him. The gap between him and the men was almost closed entirely by the time Stewart realized they were not going to stop short, or speak, or engage in any of the simian posturing that usually preceded and sometimes precluded a fight. They were here to put hands on him. That had been their intention all along, likely since well before he'd pulled to the side of the road, before they'd even begun tailing him after he left the Mill. These men were here for a reason and that reason did not involve talking.

Too late, Stewart started to raise the Maglite to take a swing, but the man on his right stepped forward nimbly at the same time and grabbed his arm and locked it against his own side in one deft move, hyperextending Stewart's elbow and causing him to drop the flashlight as though it were suddenly hot to the touch. Pain sang up into his shoulder, making him cry out. He looked at the man who held him in the armlock and saw now that he had Ronald Reagan's face, which at first of course made no sense; how could Ronnie Ray-gun be here getting ready to beat the shit out of him? Then Stewart looked to the other man and saw *he* had Ronald Reagan's face, too, and then it registered, just as the men spun him around and shoved him face-first onto the pavement, that of course they were wearing masks, and freakily realistic ones at that. He felt hands grabbing both his arms and forcing them together, heard and felt the cinch of zip ties cutting into the skin of his wrists, and then he was on his feet again being frogmarched to the men's car. Something rough and thick was pulled down over his head, and like that he was blind as a mole. Then: pressure over his ears, headphones or earmuffs or something, and now he was blind *and* deaf. One hand on his back and one on the top of his head guided him into the back seat, then those same hands lifted his legs and swung them in. As it started to sink in that he was actually being *kidnapped*, that they were taking him away to do God knew what somewhere nobody could see or hear, Stewart went into an immediate animal panic, a state of mind and body he'd never experienced, never even knew was possible. This was a complete loss of not merely control, but of one's very self. He was no longer Stewart Qualley, he was simply Fear. Heart thrashing, breath coming in rapid lizard-brain gasps that sucked in and blew out the rough fabric that had been placed over his head. He tried to beg, but just made nonsense whimpering sounds instead.

The pressure over one of his ears lifted. "I wish I could tell you it'll be okay," the man who'd shoved him into the car said. "But de truth is, it won't."

Then the door slammed shut.

The car drove. How long, it was impossible for Stewart to tell; not being able to see or hear rendered the passage of time effectively moot. Even a sense of movement was difficult to discern, except when the car hit a bump or navigated a significant turn and Stewart felt himself pulled by centripetal force to one side or the other. The panic would not relent, in part because all he could sense was himself: the frenetic, tidal rush and retreat of his breath, his heartbeat amplified by the headphones into the relentless thumping of a bass drum in his ears. The world had shrunk to the size of him, everything beyond his own boundaries obliterated. He was trapped in himself, possibly forever.

And then, Stewart thought, though he could not be sure, that the car came to a stop.

Some time later—seconds, minutes, eons?—he felt hands grip his arm once more, and he was yanked from the car onto legs that refused to work. He stumbled and collapsed. There was no direction, no space, no matter; only gravity, pulling him down (whatever "down" meant anymore). Hands under either arm hoisted and dragged.

Then, a chair. Stewart puddled in it. The headphones came off. The sack over his head was removed with one swift pull, and he was blinded by a searing light like the instant of a nuclear detonation. He felt certain his shadow was being burned into the wall. He clenched his eyes shut, heard himself moan. He pissed his pants and didn't care in the least. He wanted to die, and nothing had even been done to him yet.

"We are not your enemy," a voice said somewhere, "and you are not ours."

"Please," Stewart managed.

"Udder people have tricked you into tinking we are enemies," the voice said. "Dey used your needs, and your family's needs, to make you believe dat. But *dey* are your real enemy. And ours."

The light continued to singe Stewart's corneas, even through his eyelids. He turned his head this way and that, but there was no relief to be had.

"It's important you know," the voice said, "dat what you're about to go troo is being done by dem. Not us. *Dey* put you in dis room. Not us.

"But it's up to us to make sure you understand one ting: you no longer work at Hollingsworth and Whitney. And dat is why we're here."

"I understand!" Stewart said.

"We wish we could take your word," the voice said. "But we have to be sure."

At that instant, an amplifier somewhere in the room played the opening licks of "Sweet Home Alabama" at a volume high enough to cause Stewart's earlobes to vibrate palpably. At the same time, the chair was yanked out from under him, and he was forced to squat with his knees level with his jawline and his butt nearly touching the floor. His hands, still bound behind him, were secured to the floor with a few inches of chain, and he was left there, in the blinding light, Skynyrd rattling his brainpan, alone.

And that was it. Stewart, of course, had no way of knowing how long he squatted there, but it totaled almost twenty-eight hours, during which "Sweet Home Alabama" played in its entirety, at the same eardrum-bursting volume, 336 times in a row. The chain that tethered Stewart to the floor had so little slack that he could neither stand nor sit, and so spent the entirety of his time in the room straightening his legs while folded in half at the waist until it became unbearable, then sinking back down until the deep squat became unbearable, up and down, over and over, without end. He would never again listen willingly to Lynyrd Skynyrd (or the Allman Brothers, or ZZ Top, or the Marshall Tucker Band, or even Canned Heat), and for the rest of his life, a stray lick from any Southern rock song of the era would be enough for him to break into a cold sweat.

When the twenty-eight hours were up, Stewart was warned not to return to H&W for even one more shift, or else what he'd just experienced would seem like a Caribbean vacation compared to what would befall him next. He was given a merciful dose of propofol, which knocked him directly out, and he and his car were returned to the precise spot on 201 where he'd been abducted, just across the town line in Benton, on a slope overlooking the Sebasticook where people liked to fish from the banks.

Physically unharmed (aside from some extremely sore quadriceps), Stewart was nonetheless incoherent when two tween boys found him the following afternoon, slumped over in the front passenger seat of his car. He didn't begin speaking complete sentences until he'd been in the hospital for two days, and then he said more than enough to inflame talk all over town, put every last worker at the paper mill very much on notice, and send acting chief Bates to the Dionne house in a huff. Bates pounded on the door steadily for nearly a minute before it finally opened and Rheal stood before him.

"Where's your wife?" he asked.

Rheal popped a cashew into his mouth, chewed. "Out," he said.

"I need to talk to her. Now."

"As I said, she's currently elsewhere." Another cashew. "You can talk to me."

"I have the Portland office of the FBI calling, asking if I need any help with the abduction of Stewart Qualley. Who as we speak is sitting in a bed at Thayer hospital with his brains leaking out of his ears."

"We didn't harm a hair on his head, Bates," Rheal said. Cashew.

"No, you just scared him so badly he's practically a vegetable."

"He'll be fine," Rheal said. "Daryl, would you mind indulging me in a little history lesson?"

"Yes."

Rheal laughed. "Your police department has been crooked as a dog's hind leg since way before either of us ever came along," Rheal said. "Cops used to steal from Franco businesses as a matter of course when I was a kid. Whatever they wanted, they took, and we couldn't do shit about it."

"Like you said," Bates said, "that was before my time."

Cashew. "Yes, but the legacy belongs to you now, Daryl," Rheal said. "And I wasn't finished. The Waterville cops actually put my father out of business. He ran a little boatyard and marina for twenty years. Mostly small stuff for the lakes, you understand, given that we're a hundred miles from the ocean. But he had one big, beautiful boat that he hoped the right person would come along and buy eventually. Instead, a couple of cops waltzed in one night and drove away with it. And my dad couldn't take the hit. He went bankrupt. I was six years old. And that was when the long nightmare of my childhood really began."

"Your father should have had better insurance."

"Strangely, Franco business owners had a hard time getting insured," Rheal said. "Listen: When we started this—at your insistence, by the way—you were told our intention was to get our jobs back. You don't get to balk now because you don't care for our methods. You've got the job *you* wanted, Chief. Now it's our turn.

And just this once, Waterville's crooked cops are going to work for us, instead of against us."

"So, what, you're planning to scare everyone into quitting? You going to kidnap every person who works at the Mill?"

"Not every person," Rheal said. "We figure three or four ought to do the trick. The rest will tuck tail and go home."

"Fucking Christ," Bates said. "You can't be serious."

"As a heart attack," Rheal said. Another cashew. "In the meantime, feel free to do what you need to keep up appearances. Invite the FBI to your house for a slumber party, for all I care. We can keep our side of things tidy. Just see to it that you do the same."

When Claude told Sophie he'd secured the money to schedule her surgery, the joy (or relief, or gratitude, or just plain homely comfort) he'd hoped would blossom in place of her malaise did not arrive. Instead, she wanted to know where the money had come from.

"It doesn't matter," Claude said.

"It does to me."

He'd taken her to the Last Unicorn, Waterville's one fine-dining restaurant, where neither of them had ever eaten and where neither of them felt anything other than immensely out of place, conspicuous and fidgety in their Sunday best. His clip-on tie kept popping out of his collar on the left side, and her dress lay over her wasted body like a floral-print shroud. The food and wine menus may as well have been in Latin for all the sense they could make of them. Claude had known the moment they walked in that it'd been a mistake to come here, but had hoped the news they were celebrating would cut through the awkwardness. And now Sophie, somewhere south of overjoyed, wanted to know where the money had come from. And Claude was surprised and alarmed by his reaction: He was angry.

He tried to skip past the issue altogether: "We need to let Daryl know. The scheduler at Mass General said they could get us in within a few days, as long as Daryl's ready."

Sophie leaned in over the table. "Claude," she said, "everyone knows what Babs and Rheal are up to, and everyone knows you're working for them. A kidney's not going to do me any good if my husband's in prison."

"Who said anything about prison?"

"I did."

Claude sighed, gazed around the dining room, then looked back at his wife. "Listen to me," he said. "The money did not come from Babs and Rheal."

"Then where did it come from?"

"I sold one of *my* kidneys, okay?"

The hint of a smile, which Sophie did her best to quash as the waitress approached the table.

"Have we decided what we'd like to drink?" the waitress asked.

"Just water for me," Sophie told her.

"Still or sparkling?"

Sophie looked at her, nonplussed. "Whatever comes out of the tap," she said.

The waitress, slightly ruffled, turned to Claude. "For you, sir?"

"Miller Lite bottle, please."

"For bottled light beers we have Amstel, Tecate, or Sapporo."

"How about a Budweiser?"

"I'm afraid not."

Now Claude was irritated—at this fancy-pants place, at his own stupidity for thinking it was a good idea to come here. "Just bring me whatever," he said, pushing his tie back into his collar.

The waitress departed, and they sat staring at each other again.

"Claude," Sophie said finally, "I can't let you pay for my surgery with drug money."

"Great," Claude said. "Because it's not drug money."

"Then *whatever* kind of money it is," Sophie said. "Illegal. Ill-gotten. Dirty. Call it whatever you want. I can't do it. I won't."

Claude sat back in his chair and looked around the dining room, not wanting his wife to see what was in his eyes at that moment. Two women, seated at the table closest to them, had heard or felt enough of what was going on between Claude and Sophie that, seeing Claude turn his head in their direction, they very conspicuously kept their eyes to themselves.

"Go ahead and look," he said to them.

"Claude," Sophie said.

"No. They want to see a show, let them be honest about it." He turned back toward the women. "Hey. Hey. Yeah, you two."

They looked over reluctantly, expressions somewhere between amused and terrified.

"A question," Claude said. "Do either of you know what it's like to have someone in your life who would do anything for you?"

Both the women demurred, seemingly unsure how or even whether to answer.

"If you have to think about it, the answer is no," Claude said. "But you wish you did, don't you? Maybe you're even married, but you know in your heart he wouldn't do *anything*. He loves you, sure, but it's not that kind of love. My guess is most marriages are like that. Which means when you get right down to it, most of us are alone."

The waitress returned with their drinks, and the women looked away again, as though engaged in something illicit they didn't want the waitress to see. But when she left once more after determining Claude and Sophie were nowhere near ready to order, the women immediately turned back to him, eager now to hear where this was going.

Claude gestured toward Sophie. "This is my wife, and she's sick, and I would do anything for her."

"Claude," Sophie said again, quietly.

"Always felt that way," Claude said, "since the day we met. I would die, and I would kill, if that's what it took. I did kill, in fact. To get back to her. All the way on the other side of the world, she was what kept me going when my feet were rotting off and I had six different kinds of malaria, and it would have been a hell of a lot easier to just lay down and die."

The women's gazes softened, and their eyes glimmered with a gentle kind of envy, and then they laughed behind their hands when Sophie said, "He'll do anything for me except *shut up*."

Claude smiled. "I'll even do that, in a minute," he said. "But first I want to explain to these ladies why the one thing I won't do for you is let you die."

He turned back to the women at the adjacent table, who now looked a little alarmed. "War is pretty scary, as you'd guess," he said. "But for me, the scarier thing was ending up in a place without her. Iron sharpens iron and fear trumps fear. I'm sitting here today because I was more afraid of being without her than I was of anything else. And I still am."

Claude paused, sat back, and lifted his bottle of Amstel Light for the first time, as if he'd just remembered it was there. He drank half the bottle at a pull, as the two women and Sophie waited for him to go on. For a moment, it seemed like he might not. His eyes stayed fixed on the restaurant's back wall, seemed, for a few moments, to stare right through it.

"Sophie here does not want to have dialysis anymore to stay alive," he said finally, turning once more to the women at the next table. "Which I understand. It's a hell of a way to live. Just wears you down to a nub; I've seen it with my own eyes. But at the same time, I didn't survive January 10th, 1969, or June 23rd, 1969, or February 8th and 9th, 1970, so I could be in this world alone. I didn't survive so I could raise our kids alone, and marry them off alone. Nor did I survive so I can spend the next forty years slowly forgetting my wife's face and voice and laugh. No sir. I'll do anything, and I'll do it with a smile. But not that."

Now Claude turned back to Sophie.

"So if there's something to be done about it, I'm going to do it. And not even she can stop me."

At that moment, as the women at the adjacent table wiped delicately at their eyes, the waitress returned once more. "Have we made any decisions?" she asked Claude and Sophie brightly.

Claude yanked the clip-on tie from his collar. "You want to get out of here?" he asked his wife. "Go to the Down Under and get some nachos? And some beer that tastes like beer?"

Sophie smiled at him and stood up, slowly, unsteadily, from the table. "I thought you'd never ask," she said.

CHAPTER TWELVE

The novelist Adriaan Schade van Westrum wrote that "there are years, centuries, when nothing happens, and there are days into which a whole lifetime is compressed." He might have been referring to the week about to unfold in Waterville, during which the course of many lives, not to mention the trajectory of the town itself for the next four decades, would largely be determined.

This cascade began with the second kidnapping from the H&W mill, again in the darkest part of the night after swing shift. This time everyone knew, or thought they knew, what to expect when Duane Oakley didn't make it home from his job as a chemicals supervisor; the only question was how long he would be held before reappearing. And this time, the FBI did not wait for an invitation from Bates to come to town.

Had they asked, they would have received very little by way of response, because at the same time Oakley disappeared, Bates, Claude, and Sophie were at Massachusetts General Hospital, preparing for one of Bates's kidneys to be transferred into his sister's body. Bates was already sedated by the time Captain Farley, who'd been left in charge of the department in his absence, called the Mass General switchboard to inform his boss that another kidnapping had gone down and the FBI were elbowing in; otherwise Bates likely would have jumped off the operating table and burned rubber all the way back to Waterville wearing nothing but a hospital johnny. As it stood, the problem was Farley's to deal with, and his instructions were clear: Don't try too hard to figure out who was snatching workers from H&W, but give the *appearance* of vigorously turning over every stone. Especially for the benefit of other law enforcement.

Thus it was that Captain Farley, on the afternoon following Oakley's abduction, accompanied Special Agents Booker and Kittel of the Portland FBI field office on a canvass of Little Canada. They started at Kennebec Street, just opposite the Mill itself. Booker took the north side of the street, Kittel the south, shadowed by Farley. Captain Farley knocked on the first door they came to, and together they waited—and waited, and waited—until finally they heard the dead bolt tumbling and the door creaked open and a woman who appeared to be at least 120 years old stood peering at them, hunched over a walker with two small wheels on the front legs and two halved tennis balls coated in cat fur on the back.

"*Oui?*" this woman said. *"Qu'est-ce que-c'est?"*

"Afternoon, Mrs. Roy!" Farley shouted. "How are you today?"

"How am I? I'm blind as a bat and deaf as a stump and I'm pretty sure my cats are scheming to eat me the moment they think I've drawn my last breath. That's how I am."

"Okay, terrific!" Farley shouted.

"Qu'est-ce que tu veux?"

"I'm sorry, Mrs. Roy, I don't speak French!" Farley said.

"I asked what the hell do you want?" Mrs. Roy said.

Agent Kittel stepped forward, unsmiling. He checked a clipboard. "You're Mrs. Bernadette Roy, is that correct?"

"Oui."

"I'm Special Agent August Kittel with the FBI," Kittel said. He opened a wallet and flashed a gold badge. "We're investigating the disappearance of a worker from the Hollingsworth and Whitney Mill."

"From the what?" Mrs. Roy asked.

"The Mill!" Kittel shouted, pointing across the street to the brick facade of the boiler building.

"Okay," Mrs. Roy said.

"Did you hear or see anything unusual last night?"

"What time?"

"Around ten thirty or eleven?"

"No," Mrs. Roy said. "I didn't hear or see anything at any other time, either. Did you misunderstand when I said I'm blind and deaf?"

"Of course, Mrs. Roy," Kittel said. "Just a standard question I have to ask."

"Quoi?"

"Just a standard question!" Kittel said.

"A standard, stupid question," Mrs. Roy said.

"Let's try a different approach," Kittel said. "Have you heard any talk of who might be taking workers from the Mill?"

"No."

"Do you know of anyone who might have reason to do it?"

"Oh, sure," Mrs. Roy said.

Kittel waited a beat for her to elaborate. When she didn't, he said, "Can you maybe talk more about that?"

"Quoi?" Mrs. Roy tilted her head and cupped her ear.

"Who would want to kidnap mill workers?" Kittel shouted.

"Plenty of people," Mrs. Roy said. "Including me. You've got a prime suspect right here in front of you."

For the first time, Kittel betrayed a hint of amusement. "I don't know if I'd call you a *prime* suspect, Mrs. Roy. There are lots of factors to weigh when considering whether you think someone committed a crime. Motive is just one."

"So you're saying you don't take me seriously."

"Should I?"

"My husband worked in that mill for fifty years. My three sons and five nephews worked there, too. Until men like you came and took their jobs."

"Men like me?" Kittel asked.

"Men from away," Mrs. Roy said. "Men like the one you're looking for."

"I live in Maine, Mrs. Roy," Kittel said.

"Sure. But you're not *from* Maine, are you?"

"No, I am not," Kittel conceded.

"Well, there you go."

"And so I understand, your motive for abducting mill workers is that they took jobs from your family, or that they're not from here?"

"Yes."

"Got it."

"I'll grant you," Mrs. Roy said, "I'm not likely to have done it, owing to the fact that I'm a million years old. But you can't eliminate me as a suspect, is what I'm saying. I've got just as much reason as anyone, if not more."

"Okay, well," Kittel said, "since you put it that way, may I come inside for a moment and take a look around your house?"

"Not without a warrant, you can't."

Kittel turned to look at Farley, eyebrows raised. Farley just shrugged.

"Let me give you some advice," Mrs. Roy said. "It's the same advice I would give to any of those boys working at the Mill right now, and it's pretty simple: Go home. You don't belong here, and being here is only going to cause you and everyone else trouble. Just look at the mess we've already got."

"Well, Mrs. Roy," Kittel said, "I like to think I'm here to help clean up the mess, not to cause a bigger one."

"And that's where you'd be wrong," Mrs. Roy said. "But it's not my job to explain that you serve a master other than the law. Now if I keep standing here my cats are liable to think I've died on my feet and start trying to eat me. Maybe I'll see you again when you get that warrant."

Mrs. Roy shuffled back two steps and pushed the door closed with the same creaking slowness with which she'd opened it.

Kittel stood staring at the door for several moments, then turned again to Farley. "What the hell was that?" he asked.

Farley turned and started down the steps. "I think you'll find," he said, "that Little Canada is a bit like its own country. Like, you know how when you walk into the Vatican it seems like you're still in Italy, but you're really not?"

"No."

"Well, take my word for it, then. People around here aren't going to be impressed because you flash a G-man badge in their face. You might as well be showing them your member ID for the Mickey Mouse Club."

Kittel followed Farley down the stairs, waving to get Booker's attention as he left a house two doors down on the opposite side of the street. "If I didn't know better, Captain Farley," he said, "I'd say your sympathies seem to be with the people here, rather than us, or the law."

"Not at all," Farley said. "I'm just telling you this isn't going to be as easy as you think. If it were, we'd already have gotten somewhere all by ourselves. Without the help you've so generously offered."

Booker met them at the edge of the street. "Did that go as poorly for you as it did for me?" he asked.

"Probably," Kittel said. "What have you got?"

"Well, I don't speak French, but I'm pretty sure the first guy told me to get fucked before slamming the door in my face," Booker said. "The second one said *he* snatched Oakley and had him tied up in the bathtub."

"Did you check his story?" Kittel asked.

"Let's just say he seemed less than credible," Booker said. "So, no."

Kittel looked up and down the street. "Okay," he said, "let's keep at it."

They spent the next several hours going house-to-house through the narrow streets of Little Canada, climbing shaky exterior staircases to the third and fourth floors of tenements and dodging angry dogs—in one case, a monstrous black shepherd who appeared snarling in the open front door of a house where no one seemed to be home at all. They slowly worked their way south through the neighborhood, block by block, and this was what they heard:

From a man on Halde Street who spoke through the small gap afforded by a door chain: "I was a Company man. I did everything I was asked to do, and then some. My reward was a cut in pay and benefits in a year when the company made record profits. And then they fired me. So no, I don't know who took the guy, but if I did I wouldn't tell you. And if you put him in front of me right now I'd give him a beating."

From a woman on Carrean Street who Booker caught as she was getting in her car: "Sure I know who kidnapped the guy. The other one, too. Everybody does. And I'd be happy to tell you, except I got an appointment in Portland to sell my plasma for the fourth time this week. Maybe if my husband gets his job back someday, I'll have time to talk about what I know."

From a man on Paris Street who looked mid-seventies but who the clipboard said was only fifty-five: "They say time heals all wounds, but let me tell you something to save *you* some time: this will never heal. I have to drive past the Mill twice a day, and every time I get close I feel hate rising up in me. Real hate. The kind you kill over. They've ruined families. They've ruined this town. I know I shouldn't blame the scabs—they're being used by the company sure as we were—but I'll tell you the truth: if you find this guy floating in the Kennebec, it won't bother me even a little."

Despite the open hostility, despite the lack of both respect and actionable information, despite the ongoing threat of a dog biting one or both of them on the ass, Kittel and Booker kept at it well into the afternoon. And Farley dutifully tagged along, growing steadily more tense though he did his best not to show it, hoping they'd call it a day before they got to the Dionnes' house.

But no such luck. Kittel walked up on the Dionne place and knocked, Farley dragging his heels in the rear, taking slight comfort from the fact that Kittel didn't seem any more interested in this house than he had been in any other.

The door opened, and Rheal stood before them. "Afternoon, Farley," he said, then turned his gaze to Kittel. "Who's your friend?"

Rheal stared, and Kittel stared back. They stood that way, silent, for a beat.

"I'm Kittel, FBI," he said finally. "Wondering if we could ask you a few questions."

Rheal looked at Farley again, then stepped to the side of the door. "Always happy to help my friends in law enforcement any way I can," he said.

In the kitchen, Rheal stood at the counter with a cigarette dangling from his lips, pouring three cups of coffee. "How do you gentlemen take it?" he asked.

"Black," Kittel and Farley said in tandem.

"As you wish," Rheal said. He came to the table and set the mugs down, then took a seat and tapped his cigarette in the ashtray. "So," he said.

"Says here you're a combat veteran, Marines," Kittel said, looking at his clipboard. "Every decoration under the sun, short of a Medal of Honor. What division?"

"Fifth for a while, Force Recon after that."

"Tip of the tip of the spear," Kittel said.

"So they say," Rheal said. "You?"

Kittel smiled. "You have X-ray vision or something?" he asked. "You see my globe-and-anchor tattoo through my shirt?"

"Educated guess."

"Seventh Regiment, but I was a little before your time," Kittel said. "Just missed Korea, spent the Cuban Missile Crisis sunning myself in Puerto Rico."

"Can't all be lucky like I was," Rheal said.

"I'm hoping maybe you can be straight with me about what's going on here," Kittel said. "Marine to Marine."

Rheal smiled. "Not having much luck getting people to talk, I take it."

"None."

Rheal looked at Farley, who kept his face as neutral as possible. When Rheal continued to stare at him, Farley busied himself looking into the bottom of his coffee mug.

"I'll shoot you straight," Rheal said finally, turning back to Kittel. "Tell you whatever I can. But first you should know that all I really want is to have my job back. Put in another twenty years, get my gold watch, and retire to the garage. I've had enough excitement for two lifetimes already; I don't need any more."

"No doubt," Kittel said. He flipped pages on the clipboard until he got to a fresh one, then looked up, pen in hand. "Have you heard about the men who've been kidnapped from the Hollingsworth and Whitney mill in the last week?"

"Of course," Rheal said.

"And have you heard any talk about who's responsible?"

"I have not."

"Do you know anyone who would want to do this?"

"Aside from every last person in Little Canada?"

Kittel put his pen down. "Don't you start," he said.

"I'm just telling you how it is," Rheal said. "Everyone's a suspect, and no one's talking. As you've no doubt already learned on your own."

Kittel lifted his coffee mug and leaned back. "I spoke to a woman about an hour ago," he said. "She said something a little different than everyone else."

At this, Farley looked up sharply from his coffee, not sure who Kittel was referring to or what his angle was. Rheal, for his part, had a much better poker face, and simply raised his eyebrows, an expression much closer to indifference than alarm.

"She said she knew who's responsible for the kidnappings. She said, in fact, that everyone knows."

"She must be more plugged in than I am, then," Rheal said. "Or she's just pulling your chain."

"Seemed like she meant it," Kittel said. "I've usually got a pretty good bullshit detector."

"Well, maybe not in this case."

"No, I think it's working just fine," Kittel said. "Right now, it's telling me *you're* pulling my chain."

Rheal leaned back, smiling and holding up his hands in mock surrender. "Okay," he said. "You got me. Like George Washington, I cannot tell a lie. I know who's disappearing these guys."

"Who?"

Rheal paused a beat, still smiling. "Why, me, of course."

Farley stared wide-eyed.

Kittel smiled back now. "You."

"Guilty as sin."

"Okay," Kittel said. He gestured to Rheal's pack of cigarettes on the table—silent inquiry—and Rheal nodded. Kittel took out a smoke, lit it, inhaled, exhaled a blue cloud. He tapped the cigarette in the ashtray and kept smiling at Rheal, who continued to smile right back.

Rheal knew what Kittel intended with his silence. It was meant to create tension, which in turn—according to Kittel's gambit—would cause Rheal to eventually say something he didn't really want to say. They'd reached the point where the next person to speak would lose. And so Rheal kept quiet, too.

But it was Farley turned out to be the one who couldn't take it. "Quit fucking around, Rheal," he said. "We've been getting false confessions all day, and I'm done with the games. You said you'd be straight—so be straight."

Kittel gave Farley a look of unalloyed annoyance. But Rheal recognized Farley's play, and leaned into it.

"I am being straight," he said, shaking his own cigarette out of the pack. "We took Stewart Qualley and broke his brain, and we're in the process of scrambling this Oakley fellow's synapses as we speak. We're holding him in an old storage facility out in Sidney. I can take you there, if you like."

Kittel chuckled.

"I'm serious, Rheal," Farley said. "I'll run you in for making a false statement. See how funny you think you are then."

"I'm serious, too," Rheal said. "I'm the guilty party. Let's all take a trip out to Sidney, and you'll see."

Farley stood up and reached for the cuffs on the back of his belt.

"Okay, fine, fine," Rheal said. "I don't want any trouble, like I said. I don't have this guy and I don't know who does. But I'm glad you showed up today, because I do know something that the two of you should hear about."

Farley glared at him a moment longer, then sat back down.

"And what's that?" Kittel asked.

"Unrelated," Rheal cautioned.

"I've still got half a cigarette left to smoke," Kittel said. "Lay it on me."

"Okay then," Rheal said. "I know you've got an obligation to look into the scab stuff, but as far as I'm concerned they don't deserve the effort you're putting in. The children of this community, on the other hand, are very much deserving of your protection."

Kittel and Farley waited a beat, two, but Rheal just smoked and looked from one to the other.

"And?" Farley said finally.

"What do you know," Rheal said, "about the priest who was just assigned to Notre Dame?"

"Oh Jesus," Farley said. "No, Rheal. Don't even say it."

"I'm not saying anything. But you've got a couple of young boys, don't you, Farley?"

"We go to First Baptist," Farley said.

"I try not to hold that against you," Rheal said. "Still, I'd think you'd want to know if there was a pederast running loose in town."

Farley said nothing, but Kittel was now looking at Rheal as if trying to divine whether this was true or a ruse.

"I think the FBI has a mandate with regard to children being sexually abused," Rheal said. "Is that right, Agent Kittel?"

"Under certain circumstances," Kittel said.

"Well, how about these circumstances? A child-molesting priest has moved to town, he's been shielded by the Church for years, and local law enforcement has no interest in investigating the matter."

"That might be something we'd need to look into," Kittel said, gazing pointedly at Farley.

"Check the newspapers out of Fall River, Mass., from two years ago," Rheal said. "You'll find some interesting stories about Father Brennan. What's most interesting is what those stories *don't* say."

Since Stella's lateral move to head of community outreach, which kept her busy planning events and ordering food and clothes for the neighborhood, Carmeline had been running the till behind Grondin's Cleaners by herself—which was just fine as far as she was concerned. Carmeline was a loner by nature, not cowed in the least by working solo, and though she loved Stella she also had been ready, after only a few nights stuck in a parked car together, to bring a pillow to their next shift and use it to shut her friend up for the rest of eternity.

So she was more than happy to be parked behind Grondin's by herself on this evening. Fall's first bite was in the air, a sharp, dry wind skittering leaves across the pavement; it sounded, to Carmeline's ears, like the first mention of the inevitability of winter. She had the windows down but the engine running and the heater on, radio tuned to 92 Moose, which she usually liked, except when they played sappy shit like "I Just Called to Say I Love You," which was playing now, all treacly synth and Stevie Wonder crooning about some imaginary woman as if she was Helen of Troy, and by the way, what the hell had *happened* to him? Carmeline used to really love his songs and still had *Music of My Mind* and *Talking Book* on 8-track, but this crap, *mon Dieu*, it was enough to make you want to puke. She gave the volume knob a brisk, irritated twist, turning it down but not off.

The people she'd come to know as regulars arrived and departed, materializing out of the shadows and fading just as quickly back into them. The truth was—at least if you asked Carmeline—dealing drugs was pretty boring, just another letdown in a world full of them. Every twenty minutes or so you handed out product and made change, and otherwise you sat and waited and stretched and yawned and listened to top-40 radio until three in the morning. She'd taken to bringing a stack of crossword books and working on them, by the Accord's meager interior light, in between customers. She read Danielle Steel and *Reader's Digest* and played solitaire on the dash. She was, in fact, playing solitaire on this evening when the man who was decidedly not a regular approached the Honda.

Carmeline wasn't the nervous type, so she was not alarmed by the fact of a stranger walking up on her, even in the darkest hours of the night, even with dead leaves scraping eerily across the pavement, even when she was alone. Her ears did prick up, though, when she heard a blast of static from a walkie-talkie somewhere on his person, and she thought: *cop*. But that didn't check out; the Waterville PD had been minding their business, as per the arrangement with Bates. So what was this, exactly? Carmeline reached beneath the steering wheel, where the .38 given to her by Rheal sat in a holster taped to the underside of the dash.

"Can I help you?" she asked the man as he came up to the driver's window.

"I hope so," the man said. "I need to get a message to Babs Dionne."

Carmeline placed the deck of cards on the dashboard with her left hand as she slid the .38 from its holster with her right. "Pretty sure she's at her house," she said. "No reason you can't go over and talk to her in person."

"It may come to that," the man said. "For now, we're hoping you'll be willing to pass word for us."

Carmeline pushed the barrel of the .38 against the inside of the driver's door, angled up toward the man's torso. "State your purpose, then," she said.

"Tell Babs that Harold Aucoin hasn't forgotten about her," the man said. "And that she'll be seeing a lot more of him soon, as he's been hired to provide security for workers at the Mill. He doesn't want conflict, and he doesn't think she does either. So he's hoping she'll be willing to talk."

About what, exactly?" Babs asked Carmeline half an hour later in her kitchen.

"Didn't say," Carmeline told her.

"You should have shot the bastard," Babs said. "Doesn't want conflict, my eye."

"We could just play along," Rheal said.

"How does that do us any good?" Babs asked. "If Aucoin's got a hundred goons watching the Mill, they've taken away our ability to convince the scabs they'd be better off just going home."

"No, they haven't," Rheal said.

"How's that?"

"The Sauciers could sneak into the White House and kidnap Reagan," Rheal said. "How do you think the scabs will react when we show that Aucoin's men can't actually protect them? They'll leave town in a caravan."

Babs scowled into her coffee cup.

"Besides," Rheal said, "we can't be having an all-out war in the streets, for a dozen reasons. We're down a man for a few days with Claude gone. And now the feds have shown up. We need less attention, not more. So go talk to Harold. Let him think everything's copacetic, live and let live. By the time he realizes that's not actually the case, the scabs will be back in Dixie where they belong, and we'll have our jobs again."

Babs pulled a cigarette from her pack and stuck it, unlit, into her mouth. She thought for a moment. "A willingness to negotiate," she said finally, "implies weakness. Vulnerability. A lack of confidence in one's position, and one's ability to maintain it."

"I'll stop you," Rheal said, "when you say something that doesn't sound like exactly the position we're in."

Babs gave him a warning look. "If I agree to talk with Aucoin, it's as good as telling him we don't think we can hold our ground."

"We probably can't," Rheal said.

"Which is precisely why we shouldn't admit as much," Babs said. "Jesus, try to keep up."

"I'm keeping up fine," Rheal said. "I just disagree with you."

"Noted," Babs said. She took the cigarette from her mouth and moved to flick it in the ashtray before remembering it wasn't lit. Rheal and Carmeline exchanged a look, and Babs glanced up and noticed them noticing her.

"No negotiations," Babs said. "Let Harold spend the next few days wondering if he's going to hear from us. When he doesn't, and when another scab disappears right under the noses of his men, he'll start to get the picture."

"Fine," Rheal said. "But if you insist on ignoring Aucoin's olive branch, I have to insist on something myself."

"And what's that?"

"You have a personal security detail for the foreseeable future."

"Uh, no."

"What about me?" Carmeline asked.

Rheal looked at her. "What about you?"

"I'm the one this guy approached," Carmeline said. "I'm the one with my ass hanging in the breeze every night behind Grondin's. Why don't I get a personal security detail?"

"Because you're not the one Aucoin is after," Rheal told her.

"Says you," Carmeline said.

"Trust me, Carm," Rheal said. "I speak as the man Aucoin tried to have killed with a chain saw. You're not in the kind of danger I'm in." He pointed at Babs. "And I'm not in the kind of danger she's in."

If the Church thinks you're a big enough threat, they'll fucking kill you. That's not hyperbole. You wouldn't be the first person the Holy See disappeared, so be careful."

This was the warning Heron had given Clement before he first started taking personnel files out of the diocese and faxing them to Heron from Don's Copy Shop in Portland's Old Port. And though it had been difficult for Clement to believe he was putting himself in mortal danger, he still took the warning seriously—at first. Whether or not he believed some order of monks existed that served as a hit squad for the Vatican, he still had no desire to be caught. So he set rules for himself: He took one file at a time, and only kept it for the duration of his lunch break, returning it immediately to where it belonged when he came back for the afternoon. When he first arrived in the Old Port he would walk past Don's Copy at least twice, to check if anyone was following him, before finally going in. He went to Amato's Italian Sandwich Shop either before or after Don's, to maintain the fiction that his primary purpose on these trips was to have lunch.

But Clement was also, by now, indulging in something like despair, and it was difficult for him to muster much concern for himself, let alone anything else. And after a few days of tradecraft he came to feel, without even really giving it any conscious thought, that his precautions with regard to sneaking records out of the office were unnecessary. No one paid any attention to him, either at work or in the streets. The storage facility had no cameras or vaults, no security at all beyond the dead bolt on the front door. And the only other person ever around was ancient Father Doyon, who neither heard nor saw anything, and tended to fall asleep spontaneously at his desk multiple times a day, prompting Clement, more than once, to check if he was still breathing.

In short, Heron's warning aside, it seemed Clement had little to worry about. And so within a few days he just walked into Don's Copy on the first pass, manila file folder in hand instead of tucked into his jacket. He went to Amato's only if he actually wanted a sandwich. He stopped looking over his shoulder, both figuratively and literally. He knew this was sinful, according to Aquinas—laziness was sloth, sloth a deadly sin—and yet the cloak-and-dagger urgency of sending these files to Heron had quickly gone out of the thing, and it felt, now, like just one more mundane, meaningless task in his post-priesthood days. And those days felt, in turn, like they were never going to change, like he would spend the rest of his life doing penance in the basement of the storage facility until he was as old and ragged as Father Doyon. Nothing—not providing files to Heron, not asking God nightly to help him see where he'd gone wrong and how to repair it—would make a difference. He would die in that basement, and Babs would die with the sin of murder still on her soul.

And then, when he returned from lunch on this day, walked past the slumped and gently snoring Father Doyon, and descended the stairs, he found a man waiting for him in the basement, sitting in the chair Clement used while sorting through incoming files before shelving them in their proper place in the stacks. This man was big—not fat, but powerfully built, thick neck, wide shoulders, dress slacks taut over his thighs. He looked like he'd maybe retired not too long ago from playing middle linebacker for the Giants. This imposing physical presence was leavened by a stillness in the man's bearing, an equanimity that was hard to place but equally hard to miss.

"Whatcha got there?" the man asked, nodding at the folder in Clement's left hand.

"Personnel file," Clement said.

"Anyone I should know about?"

"That depends," Clement said. "Who are you?"

The man stood and reached into his jacket, pulled out a wallet, and flipped it open to reveal an FBI identification card and badge. "Special Agent Kittel," he said.

Clement's mind clambered to make sense of what the FBI would want with him. Was this Kittel working on behalf of the Church, somehow? Had they been watching him after all?

"Are you Father Clement Thibault?"

"I am." Clement tried to assume an air of nonchalance by tossing the file on the table as if it were nothing important. He felt his hands shaking, so to give them something to do he took off his own jacket.

To Clement's horror, Kittel reached toward the file, then paused and looked at him. "You mind?"

"Not at all," Clement said as evenly as he could. He draped his jacket over the back of the chair and sat down.

Kittel licked the tip of his index finger—a habit that caused physical revulsion in Clement whenever he saw it—and began to flip through the file. "'Father Thomas H. Maguire,'" he read. "'Currently associate pastor at St. Mary's in Dedham, Mass. Ordained 1976. Graduate work at Dallas Theological Seminary, 1973 to 1976, undergrad at same. Born and raised in Gloversville, New York, attended Gloversville schools until grade ten when he first entered seminary.' What am I missing here?"

"I'm not sure what you mean," Clement said.

"Where's the part of this file that tells me the guy's a sexual deviant?"

Clement blinked several times. "They tend not to say the quiet part out loud, in official documents," he said finally.

"So then how do you know?"

"Agent Kittel, are you here on official business?"

Kittel smiled. "Funny you ask," he said, "because I really don't know, myself."

"Basically what I'm asking is if you're here to tell me to stop digging around in Church records."

"Oh. No. That's between you and God, I suppose." Kittel leaned against the table tentatively, unsure it would hold his weight; Clement imagined testing furniture was a long-ingrained habit for a man his size. "In fact, I might be here to help you."

"You'll forgive me," Clement said, "if I don't find your lack of clarity about your intentions all that comforting."

"I'm not moonlighting as muscle for the Church. You can relax."

"So then how did you end up here?"

"Mind if I answer that question with a question?"

"It's not ideal, but if you must."

"What can you tell me about Rheal Dionne?"

Clement smiled. "Ah."

"What does that mean? Ah?"

"You're investigating Rheal."

Kittel crossed his arms over his chest. "I'm investigating the disappearance of replacement workers from the Hollingsworth and Whitney mill. You think that has something to do with Rheal?"

"I'm afraid I can't say."

"Can't, or won't?"

"Can't. I have no knowledge of what Rheal's been up to since I left Waterville."

"Could you speculate, based on what you know of his character? Let me put that another way: knowing Rheal, and knowing that someone's been kidnapping workers from the Mill, would you suspect he was responsible?"

"I would suspect every last person in Little Canada."

"I keep hearing that," Kittel said, smiling. "What *can* you tell me about Rheal?"

"That he's a war hero and a good man who's had a hard life. That he loves his wife and his community. That I would trust him to do what's right in any situation."

"I believe all that is true," Kittel said.

"Good," Clement said.

"I guess I should tell you that Rheal sent me here. Or at least, he did indirectly."

"How's that?"

"He suggested that I worry less about kidnapped workers and more about the children who attend Notre Dame parish."

Clement felt himself blanch. With the threat Brennan posed adrift in the air between him and Kittel, guilt was the chief feeling that rose in his chest. This was the first time he realized he felt to blame for endangering Waterville's children by letting himself be defrocked. And that, he realized, made him angry. Furious, in fact. As angry as he'd been at God when Simone and the baby had died. Except now he was angry at Brennan, at the bishop and Cardinal Law and the Church itself, and determined not to accept responsibility for the evil it had allowed to fester for decades.

"Open that file again," Clement said to Kittel. "I'll show you what you're looking for."

CHAPTER THIRTEEN

Aucoin's security force, one hundred men strong, appeared in a caravan of sedans and pickups descending from the interstate, snaking its way through town like the vehicles in a funeral procession. Such a display, in a town like Waterville, was sure to be noticed, and no doubt that was the point. The column particularly took its time in Little Canada, slowing to a crawl as though the whole neighborhood were a designated school zone, firearms not brandished but also, pointedly, not hidden from view. And the desired effect of all this was achieved—people pulled curtains aside and came out on their porches to watch, exchanging comments as the column rolled by and, occasionally, flipping a vigorous, deeply sincere bird. Neither side, however, said a word to the other. The locals eyeballed the interlopers and the interlopers eyeballed right back, boxers before a grudge match everyone expected to be bloody. It took a full hour for all the vehicles to make their way through the Mill gates, and once inside, the men wasted no time, taking up residence in the bunk trailers that had previously served as housing for scabs and immediately deploying the first of two fifty-man guard shifts. Within a few hours Hollingsworth & Whitney was transformed into an armed camp. Men with rifles stood watch on the walls above each set of gates, and others walked the perimeter fence in pairs. Until further notice workers were to be bused to and from the Mill like schoolchildren, each bus assigned a team of four guards, not including the driver.

No one believed that the men working for Aucoin actually met the requirements for private armed security—clean criminal records and formalized firearms training chief among them—but neither did anyone seem eager to go around checking qualifications and licensing. Certainly not Bates, who hoped from his hospital bed, perhaps naively, to keep these half-assed mercenaries inside the Mill and everyone else out of it, and thus avoid the whole thing turning into even more of a shitshow.

Security had been in place at the Mill for two days by the time Duane Oakley rematerialized in Castonguay Square downtown, within crawling distance of the police station, drooling and muttering nonsense about Steely Dan. The Mill had been hemorrhaging workers since Oakley's abduction, with over one hundred machinists, engineers, and maintenance workers packing up and leaving in only a few days; no notice and no warning, just suddenly empty spots in the lumberyard and the wash room. Pickers sat dormant, and when the rollers broke down, as they always did sooner or later, it was an open question whether anyone would answer the call to get them running again.

This presented both an immediate and a longer-term problem for Clay Sutton. The immediate problem, of course, was that his mill was down a hundred hands, which meant that, even with those who remained pulling a ton of overtime, production had inevitably slowed. This was the one thing above all else that could not be allowed to happen; if commandments had existed for the Mill in the same way they did for the church, the first stone tablet would have been inscribed *Thou shalt only ever increase paper production.* Of course, Sutton was obligated, by the terms of the agreement ending the strike, to offer open jobs to those who had been locked out. But no one was keeping tabs on whether the company actually met its obligations, and knowing that the kidnappings were intended to force him to do just that, Sutton had resolved that he'd sooner cut off his own pinkie than hire back even one person from Little Canada. Instead, he would drive the remaining workers like rented mules until replacements could be imported, and he would accept, begrudgingly, that this meant less paper would roll out of H&W for at least a short time.

Sutton's longer-term problem had a name, and now he knew it well: Babs Dionne. He'd veered from ignorant of her existence to dismissive of her ability to cause him trouble and had arrived, finally, at the understanding that she would neither be ignored nor easily dispatched. Given these facts, and given that Sutton was a businessman, he intended to approach Babs with a deal. But she was proving difficult to convince into conversation. Sutton had first imagined she'd be more likely to talk with Aucoin, because they were of a kind. But she'd rebuffed that overture with a good deal of silence. Preferring to avoid violent conflict—which was good for nobody's interests, near as he could tell—Sutton kept the leash on Aucoin, pending his own effort, today, to speak sense into this Dionne woman.

He found her in her driveway with two other women, sorting through the contents of a panel truck and talking over one another in rapid-fire Quebecois. Though Sutton was somewhere between conversant and fluent in Parisian French, and though he recognized the language they were speaking as a kind of French, he had some difficulty making out what they were saying. Based on the way they held up items for one another to consider and then tossed them into one of two loose piles, however, it wasn't difficult to infer they were sorting things to keep and things to discard.

Sutton stopped at the foot of the driveway and, when several moments passed without anyone noticing him, called out to the women. "Mrs. Dionne?"

All three turned at the sound of his voice, and stood holding winter jackets, a toaster oven, and several sets of lawn darts while they took Sutton in with identical expressions of annoyed disinterest. After a moment, the one to the far right, deepest inside the truck's interior, dropped the lawn darts in the pile that appeared to be the keepers and said, in French, "The fuck are you?"

"Are you Mrs. Barbara Dionne?" Sutton asked in French.

"You deaf?" the woman said. She bent at the waist and opened the flaps on the top of a box, peered down inside. "I asked who *you* are, and since you came to us, the polite thing would be to identify yourself first. And state your business, while you're at it."

"Fair enough," Sutton said. "I'm Clay Sutton, vice president of International Paper. And you, I now have no doubt, are the legendary Barbara 'Babs' Dionne."

"Incorrect," the woman said. "I'm the considerably less-legendary Carmeline Bérubé. But I'm still perfectly capable of slicing your balls off with this box cutter. You've got a lot of nerve, coming down here."

Now the woman farthest to the left stood up out of a crouch and stared down at Sutton. He thought he saw the hint of a smile, but in the shadows of the truck he couldn't be sure.

"I'm the one you're looking for," she said. "And you can save the hyperbole. I'm just a woman trying to do right by her family and her community."

"A woman who successfully framed poor Chief Davies, and has managed to send a good number of my workers running for the hills."

Babs shrugged this off. "Sometimes doing right by your family and community requires extraordinary measures." She leaned down into a box again and started pulling out sweaters and looking them over. "What do you want, Mr. Sutton?"

"To talk."

"We're talking. So what do you want?"

"Maybe we could speak in private?"

Babs dropped an armful of sweaters into the keeper pile. "Allow me to introduce two of my partners in the business of Little Canada. This is Rita, and you've already met Carmie. Anything you need to say to me, you can say to them."

"It's a pleasure, ladies," Sutton said.

"The pleasure's all ours, fuckface," Carmeline said in French. Rita snickered and went back to sorting without a word to Sutton.

"So, one more time," Babs said. "What do you want?"

"To reach an understanding that's mutually beneficial."

"And how do you propose we accomplish that?"

"Give-and-take."

Babs looked up again and smiled, this time broadly enough to be seen in the shadows. "We already tried that, Sutton," she said. "We gave, and you took. For years. Then when we'd had enough, you fired us. Don't come down here asking to negotiate now, as if that wasn't what we wanted all along."

"Mrs. Dionne—"

"Stop calling me that. Makes me sound like a fucking spinster."

"Babs?"

She nodded.

"Babs, what I'd like to do—where I'd like to start—is by suggesting you reframe the way you define a negotiation. Negotiations don't really begin until both sides have demonstrated the ability to make life intolerable for the other. That's when give-and-take properly comes into it. Up to that point, it's your obligation to yourself—as it is my obligation to myself and my company—to take and keep whatever you can."

"See, that's where you and I are different," Babs said. "Because I'm a decent person, and you're a shitheel whose only god is the greenback. My ethic is to start with give-and-take, and when that spirit is not returned in kind, only then does my policy change to scorched earth. Which is where things stand now."

"That inflexibility," Sutton said, "will make you a bad businessperson."

"*C'est comme ça*," Babs said. "But let's not forget—*you* came to *me* looking to settle things today, not the other way around. You're here asking me to give you something. But what *I* want I'm prepared to take. Things are going exactly as I want them to. I don't see any need to negotiate any longer."

Sutton smiled. "Well, I guess I know now that you weren't refusing to talk to Aucoin out of fear," he said.

"Nope. The time for talking is done. Now it's time to see what's what."

"It's too bad," Sutton said. "I have to admit, I've come to respect and even admire you, Babs. Part of the reason I came here today, to be totally forthright, was to make your acquaintance. Anyone who can wrest control of the police away from me and scatter my workers to the wind . . . well, I'd rather she be a partner than an adversary."

Babs stopped sorting clothes and looked at Sutton, but she didn't respond right away. Instead, she dropped a handful of T-shirts back into the box and came down the ramp that extended from the back of the panel truck. Now Carmeline and Rita stopped their work, too, and watched as Babs approached Sutton, stopping just inches away from him. It would have been obvious to anyone watching that Sutton, while ruthless in his manner, was not accustomed to being physically challenged. Though a head taller than Babs he shrank from her in the almost-imperceptible way of physical cowards: he became smaller, somehow, seemed, with her looming immediately in front of him, to displace less air. The expression on his face, however—a calm dismissiveness—did not change.

"What do you think this is?" Babs asked him. "You think you can toss a couple of compliments my way and all will be forgiven? We'll saddle up and ride together? You think I'll forget that, because of decisions *you've* made, I'm going through salvaged clothes trying to keep my neighbors from freezing to death this winter? Have you even spent a winter here, in that nice house of yours on the ocean? No, of course you haven't. Because you're not smart enough to see you have to *earn* summer here. You think you can just buy it."

Sutton tried a laugh. "Your peasant morality notwithstanding," he said, "my experience of summer in Maine is quite nice, without having to endure the winters."

Babs smiled back at him. "You people are all the same," she said. "Arrogant and stupid in equal measure. So let me explain something that shouldn't require explaining: You have left your world behind. You're in my world now. And down here, when we have a problem with someone, we don't call a fucking lawyer. *Vous me pigez*?"

Babs leaned closer, until her nose was almost touching Sutton's chin. "From our perspective, the stakes of the fight *you* started are mortal," she said. "We're fighting for our lives. That makes us more dangerous than you can imagine. Whatever means necessary, we will use. And if you're not extremely careful, you may not live to see how it turns out."

Sutton, knocked off-balance by Babs pushing into his space, fell back a step.

"It's important that you know I am not exaggerating even a little," Babs said. "I will kill you if I have to, Mr. Sutton. If you push me. I'm no stranger to it. Ask your friend Chief Davies."

"He made me aware."

"You can't end this by beating us into submission, and you damn sure can't end it by flattering me. The only way you can end it—the *only* way—is for you to do what's right, and give us our jobs back."

Sutton smiled again and regrouped. "There's something that you don't seem to understand," he said. "Even if you win this particular fight, Babs, you still lose. Let's say I let you have your jobs again. So what? I go back to my nice house on the water, and you stay here in this slum, and the world keeps turning exactly as it did before. We're still, you and me, engaged in the same bit of Kabuki theater, the plot of which is: I win and you lose. Do you know why? Because that's your *role*. You're playing the loser in a rigged game, and nothing you do will change that."

"You're right that the one who wins is the one who sets the terms of the game," Babs said. "Your mistake is thinking that it's you. See, you've forgotten your Bible, Sutton. We're made from the same stuff, you and I—ashes to ashes, et cetera. All the money in the world can't change that. We're two playthings, set to fight each other for God's entertainment. No matter who wins, in the end we both lose."

"I didn't get the impression you're a godly woman, Babs."

"Oh, I didn't learn that in church," Babs said. "I learned it when I stabbed Davies's buddy Sacha in the lung. All the scripture in the world can't make clear that we're born to die quite like killing a man will. Not that you'd know anything about that. Because people of your station always farm out the dirty work."

"Wouldn't you, if you could?"

"Never," Babs said. "When I killed Sacha, it was the first time I ever felt the presence of God. I could feel Him watching us. Not judging—watching, like we were slaves in the Colosseum and He'd just given Sacha the thumbs-down. It was better than sex. I wouldn't give that up for all the waterfront mansions in Maine. Because for just a few seconds, I saw as He sees."

"And people accuse me of having a God complex."

Babs ignored this. "When I watched Sacha kick and gasp," she said, "what I saw was an animal struggling against inevitability. I saw that we're all—you, me, everyone—trapped in a fight we can't win. I killed Sacha, but what I learned is that *I* will die, no matter what. And I act accordingly. You should do the same."

Sutton seemed fresh out of smart retorts. He crossed his arms, less a gesture of defiance and more an effort to put some kind of buffer between himself and Babs.

"And now," Babs said, "and hold on to your hat, you're going to love this—I'm pregnant."

At this, both Rita and Carmeline, who'd been listening with a mixture of anxiety and glee, straightened up as though they'd been slapped.

"Isn't that a hoot?" Babs said. "Everything is broken, everything is wrong, and in the midst of all this mess I've condemned another soul to learning what I learned that day. What a fucking idiot, right?"

Babs looked from Sutton to her friends and back again several times, as if hoping someone would confirm that she was, indeed, breathtakingly stupid.

"Anyway," Babs said finally, "you and I will fight each other, Sutton. Like there's anything to be won. One of us will die like an animal now, and one of us will die like an animal later, and that'll be that. Unless you give us our jobs back."

Sutton paused. "I will have to take time to consider," he said finally.

"Do so. But don't take too long," Babs said. "Because nothing changes until you decide. And I have every intention of continuing to make your life intolerable. You have my word on that."

Sutton nodded and walked back the way he'd come. Babs watched him go for a few moments, then turned and strode back up the ramp into the truck and began sorting sweaters again, apparently content to let everything that had just been said stand for itself.

Rita lofted a test balloon. "So, uh, you're preg—"

"You shut your goddamn dirty mouth," Babs said.

Rita chuckled. "Guess we know now why you've been chewing your cigarettes instead of smoking them."

"For your information," Babs said, "I am pregnant only for a few more days. Then I'm taking care of it."

"Babs. You can't."

"Don't give me the Holy Trinity line about this, Rita. It's 1984. Women have abortions. Stop acting so scandalized."

"Not that anyone asked me," Carmeline said, picking through loose socks, "but as someone who regularly wishes I'd aborted my shitty kids, I fully support your decision, Babs."

"Thank you, Carmie."

"What about Rheal?" Rita asked.

"When he's capable of carrying a child for nine months, I'll solicit his thoughts on the matter."

"You're ducking him, in other words," Rita said.

"It would be crazy for us to have a kid under the best circumstances, Rita," Babs said. "And these are not the best circumstances."

"You have to tell him," Rita said.

"Your opinion has been noted," Babs said. "Move on."

"Okay," Rita said. "Don't you think you might have just overstated the strength of our position?"

"Not at all," Babs said.

"He's got a hundred men in town, and we've got, what, nine people?" Rita said.

"His people are paid hacks," Babs said. "They'll run the moment things get bloody. And Sutton's scared. He came down here expecting me to roll over and let him scratch my belly. He's not ready to die for this."

"Not sure I am, either," Rita said.

"He's going to fold," Babs said. "I could see it."

"I sure hope you're right," Rita said. "Because otherwise you just signed us up for a fight we can't win."

Like Clement, since being assigned to Notre Dame Father Brennan had not received a single visitor at the rectory, though obviously he'd been there for a much shorter time. Unlike Clement, he also had not received any phone calls, nor, despite his continued best efforts, had a single parishioner stop to chat on the steps of the church after Mass, or approach him to say hello at the grocery store or the K-Mart. The comprehensiveness with which he was shunned, in fact, was enough to make him feel as though somehow everyone here knew exactly where he'd come from, and the abomination he used to be.

So when Father Brennan saw, from the rectory living room where he sat staring out the window as he did for long hours every weekday, a black sedan pull into the drive and a smallish man with sand-colored hair get out, he didn't know whether to feel delighted or terrified.

Brennan remained seated, paralyzed by these contradictory feelings, as the man approached the side entrance and disappeared from sight. Several moments later the rectory doorbell rang throughout the house, loud enough to startle Brennan even though he'd known it was coming. He sprang from the lounger and shuffled quickly through the living and dining rooms, rushing as though the house was on fire, the bottoms of his leather slippers whispering across hardwood.

When Brennan opened the door he found the man on the other side wasn't merely small, but slight, though his meager physicality was offset by an unmistakable gravity. Here was a man who had seen some shit, and come out the other side with as sure a sense of himself as a person could have.

"Father Brennan?" the man asked.

"Yes?"

"I'm Clement Thibault," the man said.

Brennan's stomach dropped like a bird shot from the sky.

"You free?" Clement asked.

Brennan gathered himself and stepped aside. "Of course," he said, betrayed by a slight tremor in his voice. "Come in."

They crossed through the kitchen and into the dining room. "I like what you've done with the place," Clement said, taking a seat at the table.

"I haven't done anything," Brennan said.

"That's what I mean," Clement said.

Brennan sat opposite Clement and asked, "So what can I do for you today?"

"I don't want to play games," Clement said. "So you'll forgive me in advance for speaking as plainly as possible."

Brennan swallowed. "I will do my best," he said.

"First, I want you to understand that nothing about this is personal," Clement said. "I have nothing against you. And I don't resent you for taking over this parish."

"I appreciate you saying so," Brennan said.

"And with that out of the way," Clement said, "I came here to tell you you should leave. To demand that you leave, in fact. Today."

Brennan's expression went flat. "What?"

"It won't be long before everyone knows what you and a bunch of others are guilty of," Clement said. "When that happens, trust me, you do not want to be here in Waterville."

"What are you talking about?" Brennan said. "Where am I supposed to go?"

Clement shook his head regretfully. “I don’t know,” he said. “If I had to guess, the archdiocese will still be invested in protecting you, if only to protect itself. Maybe start there.”

“Wait,” Brennan said. “Just wait. What’s happening? How are people going to find out?”

“It doesn’t matter,” Clement said. “You just need to be gone when it happens. I assume you’ve met Babs Dionne?”

“She approached me after my first mass and said she was going to find out who I was.”

“And when she does, she’ll gut you like a perch,” Clement said. “There’s nothing I’ve ever been so certain of in my life. That’s why I’m here. I’m not trying to pull a fast one on you. I just want the kids to be safe, and I don’t want you to die because of something I’ve done.”

“Why do you think the children aren’t safe?” Brennan asked.

Clement stared. “We both know what you are, Joe,” he said. “Let’s not bother to pretend otherwise.”

“Father Thibault,” Brennan said, “I am not a danger to the children of this community.”

“And how can you say that without any doubt?”

Brennan hesitated. “Do you really want to know?”

“I guess I do,” Clement said.

Brennan took a breath and focused all his attention on the cuticle of his right index finger, talking now without looking up. “The cardinal sent me to a treatment center in Canada called Southland. There were thirty or forty priests there. Talk therapy, mostly, but they knew none of it did any good. If you wanted something that really did work there was something else they offered. But you had to volunteer for it.”

“And that was?”

Brennan looked up from his hands. "They call it chemical castration," he said.

Clement stared. "Christ have mercy," he said finally.

"The thoughts still come," Brennan said. "But there's no urge to act on them. Believe me, I wish they didn't happen at all. But I can ignore them and do my job."

"Maybe so," Clement said. "But don't you think you'd still be better suited for something else?"

"I don't expect this to make sense to you, Father Thibault," Brennan said. "But even with everything that's wrong with me, the terrible things I did, I still know God called me to the priesthood."

"It makes more sense to me than you could realize," Clement said. "And I'm sorry to be the one to say this, but it also doesn't matter. The things you did are never going away. So you have to. It's that simple."

In his heart of hearts, Brennan knew Clement was right. Even at Southland, Brennan had known there was no coming back. He could no longer be a priest. But he had wanted so desperately to believe otherwise that he'd just gone ahead and done so. And now here was Clement, telling him what he already knew and no longer could deny.

"I don't care if she kills me," Brennan said, ashamed to shed tears for himself but unable to stop them.

"Well, I do," Clement said.

"Why?"

Clement paused, gazed at Brennan a few moments before answering. "It seems to me, Joe," he said, "that you're pretty much the embodiment of the sacrament of penance. You have admitted your sins—I would imagine multiple times and in agonizing detail, yes?"

Brennan nodded, wiping at his cheeks.

"You have shown not just sorrow, but a dedication to change," Clement continued. "And I have no doubt that you have been forgiven, at least by God."

Brennan shook his head. "But I haven't."

"How do you know?"

Brennan looked at Clement with red eyes. "Because no one's heard my confession. Not officially."

"I don't understand."

Brennan smiled, bitter as failure. "In two years, no one offered," he said. "I've spent a long time wondering why. Either they think I don't deserve forgiveness, or the Church doesn't want to hear, in an official capacity, about a problem it says doesn't exist."

"Tabarnak." Clement set his jaw and looked out the window at Notre Dame, on the other side of Kimball Street. "Unbelievable."

"So I sit here, damned," Brennan said. "And you know, maybe that's as it should be."

Clement looked back at him. "I'll hear your confession," he said.

"You can't."

"Oh, to hell with that," Clement said. "I don't think the cardinal has credibility anymore in deciding who can and cannot take confessions." He rose from the table. "Let's head across the street. You've got about a thousand years' worth of Hail Marys to get started on."

The thing Normand Saucier couldn't reconcile, squatting in a maintenance closet at the H&W mill with his brother and a corpse, was that they'd allowed themselves to get so cocked up by a bunch of hillbilly amateurs. Or, worse, actually: *one* hillbilly amateur. The Sauciers had become legends in the wet-work community precisely because no one ever got the drop on them. Among the most savage and skilled operators in the world, they were generational talents. Then, today happened. And now they had to sit here in this closet, getting intimately acquainted with their failure, for the next six hours until the shift change. And hope that they could get out of the Mill without being noticed. *Again.*

As it stood, for the time being he and Ray were stuck here with the corpse. And Normand wasn't speaking to Ray at the moment, owing to the fact that Ray had been the one who allowed the unfortunate hillbilly to become aware of their presence. Normand held a bit of a grudge about that, and probably would continue to do so until at least such a time as they were no longer trapped in the maintenance closet or the Mill. For now, they had to listen to the clash and din of papermaking in the airplane hangar–size room outside for the next several hours, and hope that no one either opened the closet door or noticed the small pool of blood on the concrete just outside of it.

"Brudder Normand," Ray said. "What time is it?"

Normand gave him the finger in response, refusing to even glance at his brother in the twilight of the closet. The unfortunate hillbilly lay on the floor between them, stretched out with arms overhead from being dragged hastily inside. One of his arms was folded up awkwardly against the molded plastic of a floor scrubber machine.

"Come on, Norm," Ray said.

"Last I checked, you got a goddamn watch on your own wrist," Normand said.

"You gonna have to talk to me sooner or later, if we want to get out of here in one piece."

"We wouldn't *be* in here in de first place, except for you. Now shut up, before dey hear us."

"No one's going to hear us over dat racket," Ray said. "What time is it?"

The finger, again.

"We might as well use dis opportunity," Ray said, "to figure out how we going to get out of here. When de shift changes dere will only be a few minutes. We should have a plan."

"You tink I don't know dat?" Normand asked.

Quiet between them once more. Then Ray said, "Okay, so whadda we gonna do?"

Normand turned a scornful look his way. "What *I'm* gonna do, right at dis moment," he said, "is run a little test to see just how stupid my brudder is. I can't proceed with a plan until I know how little I can rely on you to actually execute it. So we do a quiz. You ready?"

"Normie."

"Don't call me dat. Listen up, Brudder Ray. Fill in de blanks. Ready?"

Ray didn't respond.

"We'll start easy. Water is . . . ?"

Ray shot his brother a look, and Normand raised his eyebrows expectantly.

"Wet," Ray said.

"De sky is . . . ?"

"Blue. Asshole."

"You're doing great," Normand said. "But don't get cocky, because dis last one is harder. In order to fix de gigantic stupid mistake my brudder Ray made, we have to . . . ?"

"Get out of here without being seen?"

"Obviously. And?"

"Still find someone to kidnap?"

"Incorrect," Normand said. "Dat ship has sailed. Try again. In order to fix de gigantic stupid—"

"I heard you de first time," Ray said.

"So what's de answer?"

"I give up."

"You can't. Unless you want to stay in dis closet for de rest of your natural life."

"Fine. *Ostie de crisse.* In order to fix blah blah blah we have to find a goddamn magic carpet to fly out of here."

"Incorrect," Normand said. "In order to fix your gigantic stupid mistake, Brudder Ray, we have to somehow get not just ourselves but also dis *body* out of here. Widdout being seen or heard. You got any ideas about how to do dat?"

Ray did not, at the moment, as evidenced by his stewing silence. Of course the brothers were meant to be taking somebody out of the Mill—that was the whole reason they'd come here—but that somebody was supposed to be (1) a worker, not a member of Aucoin's security detail, and (2) alive. This guy, it was fair to say, was deader than a Texas salad bar, stabbed in the base of the skull and reaping the wages of sin before his legs went out from under him. And that was a problem not just because no one was supposed to have died on this little junket, but because it was far easier to move a live person than a dead one. Particularly if you needed to be stealthy. Dead bodies weighed a ton, were nearly impossible to carry, and frequently got dropped. Dead limbs flopped about at random, crashed into things, knocked other things over. Basically, the only thing worse than a corpse, in terms of discretion, was a pissy toddler. And at the moment, Normand might have taken his chances with the kid.

"Why can't we just leave him?" Ray asked finally.

"And like dat, you have failed the test," Normand said. "Took longer dan I tought, to be honest."

"How did I fail?"

"Weren't you de one all worried about going to jail when dis whole ting started?" Normand asked. "Now you want to leave bodies lying around willy-nilly, all de livelong day?"

"I'm just saying, now dat it's done, why bother trying to sneak him out of here?"

"Brudder Ray," Normand said, "we have a while to wait, so I want you to take all de time you need to answer your own question."

An hour passed. At some point, outside the closet, there was a noise like a sudden geyser of steam, followed by the sound of some great whirring machine coming slowly to a halt. Men groaned and cursed—something important had broken down.

"You got an answer yet?" Normand asked his brother.

"Leave me alone," Ray said. "Now *I'm* not talking to *you*. See how you like it."

"Fine by me," Normand said. "Because if dey don't get whatever dat was running again, dere isn't going to be a shift change for us to get out of here anyways."

Another hour. Men worked and hollered and clanged metal against metal, but the whirring machine refused to whir back to life. The work stopped briefly while the men conferred about something in voices too low for the brothers to make out. But whatever it was must have involved something in the closet, because a few moments after the huddle seemed to break up, the doorknob rattled above Ray's head.

The brothers looked at each other. Ray slid his Mark II combat dagger, already responsible for one death this evening, from its sheath in his boot.

"Jesus Christ," the man on the other side of the door said, mostly to himself. Then, louder: "Anyone got the key to this closet? Door's locked, for some fuckin' reason."

The call for a key bounced around the cavernous room from man to man, some close by, some so distant they could barely be heard. There was more than one additional rhetorical inquiry regarding why the fuck the door was locked in the first place, until finally it was announced over the Mill's PA system that someone with a key was on his way. In a crouch, Normand moved past the body and joined his brother at the door, his own knife—a modified Mark II with serrations halfway up the double blade—drawn and ready to slash in a reverse grip.

"I tink I have an answer," Ray whispered to Normand. The brothers stood, slowly and painfully after hours on the floor, and took up positions on either side of the doorframe.

"I tought you weren't talking to me," Normand whispered back.

"Well, it seems like we about to be in de shit," Ray said, "so I figured what de hell, let bygones be bygones."

The brothers grinned at each other. On the other side of the door, the jangling of a sizable key ring announced the arrival of a second party. This person rattled the doorknob briefly, followed by a slightly less crazed jangling of keys as he tried to find the one that unlocked the door. After a few moments this sound ceased without anyone actually trying to open the closet.

"What's the problem?" the man who'd discovered the door locked in the first place said.

"What am I standing in right now?" Keyring asked.

A pause. "Shit, it's on my shoes, too."

"What is it?"

"Probably fluid from the roller. When it shit the bed."

"How would that get way over here?"

"How should I know? Someone tracked it over, probably."

Another pause. "Except there are no tracks," Keyring said. "It's just a puddle. And it looks like blood."

"It's oil from the roller. C'mon, open the door already."

Another pause. "This smell like oil to you?"

"I didn't call you over here to play Columbo. Open the door."

"I don't know, man," Keyring said. "I think we should get security first."

"Give me the keys, and I'll open it."

As a minor scuffle broke out over the keys, inside the closet Normand whispered, "So what's your answer?"

"You tink it matters now?"

"Not once dat door opens," Normand said. "But I'd still like to hear it."

"We have to take de body wit us," Ray said, "because murder would be an escalation de police could not ignore. Babs's arrangement wit de cops depends on no one getting killed."

"Dere's my brudder!" Normand said. "Nice to have you back, Ray."

"I knew it all along," Ray said. "I was just fucking wit you."

"Likely story."

Outside, the scuffle ended in defeat for Keyring.

"Normie," Ray said.

"What?"

A key hit the lock, tried and failed to turn the tumblers, then pulled back out with a sound like the zipper on a sweatshirt.

"I'm sorry I fucked up," Ray said.

Another key, another failure.

"It's done, Raymond. Let's just get ready for what's coming now, yeah?"

"Roger dat."

The brothers freshened their grips on the knives and flexed their knees, ready to spring, as a third key rattled in the lock unsuccessfully.

"*Tabarnak*, find de right one already," Ray said. "Let's get dis over wit."

Just as the fourth key zippered into the lock, a much louder sound began, seemingly everywhere at once, above and around them on both sides of the door, and this sound was accompanied by a minute but palpable rumbling of the concrete beneath their feet. Within a few seconds the whirring of the previously broken roller was at full throttle, a crushing, seismic hum, and the brothers' eyes went from the doorknob to each other and back again several times, straining to hear if there were still more keys being tried, waiting for the door to be thrown open at any moment. After a full minute they realized that, for now at least, they'd lucked out.

Where only a few minutes before they'd been whispering almost subaudibly, with the roller running again they needed to shout at one another to be heard.

"Now what?" Ray said to his brother.

Normand sheathed his blade and shrugged. "Now," he said, "we back to de same problem we started wit." He nudged the body on the floor with a foot, then glanced at his watch. "And it's four in de morning, so we got two hours to figger it out."

CHAPTER FOURTEEN

Claude had checked everything five or six times, and he still couldn't get himself to leave.

Sophie's nightstand wasn't near big enough to hold everything she needed, so Claude had brought in a TV tray and set it lengthwise against the side of the bed, forming, along with the nightstand, a kind of L-shaped table. On it: her pill organizer; two insulated travel mugs, one with plain black tea, hot, one with cherry Kool-Aid on ice; a sixty-four-ounce plastic Dunkin' Donuts cup filled with water (the pain meds had proven to cause dry mouth of biblical intensity); a thirty-two-ounce glass bottle of lemon-lime Gatorade; a jumbo pack of Chubs baby wipes (with aloe) for cleaning around Sophie's incisions; a translucent plastic sleeve of saltine crackers (though she still had little appetite); a stack of *Reader's Digests* and *People* magazines resting atop a V. C. Andrews hardcover; a plastic device called a spirometer Sophie was supposed to breathe through five times a day to ward off pneumonia; a package of Ex-Lax and a bottle of milk of magnesia for purposes that did not require mentioning; and a pen and notepad for Sophie to write down anything worth reporting to either Claude or the doctors. She had a total of eight pillows, an aluminum walker for getting back and forth to the bathroom, and a bedpan in case she couldn't get to the bathroom in time. Rounding out her at-hand supplies were two boxes of gauze bandages, a roll of medical tape, and a pair of scissors pilfered from the kitchen junk drawer, all in case she popped a stitch or otherwise needed to change the dressings on her incisions.

Instead of leaving the house for the first time since they'd come home, as he was supposed to have done twenty minutes earlier, Claude busied himself with checking, once again, the pill organizer, as if he hadn't already confirmed it was correctly filled with enough medication to last Sophie for a week. He'd filled it from the twenty-odd bottles of medication he'd brought home from the pharmacy the day before, cyclosporine and prednisone to prevent Sophie's body from attacking the new kidney, Vicodin and Tylenol to mute her pain, Zantac to keep her from developing stomach ulcers, captopril to tamp down her blood pressure, and on and on. But he seemed to have developed, in the wake of the transplant, a kind of late-onset obsessive-compulsive disorder. No amount of confirming even the least urgent thing—the time of her first follow-up appointment in Boston, for example, which wasn't for three weeks—seemed to be enough. And he was starting to get on Sophie's nerves, even through the narcotized fog that had marked the days since she'd woken up with her brother's kidney inside her.

Later—and for decades afterward—Sophie would recall with shame her desire to be rid of Claude. Her need for a few hours' solitude, her need to just *be*, and be alone, would come to seem petty, foolish, plain stupid. She would tell herself there was no way to have known this was the last time she would see her husband. She would tell herself that anyone, having endured what she'd endured not just in the past week but for the past few years, would have needed a little time to themselves. But hadn't she been told, over and over, ever since her childhood, by those older and wiser than she, to hug people tight and always tell them you loved them, even if they were just running out to grab a loaf of bread, because *you never did know*? Hadn't she understood better than most that Claude and the kids and everyone else she loved were always a breath away from disappearing forever?

Yes, she had known, even in this moment. And yet. "Claude," she said, her voice a rasp. "Would you please just *go*?"

Claude looked over his shoulder at her, smiled, his eyes soft. "In a minute," he said.

"That's what you said half an hour ago," Sophie complained. She propped herself against the pillows with a grimace. "You're making me crazy. And I don't have the energy for crazy, right now."

"I'll be out of here sooner," Claude said, "if you stop distracting me so I can make sure all this is right."

"It's right. You've checked two dozen times."

"That's an exaggeration."

"Claude."

"Okay, all right," he said, closing a compartment with a snap and setting the organizer back in its spot on the nightstand carefully, to avoid pushing any of the other items off onto the floor. He half turned to her. "You have everything you need?"

"Everything I need, and a few things I don't. Git."

"Okay. Hey, listen, one thing."

Sophie groaned.

"I'm leaving, I swear. I just want to tell you: I talked with Rheal yesterday, and I think we might get our jobs back soon. The scabs have started leaving, and it seems like a trickle might become a flood."

"Because Babs and Rheal are driving them off?"

"They're scabs, Soph. Fair game."

"I know," she said wearily. "I'm just . . . listen, I hope you're right. I hope the scabs go home and you get your jobs back and we can forget all about the last two years."

"Back to normal," Claude said. "Won't be long now."

They sat smiling at one another.

"So," Sophie said after a moment, "you were leaving."

"I, uh, yeah," Claude said. "I guess I was. You're okay?"

"I know how it looks, but I feel better than I have in years," Sophie said. She put a hand on his shoulder. "I'm okay. I'm good. You can go. You *have* to go."

Claude placed his own hand over hers, and nodded.

"Or else I'm going to murder you," Sophie said.

They shared a laugh. And then Claude kissed his wife on the forehead and walked out of their home for the rest of time.

At the same moment, only a few streets away, Babs was already in a bad mood, having been made aware of the Saucier brothers' colossal fuckup before she'd even had a chance to pour her first cup of coffee. She didn't care about the dead man—all of Aucoin's shitstick mercenaries could rot in hell as far as she was concerned, particularly those of Franco extraction who should have known better than to fight their own people. But she did care about maintaining her arrangement with Bates, and she cared about keeping pressure on the scab workers at the Mill, as well as not giving the FBI any more reason to continue skulking around the neighborhood. In all these respects, a dead body was pretty much the last thing she needed on her bingo card. And yet, Rheal's batshit friends had produced one, so it had to be dealt with. Babs dispatched the Sauciers north, with instructions to sink the corpse in the deepest part of the Allagash River and do so in a manner that there was no chance it would ever come back up. Then, finally, as the Sauciers left with the body wrapped in a tarp in the bed of their truck, Babs poured her coffee, half hoping as she did that the brothers would fall in the drink, too, and never come back.

She sat in her usual chair at the kitchen table, and Henri the cat leaped into her lap and settled there. Rheal sat with his own coffee, keeping his mouth shut for the moment, trying to figure out when and whether to broach yet another subject that was going to piss her off. Some of her ire at the Sauciers was on him, he knew, if for no other reason than that they were his buddies and as such, in Babs's mind, the dead man was his responsibility as well as theirs. So he was already working from a considerable deficit where her patience was concerned. Babs never made an effort to hide her displeasure, and now, as they sat in silence and sipped their coffee, he could practically see the black cloud that hung over her head. Under normal circumstances he would consider himself lucky she wasn't already reading him the riot act, and keep to himself.

At the same time, Rheal knew that Claude would arrive at the house any minute, and Babs would of course want to know for what purpose he had been summoned. As he sat there, Rheal thought about the possibility of just not telling her, having Claude do his new job without Babs knowing. But he realized, even as he considered this, that it wouldn't work. First and foremost, no matter how discreet Claude was, Babs would figure it out. Second, Rheal did not make a habit of lying to or otherwise keeping his wife in the dark, and now, with everything that was swirling around them, was not the time to start. He would tell her, and she would either accept it or not, and regardless Claude would do what Rheal asked him to do, and that would be that.

Still, he had to actually tell her and at the moment, stealing a glance at Babs as she stewed, Rheal would have been more inclined to jump out of a perfectly good airplane with no chute. At the same time, he was a man who quickly lost patience with hemming and hawing, and so:

"*Ma puce*," he said.

"No."

"No, what?" Rheal asked.

"You only ever call me that when you're trying to butter me up," Babs said. "And at the moment, I'm in no mood to be buttered."

"Clearly," Rheal said, trying a smile. "But there's something we need to talk about."

"Then talk, if you must," Babs said, staring at him.

Rheal cleared his throat. "Things are getting dangerous," he said.

"You think?"

"And now they'll only get more so. Aucoin's boys are going to do a head count sooner or later, and when they do they'll realize someone's gone missing."

"Why are you telling me things I already know?" Babs asked. "Get to your point, Rheal."

He looked at her steadily. "Until further notice," he said, "I don't want you to be alone. Particularly around town."

Babs didn't respond. Another person might have imagined she'd been stunned into silence, but Rheal knew better: she was indicating her complete rejection of what he'd said by refusing to acknowledge that he'd said it.

"Obviously," he said, "I know you can take care of yourself."

"It would seem otherwise," Babs said.

"You know Claude's back from Boston . . . ," Rheal said.

"Claude?"

"I trusted him with my own life," Rheal said. "I trust him with yours."

"I wouldn't trust him to feed the cat."

Rheal put his mug down, hard, and the cat in question fled the room. "For once in your life," Rheal said, "can you try to accept someone's judgment other than your own?"

"That's nonsense," Babs said. "I trust your judgment, which I demonstrate all the time."

"Okay, so which part are you sticking on here?" Rheal asked, pulling his cigarettes from his breast pocket. "My judgment that you should have a bodyguard, or my judgment that it should be Claude?"

"Both."

Rheal smiled and shook his head. He lit a cigarette and spoke with it still between his teeth. "Listen, I know you're pissed about the dead guy—"

"*Pissed?* Your yahoo friends *killed* someone, Rheal. And now you're asking me to trust another of your yahoo friends to keep *me* from getting killed."

Rheal looked at her. "I'm not asking," he said.

"I'm sorry, what?"

"It's just us here, *chérie*, so I hope you're ready for some real talk." Rheal tapped his cigarette in the ashtray. "We're doing this thing, you and me. A life of crime, I guess you could say. We've started it and there's no going back. And it's going to take a level of trust and understanding that, forgive me for saying it, you and I don't seem to have lately."

Babs just gazed at him. If she had any kind of internal reaction to his words, she was careful not to show it.

"Claude said something the other day that's stuck with me," Rheal said. "He told me the way Soph has been sick the last few years, it's like they're living in different worlds. Like they can't reach, or even see, each other. And I realized when he said it that that's how things have felt between us, too. With them, the explanation is obvious: Soph is sick and Claude isn't, and that drives a wedge neither one of them intends. With us, I don't really know what's going on—except that it isn't me."

Babs's face remained frozen.

"I've made my peace with it, Babs," Rheal said. "Whatever's going on with you, whatever you won't let me in on, it's ultimately your business. But protecting you? Particularly from yourself? That's *my* business, whether you like it or not. And there's nobody in the world I trust to do it more than Claude. So you can accept it or not, but either way, it's happening. You owe me that, at least."

Babs continued to stare, expressionless as a doughnut.

"That's it, I guess," Rheal said. "You can speak now."

"Okay," Babs said.

"Okay, what?"

"Okay, thanks for permission to speak, okay I'll accept being babysat, okay I'll accept that my babysitter is Claude, okay I love you."

Rheal smiled. "That's great," he said, "because he should be here any minute."

Cardinal Bernard Francis Law of the Boston Archdiocese believed in making himself available to just about anyone whenever possible, a man of eminent approachability despite his high station. As such, he would, as a matter of policy, take a private meeting with a rank-and-file priest if one was requested, when most cardinals wouldn't let themselves be bothered, considering such a chore to be the responsibility of the bishop. He'd agreed to such a meeting, today's two o'clock, before realizing who exactly he was meeting *with*—Father Joseph Brennan, a name that had made a small part of Law's brain tingle with recognition when it first came across his desk the day before, but for reasons he'd been unable to place. Now, of course, he remembered: Brennan was a pederast, one of seemingly dozens that Law had been juggling ever since taking over the archdiocese, pulling them off assignments and sending them to treatment centers and halfway houses, putting out fires with parents and other clergy, the police, and unscrupulous lawyers eager to make a buck off of other people's suffering, and reinstating those priests who appeared to respond well to treatment and counseling. Sometimes it seemed that the bulk of his work was taken up, one way or another, with these sick and unfortunate men and the pain and grief and loss of faith they left in their wake.

Law's was hardly the only archdiocese with such problems, but there were few where the problem seemed more rampant. He'd gone to Rome the previous year for a closed-door meeting called by John Paul II himself on the matter. Prior to the meeting, Law had formed an alliance with the cardinal of Chicago and the archbishop of Los Angeles to raise the issue of what they considered an impossible paradox: the clash between the imperative that abusive clergy be removed permanently from the priesthood, and the unspoken expectation that cardinals and bishops prioritize protecting the Church and its reputation above all else.

Those assembled at the Vatican had, in their wisdom, declined to address this paradox.

And now here Law was, waiting to receive a man who should

have been defrocked without ceremony and sent to prison years ago, a man who came to him still wearing the clerical collar, a man who was supposedly changed, cured, however you wanted to put it, and now desired an audience with him for God knew what purpose.

Law's secretary, Clarice, poked her head in the door and announced that Brennan had arrived.

"Send him in," Law said, making no effort to seem any more enthusiastic than he felt.

A few moments later Clarice held the door open for Brennan and closed it soundlessly behind him.

Brennan bowed deeply at the waist. "Your Eminence," he said.

"Father Brennan," Law said. "Please, sit." He gestured toward the cream-colored armchairs on the opposite side of his desk.

Brennan crossed the carpeted floor briskly. "I don't intend to take much of your time today, Eminence," he said as he sat.

"Not at all," Law said. "What can I do for you, Father? It must be something important, for you to drive all the way from Maine with such urgency."

"I want to speak with you about Father Clement Thibault," Brennan said.

"I'm afraid I don't know who that is, off the top of my head," Law said.

"Formerly of Notre Dame Parish in Waterville, Maine, where I now preside. Bishop O'Leary suspended him a few weeks ago."

"What's the name again?"

"Clement Thibault," Brennan said. "He'd been at Notre Dame for fifteen years."

"Okay," Law said. "What about this Thibault did you want to discuss?"

"I believe he should be reinstated without delay, Eminence," Brennan said.

Cardinal Law paused, studying Brennan's face. "I don't understand," he said finally. "You're already in place at Notre Dame, aren't you?"

"I am. But I've decided I can no longer be clergy, Eminence. And even if I could, the congregants at Notre Dame don't like or trust me. Though I didn't ask him, I assume it took Father Thibault years to earn their trust. And now, perhaps more than ever, that community needs its priest."

Law leaned forward and put his forearms on the desk. "Well, this is now two things for us to discuss, not one. Leaving the priesthood is a serious matter, it goes without saying."

"That's decided, Eminence," Brennan said. "There's no need for us to talk about it."

Law, in fact, by this point, didn't wish to continue discussing *anything* with Brennan. The whole thing was making him uneasy, and he wanted to be shut of it.

"The people of the parish trust and love him," Brennan went on. "He deserves to be reinstated."

"If the bishop saw fit to suspend Thibault," Law said, "no doubt it was with good reason."

"He was supporting a labor strike," Brennan said. "There are greater sins, I'm sure you'll agree."

"Ah, I remember now," Law said. "Yes. The bishop had given Thibault explicit instructions, more than once, to not weigh in publicly on the strike. And Thibault defied those instructions. Coming out in support of a strike is one thing. Disobeying your bishop is quite another."

"Father Thibault attended to me selflessly and without being asked," Brennan said. "He offered a grace that no one else in the Church would. Namely, to give me absolution despite the fact that I don't deserve it in the least. He saw past his disgust, and saved me."

Law cleared his throat. "So if I'm clear," he said, "you're asking me to take the recommendation of a child molester, and reinstate a priest that the bishop saw cause to remove. Is that correct?"

"That's the easy way to do it, Eminence, yes," Brennan said.

Law frowned, not just uneasy now, but irritated. "And what's the hard way?"

Brennan didn't hesitate. "I'll tell anyone who will listen what I was guilty of. Under your watch."

Law's mind refused, at first, to process what he was being told. This man was going to out *himself*? That couldn't be. "I'm sorry?" he asked.

"You heard me, Eminence," Brennan said. "I will tell everything I did, and everything I know. How I was not just allowed to continue being a priest, but given my own parish again. And how at Southland I was not alone. Except in opting for chemical castration. Most of the others had no interest in that whatsoever. Yet they, too, have been allowed to continue ministering."

"What are you thinking?" Law asked. "*Are* you thinking? They'll throw you in prison."

"Maybe," Brennan said. "And maybe that's where I belong. But it's up to you to decide. And I need an answer before I leave here today."

Law stared at him. "Are you putting an ultimatum to me?"

"If that's how you choose to think of it, Eminence." Brennan stood and smoothed his slacks with his palms. "No doubt you need some time to think," he said. "I'm happy to wait in the reception area until you come to a decision."

The afternoon of Claude's first and last shift guarding Babs, he sat in his pickup outside the Zayre department store, where Babs had stopped for an errand she'd declined to explain to him in any detail other than saying she'd be maybe half an hour. He'd already followed her to Shop 'n' Save, the credit union, and Caswell's Liquidation Center, and now was parked next to her station wagon directly in front of the Zayre entrance. The truck's engine was off but Claude had turned the ignition to ACC so he could listen to WTOS, "the Mountain of Pure Rock," while he waited. He drank coffee, long-since gone cold, from a Styrofoam cup. He used the tip of the corkscrew on his Swiss Army knife to scrape dirt from under his nails. He lit a cigarette, smoked it to the filter, lit another. He was bored, but one of the things war taught a person was that boredom and attentiveness were not mutually exclusive—or at least they better not be, if you meant to survive. He still kept a close eye on the comings and goings at the front of the store, as well as giving every vehicle that parked nearby a once-over. If Rheal thought there was reason to worry, there was reason to worry, so Claude stayed frosty.

And he found, as he waited half an hour and then longer for Babs to emerge from Zayre, that he was happy. Happy to be bored, happy to be useful to his oldest and closest friend, happy that WTOS was playing "Hells Bells" by AC/DC for the fifth time that day. Everything—the gunmetal sky, the tired and dingy facade of the Zayre store, the first few yellowed leaves on the juvenile elm trees in the parking lot dividers—was limned with the glow of new and unexpected hope, the near-assurance that he and Sophie would watch their kids grow up, that they would greet their future grandchildren together, that they might, with any luck, spend their dotage together, side by side on the front porch in matching Canadian rockers.

All of this was wonderfully, improbably within reach. And the hard part was done, or nearly so. Now Claude just had to do whatever he could to help get their jobs back, and everything would be well again.

Babs emerged with plastic Zayre bags in either hand, contents unclear and probably, for Claude's purposes, irrelevant. He smoked as he watched her wait for two cars to cross in front of the store—taking careful note, as he did, of the cars' occupants and general vibe. After the second car passed, Babs stepped down off the walkway and crossed toward her station wagon. Claude's window was cracked to vent smoke, and as she approached, he rolled it the rest of the way down.

"I assume your shopping experience was uneventful?" he asked.

"It was," she said, opening the tailgate and lifting the bags in.

"Where to next?" Claude asked.

"Home," Babs said, smiling. "I'm done for the day."

The smile jolted Claude, though he didn't immediately understand why, and then it came to him: Babs had never, in over a decade, smiled at him that he could remember. "Lead the way," he said after a moment, rolling his window back up.

Babs backed out of her space and Claude did the same, following her to the southern exit of the shopping plaza, where they waited for the light then drove directly across the intersection onto Silver Street. Babs made her way at a leisurely twenty-five mph, past the Daughters of the American Revolution chapter, the Redington Museum, several apartment buildings, and a hair salon. Claude kept one eye on her and the other on traffic approaching in the opposite lane, as well as vehicles waiting to turn off side streets as they passed. Part of his brain was also busy anticipating Babs's most likely route home—she would pass through the light where Silver met Elm Street, then continue another quarter mile and turn left onto Gold Street, which descended into Little Canada.

Thus effectively distracted from the top-line imperative of his job—paying close attention to Babs herself—Claude failed to notice right away when, as the light at the intersection of Silver and Elm flashed yellow, Babs sped up rather than slowing down. She blew through the red doing forty, and Claude hit the gas to run the light himself but had to slam on his brakes when a line of traffic from Elm crossed his front bumper. He watched as, like he'd anticipated, Babs banged a left onto Gold Street and disappeared. Spitting curses around his cigarette, he swung the truck in a half circle and turned immediately down Sherwin, speeding parallel to Babs's path into Little Canada, V-8 bellowing. A cat crossing the street in that leisurely, fuck-you-all cat way broke into a sprint, just making the sidewalk as Claude barreled past.

He reached the bottom of the hill, the Chez Paree on one side, Scottie's Pizza on the other, and made a screeching right onto Water Street, more irritated than alarmed at this point. Even if he couldn't catch up with Babs right away, he would be at the Dionne house within two minutes, and if she thought Claude wouldn't scold her for her carelessness (or gamesmanship, or whatever the hell she was up to), she had another thing coming. As of this moment, speeding around the bend where Water Street straightened out as it entered Little Canada proper, he intended to read her the riot act, chapter and verse. He would follow her into the house to do so, if he had to. That, surely as anything else, was his obligation to Rheal.

Except when he came careening into the driveway, Babs's car wasn't there.

It took a few moments for his mind to process that she'd actually given him the slip. On purpose. For reasons he had no idea about and that she obviously didn't want him to know. And now Claude was going to have to tell Rheal that he'd lost his wife only hours after being asked to guard her in the first place.

At that same moment, Doc Belanger waited in her exam room for Babs, who was already fifteen minutes late. Doc's irritation grew with each glance at the clock above the door, but irritation was mixed with another feeling she couldn't immediately identify—concern, maybe? Dread? Something that created a ball of tension right where her throat met her chest, like she'd swallowed something sideways and it was stuck there. It was possible, of course, that Babs had changed her mind yet again about the abortion; the woman had walked out of her first appointment after she already had her feet in the stirrups, and threatened to beat up a nurse for good measure. So the most obvious conclusion to reach was that she'd had a change of heart this time, too.

But that didn't feel quite right. Doc read people extremely well, an ability honed by decades of intuiting the gap between what her patients told her—about their symptoms, their worries, their diets and drinking habits, their sex and work lives, you name it—and what was really going on. And when Babs had come to her the second time, contrite, chagrined, even a little scared, she had seemed to Doc's eye and ear to be as sure as anyone could be about the decision she'd made. Plus, she'd resolved, through a conversation with Father Clement, the last thing that was keeping her from following through on ending the pregnancy. Otherwise, Doc wouldn't have made the appointment.

And yet: twenty minutes late now.

Doc stood up from the little stool and walked out to the reception desk, where Tonia sat working on the Infinite Stack of Insurance Paperwork. The waiting room was empty, the office, at this point, technically closed.

"She hasn't called?" Doc asked.

Tonia answered without looking up. "You hear the phone ring?"

"I have not," Doc said.

"Then she ain't called," Tonia said, setting aside the file she'd been scribbling in and opening a new one.

Doc moved next to Tonia at the desk and lifted the phone receiver herself, scanning, as she did so, Babs's open file for her number. Doc dialed, waited, listened to it ring, waited, heard the click of the answering machine picking up and Babs's recorded voice: "You've reached 872-758—"

Doc put the receiver back in its cradle. "We'll give her another half hour," she said.

"The Infinite Stack of Insurance Paperwork is, by definition, infinite," Tonia said, still not looking up.

Instead of returning to the exam room, Doc Belanger went to her office in the back of the building. While it was true that Tonia could stay there until the universe collapsed and still not be done with her work, Doc intended to send her home when the half an hour had passed. She, on the other hand, was going to stick around until she got some sense, one way or another, of what was going on with her patient. Because something wasn't right. She'd known Babs longer than literally anyone else on earth, having been the physician who delivered her, and Babs didn't flake. Plus, after the winding path Babs and Doc had walked together to arrive at this day, the very least Doc expected was a phone call by way of explanation. So something was up. And Doc would keep waiting, and keep calling, until she found out what.

For whatever reason, Rheal had felt like drinking somewhere he didn't know every bit of bathroom graffiti verbatim, so instead of the Chez Paree or You Know Whose Pub, he'd driven uptown to Pete & Larry's, a nightclub favored by rednecks from the constellation of townships that surrounded Waterville because it sat at the northern edge of the city and as a result one was less likely to get picked up by Waterville cops for drunk driving at closing time. Rheal had two hours or so before he needed to be out on the road covering Carmeline, Bernette, and Rita, and he intended to spend it drinking whiskey alone at Pete & Larry's bar. But he only got half an hour to himself before Kittel straddled the stool next to his and ordered a Bud Light.

"Normally," Rheal said, stirring his whiskey rocks with one finger, "I'm pretty on top of when I'm being tailed."

"You get tailed a lot?" Kittel asked.

"Not lately."

"It's maybe something you should get used to again, in your new line of work," Kittel said.

"I didn't know the FBI had jurisdiction in small-town drug cases."

"We don't," Kittel said. He put a five down as the bartender arrived with his beer. "And I couldn't care less about that."

"Then why are you following me?"

Kittel dug one big hand into the bowl of bar snacks to his right. "I put in a request yesterday for files on ten priests, including Brennan," he said. "Today, instead of the files I get a call from the executive assistant director—who, I can assure you, had no idea I existed before my request hit his desk."

"Movin' on up," Rheal said, indicating with a nod and raised eyebrow that Kittel should slide the bar snacks his way, which Kittel did.

"He gives me a twenty-minute lecture," Kittel said, "about how my job is not to freelance, my job is to investigate the things my superiors hand down to me, no more and no less. That I don't get paid to be creative, or to make more work when we have plenty of outstanding cases waiting for someone to figure them the fuck out."

"That a direct quote? 'The fuck out'?"

"I ask myself," Kittel said, "why would the executive assistant director take twenty minutes of his day to chew my ass about this?"

"You looking for my input?"

"I've reached my own conclusions, but shoot."

"Sounds to me like your boss's boss's boss is worried you might find something he doesn't want found," Rheal said.

"Bingo," Kittel said. He took a swig of beer. "But. There's another question that comes right on the heels of the first one: Why? Why would he be so keen to make sure I don't start sniffing around a bunch of priests?"

"You looking for my input?"

"This time, yeah."

"You must be a Protestant," Rheal said.

"I assume you won't hold that against me."

"I one hundred percent will," Rheal said. "But reason I ask is you don't seem aware of just how influential the Catholic Church is."

"Never really thought about it."

"Well," Rheal said, popping a pretzel into his mouth, "now you know."

Kittel lifted the bottle to his lips, held it there, pondering.

"I think of it this way," Rheal said. "Power protects power. They can't help themselves—it's a reflex. The upper reaches of the FBI are going to cover for the upper reaches of the Church, just as surely as it covers for criminal yuppie assholes on Wall Street, or anyone else with enough money that it makes questions of legality irrelevant."

"Seems like you've spent a lot of time thinking about this kind of thing," Kittel said.

"I bore easily." Rheal grabbed another handful of snacks. "You still haven't said why you're following me."

"Haven't I?"

"Nope."

"You see this?" Kittel asked. He took a yellowed, brittle slip of paper from one of the photo sleeves in his wallet and laid it carefully on the bar. Written on the paper, in elegant cursive, were a dozen or so names.

"I do," Rheal said. "What is it?"

"My grandmother's scab list. From the Chicago garment workers' strike, 1910."

"No shit," Rheal said, leaning down for a closer look.

"You'll notice all the names are of men," Kittel said. "That's because the women walked out first and the men refused to support them, stayed on the job. Some came around eventually, but these ones didn't. My grandmother got her head split open and lost the use of one of her hands fighting in the streets. And she was not a woman inclined to forgive."

"I know a woman like that," Rheal said.

"So when she got old, she gave my father this list she'd been carrying around for forty years, with instructions to stomp anyone he ever met from any of these families. And he did. And then, eventually, he gave the list to me."

"That's a long time to hold a grudge."

"Solidarity forever," Kittel said. "I played football with three guys who were related to the men on this list, and I had to keep the fact that we were buddies from my grandmother. She would have had my balls."

Rheal laughed and polished off his drink. Across the room, a band was setting up for an evening of classic-rock covers, lugging amps, guitar cases, parts of a drum kit.

Kittel shifted gears. "There was an old lady I interviewed last week in Little Canada who said something I've been troubling over ever since. She told me I serve a master other than the law."

"What do you suppose she meant?" Rheal asked, waving a hand to get the bartender's attention, then pointing down at his glass.

"Well, all this is related, right?" Kittel said. "Power protects power. If my boss's boss's boss is helping shield child molesters, then so am I."

Rheal looked at Kittel, pausing a moment before he responded. "It's a hell of a thing, isn't it," he said, "when you realize 'America the Beautiful' is just a tune they play to get you to do awful things without thinking too hard about it."

"You remember when you first had that realization?"

"I do," Rheal said, and did not elaborate any further.

"I don't give a shit about the workers you've taken," Kittel said, "as long as they keep coming back with all their anatomy in the right place. Scabs are scabs. Just don't make it impossible for me to ignore this. Don't fucking kill anybody."

"I'll do what I can," Rheal said.

"That's not very reassuring."

"Look, the stakes are mortal here," Rheal said. "Your grandmother understood that. We didn't choose this fight, and we didn't set the terms. But we're going to see it through, whatever comes."

"I have no doubt," Kittel said. He upended his beer and drained it, glanced around. "This place is kind of a shithole, huh?"

"If it's white tablecloths you're after, you'll need to head to Portland," Rheal said. The bartender arrived and poured whiskey. "You want another one?" Rheal asked Kittel. "On me."

"Nah, I should go. When I hang around bars longer than one drink, I tend to wake up the next day feeling like every decision I've ever made was the wrong one."

Kittel rose from his stool just as Claude came in. He stopped inside the front door, scanned the barroom like a quarterback being blitzed, then came over to them at a jog, shoving other patrons aside as he went.

"For Christ's sake," Rheal said to no one in particular. "What the fuck is this."

"Someone you know?" Kittel asked.

"Someone who's very much supposed to be somewhere other than here," Rheal said.

A moment later, Claude stood before Rheal and Kittel, breathing hard. He looked at Kittel, unsure what, if anything, to say in front of him.

"Speak," Rheal said. "Don't make me guess."

"I lost her," Claude said.

CHAPTER FIFTEEN

Acting chief Bates was acting again, though forced to do so, for another week, from the La-Z-Boy in his living room. Still heavily doped up and arguably of questionable judgment as a result, he probably should have taken that time off, too. But there was no way he was letting Farley run things for a minute longer than necessary. Not that Farley was incompetent, but things were just too volatile and fluid for Bates to wait any longer to resume his duties.

And as stressful and insane as this new, decidedly illegal enterprise had already become, Bates was glad of the distraction from how he felt. He'd anticipated, of course, the pain and physical infirmity that would follow having one of his kidneys yanked out, but what he hadn't counted on—and what none of the supposed experts had mentioned—was the mental effect, currently far more agonizing than the physical. It was as though in giving away a kidney, the part of Bates's brain that experienced pleasure, the part that anticipated the possibility of a happy future, had turned off. Gone dark. Everything seemed futile, utterly without a point, and he had no idea why or what to do about it. He couldn't recall ever feeling so bereft. He was depressed, in a word, though Bates wouldn't have known to call it that and likely wouldn't have accepted it if he had known. This was the '80s, after all; men generally, and men like Bates in particular, did not suffer *mental illness.* That was a tag only properly applied to the schizophrenics and psychotics and other unfortunate souls who had been released en masse from asylums all over the country a decade back, and that cops from coast to coast had been dealing with ever since.

Melinda came into the doorway between the living room, where Bates sat, and the kitchen. "Farley's here," she said. "How you feeling?"

Bates tried a smile. "Not bad," he said.

"You're a lousy liar," Melinda said. "I'll tell him he's got five minutes."

She disappeared into the kitchen again. Bates coughed gingerly, shifted a little in his chair. All this sitting. He was half convinced he'd need to send Melinda to the pharmacy for diaper rash cream soon.

Farley came in wearing his patrol uniform and jacket, looking as though someone had just run over his dog.

"Chief," he said. "How are you doing?"

"Not as shitty as you, by the looks of it," Bates said. "Why the long face?"

"More trouble at the Mill," Farley said.

"I bet you're glad I'm back."

"It's just a rumor, as of now," Farley said.

"Tell me," Bates said.

"One of the guys they brought in from Lewiston, for security, has gone missing," Farley said.

"Okay," Bates said. "That's, what, the fourth person Babs has taken? They always come back. What's the big deal?"

Farley looked chagrined, as though somehow he was personally responsible for what he had to report to his boss. "Well, they found blood, Chief. A lot of it."

"*Inside* the Mill?"

"Affirmative," Farley said.

"Fucking Christ," Bates said, struggling up out of the lounger. Farley half moved to lend a hand, then backed up again, gladly, when Bates waved him off.

"How long?" Bates asked. Upright now, he put his hands on his hips and caught his breath.

"Call came in from the shift manager fifteen minutes ago."

"And they were told not to touch anything? You've got officers over there?"

"Cordoning the room off as we speak."

"Good," Bates said. "Get my coat out of that closet. You're driving."

"You sure you should be going anywhere like this, Chief?"

"I'm sure," Bates said. "We've got to do an A-plus job of making this look good, or we're going to be in deep shit. I swear to Christ, that woman is bound and determined for us all to end up in state-issued jumpsuits."

Just as Bates had returned to the job, so had Father Clement returned to his, against all logic and without explanation from the people who'd made the decision. The previous afternoon had been like any other, Clement at his little desk in the basement, when Father Doyon clomped halfway down the stairs and announced a call had come in and Clement was to report as soon as humanly possible to Notre Dame in Waterville.

Clement at first assumed he'd misheard the wheezy old priest, and he rose from his seat and went to the foot of the stairs and asked Doyon to repeat himself. Father Doyon, fully given over to the impatience of extreme old age, made a show of coming down several more stairs, his lame right leg bonking each of the risers as though itself made of wood. Eyes wide with comic exasperation, Doyon looked at Clement and said, "You got your job back, jerkoff. That clear enough?" Then he executed something like a six- or seven-point turn, *clomp clomp clomp*, and began the long, slow ascent of the stairs again.

Clement, for his part, once he'd processed the actuality of his return to Waterville, had wasted no time. He left a message with Heron that he would no longer be reachable at the storage facility, packed his secondhand hockey bag, and walked into Portland proper to rent a car for the hour's drive north. And now here he was in Waterville, daylight having confirmed the impression he'd gotten when calling on Brennan that the rectory was entirely unchanged. It was as if the place had been vacant in Clement's absence. No trace of Brennan existed—except a note, addressed to Clement, left on the entryway table.

It was through this note—only two handwritten lines—that Clement gleaned the first and perhaps only clue he would get regarding why he suddenly had his old job back. In the opening line, Brennan thanked Clement for saving his eternal soul when no one else could be bothered. In the second, Brennan expressed confidence that, as long as he was still drawing breath, Clement's position at Notre Dame was secure.

He offered no further elaboration on this point.

After rereading Brennan's note several times over coffee, Clement unpacked his few belongings, took a shower, and resumed his priestly garments, still hanging in the bedroom closet, like a superhero's uniform forsaken in a crisis of confidence and now reclaimed: black slacks, black oxford, white tab collar. He checked himself in the mirror on the back of the closet door, decided that he hadn't entirely forgotten how to look the part. But then he realized: He had no idea what he could or should do next. He did not know what was happening in Little Canada, or who might benefit from his presence and counsel. But he did know where he could most quickly find out.

Sophie was startled out of an uneasy sleep by the shrill jangle of the pink rotary phone on Claude's nightstand. She glanced at the clock radio, saw the red digital readout said 9:30, and at first imagined it was 9:30 at night. But a few things didn't add up. For one, she had a distinct if drug-fogged memory of waiting for Claude to come home until at least 10 p.m. before drifting off. For another, it was light out. She looked more closely as the phone continued to ring and saw the little red dot to the right of the numbers, which indicated p.m., was off. It was 9:30 in the morning, and Claude still wasn't home, and it had been long enough since her last dose of painkillers that merely sliding across the bed to reach for the handset nearly caused her to cry out.

"Hello?" she gasped, collapsing onto her back and trying to untangle the forever-tangled cord that attached the handset to the base.

"Soph." Claude's voice, cool salve on a burn. "You okay?"

"Where are you? It's past nine in the morning."

"I know what time it is," Claude said, and now Sophie heard

the darkness in his tone. "Something's come up. Are you all right? Do you have everything you need?"

"What's happening, Claude?"

"Babs is missing."

"Why is that our problem?"

"Soph."

"Really, Claude."

"Because I was supposed to keep an eye on her."

Sophie felt her breath catch in her chest. "Are you . . . in *trouble*?"

"No, nothing like that," Claude said. "I just have to help look for her. The Sauciers are coming back down to help out, too. Carmeline, Bernette, Stella, Rita. It's all-hands-on-deck."

"Okay," Sophie said. "Well, I'm probably going to need someone to help with a few things before the day's out—"

"I called your mother already," Claude said. "She should be on her way there by now. Said she'd head over once she got the kids off to school."

A moment's quiet between them. "Okay, well," Sophie said.

"I'll be home as soon as I can," Claude said.

"You sure you're not in trouble?" Sophie said.

"I'm sure," Claude said. "This is on Babs. She gave me the slip on purpose."

Another pause. "Okay," Sophie said. "At least call me when you can."

"Don't worry, Soph," Claude said, and hung up. It was the last time they would speak.

Privately, Claude did not feel so certain that he was in the clear with Rheal. He knew he *should* be—Babs had, after all, deliberately lost him, that was the plain truth, and it was hard to successfully tail someone when they pretended to be a willing surveillance subject but were not. But the emanations from Rheal as they searched through the night had been darker and more volatile than anything Claude'd ever seen from his oldest and closest friend, even at war. He was put very much in mind of the worst possible thing: Rheal's father, Phillipe, as nasty and conscienceless a man as Claude had ever had the misfortune to know. All night, as they searched, whenever Claude looked at Rheal he saw Phillipe; it was something to do with the eyes, as if the father, denied entrance to either heaven or hell, had come back to possess his son's body. And though Rheal hadn't yet turned to blaming Claude for Babs's absence, Claude knew that the longer she was missing, the more likely that was to happen.

Now, this morning, as they sat at the kitchen table gulping black coffee, their hair mussed and clothes rumpled, Rheal asked him to explain once again what had happened.

More than a little indignant, Claude thought to tell Rheal he didn't appreciate being cross-examined. He knew Rheal was asking to hear his story for the eighth time not because he couldn't remember it from the first seven, but to seek out the inconsistencies that inevitably cropped up when someone told a lie over and over, and that was a bunch of bullshit, as far as Claude was concerned. But he looked at his friend and saw Phillipe and wisely decided to park his anger.

"We left Zayre," Claude said, shaking a cigarette from his pack and lighting it with his Zippo. He dragged, inhaled sharply, snapped the Zippo shut. "She told me she was heading home. I followed her to the intersection of Silver and Elm, in front of the U. U. Church. Babs blew the light, and for a minute I thought she just wasn't paying attention. Then I realized she's always paying attention, and she'd done it on purpose. She went left onto Gold Street, I flipped a U-turn down Sherwin and right onto Water to cut her off. But I never saw her again. When I got here, she was nowhere to be found. I circled the neighborhood four or five times, nothing. And that's it."

Rheal stared steadily at Claude the entire time he spoke. "Was it four or five?" he asked now, his gaze still unwavering.

"I don't know for sure. I was looking for your wife, not counting laps."

"Why would she want to lose you?"

Claude dragged on the smoke again and tapped it in the ashtray. "I imagine you'd know better than I would," he said.

"What's that supposed to mean?"

"I'm just saying, common sense says if she wanted to lose me it's because she's up to something she doesn't want *you* to know about."

"You were supposed to be keeping her safe, not monitoring her activities."

"That's your perspective. What's hers?"

Phillipe came through his son's glare. "You want to be careful right now how you talk about my wife."

"I'm sorry," Claude said, rolling the cherry of his smoke against the bottom of the ashtray to avoid meeting Rheal's eyes. "I don't know why Babs wanted to lose me. I just know that's what she did."

"So she dropped your tail and spent the entire night . . . where? And for what purpose?"

"I just told you, I don't know."

"Then let me ask you something you do know, Claude," Rheal said. "Where'd the money come from?"

Silence. The air in the kitchen quivered like the moment after a gunshot. Now Claude's eyes caught fire, and he met Rheal's gaze.

"The money for what?" he said.

"You know damn well."

"You just warned me to be careful how I talk about your wife," Claude said. "Now let me return the favor. Do *not* make this about Sophie, Rheal."

"Fine. Just tell me where the money came from."

Claude cursed in French under his breath. "If you're accusing me of something," he said, "you go ahead and come out with it. But I don't think you want to, because you know how ridiculous it'll sound the moment the words leave your mouth."

"I think," Rheal said, "that you gave up my wife to save your own."

"If you really believe that, then we've got nothing else to talk about. But before you do me in, you might want to go into the bathroom and take a look in the mirror. I don't think you'll like what you see."

"And what will I see?"

"The man you hate more than anyone," Claude said. "The man you swore you'd never become."

Rheal looked away, sat back, lit a cigarette, and held it in his lips. He smoked that way, slumped and exhausted, his arms hanging down on either side of the chair.

"Maybe," he said, "the old man was the role model I needed all along. Because we're going to find out where Babs is, Claude, and if it turns out to have something to do with Harold Aucoin, I'm going to assume that's where the money came from. And deal with it exactly like Phillipe would have."

Claude shook his head. "As you wish, friend," he said.

They stared at one another over their coffees, stags in a field ready to lock racks.

And then they both startled at a knock on the door.

Charlie St. Pierre had roughed Babs up pretty good, and taken more than a little pleasure in doing so, especially with her hands bound behind her back so he could work her over at his leisure. Her right eye had swelled completely shut—Charlie being a southpaw—and her left stood at half-mast. Blood from a cut on her brow, courtesy of a rough seam on one of Charlie's gloves, had dried to a crust on her cheek and throat, and her nose had been rendered a pulpy mess useless for breathing, broken in three or four places. But as far as she was concerned, Charlie could do all the damage to her face that he wanted, so long as he didn't get the idea of turning to body shots.

They were in the sticks somewhere—Burnham, maybe, or even farther out, judging by the lack of highway noise—and her holding cell was a post-and-beam barn of mid-nineteenth-century vintage, the kind of structure that regularly went up in flames around the state, owing to hundred-year-old timber's eagerness to burn. As Babs sat alone in the barn, still bound wrist and ankle to an old wooden chair, she experienced a feeling altogether unfamiliar to her—fear. But this fear was not for herself. Because it was clear now: She hadn't waffled back and forth with Doc Belanger and talked to Clement for hours about what happened to an unborn baby's soul because she was trying to reach a decision about whether to keep the pregnancy. She did it to avoid acknowledging that the decision had been made the very moment she saw the blurry little + on the plastic stick weeks earlier. She wanted this baby, and had all along, in spite of herself. With every day that passed, her soul and her heart had been more completely and profoundly hijacked as surely as her body. There was no denying it.

Still, Babs being Babs, she tried. For years, when people had asked why she and Rheal didn't have kids, she'd replied that she loved her children the best way she knew how: by not having them in the first place. She was determined not to inflict life on anyone else. Besides, pregnancy made you weak, pregnancy made you vulnerable physically and emotionally, and this was not a time when she could afford to be any of those things. Worst of all, pregnancy made you *dependent.* In six or seven months she'd be waddling around like a wounded penguin, relying on Rheal for the most basic things and waiting for this person she had never met but would love irrationally, consumingly, to finally arrive and fuck up her judgment for the rest of time. She would not—could not—allow it.

And yet, the feeling persisted, as certain and pure a self-understanding as she'd ever had: She wanted this baby. And she wanted it even more now, bound tight in this barn, beaten up, exhausted, and afraid for her child as she'd never been frightened before.

But what could she do? With no real idea where she was or even how long she'd been there, she could only keep breathing and, whenever Charlie returned for another round, continue to encourage him, with her words and posture, to hit her in the face instead of the belly.

"My suggestion?" Babs's mother said, appearing suddenly on a built-in bench attached to the wall nearest her daughter. "You need to find out who's really in charge. Because it isn't that fat *crétin* who's made such a mess of your face."

"What good will that do?" Babs asked. She turned her head to spit blood onto the dirty floorboards.

"Whoever it is calling the shots, they want something. It's hard to know what they want until you know who they are."

"There's no one else," Babs said. "It's Charlie. And what he wants is for me to be pushing up daisies."

"You're wrong about either one thing or the other."

"What do you mean?"

"Either he's not in charge, or he doesn't want you dead."

"He definitely wants me dead," Babs said.

"Then he's not the one making the decisions," her mother said. "Otherwise, you'd already be in a hole."

Babs thought for a moment. "Oh Jesus," she said. "There's something else."

"You don't have enough problems already?"

"Rheal's going to think Claude had something to do with this."

"Did he?"

"No. But Rheal won't believe that. *Maman*, I've got to tell him."

"Seems to me that brings us back to the original issue," Babs's mother said. "You need to find out who's in charge, and give them what they want in exchange for a phone call. Fast."

The door to the barn rattled open along its track, and a blade of sun sliced through the dusty twilight inside, nearly blinding Babs's one good eye. After a moment the light was eclipsed almost entirely by a hulking shadow like a boulder come to life: Charlie. He slid the door closed behind him and came toward Babs, smiling.

"I need to talk to your boss," Babs said.

"I am the boss," Charlie said. He lifted the blood-crusted leather gloves he wore to protect his hands and slid one on. "It's just you and me here, Babs."

"Bullshit," Babs said. "You're not smart enough to tie your own shoes. Let alone put this operation together."

Without warning, Charlie wound up and unleashed a mammoth left cross to Babs's temple. Her head lolled, and fresh blood gathered and ran down the side of her face as Charlie gloved up his other hand.

"Got any other smart comments you want to make?" Charlie leaned down at the waist, peering at her inquiringly. "No? All talked out? Okay then."

Babs hung her head and breathed as Charlie stood up straight once more, pacing a short, lumbering path around her chair. "Nope," he said, "you're dealing with me, and me alone. Get used to it, and start loving it."

"It's good that you've only got yourself to answer to," Babs said. "Because if you *did* have a boss, I'd hate to think what they'd do when they found out I was ready to give them whatever they wanted, and you didn't put me in touch."

Charlie stopped pacing, his pig eyes registering concern. "What do you think he wants?" he asked.

"I thought there is no 'he'?" Babs said.

"Well, there might be."

"Charlie," Babs said, spitting blood again, "just get Harold on the phone, you half-wit. Before you fuck this up any worse."

Bates and Father Clement had arrived at the Dionne house almost simultaneously, and now the two of them sat having an extremely tense coffee klatch with Rheal and Claude.

"So that's the plan?" Clement asked. "Find out who took her, and kill them?"

"That's the plan," Rheal said.

"How do you know she didn't just disappear for her own reasons?" Clement asked.

"She didn't."

"How do you know?"

Rheal turned his gaze on Clement. "You got something you want to tell me, Father?" he asked.

"I asked a legitimate question, Rheal," Clement said evenly. "Regardless of what I do or don't know."

Claude, for his part, smoked in silence.

"You know I can't let you turn this town into a war zone," Bates said to Rheal. "I'm already dealing with very compelling circumstantial evidence that someone's been murdered."

"Can't have a murder without a body," Rheal said.

"And how can I be assured there won't be a body?"

"You ever try to find something in the Allagash?"

"Don't be cute."

"Trust me," Rheal said. "Even if you knew right where to look, you'd never find it."

"Either way," Bates said, "enough is more than enough. Whatever's happened to Babs, let me deal with it."

Rheal just laughed.

"This is not a request," Bates said. "I can cuff and stuff you right now, if you give me reason."

"You couldn't cuff and stuff a little girl. And if you think I'm leaving this to you and the Keystone Kops, you're out of your mind."

"Listen," Bates said. "If someone took her, why haven't they reached out? Made demands? Asked for a fucking ransom?"

"That's what we're sitting here waiting for," Rheal said.

"And how long has it been?"

All eyes turned to Claude. After a pause he said, "Sixteen, seventeen hours."

"Normally," Bates said to Rheal, "kidnappers don't wait that long to announce their wish list."

"Well, these ones have."

"You've checked your answering machine, naturally," Bates said.

Rheal's flat, impenetrable expression suddenly gave way to something else—a mixture of surprise, embarrassment, and alarm.

"Are you kidding me?" Bates said. "Where is it?"

But Rheal didn't respond. Instead, he stood without a word and headed to the bedroom, and the other men followed.

On Babs's nightstand, next to the phone, the display on the answering machine strobed an urgent red: five messages. The men huddled around as Rheal pushed play.

First—inexplicably, from Rheal's perspective—there were four messages in a row from Doc Belanger asking where Babs was and whether she planned to keep her appointment, but being very careful to offer no hint of what, exactly, the appointment was for. As the third of these messages began to play, Rheal looked at Clement.

"The answer's the same," Clement said. "I can't tell you anything."

And then the fifth and final message played. "Rheal Dionne," a man's voice boomed, faux-friendly, "this is Harold Aucoin. We need to talk about Babs. Call me." *Beep.*

Rheal slammed the stop button and turned to Claude as if they were the only two people in the room. "You want to tell me again," he said, "how my wife just up and disappeared of her own volition?"

WE WILL SEE YOU BLEED

Steve Heron had occasion to reflect, as he cleared his desk into bankers' boxes well after everyone else in the newsroom had gone home, that it was always bound to end this way. The Church that had abided for nearly two thousand years, outlasted pagan chieftains and duplicitous kings, absorbed empires and prosecuted not one or two but eight crusades, and continued to thrive even in the midst of modernity, was not now going to fold because of a single radical reporter from the *Globe.* His bosses had seen to that earlier in the evening, when they'd fired him, officially for repeated insubordination, unofficially for continuing to chase a story literally no one but Heron was interested in knowing about. He'd been given a dozen warnings, more, and now he was out on his ass, and the only surprise was that he'd ever been able to convince himself, in the heat of pursuing the righteous truth, that the world would actually want to hear it.

Not in this lifetime, it turned out.

His bosses' confidence that no one would publish the story was so absolute that Steve had been allowed to pack up at his leisure, without supervision or security, so long as he was gone for good by nine the next morning. He was free to take all his notes and transcripts and drafts, for all anyone cared.

In one bankers' box he'd placed all the things he planned to take and keep: word processor, several coffee mugs, a bunch of random pens and pencils, a stapler he was almost certain he'd bought with his own money, several half pouches of Big League Chew, two framed pictures of dogs he'd owned and lost, a can of Right Guard deodorant, and a paperback copy of *The Essential Lenny Bruce,* which he'd forgotten about and was glad to now have the time to finally finish.

Because fuck it, and fuck them. Someone else could tell this story, when the time was right, if it ever was, but for his part, Heron was washing his hands of the whole thing. To that end, the other bankers' box held every last page of all Steve's work in the previous twelve months: Church records, interview and court transcripts, copies of lawsuit filings and settlements, written intradiocese communications, and so on. Everything cross-checked and collated and cited, every last dot connected for whoever might be in charge of the Spotlight investigative team fifteen years from now.

When he left here for the last time, Heron would take one box home, and the other would go to the nearest branch of the First National Bank of Boston, where Heron would place it in safe deposit. The key would go in an envelope, along with a short note from Heron, and that envelope would be given to a notary public of Heron's acquaintance, along with instructions to deliver it to the head of the Spotlight team on January 1, 1999. Maybe then, enough time would have passed. Maybe then, the right decision-maker would be in charge.

In the meantime, on his way out the door Steve decided to engage in some small, private acts of civil disobedience, a little throwback to his student days. First, he went around the newsroom and into all the managers' offices and removed every writing utensil. When he was finished three hours later, no one at the *Globe* had a single pen or pencil. Then he took a smoke detector with a low battery that had been driving him crazy for weeks, opened a ventilation duct in his former boss's office, and put the smoke detector inside. Finally, he wrote a sign that read NOW VOICE-OPERATED and taped it to the front of the photocopier. And then he stacked his two bankers' boxes one on top of the other, lifted them, and headed to the elevator for the last time.

Babs had no clue how long it had been between when she spooked Charlie into calling Aucoin and Aucoin showing up at the barn. Might have been twenty minutes, might have been two days—she'd browned out after the last beating from Charlie and had fun-house-mirror recollections of coming to a handful of times, or maybe just the one time, or possibly not at all. In fact, she wasn't even sure she was awake now as Harold walked in, flanked by a sober and servile Charlie. Maybe this was a dream, or a hallucination. Maybe she'd died and would spend eternity in this barn. There was no way to know.

As the two of them came in and slid the barn door closed behind them, Babs was struck by another recollection that she hoped quite fervently had been a dream: a feeling like her guts were being twisted by unseen hands and—when she'd managed in her panic to free one of her wrists and looked—blood in her underwear. This memory came back unbidden, and at first she assumed, with relief, that it had been fevered imaginings—until she realized that her left hand was, in fact, no longer bound behind her.

Despite her wooziness and worry, Babs had enough presence of mind to pretend to be unconscious as the two men approached, on the chance they might say something useful believing she couldn't hear.

"Jesus Christ," Aucoin said, "you think you could maybe get her a little closer to dead without actually killing her?"

"I didn't think you'd mind if I had a little fun," Charlie said.

"I don't," Aucoin said. "But the man who's paying for all this will."

Charlie didn't have anything to say to that, but his silence felt swollen with chagrin.

"Wait," Aucoin said. "Is she actually dead?"

"She wasn't when I was in here last," Charlie said.

"Imbécile," Aucoin said. He put two fingers to the side of Babs's throat, felt the thrumming there. Then he took her by the shoulder and shook her. "Babs. Wake up."

She waited through a couple more jostles, then made a show of coming around.

"Do you know where you are?" Aucoin asked her.

"No," she said. "But I didn't to begin with. Charlie here was at least smart enough to blindfold me."

"Miracles never cease," Aucoin said.

"What do you want, Harold?" she asked. "I've got a terrible headache, as you might imagine, and breathing has become something of a chore."

Aucoin glowered at Charlie for a moment, then turned back to Babs. "Maybe you don't remember," he said, "but *you* asked to speak to *me*."

"Ah. So I did," Babs said. "I wanted to ask a favor."

"A favor?" A slight, incredulous rise of the eyebrows. "From me."

"Hard as that might be to believe," Babs said. "After all, like it or not I'm at your mercy. At least for the time being."

"You've always been the consummate realist, Babs. Which is why this conflict between us makes no sense. What's the favor?"

"I'd like to speak to my husband."

Aucoin crossed his arms atop his belly and gazed at her. "Now there's a difficult man to reach," he said. "I had to call him a dozen times before finally getting a call back."

"One imagines he's busy," Babs said.

"Indeed he is," Aucoin said. "He's got big plans."

"Yeah?"

"He said he was going to kill me, my crew, my entire family, all of my friends, every person I've ever had coffee with, anyone who owes me money, and whoever walks my dog."

"And if you'd like to keep that from happening," Babs said, "you should let me talk to him."

Aucoin lowered himself onto the bench where Babs's mother had sat earlier; the old boards popped and groaned under his weight. "What is it that you need to speak with Rheal about so urgently?"

"A private matter. Husband-and-wife stuff."

"Ah, I see. Far be it from me to stick my nose in someone else's marriage," Aucoin said. "But I hope it's nothing to do with Rheal's friend Claude."

Babs stared with her one good eye. "What do you know about it?"

Aucoin examined the nails of his right hand, picking at something he found there. "Back when you sent Claude to break into my house and deliver a message, I thought it would be easy to turn him. I offered him a job, to pay for his wife's medical care, you name it. But the man is incorruptible. There was not enough money on earth, even with his wife so sick, for him to betray you."

Babs continued to stare at Aucoin for a moment, then hung her head.

"Unfortunately, now Rheal is convinced that's exactly what happened," Aucoin said. "He thinks Claude gave you up. Of course, I could have disabused him of the notion. But I didn't want to insert myself into, as you put it, a private matter. So I thought I'd just let two old friends sort it out."

Just outside Lewiston's city limits, Rheal pulled the Mustang into the parking lot of a boat launch with Claude in the passenger seat next to him. The lot was little more than a patch of dirt overlooking the Androscoggin River, no lights and no one else around, although Claude did take note of a U-Haul panel truck parked on the other side of the lot when the Mustang's headlights swept over it.

Rheal shut off the car and turned to Claude.

"You ever have someone you love lie to you, Claude?" Rheal asked.

"Hasn't everyone?" Claude said.

"Who was it?"

"My entire family. For the first eighteen years of my life."

"What kind of lie lasts eighteen years?"

"They lied about me being a Rancourt," Claude said. "Turns out I was adopted."

A pause. "You never told me that," Rheal said.

"I never told anyone that. Not even Sophie. Because it didn't matter. I was raised a Rancourt, and I love my family."

"But it broke your heart, didn't it? That they'd lied to you that whole time?"

"A little, sure."

"Then you know how I felt when you lied to me about selling information to the company," Rheal said. "It wasn't that you did it. It was that you lied about it."

Claude looked around through the Mustang's windows, at the trees and the river draped in night. "We're not going to Aucoin's place, are we?"

"No we are not," Rheal said. He pulled out his pistol and leveled it at his friend. "Give me your weapon, and get out."

Claude reached slowly behind him and pulled out his own 9mm, placing it on the dashboard.

"I said hand it to me," Rheal said.

"Don't worry," Claude said, raising his hands in surrender. "If this is how you're going to play it, Rheal, you'll get no fight from me."

Another pause. Rheal's eyes glazed with tears. He motioned with his gun, waited for Claude to climb out of the car, then opened his own door and followed. "Down to the river," he said, pointing again with the gun.

They walked down the slope, Rheal a step behind Claude, their feet crunching a slow rhythm over gravel. As they approached the water's edge, the Sauciers materialized like wraiths and took up positions on either side of Claude.

"I assume the U-Haul means you got what I asked for?" Rheal said to the brothers.

"Dat is correct," Normand said.

"Turn around, Claude," Rheal said to his friend, and Claude did.

"Let's knock it off with the pageantry," Claude said. "If you're really going to kill me, just go ahead and do it."

Rheal stared at Claude for several seconds, gripping and regripping the pistol.

"Rheal?" Ray said.

"Not interested in talking at the moment, Raymond."

"Well, dat may be, but we need to wedder you like it or not."

Rheal glared at him, and Ray hooked a thumb over his shoulder and walked off toward the trees. After a moment, Rheal followed.

"Are we really doing dis?" Ray asked.

"That's up to Claude," Rheal said.

"No, I'm pretty sure it's up to us."

"If you don't have the stomach for it," Rheal said, "feel free to go."

Ray put a hand on Rheal's shoulder. "You know we're wit you

no matter what," he said. "But dis is crazy, Rheal. Claude is family, sure as you and me."

"Not anymore," Rheal said. "He made a different choice."

Ray looked over at his brother and Claude, then back at Rheal. "You better be damn sure about dat," he said. "What you're about to do, dere ain't no takebacks."

"You think I need to be told?" Rheal asked.

"Just tought someone should say it out loud."

"If there's nothing else, Ray?"

Ray shrugged, and Rheal turned and walked back, Ray trailing a step behind. They rejoined the other men, and for a while no one spoke.

"When you lied to me the first time," Rheal said to Claude finally, "Babs told me I could never trust you again. That if someone's willing to deceive you once, you can never know they won't do it a second time, no matter how sorry they are, no matter how much they regret it. But I told her she was wrong. That it's never that black and white. That people fuck up under tough circumstances and that all the rest of it aside, she just didn't *know* my friend Claude the way I do. We grew up together. We went to war together. We know each other's souls. So I kept you on, and kept trusting you, even when she told me I was a fool, even when she invited me to sleep on the couch. I trusted you with her life, when she insisted I couldn't."

Rheal looked up at the sky, his face locked in silent entreaty like a death mask, and he turned away from them. For several long moments he was still, and then his fists clenched and his arms and shoulders began to tremble with the approach of something terrible that could only be expressed as a scream, and so that's what he did, screamed across the river loud and long enough for God to hear. Neither Claude nor the Sauciers made a sound.

Finally, Rheal turned back to them, and tears had fallen to his cheeks. "But Babs was right," he said. "She always is. You'd think I'd know that by now, nearly six years of being married. But I had to learn one more time: Babs is always right. And now I know what I have to do, but I can't bring myself to do it. So I need to ask you a favor, brother to brother."

"And what's that?" Claude asked.

"Admit what you did," Rheal said. "That's all. Just tell the truth, and I'll let you live. You'll have to leave town, and you can't ever come back. But you'll be alive. Anna and Julien will still have a father. You can finish raising them and grow old with Soph. You'll just have to do it in Nebraska, or some other big empty place I can never find you."

"No," Claude said flatly.

"Claude," Rheal said, "there's nothing you could do or feel that I can't understand. But I need to hear you say it."

"No," Claude said. "I won't tell my best friend I betrayed him when I did not."

"You're gonna make me orphan your kids? Make a widow out of Soph?"

Suddenly Claude grabbed Rheal by the jacket and yanked him close enough to kiss. "I'm not making you do shit," Claude said. "You know how when your old man would lock you in the shed until you just about froze to death, and you'd come over after he let you out and talk about how every one of us is alone in the world, and I'd say 'No you're not alone, not as long as I'm alive'? I take it back, Rheal. I was wrong. I'm still alive, and it turns out you *are* alone. We all have our choices to make. So go ahead and make yours, and let's get on with it."

Rheal slapped Claude's hands away. "So that's it?" he said.

"That's it," Claude said.

Rheal closed his eyes, heaved a deep breath, let it out. When he opened his eyes again, they were dry.

"Goddamn you, Claude," he said.

"I'm sure he will," Claude said. "Just promise me one thing."

"What?"

"Take care of Sophie and the kids."

Rheal stared at him. "It's an insult," he said, "that you think you need to ask me for that."

CHAPTER SIXTEEN

All operations at the Hollingsworth & Whitney mill had ceased, even before Rheal and the Sauciers stormed the place. Aucoin's security detail was still mostly on the job, but more than half the replacement mill workers had left after word of the blood in the roller room circulated. The other half, unable to do their jobs and sensing they were in the middle of something about to spin out of control, were giving serious thought to joining them.

There was little finesse and no stealth whatsoever to the way Rheal and the Sauciers seized the Mill; the only thing they took pains to conceal was their identity, each of them wearing a foam latex Ronald Reagan mask that was spooky realistic when seen at a glance. They drove right up to gate number one like they were delivering a load of logs, put a pistol to the guard's head, and invited him to consider whether he'd rather open the gate or meet Saint Peter. When the guard chose the former, Ray Saucier piloted the box truck into the lumberyard, Rheal closed the gate behind them, and that was that. The outside world was sealed out; inside would presently belong to them.

The principal assumption of the plan—that Aucoin's men would fold like banquet tables when faced with the prospect of the real-deal life-or-death violence Rheal and the Sauciers were expert in—proved almost entirely correct. As they swept the lumberyard and exterior wall, then made their way inside building number one and began clearing rooms, they spent most of their time zip-tying guards who'd dropped to their bellies at the first sight of three Reagans brandishing AKs. This uniform lack of resistance did not, however, prevent Rheal from breaking operational discipline and doling out the occasional head shot with the butt of his rifle. More than once Ray Saucier had to yell at him to cool it and move on, even physically hauling Rheal off a guard to keep him from stomping the man to death. But just as surely as to liberate the Mill, Rheal was here to level punishment—for Babs and for Claude, certainly, but also for the mortal sin these men had committed in taking the Mill away from the people who'd always worked and cared for it. Rheal was completely in control of being out of control, and this was, in the end, a reckoning.

With all the security in the first building subdued, the three rounded up the workers and locked them inside, then moved on to building number two. Here, it went much the same as in the Mill's first building—until it didn't.

The master control room for the rollers that pressed pulp into paper was overhead, part of a system of steel staircases and catwalks that lined the inner wall of the building and provided an elevated view of the machines. This was the final space in the Mill to be cleared, and nothing about it, as Rheal ascended the southern staircase and the Sauciers the northern staircase, across from the control room, gave any indication this would go differently. That was, until a bullet cut the air between Ray's and Normand's heads and ricocheted with a whine off the concrete behind them, sending the brothers sprawling to the deck while Rheal pressed himself into a corner away from the control room's line of sight.

Still prone on the steel mesh, the Sauciers craned their necks and saw one large pane of the control room's windows spiderwebbed, a small hole at its center. The round had come from inside, and whoever it was could see but not be seen, hidden behind the mirrored, one-way glass. The brothers exchanged a look freighted with meaning: they were sitting ducks. Nowhere to run and, up here on the catwalk, nowhere to hide. The best they could do was keep themselves pressed flat and hope Rheal had something up his sleeve.

But when Ray looked across the catwalk to the other staircase, he saw that Rheal was, in fact, gone.

Before taking the Mill, Normand and Ray had exchanged a private word about Rheal's state of mind, and agreed he was not just upset but *off*, way far removed from his tree. Neither of them had ever seen anything like it from Rheal, but they had seen it in other men, and in most cases those men were no longer alive. Accomplishing an objective and returning intact was not about what was thought of, in the popular imagination, as courage, boldness, abandon. Quite the opposite, in fact: courage usually did little other than making you, and often others, spectacularly dead. And now here was Rheal, filled to the eyeballs with the worst kind of courage, that which piggybacked on grief and fury. Could he be counted upon? Could his judgment? Normand, in particular, had been skeptical, but in the end Rheal was their guy, had always been their guy. He was an objectively peerless leader whose word was old-growth oak, he understood better than most what it took to kill and stay alive, and they would follow wherever he led, for better or worse.

Now, here was worse. Rheal had vanished, and as Normand tried to crawl backward, away from the control room, while remaining flat on the floor, another round pinged off the steel in front of him and a third sizzled past his left ear and lodged with a sickening thump in his calf. The sensation—instantaneous and searing—was of having been stung by a hornet the size of a cardinal.

It was hardly the first time Norm had been shot, but he was dismayed nonetheless, not least because the fusillade continued, with no way for them to escape or stop it. The next round might catch him in the forehead, and all he could do was wait to see if that would in fact be the case.

"I took one," Normand called out to his brother, directly behind him but, given their posture, out of sight.

"You okay?" Ray yelled over the din.

"You tell me," Normand said. "You're closer to it den I am."

A pause, and Normand could feel his brother futzing around with his pant leg. "Bleeding's superficial," Ray said. "Looks okay."

"Where de hell is Rheal?" Normand asked, then threw his hands over his head as another series of bullets zipped past, pinging and whining around them.

Finally, the shooting let up for a moment. The brothers looked across the catwalk and saw the pane of glass that previously had been splintered was now almost completely gone, providing a view of the inside of the control room. They could see the top of someone's head poking out above the window frame, probably reloading. And directly above this person, clinging to the underside of a ventilation duct, was a black-clad figure in a Ronald Reagan mask.

Reagan dropped, like a spider onto its prey.

The Sauciers clambered to their feet, Ray in a dead sprint, Normand hobbling behind him, their boots ringing against the steel.

When they reached the control room they found Rheal atop someone who was little more than a boy, nineteen or twenty perhaps, eyes wild with fright as Rheal pressed the blade of a knife against his throat with enough pressure to draw blood.

"Easy dere, Ronnie," Normand said to Rheal. "You got 'im. Let's just tie de poor kid up."

But Rheal didn't respond, didn't even turn his head to look at the brothers. Instead, he leaned into the blade, and the boy cried out.

Ray leaped forward and slipped his arms under Rheal's shoulders in a full nelson, hauling him off the boy as Rheal kicked and cursed. The two men fell backward in a heap, and Rheal's knife skittered away across the floor.

"Ease up, dere," Ray said to Rheal, patting his shoulder but still keeping a grip on his friend. "Let's not go killing children now, yeah?"

Several 9-1-1 calls had gone out from the Mill to Waterville's Emergency Dispatch Center, an operation that sounded like a lot more than what it actually was: a single desk at the police department in a room the size of a walk-in closet. That Waterville had its own dispatch, however modest, was a stroke of luck for Bates, however—it meant that rather than alerting the Sheriff's Department or the State Police to what was happening inside the Mill, these calls didn't go beyond the sphere of his control. At least for the moment.

Bates sent half a dozen cruisers to the Mill with instructions to set up a perimeter and then do absolutely nothing—even if someone started shooting at them—until they got word from him. He had Farley call the newspaper and the mayor's office to tell them that, in light of recent events, the department was conducting an unscheduled emergency response drill at Hollingsworth & Whitney. And then Bates sat down at his desk as his hands trembled and the incision in his side itched and ached, thinking frantically about what, if anything, he could do to unfuck this situation.

He believed—or rather hoped to Almighty God—that he'd be able to keep a lid on this, at least for a short time, and for the same reason that crime had always been allowed to flourish among society's lower castes: no one cared what poor people did to one another. Nobody who mattered—i.e., no one who could cause trouble for Bates—was concerned about the fates of scab hillbillies from Virginia, or about Francos cutting other Francos' throats. These kinds of shenanigans, properly contained, would fly under the radar of polite society, as they had from time immemorial, so long as blue blood wasn't spilled.

An exploding paper mill, though, people might just take notice of.

The report was as simple and straightforward as it was incredible: Rheal had a box truck loaded with half a ton of TNT, and he meant to use it if his wife wasn't returned within twenty-four hours. Bates thought he knew who was really responsible for Babs's disappearance, and it wasn't Harold Aucoin. He just had to convince that person to let her go.

He thought, in his desperation, that maybe the FBI could help.

Kittel had, in the course of his professional life, been to plenty of rich people's houses, but he'd never seen anything quite like Sutton's Kennebunk compound. The guesthouse, the boathouse, the three-hundred-degree view of the Atlantic, along which one could actually discern the curvature of the earth—even as somebody who believed that massive individual wealth was a sin, Kittel couldn't help feeling a twinge of envy. It had to be something, to live like this. The cul-de-sac at the entrance to the main house, festooned with Greco-Roman fountains and kinetic art, seemed a bit much, but Kittel figured it best to keep that criticism to himself.

A gigantic, grim-looking man in a suit met him at the door. "Kittel?" this man asked simply.

"Special Agent Kittel."

The man, who achieved the improbable feat of making Kittel seem small, looked at him in a way that made clear he couldn't be more underwhelmed by the title. "Mr. Sutton's waiting for you," he said.

"Well, then," Kittel said.

He smiled brightly at the man, whose scowl deepened in response. Without another word he led Kittel inside, past the entryway, and into the cavernous sitting room, where Sutton rested primly on his chocolate lounger.

"*Special Agent* Kittel," the man announced to Sutton.

"Thank you, Karl. That's all."

The man left the way they'd come in, and Kittel and Sutton were alone.

"Thanks for agreeing to meet with me," Kittel said. He motioned to a wing chair opposite the lounger, and took a seat when Sutton nodded.

"I always have time for the brave men and women of law enforcement," Sutton said.

For a few moments, the two men gazed at each other across what Kittel imagined had to be an obscenely expensive area rug, possibly one that belonged in a museum. Finally, Sutton broke the silence.

"What is it you want my help with today, Agent Kittel?" he asked.

Kittel playacted confusion. "Your help?" he said. "No, Mr. Sutton, you misunderstand. I'm here to help *you*."

Sutton smiled. "But what do you think I need help with?"

"Extricating yourself from the shitshow you created in Waterville."

Sutton shifted in his seat, appraising Kittel anew. "Are you here in an official capacity?" he asked.

"Not exactly," Kittel said. "Just doing a favor for a friend."

"I see," Sutton said. "And does this friend happen to also be the person threatening to blow up my mill?"

"I don't know who's threatening to blow up the Mill," Kittel said. "The assailants are masked and, near as I know, have not been identified."

"Right, of course," Sutton said.

"It's not my investigation, you understand," Kittel said, "so I have very little knowledge about the details. You know how it is with jurisdictional boundaries."

"I suspect you know a lot more than you're letting on, Agent Kittel."

"And you're free to suspect whatever you like," Kittel said. "In any case, my friend, who may or may not be the person threatening to blow up your mill, has two conditions you can easily accommodate. Without costing yourself a thing."

"And those are?"

"He wants his wife and his job back."

"Giving him his job back will cost me quite a bit, actually."

"Oh?"

"Is your friend a union member?"

"It happens that he is."

"Unions are very demanding, and very expensive."

"Mr. Sutton, let's be plain. You're ruthless, I'm sure, in your way—but not like the people you're dealing with. You won't go as far as they will. All your money and power aside, you're out of your depth. And it's best for you to cut bait before this reaches a point we can't come back from. Because then I *will* need to get involved in an official capacity, and I will make a point of seeing that does not turn out well for you."

"Are you sure, Agent Kittel," Sutton said, "that my wealth and power aren't sufficient to make a problem like you go away?"

"Not at all," Kittel said. "But what I do feel assured of is you have little interest in finding out. See, I think this has already gone way farther than you ever imagined. You're a businessman, not a gangster. Your workers are already gone, and even if you had workers, they wouldn't be able to do much with a pile of broken bricks. In short, Mr. Sutton, you've lost. You know it, and I know it. Inside, behind that businesslike exterior, you're just begging for someone to show you a way out. And here I am. Your white knight."

Sutton stared for a moment, then looked out through the floor-to-ceiling windows at the ocean. He blinked several times behind his glasses, then turned back, finally, to Kittel.

"Feel free to say thank you," Kittel said, smiling.

The first sign of the turn events had taken, for Babs, was the reappearance of Aucoin in the barn that afternoon. She hadn't asked for him to come, because she had no further need of him.

She'd bled into her underwear off and on through the night, and she was certain that could mean only one thing: the baby she'd never planned on but had come to love so desperately was gone.

So she had sat in silence and grief, indifferent to whatever else might come to pass, desiring nothing, hoping for nothing. And that was when Aucoin returned to the barn, accompanied by a man Babs did not recognize. This man carried a large black bag with a metal-clasp top, like the doctors who still made house calls when Babs was a girl, as well as a small hard-shell briefcase. Charlie St. Pierre was nowhere to be seen, praise God for small favors.

Aucoin looked grim, which pleased Babs even through her sorrow. "Bad news," he said to her as he approached. "You're going home."

"Poor Harold," Babs said. "Did your master yank your leash?"

"If I had my way," Aucoin said, "I'd toss you down the well out back and brick it up."

"I'll miss you, too."

"This is Dr. Derosier," Aucoin said, indicating the man with him. "He's here to check you over and make sure it's safe to move you. If it is, he'll take you to CMMC in town. Based on how you look, I imagine they'll want to admit you."

"I'm going home," Babs said.

"Not until you've been checked and cleared," Aucoin said. "Those are my instructions. Your Father Clement will meet you at the hospital. He's being sent down from Waterville to confirm your release."

"For who?"

"Who do you think?" Aucoin said. "That lunatic husband of yours."

"Why isn't Rheal coming himself?"

Aucoin smiled down at her. "That's all I'm going to tell you," he said, "except for this: Don't imagine you've won just yet. Sutton may have rolled over, but I still have one card left to play."

With that, Aucoin turned and went out, leaving Babs alone with this Dr. Derosier. He set his bag down and crouched on the floor in front of her, fumbling with the restraints on her legs. "*La vache*, they did a number on you," he said.

"I know it looks bad," Babs said, "but trust me, it's even worse than it looks."

Derosier stood and moved behind her, worked on the rope that remained around her right wrist. "What do you mean?" he asked.

"Well, I'm pregnant. Or at least I was, before they used me as a heavy bag for two days."

"*Sacrebleu*," Derosier said. He crouched again, flipped open the clasps on the suitcase, and began screwing together an aluminum pole to hang one of two saline IV bags also contained in the suitcase. "How far along?"

"A couple of months, I guess."

"You've been bleeding? Cramping?"

"Both of those things."

"Any pressure? Does it feel like you've dilated?"

"I don't know," Babs said. "Is the baby gone?"

Derosier hesitated a beat. "It's hard to say," he told her. "We need an ultrasound to know for sure."

They were quiet for several minutes as Derosier started an IV and hung the saline. He took Babs's blood pressure and listened to her heart and lungs, then set about examining the mess of her head and neck.

"This will need stitches," he said, gently probing the cut on her brow. "And this," he said, moving to a gash below her left ear.

"How long have you been cleaning up Aucoin's messes?" Babs asked.

"I'm a doctor," Derosier said. He took out a penlight and flashed it in Babs's good eye several times. "When people are hurt, I do what I can to fix them."

"Sure. But taking your pay from the person who does the hurting . . . it's a bit dicey, Hippocratically speaking, isn't it?"

Derosier paused and looked at her. "And what did you do, pray tell," he said, "that you're in this barn tied to a chair, in need of my help?"

"When you put it that way, I guess none of us is in line for sainthood."

Derosier laughed. "*C'est peu dire*," he said. "Can you walk? We need to get you out of here."

Bates limped in through gate number one believing that, against all odds, he'd engineered a way for this to end that wouldn't involve chunks of brick being blown into orbit. Sutton had caved, and initial reports were that Babs was alive and on her way to the hospital in Lewiston; Clement had already been dispatched to confirm this was the case. On top of that, Sutton had agreed to let Little Canada go back to work. Everyone had their job again, and once Bates delivered the news to Rheal and he got the Christ out of the Mill, everyone would get to stay out of prison.

Not bad for a guy with just one kidney.

In a just world, Bates thought as he followed a man in a Ronald Reagan mask carrying a Soviet assault rifle across the lumberyard, they would have renamed a street in Little Canada after him. Or at least thrown him a parade. But in this world, he would have to settle for delivering the good news in person to Rheal. And then maybe—just maybe—these people would behave themselves long enough that he could go home and put his feet up for a week, like the doctor had told him.

The man in the Reagan mask led him into the building that housed the massive paper rollers. Bates had been in here a handful of times, and on each occasion had been required to wear hearing protection. Now the cavernous room was silent except for their footfalls as they crossed the floor and mounted the stairs to the control room, where two other men—both wearing the same Reagan mask as the first—waited for them.

Bates looked around, and for the first time he had occasion to wonder if any of the men was his brother-in-law, Claude. "Which one of you is running this chickenshit operation?" he asked.

The Reagan who was seated spoke up, and Bates instantly recognized the voice, muffled though it was, as Rheal's. "That's me," he said.

"Where is everyone?" Bates asked. "Where are the workers?"

"Everyone's alive and well and locked in the boiler building," Rheal said. "Mill hands, as well as Aucoin's security."

"Can we maybe let them go?"

"That depends. What do you have to tell me?"

"You're getting everything you asked for. Babs has already been released, and Clement is on his way south to confirm. The replacement workers will be fired and, according to law, those jobs will be offered first to the strikers who had them previously."

"Fine," Rheal said.

"You're not as happy as I thought you'd be."

"This has been the worst twenty-four hours of my life," Rheal said. "And I've had some bad ones. Forgive me if I'm not turning cartwheels."

"Well, happy or not, this needs to end," Bates said. "There's only so long I can keep a goddamn armed takeover under wraps. I got you what you wanted. Now it's time to do what's right—for yourself and everyone else—and clear out of here."

"I'm not going anywhere until I hear from Clement that my wife is safe."

"Rheal—"

"That's it, Bates. Nonnegotiable. Once I get the call, we'll leave. Not before."

Satisfied that he'd double-knotted the last loose end of this mess in time for dinner, Bates was almost to his car outside the Mill when, back inside the control room, one of three phones began to ring. Normand, who by now had taken off his Reagan mask, raised his eyebrows at Rheal, who nodded. Normand lifted the receiver, listened a moment, then handed it to Rheal. "Aucoin," he said simply.

The brothers could only hear one side of the conversation, but that was all they needed to know it was not going well. It concluded when Rheal said, "You're a goddamn liar," and slammed the receiver down hard enough to crack the phone's molded plastic base.

"Get out," Rheal said to the Sauciers.

"What—"

"I said get out," Rheal said. "And don't come back in here unless I call for you."

CHAPTER SEVENTEEN

When Babs woke to a screaming headache in a bed on the third floor of Central Maine Medical Center and saw Clement seated to her right, she felt as though she knew nothing. She didn't know where her husband was or what he was doing or whether his best friend, Claude, who Babs had insisted he not trust, was dead. She didn't know how Clement had returned from exile or what that might mean. She didn't know what was happening with their businesses at home—that of dealing drugs and that of providing for the neighborhood, which of course were bound up in one another. She didn't even know if anyone was around to feed Henri the cat.

And she found, as sleep fell away and the pain behind her eyes began to throb steadily, that she didn't have a particular need to know any of those things. Even though Clement likely had all or at least most of the answers, she felt she could live the rest of her days without them, so long as she learned one thing: whether or not she was still pregnant.

Naturally, it turned out that was the subject Clement knew nothing about.

"They didn't say," he told her. "I don't know if that's because they haven't determined, or because they were waiting for you to come around to talk about it."

Babs put her head back on the pillow, looked up at the ceiling with her one good eye, and sighed.

"You want some water?" Clement asked. "Or something else to drink? I can get the nurse."

Babs waved a hand, *Non*. "How do I look?"

"Like you made God angry."

"He's just that way. Got nothing to do with me."

Clement smiled. "You should call your husband, let him know you're all right. Sort of."

"I don't want to talk to him right now."

"Why not?"

"Have I ever mentioned," Babs said, "that you are nosier than any old *mémère* could ever hope to be?"

"I'm your priest," Clement said. "It's my job to be nosy. So you still haven't told him?"

"No," Babs said, "but that's not it."

"What is it, then?"

"I think he did something terrible he's going to blame me for."

"I see. And you're planning to live the rest of your lives together without talking to him about it?"

"No. Just tonight."

"Fine," Clement said. "Your business, not mine. But I have to call and tell him I've put eyes on you."

"Do what you must. If he asks, I'm out dancing."

Clement pulled a slip of paper from his hip pocket and reached for the phone on the nightstand just as a doctor came in.

"Barbara Dionne," the doctor said, flipping through pages on a clipboard as he walked to the bedside. He looked up from the file and noticed Clement just as the priest put the phone back in its cradle. "Oh. Hi. I know she looks terrible, Father, but I don't think she's in need of last rites just yet."

"She might be soon, she keeps getting on my nerves," Clement said.

The doctor laughed, more than a little uncomfortably; it seemed he wasn't accustomed to priests making jokes about killing his patients. "Okay," he said, going back to the clipboard, "let's see, has anyone talked to you yet about where things stand?"

"Not that I remember," Babs said.

"You didn't see Dr. Berry before he left for the night?"

"What did I just say?"

"You can proceed," Clement said, "as if neither of us knows anything about her condition except what's obvious."

"Right," the doctor said. "Well, a lot of it *is* what's obvious: You've got multiple lacerations that took both sutures and staples, as well as contusions too numerous to count. It looks like the damage to your right eye is superficial, if spectacular; the orbital bone's intact, miraculously enough, and all the structures of the eye itself appear to have held up. Nose is broken in two places; we set that and it should heal. You're concussed, obviously, but you've got no cerebral swelling, which is what we'd worry about most with this kind of thing. How did you say you wound up like this, by the way?"

"I didn't."

"That must be why there's nothing in the chart. What happened?"

"I made God angry."

The doctor looked at Clement, who shrugged. "I see," the doctor said.

"She was wondering," Clement said, "about her pregnancy."

The doctor snapped his fingers. "Ah, right," he said. "Either you or that kid is extraordinarily tough, because you are still with child, I'm happy to report." He looked up at Babs. "Assuming that's the news you wanted to hear."

Now Clement turned and looked at her.

"It is," Babs said, her voice suddenly little more than a whisper.

"Then all is well," the doctor said. "We'll want to keep you overnight, but assuming nothing's changed for the worse come morning, I don't see any reason you won't be able to go home."

Babs turned her face away, toward the window, where dusk was falling over Lewiston, stars beginning to reveal themselves against the twilight. "Thank you," she said, again barely audible.

"You're welcome." The doctor shuffled back to the hallway, turned right, and was gone.

"Babs," Clement said when they were alone again. "I'm so pleased."

"I figured you would be."

"I'm going to call Rheal," he said. "You really should talk to him."

"No," she said.

"Fine," Clement said. "But you should know, at least, why it's important that I talk to him. He's taken the Mill, and is threatening to blow it up unless you come home safe and everyone gets their job back. The second of those conditions has already been met."

"Then we've won," Babs said.

"It would seem so."

"And all it cost me was my marriage."

A pause. "You sure you don't want to tell me what's going on?"

"Just call him, Clement," Babs said. "Tell him I'm okay."

"He's going to ask to talk to you," Clement said.

"So be it."

Clement pulled out the slip of paper again and dialed, then lifted the base of the phone and walked away until the line from the wall stretched taut. In the quiet of the room, Babs could hear Rheal pick up on the other end.

"Babs is okay," Clement told him. "We just talked to the doctor. She's beat up, but nothing that won't heal."

A pause, Rheal speaking too low for Babs to understand.

"She's sleeping. I can have her call when she wakes up."

Another pause.

"She really needs to rest, Rheal."

This time she heard her husband just fine, clear across the room: *"I said put her on the fucking phone."*

Clement dropped the handset to his side, turned, and came back to the bed. "I tried," he said, holding the phone out to her.

"I heard," she said. "No point delaying the inevitable."

Babs took the phone and raised the handset to her ear. *"Allo, chéri,"* she said.

"Clement says you're okay."

"You're not going to be pleased when you see the state I'm in," Babs said. "But yes."

"I need to ask you a question."

Babs's mouth went dry. "Okay," she said.

"Aucoin called. Said after thinking about it, he wanted to make sure I knew Claude wasn't working for him. Said it would be a shame if there was any confusion about that and someone got hurt."

"*Chéri,* did you do something terrible?"

"Just wait. Claude told me you lost him on purpose. Is that true? Or did he hand you over to Aucoin?"

"Rheal," Babs said, "we did it. We won. Just come home."

"Not until you answer the question."

"Come home, and we can talk about it."

"Why did you lose him? What were you hiding?"

"Just . . . I'll tell you everything, but you have to—"

"I *killed* him, Babs. I put a bullet in my best friend and threw him in the river. Because you said he couldn't be trusted. But *you* were the one who was lying to me. Not Claude."

Before Babs could say anything else, the line went dead.

Bates had barely settled into his La-Z-Boy again, a plate of shepherd's pie on his lap, when the phone rang. He heard Melinda pick up in the kitchen, and allowed himself to hope that the call was for her, one of her girlfriends asking for a ride to ceramics class tomorrow or something. After a moment, when she hadn't called for him to pick up like she usually did, he thought maybe he'd lucked out. But then Melinda came into the living room, looking spooked.

"It's Sophie," she said. "She's crying."

Bates sighed, put his fork back on the plate, put the plate back on the TV tray next to the lounger, and picked up the phone from the end table.

"Soph," he said. "It's me."

"I'm sorry to call so late," Sophie said, her voice indeed hoarse with tears.

"It's not that late. What's wrong?"

"I don't know where Claude is."

"What do you mean?"

"He went out two days ago with Rheal and hasn't been back."

"I think he's probably okay, Soph," Bates said. "You haven't heard from him at all?"

"Not since yesterday morning," Sophie said. "He called and said he was supposed to be looking after Babs, and she'd gone missing. It sounded like maybe he was in trouble with Rheal."

Bates flipped the footrest down on his chair and sat upright, not even noticing the pain in his side. "This was yesterday morning?"

"Yes. Around nine."

"And nothing since then?"

"No." Sophie's voice cracked, the harbinger of more tears.

"Soph, listen, I'm sure Claude is fine," Bates said, though he himself no longer felt nearly as certain about that as he had ten seconds earlier. "I'm going to take a drive, ask around, see what I can find out. But don't worry, okay? We'll find him."

"Okay."

"I'll call you back soon, whether I hear anything or not. You've got everything you need?"

"Ma's here."

"Okay, good. I'll call you back. Hang tight."

CHAPTER EIGHTEEN

Clement had never been a lead foot, even before the taming effects of maturity and the priesthood, but he did near a hundred miles per hour northbound on I-95 heading back to Waterville, steering wheel gripped tightly enough that his hands would ache for several days afterward. Babs had explained everything, making clear that in his current state of mind Rheal might actually make good on his threat to blow up the Mill. And though Clement doubted there was anything he could say or do to forestall disaster under such circumstances, he still figured he had a better chance than anyone else. It would require that he violate the most central of his priestly oaths, but compared to what might happen if he didn't, that was almost beneath consideration.

And he had to get there fast. The old Lincoln that came with the rectory didn't look like much, but it had a V-8 under the hood, and Clement drove it so hard and so fast that when he pulled into town off the highway he had no real memory of the drive itself. He'd been all fear and reflex, the frontal lobe of his brain of no use and thus mostly dormant. But now, as he approached the Mill gate, he endeavored to turn it back on, and at full power. Whatever came next, however meager the chances of avoiding the worst, he would need his wits.

Half a dozen police cruisers held down the four corners of the Mill perimeter, strobes painting the night electric blue. Clement got out of the Lincoln and stepped toward the gate, but two uniformed officers came at a run and stopped him.

"No one in or out, Father," one of them said. "We've got orders."

"Call Bates," Clement said.

"Chief Bates is here. Over at gate two."

"Then go get him. Now."

The officer was moved by something, whether Clement's authority as a priest or simply the urgency in his voice, and within two minutes he came back on the double, accompanied by Bates, who hobbled two steps behind.

"I have to get in there," Clement said to Bates.

"You and everyone else," Bates said, holding his side with one hand. "He's not talking."

"He's not talking to you."

"He won't talk to anyone if he doesn't pick up the phone to find out who it is," Bates said. "Do you know what he did to my brother-in-law?"

"I know what he might have done," Clement said. "As awful as that is, I'm more worried about what he might do next." He looked around, at the gate and the wall and up at the Mill's smokestack, mammoth and ghostly against the dark. "You got a bullhorn?" he asked.

Ten minutes later the gate opened and Clement was escorted to the roller building by Normand, in his Reagan mask once more. Clement had an inkling that this was one of the Sauciers, but didn't know for certain until he spoke.

"He's gone around de bend, Fadder," Normand said without preamble, as they walked past the box truck full of TNT.

"He was wrong about Claude," Clement said.

"He knows. Why do you tink he's gone crazy?"

"Can you stop him, if you have to?" Clement asked.

"I could drive dat truck out of here right now," Normand said.

"Then why don't you?"

"*Fidélité*," Normand said simply.

Rheal had removed his own mask and sat slumped in a chair near the control panel. The phones next to the control panel had all been taken off the hook, handsets resting on their sides, still tethered to their bases by curlicue cords.

"Father," Rheal said. "Nice of you to join us."

"Sadly, I can't stay long. Just wanted to pop in and see how you're faring."

"Poorly."

"No doubt."

"This is happening, Father. I'd recommend you go."

"If that's the case," Clement said, "if you cannot be swayed, then why did you let me in here in the first place?"

Rheal didn't respond.

"You think you want revenge. I understand. But this isn't the way."

Rheal laughed bitterly. "Revenge," he said.

"No?"

"Father, there are no words for what this is."

"Sure there are," Clement said. "Nihilism, for one. Despair. Renunciation. Cowardice. Contrition. I could go on."

"Contrition?"

"What else would you call it? You made a terrible mistake, and you're so sorry for it you're determined to make a worse one."

Rheal looked at him. "You ever kill anyone, Father?"

"You know I haven't."

"Then don't talk to me about contrition."

"Ah, I see," Clement said. "I have no authority to speak on the matter."

"Not that I can see, no," Rheal said. "You think you know God so completely that you can tell *me* who He is and what He wants. But the truth is, Father, you can't really understand God until you've killed."

Clement thought for a moment. "Maybe you're right," he said. "God's done plenty of killing, no sense disputing that. So maybe you have to kill to really know Him. If that's the case, I'll have to settle for my incomplete understanding of the divine."

Rheal stared balefully, surprised by Clement's concession and unsure what to do with it.

"On the other hand," Clement said, "it's possible that I understand something equally important about the nature of God that *you* have no inkling of."

"And what's that?"

"God doesn't just kill, Rheal," Clement said. "He creates life, too, of course."

"And what could a man sworn to celibacy," Rheal said, "know about creating life?"

Clement smiled. He grabbed the top of an empty chair nearby, rolled it over to himself, and sat. "Doesn't matter," he said finally. "I'm not here to tell you my sad story. I'm here to offer you a way out, Rheal. You've done an awful thing, so awful you think you have to die and take a chunk of this town with you. But what you really need is to confess, and be absolved."

Rheal laughed again and threw his hands skyward. "Confess! Confess! Why is that always your answer to everything?"

"Because," Clement said, "that's the answer to everything."

"Not here in the real world," Rheal said.

"Yes, let's talk about the real world," Clement said. "Here in the real world, you don't yet know anything about creating life. But you're about to learn. Assuming you come to your senses in time."

A pause. "I don't understand," Rheal said finally.

"Don't be coy," Clement said. "You know what I'm talking about. You've known it all along. Babs is pregnant. And regardless of what happens here tonight—regardless of whether you accept God's mercy or not—you will have brought a child into this world."

Rheal just stared.

"Of course, it goes without saying that bringing a child into the world is very different from *being a father*," Clement said. "So if you want to do *that*, I'd recommend you pull yourself together, stand the fuck down, and confess."

Silence. Rheal's face had collapsed into a grief beyond tears, and Clement got the briefest, crystalline glimpse of what this man had looked like as a boy himself, forsaken by those who were supposed to love him, believing himself alone on the earth.

"A baby?" Rheal asked.

"A baby," Clement said. "One that's not going to know or care about any of the heartaches you've had to endure, or accept those heartaches as an excuse for failing to do right by him. The only thing that kid's going to care about is feeling your arms hold him close and hold him up. Everything has changed completely and forever, Rheal. Your life has nothing to do with you anymore."

A long pause. "Thank God," Rheal said finally.

Clement smiled. "So. Are you ready to confess what you did?" he asked.

Rheal looked at him. "Here?" he asked.

"It's as good a place as any," Clement replied.

CHAPTER NINETEEN

Several months later, when Babs called on Sophie, she found her seated at the kitchen table under a cheap six-bulb light fixture and ceiling fan Rheal had helped Claude install the previous summer, during which project each of them had been zapped on separate occasions to the other's great amusement. The kids were at school, and Sophie looked, seated by herself at the table with a coffee mug and a pile of paperwork, as alone as anyone Babs had ever seen.

"Hey, Soph," Babs said. "Mind if I grab a coffee?"

Sophie blinked slowly, seemed to take several moments to process the fact of Babs's presence, then simply nodded toward the coffee maker on the counter in response. Babs took a mug from the cabinet at random and poured. She came back to the table and moved to sit down when, suddenly and sharply enough to make her startle, Sophie spoke up.

"Not there!" she hissed.

Babs froze in mid-squat. "No?"

"That," Sophie said, "is where Claude sits. Do *not* use his chair."

Babs shuffled over to the next seat, directly across from Sophie, and sat down.

"So," she said after waiting a moment for Sophie to start the conversation. "You wanted to talk to me?"

"Where is my husband, Babs?"

Babs gazed coolly at her. "Getting right to it," she said.

"Did you think I wanted to swap recipes and gossip about bowling league?" Sophie asked.

"Just be careful," Babs said. "Experience tells me most people who demand brass tacks aren't happy when that's what they get."

"Where is he?"

"I don't know," Babs said.

"Is he alive?"

"I don't know."

"You're a goddamn liar," Sophie said.

Babs looked at her. "You really think you want the truth?" she asked.

"It's all I've ever wanted," Sophie said. "I didn't get it from your husband. I was hoping you might have the courage he lacks."

Babs considered this. "Then let me tell you exactly what's going to happen," she said. "I'm going to give you the truth. And you're going to keep your mouth shut about it. For the rest of your natural life. You will never tell anyone else. Anyone."

"Or what?"

"Or your kids will be orphans."

Sophie narrowed her eyes and was about to say something with heat. But then she recovered herself, took a breath, and spoke evenly.

"When Claude first came up with the cash for my transplant, I was sure it came from you and Rheal and your new . . . enterprise," she said. "Where else could he have gotten it? And I thought, no good can come of this. I didn't want it. I told him so. But he insisted it wasn't what I thought, there were no strings attached, no one was going to jail. 'Then tell me where you got it,' I said. But he wouldn't. 'You just have to trust me,' he said."

"I don't know where the money came from," Babs said. "All I can tell you is it wasn't us."

"Oh, I know that now."

In Sophie's expression Babs saw something that she immediately recognized: The counterintuitive strength that blossoms when the worst has come to pass and there's nothing left to be afraid of. A calm, sad, resigned sturdiness.

Sophie put a hand on the papers next to her and pushed them toward Babs. "Take a look at that," she said.

Babs pulled the stack closer and read the top sheet. It was a contract for the sale of two hundred wooded acres near Mount Katahdin, from Claude to a development company out of Portland.

"Did you know about this land? Claude ever tell you about it?"

"No," Babs said.

"His father bought it forty years ago, when he came back from the Pacific. It's where Claude learned to shoot and fish. His dad started building a house there but never could afford to do anything beyond framing it up. More than just about anything in the world, Claude wanted to finish what his father started, and finally build that house. Share the place with the kids, same as their grandfather had shared it with him. Instead, he sold it. To save my life."

Babs said nothing.

"Claude told me something a while ago," Sophie said. "Before the strike ended, before all this. He said he'd screwed up, and you didn't trust him anymore. That he was on probation, of a kind. He said he thought Rheal understood why he'd done what he did, but you never would. You'd always think he was a traitor. He worried the next time something went wrong, no matter what it was, you'd put the blame on him. And Rheal would follow your lead."

"Dieu aide-moi," Babs said, more to the air than to Sophie.

"So I'll ask you one more time: What did you do to my husband?"

Babs looked at her. "We made a mistake," she said.

"A *mistake*? Are you fucking kidding me?"

Babs sighed, leaned forward, and pulled an envelope from the pocket of her parka. She put the envelope, fat with bills, on the table between them. "We've been mailing this up until now," she said. "But I wanted you to know where it's coming from."

"I know where it's coming from. And I wish to hell I didn't need it."

"This isn't a handout," Babs said. "It's profit-sharing. Claude's cut. And it'll continue to be paid, in perpetuity. Neither you nor the kids will want for anything ever again."

"I suppose you expect me to be grateful," Sophie said. "To kiss your ass and say thank you, thank you. Well, keep holding your breath."

Babs sat back and laced her hands over her belly. "Soph, we haven't seen each other for a few months, so let me explain something that everyone else understands by now. There was a time when I would have cared about your grief and anger, felt bad about it. But that time is gone. Even saying we made a mistake is a concession I don't really believe. It was Claude who made the mistake. When he took the company's side against his own people. Whatever happened after that, don't try to pin it on me. Or my husband."

"You cold-blooded bitch," Sophie said. "What if I just lost it right now and put you on the floor and kicked you in the stomach? You're not the only one who can do terrible things."

Babs jolted forward in her seat, her eyes suddenly aflame. "But that's just it, Sophie," she said. "I *am* the only one. There's nobody here better than me at doing terrible things. Not even close. So, Claude is gone. It could have turned out different, but it didn't. And I don't want to hear you, or anyone else, bitching about it ever again."

Sophie stared wide-eyed now, incredulous—and afraid.

"I need you to understand, before I go," Babs said, "that there's only one rule in Little Canada now, and it's this: Like God, I am above reproach. If you want to go on living here, under the blanket of protection I've created, you will live by this rule as if it were your idea to begin with. On the other hand, if you want to go on blaming me for Claude's death, you're welcome to do so—somewhere far away from Little Canada."

Sophie absorbed this, quiet for a moment. "I see," she said finally. "I might stay, or I might go. But before I decide, may I speak freely one last time?"

Babs nodded.

"Christ have mercy on that baby you're carrying," Sophie said. "Now get out. You may own this neighborhood, but this is still my house."

ÉPILOGUE

Here's the thing about America: we're never what we were, or even what we are, but only and forever what we *will be*. Our eyes don't linger on the ground where we stand, and we rarely if ever spare a glance backward. Thus severed from our past and disinterested in the present, we fixate on the horizon, even as it remains eternally beyond our reach. We live in the dream of a future that, by very definition, never arrives.

You, for instance, the firstborn and only son of Rheal and Babs Dionne, are born Jean-Louis Lebris de Yonne, but despite the Old World heft of your name, you will quickly be subsumed into the great homogenizing machine of American culture. This is neither good nor bad, but simply is. Being stoutly American will seem as natural to you, and as essential, as breathing. You will become a child of John Rambo and Levi Strauss just as surely as of Babs and Rheal, and by the time you're seventeen years old, you will feel yourself so fully American that when the Twin Towers collapse you'll speed to the armed forces recruiting office next door to the Subway franchise across town, and within a few years you'll be part of a tank crew in Ramadi, a God-and-Country jarhead who goes by Jack and *only* Jack and hasn't spoken a lick of French since you got to boot camp.

Though named for your uncle Jean, you will remind your mother of no one so much as her grandfather Leonard, quiet and kind and oversize and flatly dismissive of any suggestion that he was anything more, or other, than American. Your great-grandfather made a point of speaking English at all times, even well before he was fluent, and ate nothing but American foods, burgers and spaghetti and fried chicken and macaroni and cheese—no *tortière or cretons* for him, not even at the holidays, once he'd crossed the border in 1918. And he never went back across that border, not for a visit, not to see family or erstwhile friends. To him, there was a reason he'd left everything he'd known behind. To him, as hard as life could be here it was still better, in every way, than it had been before. Why indulge nostalgia? Why pretend there was anything worth going back to, even for a minute? Why look anywhere but forward?

So in this way, you will be exactly like your great-grandfather Leonard: American through and through. But in one important, intractable way, you will be the same as your namesake: like Uncle Jean, you will be killed far from home on a day that seems like any other until the thunderclap moment God's judgment arrives, and like Uncle Jean you will fly home in a flag-draped casket, to be met on the tarmac by your mother.

Before that, though, she will love you and you will love her and you will both strive and fail to understand each other.

In the wake of all that happened, your parents will learn that some ruptures between people cannot ever be completely healed, no matter how much they love one another. Forgiveness is what's needed, absolute and unconditional, but true forgiveness is among the most difficult things a person can endeavor to know. Your mother will manage it, because she is stronger than anyone else you will ever meet, and real forgiveness requires her kind of strength. But your father will never quite get there, never forgive your mother or himself. And over the years he will drink more and more, and then, when they start dealing it in the years to come, will develop an on-again, off-again heroin habit. Your mother will tolerate the distance between them, with the understanding that it not grow any wider. That when your father goes out to play cribbage with his drinking buddies for fifty dollars a game, or even when he visits a whore, he will never sleep in a bed other than theirs. This will be their arrangement, unspoken but ironclad, until the day your father dies in that very bed.

Daryl Bates will never achieve forgiveness for what he knows but cannot prove your father did, and he will not even try. He will be motivated to let Claude's death pass unpunished for an altogether different but equally powerful reason: self-interest and -preservation. Daryl is nothing if not a practical man, and he knows his fate is now inextricably bound up in that of your parents. They rise and fall together, and as such, to pursue and prosecute your father, even if Daryl could do so successfully, would be to cut his own throat. So even as his sister grieves and burns for decades, he will let Claude's ghost wander the earth for want of justice.

For Harold Aucoin your father will have no forgiveness or mercy; for Harold Aucoin your father will have only patience—the patience to wait through four years of peace between them, Harold tending his side of the fence and your parents tending theirs, bygones to all appearances definitively bygones, and then, on Devil's

Night in October 1988, Harold will startle awake in the darkness of his bedroom and feel, but not see, your father's presence, vengeful and omnipotent, and that will be the end of Harold for all time. His body will never be found, and your father and mother will never speak of him again.

It will go on like this—people being dragged screaming into this world, people breathing their last, the grievous rise and fall of life—as it always has. You will be joined by two sisters, and the fiercest love of your brief existence will happen among the three of you. In the end, of all the people you know and love in your time, your sister Lori will suffer the most for her own attachments. Being the heir to your mother's otherworldly toughness will seal Lori's fate in this regard—she will survive all that does the rest of you in, and alone and grieving she will run from this place, cursing her own inability to die. But then she will have a child—your niece Evangeline—and by and by she will return to reclaim your mother's legacy, and Evangeline will be heir to the throne. And every week without fail, through all their troubles and triumphs, they will come together to the cemetery and put a clutch of fresh irises on your grave, and when the great and terrible Lori is finally gone, Evangeline the Queen will come alone, with two bouquets.

And so it will continue.

ACKNOWLEDGMENTS

The author gratefully acknowledges the tireless support, belief, and work on behalf of Babs and her crew by the crack team at Penguin Putnam:

Tal Goretsky, who laced two first-pitch grand slams with the covers.

Nicole Biton, indispensable (and very patient) doyenne of publicity.

Brennin Cummings, ditto of marketing.

Andy Dudley, fellow old man of publishing.

Megan Mills, who brought Babs to great prominence where it counts.

Brianna Fairman, without whom all would be lost, or at least disorganized and way late.

Alexis Welby, who graciously brought Babs out on her first tour.

Ashley McClay, who keeps the wheels turning for everyone.

Lindsay Sagnette, who lent me her reading glasses at an absolutely critical moment.

Ivan Held, who runs the whole show.

Finally, Daphne Durham . . . we've talked about this, but it bears repeating: without you, Babs is still sitting in a file somewhere, unread and unknown.